PRAISE FOR HAROLD ROBBINS'
THE RAIDERS

"Harold Robbins, the world's bestselling novelist, has quietly completed a sequel to his classic 1961 novel, *The Carpetbaggers*. . . . THE RAIDERS tells the further adventures of ruthless mogul Jonas Cord—a thinly veiled Howard Hughes. . . ."

—Liz Smith, *New York Newsday*

"A sequel [to] one of the bestselling novels of all time . . . Readers will welcome historical cameos (from the likes of Jack and Bobby Kennedy, to Jimmy Hoffa and Jack Benny) and the reappearance of Cord's sidekick, Nevada Smith. . . ."

—*Publishers Weekly*

"*The Carpetbaggers* made Robbins' name a household word. . . . Will *THE RAIDERS* be in demand? You bet."

—Donna Seaman, *Booklist*

"Scandals, sex, and skulduggery . . . Appearances by such real-lifers as Jack Kennedy, Che Guevara, Jimmy Hoffa, Tallulah Bankhead, and Danny Kaye add some spice and historical context."

—*Kirkus Reviews*

"Harold Robbins' *THE RAIDERS* prove[s] he has not lost his knack for great storytelling . . . a story of backroom deals, bedroom betrayals and dark family secrets. You won't put it down until you're on the last page."

—Alan Caruba, *Bookviews*

Books by Harold Robbins

The Raiders
The Piranhas
The Storyteller
Descent from Xanadu
Spellbinder
Goodbye, Janette
Memories of Another Day
Dreams Die First
The Lonely Lady
The Pirate
The Betsy
The Inheritors
The Adventurers
Where Love Has Gone
The Carpetbaggers
Stiletto
79 Park Avenue
Never Leave Me
A Stone for Danny Fisher
The Dream Merchants
Never Love a Stranger

HAROLD ROBBINS

THE
Raiders

POCKET BOOKS
New York London Toronto Sydney Tokyo Singapore

This book is a work of fiction. Names, characters, places and incidents are products of the author's imagination or are used fictitiously. Any resemblance to actual events or locales or persons, living or dead, is entirely coincidental.

POCKET BOOKS, a division of Simon & Schuster Inc.
1230 Avenue of the Americas, New York, NY 10020

ISBN: 0-671-87293-1

First Pocket Books printing September 1995

10 9 8 7 6 5 4 3 2 1

POCKET and colophon are registered trademarks of Simon & Schuster Inc.

Cover photo by Robert Olding / Photonica

Printed in the U.S.A.

*For my wife Jann,
with all my love.*

You don't have to deserve your mother's love. You have to deserve your father's. He's more particular.
—*Robert Frost*

No man is a hero to his valet.
—*Madame Cornuel*

Or to his father.
—*Jonas Cord*

PROLOGUE

PEOPLE HAVE RECURRING DREAMS. JONAS CORD HAD them. Memories are often distressing. Dreams, bringing memories to life, are worse; emotions that are dull in memory come back sharp and tormenting in dreams.

The one that came most often began with the words "Jonas—my son." "Jonas—my son," his father had muttered as he toppled into his son's arms, dead of an abrupt, massive stroke. One moment Jonas Senior was a powerful, domineering man. The next moment he was dead.

He had died without ever having told his son he loved him, or that he was proud of him. He had died without ever hearing any such words from his son. The old man and the young man loved each other, but neither could ever bring himself to say so, and neither ever felt confident of it. Jonas resolved he would never let things be that way with a son of his own—if he ever had one.

It was Rina who first made it clear to him that his father had cared for him. Rina: the young, voluptuous Rina. Jonas had almost hated his father over Rina. He had decided to marry her and had announced his decision to Jonas Senior. His father had opposed the marriage on the ground that the boy was too young to marry; and he had blocked it in the most effective way he possibly could, by marrying her himself. Jonas had called the old man a fool who had fallen for a scheming, avaricious gold digger.

Within hours after his father's death, Rina had explained that the old man had not been a fool at all. He had demanded a prenuptial agreement from her, in which she accepted a settlement but would not inherit stock in the Cord family businesses. If she had borne the old man a child, that child would have inherited stock and Jonas would have had to share control. During a whole year of marriage to the luscious and licentious Rina, the old man had resolutely avoided getting her pregnant—to preserve Jonas's status as sole heir.

The next person who made Jonas understand his father was Nevada Smith, the best and wisest friend either of the Jonases ever had. The leathery, straight-spoken Nevada Smith had shown up at the Cord ranch one day sixteen years before the death of Jonas Senior and asked if there was a job for him. There wasn't, but Jonas Senior was a man who sized up other men quickly; and he had hired Nevada to teach his little boy to ride and shoot—in short, to make a man of him. After Jonas Senior died, Nevada moved on. He starred in his own Wild West show and then became a major star of Western pictures. But he remained a friend and saw Jonas often. He told Jonas things the old man should have told him.

Jonas never told anyone else, but he pledged himself that if ever he had a son, the boy would know he loved him, would know it all his life, would know it before it was too late.

* * *

In another dream that often came, the year was 1945, twenty years after the death of his father, and Jonas was proudly and exuberantly flying *The Centurion,* the huge fiberglass-hull flying boat in which he had invested seventeen million dollars of the assets of what the *Wall Street Journal* called "the Cord Empire." It had been at the time the biggest airplane ever built, designed to carry an entire company of soldiers with two light tanks and all the other equipment they would need to invade a Japanese-held island.

The conventional wisdom was that he could never get the thing to lift off the water, but he was in the air. *The Centurion* was one more example of how Jonas Cord—no longer ever called Jonas Cord Junior—repeatedly defied expert opinion, went his own way, and made things work the way he wanted them to work.

For example, at the time of his death, Jonas Senior had been about to launch the parent company, Cord Explosives, into the manufacture of an exotic new product said to have thousands of potential uses in industry and in consumer goods. For want of a better name, the product was called plastics. Jonas had picked up on this idea and carried it forward. Cord Plastics was one of the biggest names in the industry. A Cord company manufactured airplanes, and another ran an airline. Cord Productions had made movies for some years, but later Jonas had decided to get out of that business and use the soundstages as rental properties.

For the test flight of *The Centurion,* Amos Winthrop, Jonas's father-in-law, who had supervised the building of the plane, sat in the co-pilot's seat. They had taken off, and the huge plane was flying, but suddenly everything went wrong. In the dream it was as if the plane had been rigged backward. If he turned

3

the yoke to lower the right wing, the left wing dipped. If he shoved in the left rudder pedal, the plane turned right. And then the engines began to fail, one by one . . .

Then, invariably, the telephone rang. It rang once, just once, enough to wake him and interrupt the dream, mercifully sparing him from having to relive what had really happened in 1945—the failure of the engines one by one, the plunge into the sea, his escape from the buckled fuselage with doors jammed shut, shoved through a port by Amos, who was himself too fat to squeeze through, and finally the sinking of *The Centurion,* carrying the older man down with it.

Two weeks later, while Jonas was still in the hospital recovering from injuries he had suffered in the crash, the atomic bomb brought the war with Japan to an end; and Jonas had to give up plans to build *Centurion II.* Fortunately, Cord Aircraft had also just delivered to the Air Force its first jet fighter. The luck of Jonas Cord, someone commented acidly.

A son. He'd never had a son. He had been married twice, twice to the same woman. Monica Winthrop. By a sad, stupid error he had decided that the daughter she bore, Jo-Ann, was not his. He left Monica, and she divorced him. Fourteen years passed before he learned he had been wrong. Then, thank God, it was not too late. He remarried Monica and happily accepted Jo-Ann as his daughter. Jo-Ann said she wanted a little brother, but five years of trying had not yet produced one. The fault wasn't his. He had established a trust fund for a daughter born to his secretary in 1948. It was Monica's fault. Doctors said there was something funny about her. Monica was forty-three, a pregnancy was not impossible, just

4

unlikely, and if they really wanted another child they should keep trying.

Anyway, he had bought a home in Bel Air, and Jo-Ann was going to college at Pepperdine. Monica had not given up her career and spent a lot of time in New York—as he spent a lot of time flying here, there, and the other where—but they were together enough to have plenty of chances to make something happen.

Jonas was happy. He insisted to himself that he was happy. Why shouldn't he have been? He had inherited Cord Explosives and built it into a billion-dollar conglomerate that was still growing. He was notoriously successful. He had the luck of Jonas Cord. He was forty-seven years old and had done just about everything he had ever wanted to do in life—

Except that he had never told his father he loved him and never heard his father say it to him. And he had never had a chance to make it right in some sense by treating a son of his own a different way.

1
============= 1951 =============

1

AN ODDITY OF THE RECURRING DREAM ABOUT *The Centurion* was that the telephone ring that interrupted it always happened forty-seven minutes past the hour. It could be 1:47, 2:47, or 3:47; but when he woke and looked at the clock it was always forty-seven past something.

This was not the same. The telephone did not ring once. It persisted. And when he opened his eyes and looked at the clock, the time was 2:06.

The phone had rung maybe six times when he picked it up. He was groggy. He'd eaten well, drunk a little more than usual, and had finished the evening with a round of good sex with Monica. Waking was not easy.

"Yeah . . . ?"

"Jonas, this is Phil."

"You know what time it is?"

"What time you think it is in Washington? Listen to me. A friend—never mind who—woke *me* up to read me a highly confidential document. Plan on a visit from a United States marshal. He'll be early. He means to get to you before you leave the house."

Jonas switched on the bedside lamp. He lifted

himself to a sitting posture. He was stark naked. He didn't own such a thing as a pair of pajamas, and it took a cold night in a badly heated bedroom to make him sleep in his underclothes.

"Phil . . . What the hell are you talking about?"

"The airline hearings, for Christ's sake! They've issued a subpoena for you. They want to grill your ass, Jonas. You didn't appear voluntarily in response to their request, so—"

"Bunch of two-bit politicians want to make names for themselves by cross-examining Jonas Cord."

"Maybe. But they're United States senators, and they've got subpoena power. If you don't show, you're in contempt of Congress. People have gone to jail for contempt of Congress."

"I hold Congress in *complete* contempt."

"You're not in the world's best position, Jonas. If those contracts for gate positions in New York and Chicago were in fact rigged the way—"

"Phil. Never mind. I know what they accuse me of. I don't want to talk about it."

"Yeah? Well, if the senators subpoena you to talk about it, you're going to have to talk about it. You don't have any choice."

"Except one," said Jonas.

The lawyer was silent on the phone for a moment, then said, "As your lawyer, I can't advise you to take that option."

"As my friend . . . ?"

"That's why I called you in the middle of the night."

"I'll be in touch, Phil. I won't tell you where I'm going. If they ask, you really don't know. But I'll be in touch."

Monica had wakened, had sat up, and was squinting curiously at him. She was naked, too, as Jonas noted in a quick appreciative glance. Her boobies, that had always been a pleasure to look at and fondle, had grown plumper and more rotund since she had gained a little weight in her late thirties. Her belly was cute and roly-poly now, like a smooth little melon riding in the bowl of her pelvis. Her legs remained thin and sleek, and she had put on no new flesh around her neck or jawline. Her dark-brown hair, now pillow-tousled, framed her face, which was as strong as always, maybe a little stronger as the years had imposed character.

"Do I hear that you're going somewhere?" she asked.

"I have to scram for a while," said Jonas. "A marshal is coming to serve me a subpoena. A couple of senators want to grill me in the Senate airlines hearings. I really don't want to testify. I can't afford to testify."

"What have you done?" she asked.

"Nothing illegal," he said acerbically, annoyed that she would even suggest he'd done something crooked. "Competent counsel have advised me at every step. But congressional investigators like nothing more than making a businessman look bad, particularly if the businessman is one who gets newspaper coverage. They might even pressure the Justice Department into going for an indictment. I have done nothing illegal and would be acquitted for certain—but that would be after an ordeal of two or three years."

"But what are you going to do?"

"I'm just going to make myself unavailable for a while."

Monica sighed and glanced around their bedroom, at new furniture she had not yet grown accustomed to think of as hers. "I can't believe this! Goddammit! We've only been in Bel Air four months. Jo-Ann is just getting settled in at Pepperdine and—"

Jonas was out of bed now and was dressing. "This has got nothing to do with where we keep a home or where Jo-Ann goes to school. You're staying here. Both of you. Those bastards might force me to duck their process server, but they're not forcing us out of our home or Jo-Ann out of her university."

Monica got out of bed. She reached for a lavender dressing gown with white lace trim—not quite sheer but not quite modest either. She pulled it on.

"How long is this going to last?" she asked.

"Not very long," he said. "I can get it straighted out in a few weeks, maybe two or three months. The lawyers will talk for me. I've got a few political contacts, after all."

"Why don't you just accept the subpoena and face it?" she asked.

She picked up a pack of cigarettes from the night table on her side of the bed, shook out a Tareyton, and lit it with a paper match. "If you've got nothing to hide—"

"I didn't say I have nothing to hide. I said I haven't done anything illegal. This kind of thing—a congressional hearing, maybe having to defend myself in court—could damage some of my businesses. Severely."

"More than skipping?" she asked skeptically, even a little scornfully.

He zipped up his pants. He smiled wryly. "Business people will see skipping as smart."

"But—"

"Look. If I'm compelled to testify, I'll have to tell how things are done. Inter-Continental Airlines wasn't built by chance. You have to be smart. You have to find ways and means of doing things. We have business secrets. Understand? Do you understand, Monica? It's business."

"Is there something wrong with your SEC reports, Jonas?" she asked.

"Not unless the smartest lawyers on Wall Street have fouled them up. And taxes . . . Our accountants are meticulous. We don't fudge on taxes."

"What could they indict you for? You said they might indict you. What would that be for?"

"Inter-Continental has been getting good gate slots at major airports. Do you understand that? An air terminal can only receive so many flights a day. There are only so many gates. Some of the airlines we shut out are furious and have suggested we rig contracts, that we pay kickbacks, and so on. No one can prove we do. The truth is, we don't. But we do have ways of— Well. You can see what I mean. Another question is Do we make deals with other airlines, violating the anti-trust laws? Again, no. But it's not all cut-and-dried stuff, not black and white. They'd love to grill me. Some of them would love to tie me up in knots for two or three years."

"Jonas . . . This is the same damned thing that—"

"Look," he interrupted firmly. "A U.S. marshal may be here to serve me before dawn. I've got to throw a few things in a briefcase and get going."

"Where?" she asked. "Where the hell will you go?"

"The marshal will ask, and you can answer very honestly that you don't know. I'm not one hundred percent sure myself. I'll call you as soon as I get settled someplace and let you know."

She followed him out of the bedroom and along the hall to his little home office. He opened a big briefcase on his desk and began to shove papers into it. He shoved in a quart of bourbon, too.

11

"What am I supposed to tell Jo-Ann?" she demanded. "That you disappeared in the middle of the night, two skips ahead of a U.S. marshal? What's the kid supposed to think?"

"Tell her the truth. Tell her just what I told you."

"That her father's on the lam? Is that what I'm supposed to tell her? That—"

Jonas jerked his head around. *"Don't put it that way!"* he barked. "Not to her. Not to yourself. Business is business, Monica, and sometimes it makes us do things we don't want to do. Jo-Ann's going to be eighteen years old before very long. She's old enough and smart enough to understand."

Monica had carried her cigarette with her from the bedroom, and now she crushed it in the ashtray on his desk.

"Monica, I'm sorry," he said. The lavender dressing gown that didn't quite conceal, didn't entirely reveal, clung to her hips and reminded him of the firm smoothness of her buns, which he had been fondly caressing only hours ago. "I wish I could take you with me. We'll be together again as soon as possible."

"Sure," she grunted. "You walked out on our first honeymoon. Business called. What else have you missed? Anniversaries. Birthdays. Even Christmas afternoon last year. Business called."

He had withdrawn from the conversation. He grabbed up his briefcase and walked out of the room.

She followed him downstairs, toward the door. His Cadillac convertible sat in the circular driveway before the house. He opened the door and tossed in the briefcase.

Then he came back to kiss her.

"Baby, it won't be long," he promised. "I'll probably be on the phone with you tomorrow."

She accepted his kiss, but accepted was the right

word for it; she was not hungry for it, and she was rigid in his arms. He patted her shoulder and her backside.

"Tomorrow. I'll call you tomorrow if I possibly can."

"Sure," she whispered, resigned.

"Monica, I'm *sorry*. What the hell else can I say?"

"Nothing."

He broke away from her and strode to the car.

2

Monica stood outside for a while, first watching the red taillights of the Cadillac disappear, then looking up at the points of starlight in an unusually clear sky. A tangle of emotions suffused her, and she was not sure if she wanted to cry or curse. Or both.

Damn him. Damn Jonas Cord! He had abandoned her on their honeymoon . . . because of a business emergency, he'd said. Then he'd got it in his head that Jo-Ann was not his daughter. When he learned the truth he had begged them to return to him. After fourteen years. And she, like a fool, had gone back to him. Because she loved him. And he said he loved her. He said they'd have another child. Lucky they hadn't.

Because he hadn't changed. He was the same intriguing, fascinating, loving . . . egocentric, insensitive, disloyal son of a bitch he had always been. He was obsessed with money and power, especially power. She couldn't compete with money and power. Neither could Jo-Ann. They always lost.

She began to shiver and realized it was not because the night was cold, which it wasn't, but because she was frustrated and disappointed and angry. She went inside the house and went to the bar. She poured herself two fingers of bourbon and jerked the glass back for a quick swallow. She could feel it all the way down, burning, warming. It stopped her shivering.

She jerked off her dressing gown and stood at the bar naked, even though she could be seen by anyone who walked up the driveway. That was somehow defiant, and she felt defiant.

Jonas . . . It probably really had been Phil, calling from Washington. For a moment she was tempted to dial him and find out. Of course he'd lie for Jonas. A lot of people would lie for Jonas. He may have told Jonas to duck service of a subpoena, or he may have been calling to say something like "If you get your ass to Frisco before dawn, you can get in bed with Marlene Dietrich."

Of course . . . If a United States marshal really showed up on the doorstep in the next six or eight hours, she'd know.

Actually, she wouldn't know, not really. If it was true he was going somewhere to hole up and let an investigation cool down, he'd for sure be taking some girl with him. A "secretary." He'd no more travel without a female to attend to his needs than he'd have forgotten to stuff that bottle of bourbon into his briefcase. She wondered which one it was this time. She'd identified three. He'd stop at a phone booth somewhere. Then he'd pick the girl up.

She tipped the glass and swallowed the rest of her whiskey. So, now she would go back to bed. She'd take a shower first, to wash his sweat off her body. And then she would go to bed. Not in the bed where they had struggled and twisted the dampened sheets into knots. She would sleep in the guest room. Alone. Alone again.

"Fuck you, Jonas Cord," she said aloud in the shower as she washed his come off her legs. "Fuck you," she said again, this time tearfully, as she dried herself and walked out into the bedroom.

To hell with this way of living. To hell with *him*. She didn't have to live this way, and she wouldn't. Two could play this game. She glanced at the clock and decided it was too early to waken Alex in New York. She would call him later. By God, two could play this game!

"Fuck you, Jonas Cord! I got a big surprise for you. You're gonna be served with some different legal papers. Monica's getting a new divorce!"

2

1

NEVADA SMITH WOKE. WHO COULD SLEEP WITH AN AIR-plane buzzin' the house? Airplane . . . buzzin' . . . ?
Oh, God! It had to be Jonas, he decided. Who else
would buzz the house before dawn?

He rolled out of bed. His wife Martha hadn't
wakened. A pair of faded blue Levi's lay on the floor,
where he had kicked them off last night, and he pulled
them up over his long, muscular legs that had never
been anything but thick and strong, all his life. He
slipped into soft moccasins. With a backward glance
at Martha, to be sure she was still asleep, he trotted
from the bedroom and through the house to the gray
steel box that contained the switch for the runway
lights. He pulled the switch.

He hurried out on the porch. The yellowish-brown
lights were on, two parallel lines of them, defining the
thousand-foot landing strip. The only other lights
were a pair of floodlights on the windsock. It was a
primitive strip, for sure, but it had proved enough for
Jonas, even in bad weather. Nevada had been his
passenger many times, day and night, and he had
marveled at Jonas's uncanny knack for finding this
ranch and this house and the landing strip, seeing
landmarks that were invisible to anyone else. The old
man had never been proud of his son's instinct for

flying—had, in fact, disapproved of it as dangerous foolishness—but that was because he died before he could experience it and learn to appreciate it.

The strip was not paved. Nevada had gone out and walked it only yesterday, carrying a shovel and looking for any holes animals might have made. It was smooth. An ill-tempered rattler had threatened, but Nevada had let it go, had not killed it. If it was lying out there now, it had a big surprise coming from the onrushing wheels of the heavy airplane that was about to land.

He stood on the porch and watched the red and green lights on the plane's wings as Jonas circled for his approach. Nevada had first seen him fly in 1925 when he had flown to the landing strip at the Cord Explosives plant in an ancient wood-and-wire Waco he had won in a crap game. Nevada had called him Junior then, and Junior had demonstrated a natural aptitude for flying, more aptitude for it than for riding, which Nevada had taught him. Maybe not more aptitude than he had for shooting, which Nevada had also taught him.

Nevada had come to the Cord ranch in 1909, looking for work as a cowhand, and the old Jonas had hired him as a nursemaid. Teach the boy to ride. The old man never used many words. Teach him to ride had meant a lot of other things. Make a man of him was what he'd meant. Nevada'd had sixteen years to do it before the old man died—on that very day when Junior flew to the plant in the Waco. Nevada had been unsure just how well he'd done with the boy until he heard Jonas abruptly and coldly announce to the directors of Cord Explosives that no one was to call him Junior, ever again.

The airplane was a mile east of the runway when it turned and began to lower toward the dusty strip.

When he was maybe a quarter of a mile out and maybe a hundred feet above the ground, Jonas switched on the airplane's landing lights for about two seconds, just long enough to make sure there was not a big animal on the strip. Nevada understood that Jonas's eyes were adjusted to the dark, so he did not want the glare of landing lights as the plane settled on.

The tires squawked as they touched the hard ground, and the airplane rolled down the strip almost to the end. A thousand feet was little enough runway for the Cessna Skyknight, which weighed two tons and had hit the ground at more than eighty miles an hour.

As he turned the airplane toward the house and taxied, Jonas switched on the landing lights and illuminated the porch and Nevada—and Martha, who had now come out. Martha waved. Nevada waved. But he had a big, troubled question—

Why?

2

The sun wasn't up, but Nevada sat down with Jonas on the porch with a bottle of cognac and poured them two generous drinks. Martha was in the kitchen, happily making a big breakfast.

"So you see how it is," Jonas said. He had just told Nevada about the telephone call from Phil in Washington and what he had done about it. "I figured I'd hole up here with you for a little while—that is if it's okay with you."

Nevada had gone to the bedroom and pulled on an old buckskin shirt. He had wrapped a red-and-white bandanna around his neck in anticipation of the heat of the day and of the sweat it would catch. The man didn't seem to age. His shoulders remained broad, his posture straight, his chest deep, his belly flat, his arms muscular, his hands deft and quick. His hair was white. The old story was that Indians' hair did not turn white, which was foolishness; but Nevada's had turned white. Of course, he had blue eyes, too. He was only half Kiowa. He was almost seventy years old.

It would have been easy for Jonas to say that Nevada was Nevada because he had stayed away from cities, that he was a product of the open country, of the blood of his Kiowa mother, of an outdoor self-reliant way of life. The truth of course was that Nevada had seen his share of city living. He was Nevada Smith of the movies, Nevada Smith of the Wild West shows. He'd lived in New Orleans and Los Angeles.

Jonas's father had died with Nevada's secret in his heart, never disclosed. Jonas, who had discovered it accidentally, had kept it since. Nevada's real name was not Nevada Smith but Max Sand—the initials on his old revolver: MS. He'd killed the men who killed his parents, tracked them down and killed them without mercy. He'd spent time in prison and had escaped. He'd done other things the law did not allow. Technically, he was perhaps still a fugitive. But for more than forty years he had been Nevada Smith and—among other things—the hero of Western pictures the whole world respected. To Jonas he had never been anything but a hero and the best friend a man ever had.

"I don' hardly have to tell you," Nevada said, "that you're welcome to stay here as long as you want to. Nothin' would pleasure me more, and nothin' would make Martha happier. Nothin' but having Monica and Jo-Ann here with you. But we gotta figure that there'll be a problem."

"I think I know what you have in mind," said Jonas.

"Well, let's suppose I was a law feller, a United States marshal," said Nevada, "and I come to your house and find you've skedaddled. Now, where'd I go lookin' fer you, if I was a law feller?"

Jonas took a swallow of Nevada's fiery brandy. He stared out at the eastern mountains, where the sky was turning and the sun was about to show itself. In the red light now blooming on a few gentle clouds that had developed overhead he could see a big old rattler coiled alongside the runway, probably moved into a defensive posture because of the mysterious disturbance that had shaken the land half an hour ago. A silly tiny animal skipped past, but the rattlesnake was apparently still so alert for danger to itself that it took no notice of what otherwise would have been a tasty meal.

"I see what you mean."

"I'd say, 'Jonas Cord, where'd he go?' And I'd say, 'What you bet out to Nevada Smith's place?' I could hide you here. I got places where we could hide you. Course, we'd gotta get rid of the airplane. But, problem we got is that that plane was see'd landin' here. Hands that work the place. Folks around. An airplane landin' on my strip before dawn . . . The word's all over. Now, if you'd druv—"

"They'd still look for me here," said Jonas.

"I'm afeard so," said Nevada.

"It's not so easy, is it? I mean, running away from the law."

Nevada turned toward Jonas with a small ironic smile on his lined face. "No, it ain't. But it can be done. Some folks do it for a lifetime."

"I'm not planning on doing it for a lifetime," said Jonas.

"Fellers don't, generally," said Nevada. "Question is, just what have you done so far? Like, did you tell Monica where you were goin'?"

"No. I told her I'd be in touch."

"That airplane out there belongs to you. They'll look for it. First place they'll look for it is here. We got . . . what? Two, three hours? You gotta eat, then take off. I got drums of aviation gas on hand. We'll pump your tanks up, like usual."

"Going where, Mexico?" Jonas asked.

"No. You fly 'cross the border, they track you. No. You gotta go somewheres else."

"I guess an airplane's an impediment," said Jonas. "Wherever it sits, it's got its numbers painted on it. You can hide a car, but—"

"Right."

"Shit," said Jonas. "I got away for a few hours, but—"

"You got a problem, Junior," said Nevada. "You're business smart. You turned out to be surprisin' business smart. Your daddy never guessed how business smart you were . . . or how fuckin' stupid you can sometimes be about life-type things. I don't know if you should've tried to duck that subpoena. That ain't a judgment for me to make. I know one thing. You gotta lam, and you gotta lam smarter than you've done so far."

"Can you help me, Nevada?"

Jonas reached for the cognac bottle, and Nevada caught his hand short of it and pushed it back. "You gotta fly, so you don't need no more of that. I gotta make a telephone call or two. What I think you oughta do is eat what Martha's cookin', then stretch out on a bed and get some shut-eye. Hour or two, you'll have to take off. By that time I may know where you can go."

3

Jonas lay in a cool dark room and tried to sleep. He dozed only, and odd, half-real dreams ran through his head. In his dream his father was still alive, and they were very angry with each other. About Rina. The old resentment.

In the waking part of his dream, when he was aware of himself and where he was, he regretted never forgiving his father. More than that, he regretted that his father had not lived to see him take over the company and expand it into what some people called the Cord empire. Of course . . . if his father had lived, his son would never have had the chance to do it.

Jonas didn't believe his father was in heaven or the other place, or somewhere out there watching him. But he wished he were. God, how he wished that! Everything he did he measured against one standard: Would his father have approved? He tried not to. He tried not to think of how his father would judge. But he caught himself constantly asking, "Did I do it right, old man?"

It was no easy standard. What would his father say, if he knew, about ducking this subpoena? What would the old man think?

He went to sleep finally and was asleep when Nevada entered the room and told him to wake up.

Jonas sat up and put his feet on the floor. He hadn't slept enough and felt as if he had a hangover. Nevada handed him a mug of strong black coffee.

"I found a place where you can go," Nevada said.

"Where?"

"Las Vegas."

"Las Vegas? There's hardly a more public place in

the world. Besides, the town swarms with federal agents, all kinds."

"Don't call an idea dumb before you even heard it," said Nevada. "I'm goin' with ya to set things up. The first thing we've gotta do is fly that conspicuous airplane out of here. There's a private field in Arizona where they'll shove it into a hangar for us. Then we'll drive to Vegas. After dark. Tonight. This is gonna cost you some money. You carryin' any?"

"Not much."

"I'll take care of things till you get some funds transferred."

"Where'm I gonna be living, Nevada?"

"Did you ever hear of a casino-hotel called The Seven Voyages?"

"Of course."

Nevada nodded curtly. "Well, that's where you're gonna be livin'. You got the whole top floor, and nobody but nobody is gonna know you're there."

"How'd you arrange that?"

"Over the years, a man makes friends," said Nevada.

4

They hand-cranked a primitive pump to transfer aviation gas from drums into the wing tanks on the Cessna. As Jonas shoved in the throttles and the airplane roared down the short runway and lifted off, a pair of black cars turned in at the gate and drove toward the house.

"We played that one a little too close," Nevada remarked. "If I was flyin' this airplane, I'd turn like we was headin' east. I'd wanta be well out of sight of those fellers before I turned the right way."

Jonas did exactly that. He did not turn south until he was east of the Utah state line, after which he flew over the Grand Canyon, then turned west. He navigated the way he'd done in the old days, before technical types mounted all kinds of radio-navigation equipment in airplanes. He didn't even refer to his charts but constantly compared what he saw on the ground to what he saw on state highway maps. The little private airport was where Nevada's friend had told him it was: eighteen miles northeast of Dolan Springs and a mile east of a narrow rural highway. He overflew once to have a look at the runway and windsock, then throttled back in a left-hand pattern and touched down just over the threshold, leaving himself plenty of room to bleed off speed and come to a stop before the end of the runway.

A large but rusting and ramshackle corrugated-steel building sat alongside the runway. Jonas and Nevada had hardly stepped down from the Cessna when a tractor backed up to it and towed it inside the building. The tractor guided it into place in a row of expensive twin-engine private planes. Powerful electric motors pulled the big doors shut.

Jonas and Nevada walked into the line shack, where Jonas asked the man on duty to top off the tanks on the Cessna.

"Okay, Mr. Cord. Nice-lookin' airplane. We'll take good care of it. We've got a car waiting for you. Understand you don't want to leave for a while. The house at the end of the ramp is a private club for owners and pilots."

Jonas nodded. "Fine. We'll pay it a visit."

5

Jonas and Nevada did not want to drive into Las Vegas until after sunset, when they would be far less likely to be recognized by chance. They knew the town. Both of them had been there before, often.

Jonas in fact had a business connection with the city. It resulted from the peculiar history of the State of Nevada and of Las Vegas.

The Nevada legislature had legalized casino gambling in 1931, as a measure to pump up the state's Depression-stricken economy. A few hotels and casino-hotels opened, but the business was modest. The problem was, Las Vegas was too remote. Los Angeles, the nearest city of any consequence, was three hundred miles away, a daylong drive in daunting desert heat in cars that were not air-conditioned, or a bumpy, adventurous two-and-a-half-hour flight over deserts and mountains. San Francisco was six hundred miles away, the East Coast as remote as China.

The casino-hotels operated like dude ranches, on a howdy-pardner basis with rustic accommodations and fare and no entertainment but the gambling. Sophisticated nightclubs operated in Los Angeles, and a few enterprising men developed the idea that Las Vegas should offer a combination of casino gambling, first-class accommodations, and top-notch entertainment.

The problem was, banks were reluctant to lend money to build casino-hotels. One Benjamin Siegel, better known to the world as Bugsy Siegel, solved that problem. With money of his own from his bookmaking operations in California, plus money from such investors as Meyer Lansky and Moe Greenbaum,

Bugsy built the Flamingo. It opened on December 26, 1946, with Jimmy Durante and the Xavier Cugat band on the stage.

The Flamingo made no profit with the flamboyant Bugsy managing. Besides, he had a furious temper and more than once attacked and injured men who called him Bugsy—in full view of casino clientele. A person or persons unknown—who would permanently remain unknown—solved the Bugsy problem on June 20, 1947, by shooting him in the head with a .30-caliber rifle as he lounged on a chintz-covered sofa in the Beverly Hills home of his girlfriend Virginia Hill. With him out of the way, banks were more willing to lend money to finish the Flamingo and to construct other casino-hotels. The Las Vegas boom was on its way. New hotels went up all along what they began to call The Strip.

A major problem remained. Access. Las Vegas was still difficult to get to.

Jonas Cord had contributed significantly to the solution of that problem. In 1947 he had instituted daily Inter-Continental Airline flights to Las Vegas from Los Angeles and San Francisco. Shortly he made that two daily flights. His airplanes flew at high altitudes, in the smoother, cooler air. They flew faster. On Inter-Continental, Las Vegas was only ninety minutes from Los Angeles. Players could fly to Vegas on an afternoon flight, gamble all night, and return on the morning flight. Hostesses served drinks during the flights.

Airline hostesses had originally all been nurses, expected to hover over passengers and to help them through likely bouts of airsickness. Even after they were no longer nurses, hostesses remained treacly solicitous. The Vegas flights were supposed to be fun, and Jonas asked his hostesses to wear shorts. They were the first airline hostesses in the world to wear shorts. They wore T-shirts too, lettered INTERCONTINENTAL—LAS VEGAS. Most flights were full, or nearly so. Other airlines saw the profitability of the market, and in 1948 other flights began to come in from as far away as Denver, Dallas, and Chicago.

Jonas Cord had made a major contribution to the success of Las Vegas, and his name was known there. He had never paid for a room, had never paid for a drink or a meal, on any visit.

He would never have thought of coming to Las Vegas to stay while the enthusiasm for subpoenaing him died down. That had been Nevada's idea. He knew Nevada would have made good arrangements.

6

The little frame house at the end of the ramp was indeed a private club for owners and pilots. They could eat, drink, play one of the dozen or so slot machines in the hall, or visit rooms upstairs with one of the girls who sat in the bar.

"Don't know about you," said Nevada, "but I could stand a nice thick steak."

They took a table by a window overlooking the runway and ramp. The table and chairs were solid maple furniture. The tablecloth and the curtains on the window were of red-and-white-checkered cotton. A candle had been allowed to burn down and cover with wax the neck of a Chianti bottle in a basket. The napkins were paper.

Jonas asked for a bottle of bourbon and two thick steaks, rare, with potatoes.

"Who's renting me the top floor of The Seven Voyages?" Jonas asked.

"The man who owns it," said Nevada. "His name is Morris Chandler."

"I've heard the name," said Jonas.

"Maurie and I go back a long, long way."

"Longer than the time you've known the Cords?" Jonas asked.

"Longer than that."

Jonas did not pursue the subject further. A part of Nevada's life was a closed book. Jonas knew the broad outlines of it, as his father had known, but Nevada Smith was not the kind of man you cross-examined.

One of the girls from the bar came to the table. She was a short bleached blonde wearing too much red lipstick. She wore a white peasant blouse to show off her oversized breasts.

"You guys bored?" she asked.

"As a matter of fact we're not," said Jonas. "And we've got business to discuss."

"Oh. Well, if business gets boring, I'll be in the bar."

When she was out of earshot, Nevada said, "Maybe you oughta take her up on it. Settle your nerves."

"The bourbon will take care of my nerves. I suppose I should call Monica and tell her where I am."

"Wait till you're in your suite," said Nevada. "Chandler has got the phones hooked up so they relay through an office in San Diego, which makes it impossible for somebody to trace your call and find out where you are. Besides, whatta you wanta bet they got your home phones tapped by now?"

"How am I going to talk to my offices?"

"Trust Chandler. He'll put scramblers on your phones, too. I talked to him about it. I told him you'd have to be able to reach the people that work for you.

Hey! You're not the first guy that's holed up on the top floor of The Seven Voyages."

" 'Trust Chandler'?"

"I do."

As they talked, Jonas watched the tractor pull a Twin Beech out of the hangar. Shortly two black cars drove onto the ramp. Five men got out and climbed into the Beech. It taxied to the end of the runway, turned, and came roaring back. It needed all the runway available to take off and rose into the air just before the pavement ended.

"We're staking a lot on this Morris Chandler," said Jonas.

"Don't worry about it," said Nevada. "Maurie and I go back a long way."

3

1

THE DESERT SETTING OF LAS VEGAS INSPIRED SOME OF the men who came to invest to give their hotels fanciful names from the Arabian Nights—fanciful Arabian Nights films being a Hollywood fad in those years. The Seven Voyages was a reference to the Seven Magic Voyages of Sinbad the Sailor. The hotel was built in a Moorish style, actually in what Morris Chandler's architects had adapted from the style of a dozen movie sets. It was in the middle of a vast irrigated green lawn where twenty luxuriant palm trees swayed on the desert wind. Long three-story wings angled away from the five-story central building.

Water played an important role in the character of The Seven Voyages. Jets of bubbling water shot up from fountains in front. A swimming pool dominated the rear. As Jonas was to see when they were inside, fountains and pools were important elements of the interior decor.

At night everything outdoors was lighted. Underwater lights gleamed in the pool. White lights shone on the palms. Colored lights played on the fountains. Warm-yellow floodlights lit the facade of the hotel.

Jonas parked the car in the lot behind the hotel, and

he and Nevada entered through a rear door. Nevada knew his way around in The Seven Voyages and led Jonas directly to Chandler's executive office on the second floor.

A dark-visaged man in a black suit stopped them for a moment but only for a moment, since he recognized Nevada. He opened the door to the inner office and said he would go and find Mr. Chandler, and they should be comfortable in the meantime.

The style there was not Arabian Nights. To the contrary, Chandler's office reminded Jonas of his father's office—his own for many years now—at the Cord Explosives plant. The furniture was heavy dark oak, the chairs upholstered with black leather fastened down with ornate nails; the drapes and carpet were green; and a brass banker's lamp with a green glass shade sat on the desk. The office was old-fashioned, functional, and unglamorous.

Morris Chandler was not the man Jonas had expected to meet. He was about seventy years old, at a guess—about the same age as Nevada. Though he was erect and looked well put together, he was short and thin—a little man. Silver-gray streaked his black hair. His brows arched above weary brown eyes. His nose might once have been long and sharp, but it was flat now, undoubtedly broken at some time in his life. His face was asymmetrical; his eyes didn't match; and Jonas guessed his right cheekbone had been fractured. His mouth was wide, and the lower lip was heavy. Deep wrinkles scored his flesh at the bridge of his nose, under his eyes, and around his mouth. The skin on his neck sagged. He wore a conservative dark-blue pinstriped double-breasted suit, precisely tailored to fit him perfectly.

As he entered the office and extended his hand to be

shaken, he pulled a thick black cigar from his mouth with his left hand. The sharp, strong smoke swirled around him and reached Jonas's nose. The cigar was not just strong but cheap.

"Mr. Cord," he said, taking Jonas's hand in a firm grip. "I am pleased to meet you." He turned to Nevada. "Hello, Nevada. It's good to see you again."

"H'lo, Maurie," said Nevada.

2

It was true that Nevada Smith and Morris Chandler went back a long way, back in fact to September 21, 1900. They met in a state prison camp just outside Plaquemine, Louisiana. Morris Chandler was then Maurice Cohen. Nevada Smith was Max Sand.

That day was the worst day of Chandler's whole life. He had arrived from Baton Rouge on the back of a wagon—chained to the back of the wagon. In the yard, in view of anyone interested, he'd had to strip and put on a prison uniform: black-and-white-striped pants and a shirt much too large for him. Then he'd sat on a bench, put his legs on an anvil, and watched in horror as a guard *riveted* shackles on his ankles: steel bands joined by about a foot and a half of chain, with a large steel ring in the middle. They gave him no shoes, and he was barefoot as he lurched across the yard toward the warden's office.

The warden was a big ruddy-faced man who wore round steel-rimmed spectacles and now pulled them off as he squinted over a paper that had been handed him by a deputy. He read what was on the paper and looked up. His face was not unkind, not even stern. He shook his head.

"Boy," he said, "you gotta be some kind of dumb. Some kind of dumb to get yourself a year in a place like this for no more'n the petty racket you was runnin'." He shook his head again. "Jew-boy from N'Yawk. That ain' gonna make it no easier for you, boy."

"He's a fancy dude." The deputy laughed. "Prettiest little suit of clothes you ever see. Celluloid collar. Pink satin necktie. High button shoes, with spats. An' he greased his hair down with some kind of stickum that smelt like geraniums. Personally, I like him better in what he's got on now. Th'other way kind of made a man sick."

The warden read from the sheet of paper. " 'Maurice Cohen. Grand larceny by fraud.' Hell, boy, you shoulda robbed a bank. You'd had a better chance of gettin' some real money, and you'd done better time here. Ol' boys'd respect you if you was a bank robber. You gonna do bad time, Maurice Cohen."

Maurie trembled. He was on the verge of tears. He was afraid his legs would fail him and he would fall on the floor.

"Well, okay then," said the warden. "Mike, you take him out and give him ten stripes. Then he can have his dinner."

"Ten stripes!" Maurie shrieked. *"Why?* What have I done to get— Sir! Sir! Why?" He wept, and his words blubbered out of him. "Oh, please . . ."

"Insurance," said the warden gently. "Seems like a man that gets ten the first day behaves better and doesn't think about tryin' to escape. Some way, they remember the feel of it, an' it makes better men of 'em."

Mike was a huge Negro. He was a trusty. As he led Maurie out across the porch and toward the whipping post in the middle of the yard, he spoke quietly. "Don' you worry none, boy," he said. "I'm very good at what I do. It ain' gonna hurt like what you think."

The big black man ordered him to strip off his uniform. He couldn't of course get his pants all the way off; he could only drop them down to his leg irons. When Mike lashed him to the post, Maurie was naked. He had an hour to stand there, bound to the post, before the work gangs came in and assembled in the yard to watch the whipping.

The convicts found him a curious figure. He was a little man, short and slight, and his skin was almost white. Many of them had never seen a circumcised man before, and they walked around him, staring and commenting—

—"Jeez Chrass! Somebody's cut th' end off him!"

—"God, it must hurt like hell t' have that done!"

—"It's what the Jews do. Talks about it in the Babble. Y' ever read the Babble, y'd find out where it tells the Jews to cut their boy babies like that."

—"Makes m' flesh crawl!"

Hanging in his bonds, Maurie saw a man as bad off as he was: naked as he was and locked inside a small cage in the middle of the yard, a short distance from the whipping post. The cage was so small the man could not stand up and could not stretch out. He was curled in a fetal position in a corner of the cage, confined with his own excrement, which lay about him on the ground. He seemed oblivious to the flies that crawled over his sweating body.

When the work crews were all in, fifty or sixty men formed a circle around the whipping post to witness the lashing about to be given to Maurie Cohen. His knees kept buckling, and he hung on the rope that bound his wrists to the post. He glistened with sweat, and when the wind blew he shivered. He knew he was earning the contempt of the men he was going to be locked up with for a year. He dreaded that, but he couldn't do anything about it. When he saw the warden step out on the porch, his bladder let go. They all laughed.

Then Mike, the big Negro, stepped up behind him. Maurie twisted his neck and looked. Mike was carrying the snake, a fearsome, threatening instrument of torture.

Maurie looked at the warden. The warden nodded, and instantly Maurie felt the snake crack across his shoulders. It hurt like being seared with a hot iron must hurt—worse because he felt its cut. He opened his mouth to scream—

Cold water crashed against his face. A lithe, muscular man with black hair stood staring curiously at him, empty bucket in hand. Oh, God, he'd passed out, and they'd revived him so he'd feel the remaining nine stripes! The man with the bucket wore a small quizzical smile. Maurie glanced around. The warden was gone from the porch. The convicts were in a moving line, going in the mess shack to pick up their food. All wore stripes the same as his. All wore leg irons. Except for the man with the bucket, no one was paying attention to him anymore. Maurie was still tied to the post. His back was . . . What was it? It felt like it was on fire, and yet it ached, too, a deep, agonizing ache in swelling flesh.

"Felt that fust one, din't ya?" asked the man. "But none of the rest. Like Mike tol' ya, he knows how to do what he does. That first shot went across your shoulders all right. But when he give ya the second one he made the tip hit ya sharp and hard on the back of the head an' knock ya out. Ya got th' other nine while ya wasn't feelin' nothin'. Ya didn't even have to feel the sting of the liniment Mike poured on to keep th' stripes from festerin'. You lucky. You git stripes ag'in, y'll git 'em the reg'lar way. Think on't."

Maurie moaned.

"It was nothin' special, got nothin' to do with you bein' a Jew-boy. They done it to me my first day here. My name's Max Sand. The Man ordered me to take care of you fer a while."

Max untied him, and Maurie dropped to his knees.

"That's th' way, boy. Pull them pants up and come on."

Maurie followed him. He couldn't imagine trying to pull the shirt on over his back. Max led him to a shack, where there was a cot and a bucket. A chain ran from a ring set in a heavy block of concrete. Max padlocked that to the chain between Maurie's leg irons, and he went away and left him.

Maurie sat on the cot. He couldn't lie down. He sat and wept.

A little later Max returned. He brought a tin cup full of coffee and a tin plate heaped with food. Without a word, he put the cup and plate down and left, latching the door outside.

Beans. Beans cooked in some kind of congealing grease that was almost certainly lard. The few little flakes of meat among the beans were undoubtedly pork. Forbidden food. But Maurie had learned from his days in jail that even mildly suggesting they should not serve him pork would win him laughter at best, a backhand slap across the mouth more likely. He picked up the spoon that was the only utensil they provided and ate a couple of mouthfuls of the unappetizing mess. He'd starve if he didn't eat whatever they gave him; he knew that. God forgive, he prayed as he shoved some more into his mouth.

And then he wept some more.

3

The horror of his year's imprisonment had only begun.

They left him in the shack for five days: time for his back to heal, or begin to heal. He was let out only when he carried his slops bucket to the latrine and poured the contents in. Max came to take him out. Max brought his food. Max was no trusty, as Mike was. He wore stripes and leg irons as most of the other men did, but Maurie noticed that Max didn't stumble. He'd learned how to walk in chains.

Max sat down in the doorway of the shack and talked to him. He asked him what fool thing he'd done to get himself a year in this place.

"They say ya done somethin' stupid. How stupid? What stupid?"

Maurie sighed heavily. "I was selling insurance," he said.

Max grinned. "Oh, yeah. And there wasn't no insurance company, right? I guess you just had a printer print up some fake policies for you, and—"

"Right," said Maurie.

"That's dumb all right. That *is* dumb. To risk being sent to a place like this . . . That's dumb."

"What are you here for, Max?"

"Two years. Illegal use of a firearm."

"What'd you do with it that was illegal?"

"I killed a man."

"You don't go out with a work crew."

"I will, next week. A cottonmouth got me on the leg. I'm on half duty right now."

At the end of the five days they took Maurie out of the shack. He was assigned to a cot in a barrack. At night they ran a long chain the length of the barrack, passing it through the ring in the middle of the chain that linked each man's leg irons. That confined them. The guards didn't even close the doors and windows, which were left open so air—and mosquitoes—could come in.

The warden really was a man of kindly disposition. Realizing Maurice Cohen did not have the physique to work all day in the fields, he had him assigned to the kitchen.

Routed out of bed and off the long chain before dawn, he shuffled around the kitchen shack, helping the trusty cook to bake cornbread and boil coffee. The convicts began their day with platters of cornbread soaked in molasses, a sticky-sweet mélange that filled out their stomachs but rotted their teeth. Maurie managed to put aside some cornbread without molasses for himself. The cook noticed but said nothing. Similarly, Maurie kept the cook's secret: that he kept pots of molasses and water fermenting in various hidey-holes and in midafternoon ran a still that produced a fiery, heady kind of rum.

His back healed, and he learned to sleep in a long room filled with the oppressive stench of unwashed men and unwashed clothes, blowing wind from the meals of beans, the night loud with their snoring and cursing, violent with constant jerks on the chain between their legs. He learned to live without baths or clean clothes. He learned not to vomit as he relieved himself as fast as he could in latrine shacks over reeking holes of excrement alive with flies. He learned to walk in leg irons. He began to believe he might survive his year.

Then Big John LeBeau came for him.

It was in the evening, the first time. The prisoners were allowed to sit around in the dust of the yard, smoke, and talk for an hour before they were herded into the barracks and the chains were passed between their legs. Maurie's work was not finished. He was still in the kitchen, scrubbing tin plates.

Big John was a trusty with no chains on his legs. He was a gargantuan man, obese but with swelling muscles. Although men were allowed to shave—under supervision—twice a week, he shaved once a month. His arms were blue with tattoos of snakes and dragons. The convicts called him Boss.

He stalked into the kitchen shack, grabbed Maurie by the collar, and shoved him into a pantry stacked with bags of cornmeal and five-gallon cans of lard. Inside, with the door closed, he unbuttoned his pants and pulled out his long, thick penis.

"Okay, Ikey," he said. "What I hear, Jew-boys are better'n anybody at sucking off. Well . . . better'n anybody but Jew *girls*. An' they ain' no Jew girls here. So, get at it. Let's see what you can do."

He put his hands on Maurie's shoulders and pushed him down to his knees.

Maurie whimpered. Big John shoved his wet, stinking phallus against Maurie's face. "Get goin'," he growled.

The door opened. Maurie nearly fainted. The penalty for doing what he had not yet begun to do—but surely *looked* like he was doing—had to be something brutal.

"Whatcha doin', John?"

Maurie looked up and through his tears saw Max Sand.

"You kin have yours after he gits finished with me," said Big John. "I kinda figured on the kike bein' mine, but, what the hell, I'll share with one man. In the spirit of Christian charity."

Max shook his head. "I don't figger it that way,

John," he said. "I figger we oughta leave the Jew-boy alone. You an' me, we're tough enough t' handle th' Loo-zeeanna prison system. He ain't. There's plenty of men be glad to do what you got in mind. Git it from them. Let's let this poorly little fella alone."

Big John stepped around Maurie. His erect penis was still sticking out as he confronted Max Sand.

"You gone tell *me* who gits let alone, who don't?" he asked, squinting and bouncing a little on the balls of his feet as if he were ready to attack.

Max didn't wait to see what Big John had in mind. With his right hand he slapped him hard on that erect penis; and while Big John stood startled, even a little stunned, grabbing at himself, Max drove his left fist into his belly. Big John grunted and staggered, and before he could recover himself Max began pounding him, left fist and right fist, in the gut. Big John dropped to his knees, gagged and heaved, and spit out a mess of beans and grease.

Max had been smart. If he'd bloodied the big man's face with his fists, the fight would have become known to the guards, and both of them would have been lashed and locked in a cage. As it was, Big John was defeated but unmarked.

"Figger I'm right, John?" Max asked as the big man struggled to his feet.

Big John nodded. "See you again sometime, Max."

Maurie couldn't express his gratitude. He didn't have a chance to try. Max led Big John back into the kitchen and pumped a tin cup of water for him. Then they left the shack.

Five months later something terrible happened. Max Sand escaped, together with Mike the big Negro trusty and a prison hustler named Reeves. The common story was that no one had ever escaped, but those three did. It caused a burdensome clampdown on security for a while: constant strip searches, more whippings, in general a tougher life for all the convicts. Then things went back to routine.

Something terrible . . . It was terrible for Maurie. Immediately, Big John came back and began again where he had left off when Max stopped him. For all the remaining months of his sentence, Maurie was compelled to service Big John LeBeau.

Big John knew the prison routine and was a trusty besides. He found times and places, sometimes twice a day. Maurie had no choice. What he had to do made him sick every time he did it. He hated Big John and in his fantasies killed him a thousand times, a dozen ways.

Killing him would have been foolish, even if Maurie could have done it and gotten away with it. It would have meant only that other men would have demanded the same of him. Big John called him his wife and demanded that other men keep away from him. Maybe it was better, Maurie had to concede, that he was Big John's "wife." Not only did other men not dare intrude on what was Big John's; they didn't dare in any way abuse the little Jew who was under his special care.

For whatever reason, Maurie survived.

4

The familiar hard lines of the face were obscured by a thick black beard. The clothes were very different— no black-and-white stripes but a fringed buckskin jacket and Levi's, cowboy boots, and a champagne-colored cowboy hat, one of those with the tall crown and the broad brim. The man wore a pistol on his hip, too. He was tall and hard. He walked with complete self-confidence up to the bar, where he ordered whiskey.

It was the man who was with him that confirmed the identification. He hadn't changed, maybe couldn't change. He was Mike, the big Negro who had knocked Maurie unconscious with the second blow of the lash and had whipped him while he was unconscious. He wore the same kind of clothes and carried a gun.

If that was Mike—and it sure as hell *was* Mike— then the man with him was Max.

Sure. Max Sand. You could tell by the blue eyes.

Maurie gathered his chips, nodded farewell at his playing friends, and walked up to the bar. Max wouldn't know *him,* either. Max's clothes were handsome, conspicuously expensive; and Maurie's were too, in a style as different as two styles could be. Maurie's fine gray suit, narrow-tailored with a four-button jacket and thin lapels that ended at the level of the armpits, had set him back a few dollars. He wore a white shirt and celluloid collar, a pink satin necktie with a genuine diamond stickpin, high shoes and spats—pretty much what the deputy had laughed at when he described Maurice Cohen's clothes to the warden.

"Max."

Max Sand's head snapped around. Apparently he did not like to be recognized.

Maurie sensed danger and spoke quickly. "Maurie Cohen." He nodded then to the big Negro. "Mike."

Max's eyes, which had focused on him glittering hard, now softened. He raised his chin and looked down at Maurie. "Yeah," he said to Mike. "It's Maurie. Figured him for dead, didn't you?"

Mike shook his head. "Man lives through his ten stripes ain' gonna die of suckin' John."

"More nearly," said Maurie bitterly. "Can I buy you two gentlemen a drink."

"Why not?" said Max.

"Bottle of the better stuff for my friends," Maurie said to the bartender. "And my usual."

The bartender shoved a quart of whiskey across the bar toward Max. He poured a small glass half full of an odd yellowish fluid, and Maurie lifted a pitcher and added some water to it. The stuff turned milky green.

"What the hell's that?" Max asked.

"Absinthe," said Maurie. "It's made in France. I picked up the habit in New Orleans. Well . . . cheers. What's it been, eight years?"

Max nodded. "Way I count it."

"Uh . . . Figure Louisiana's still looking for you?"

Max shook his head. "Maurie . . . I ain't never been in Loo-zeeanna in my life."

Maurie stiffened. "Uh— No. Me neither."

"You look prosperous," said Max. "Han'some-lookin' suit."

Maurie smiled and shrugged. "Pinchbeck," he said. "But I'm doing all right. There's money here. This is a boomtown. They drill in new wells every day. This country's *afloat* on oil."

"You still sellin' fake insurance policies?" Max asked.

"No, sir," said Maurie. "They'd hang a man for that here. They ain't got *no* sense of humor in Texas. But you can make money playin' cards honest. I got my method. Somebody says, 'You cheatin',' I says, 'Search me, friend. You'll find no gun, no knife, and no extra cards.' And they do, and they don't find them. Then I say, 'Call for a new deck of Bicycles, friend—just in case you think I got 'em marked.'

Then we play some more, and I win some more. Then if I see the man's gone bust, I say, 'Friend, I wouldn't never want a man to walk away from a table busted from playing cards with me. I believe I won a hundred fifty off you. Here's fifty back. Matter of principle with me.' "

"How you do it?" Mike asked.

"I play all the time, and I play smart. I don't drink when I'm playing. Besides . . . word's around. It's a challenge. Beat Maurie Cohen. That proves you're smart. I've been paid as much as two hundred to sit with a man and lose a hundred to him. Gives *him* a reputation. What he does with it is up to him. Anyway, what are you guys doing in town?"

"We been runnin' cattle down in Mexico," said Max. "Once in a while we come up to Texas to put some of our money in an American bank."

"That's smart," said Maurie. "You like to have supper? And I know where I can find a couple of real nice young girls."

"That's friendly of you, Maurie," said Max gravely. "We've got to talk to a couple of men, then we'll be back."

5

A nightmare. They didn't knock on his door. They broke it down in the middle of the night. By the time he was awake, their heavy handcuffs were on his wrists, and he was being hustled out of his hotel room in his nightshirt—totally mystified as to why.

"Gentlemen!" he protested. "I don't cheat! Any man who has played with me can attest—"

One of the deputies shut him up with a hard fist to

the jaw. He was dragged into the sheriff's office bleeding from the mouth.

They shoved him into a chair.

"All right, Cohen. Who are they? Where are they?"

"Who?"

The deputy slapped him. "You bought a bottle for two guys, one of them a nigger. You bought 'em supper. You bought two whores for 'em. That's who!"

"Friends," said Maurie. "Friends from years back. I hadn't seen them in eight years. What—?"

"They didn't get into the safe, you know," said the sheriff. He was a fragile little old man, pallid, with an outsized hat he did not take off. "The one they kilt was one of *them*. Now, you tell us why, Cohen. Why'd they kilt that man? *And that way?* What the hell was goin' on?"

"I don't know!"

"Don't? Well, let's fill you in. They tried to rob the Merchants and Mechanics Bank. Only thing, the clerk on duty din't have the combination to the vault. They threatened to burn his eyes out with a hot poker they'd heated in the office stove. Instead, the big one, the mean one, burnt out the eyes of one of *them*. I mean, he blinded his partner with a red-hot poker he shoved in his eyes. The man ain't gonna live, I don't think. No difference. We'd hang him anyways."

"I don't know anything about this!" Maurie cried.

"Don't? The one they blinded was called Ed. What's his last name?"

"I don't know! I never met no Ed."

"Who's the others? Who's the men you bought drinks and supper and whores for?"

"I—"

The deputy slapped him hard, so hard Maurie wondered if his neck hadn't snapped.

"Names, goddamn ya!"

Maurie bent forward and vomited. "Max!" he spluttered. "And Mike! The nigger is named Mike!"

"Their last names?"

"I don't know!"

"Where you get to know 'em?"

"In Louisiana."

"Where in Loo-zeeanna?"

"I had to do time on a prison farm. They were there. Mike give me stripes. Look on my back. You'll see I'm tellin' the truth."

The deputy lifted Maurie's nightshirt. He nodded at the sheriff. "Marks of a Loo-zeeanna prison snake if ever I seed any." He stared at Maurie with a new eye, with a sort of grudging respect.

"Cohen, where are these two men?" the sheriff asked.

"If I knew, I'd say," said Maurie. "I don't owe them nothin'."

The sheriff frowned at the deputy. "Well . . ." he mused, pushing his hat back on his head but not taking it off. "I figger they'd-a got the fifty thousand out of the vault, you'd-a got a share. On that basis, we'll hold you for bank robbery and . . . if the one they called Ed dies, for murder. Hangin' you might not be *technical* right, but it'll rid the world of one slick little Jew. Welcome our kike-boy into a cell, Brewster."

6

Nightmare. They took away his nightshirt and locked him in their cell naked, saying they'd bring his clothes from the hotel tomorrow. He wrapped himself in the skimpy, threadbare gray blanket from his cot and sat there shivering the rest of the night and all the next day. They didn't bring his clothes. They brought newspaper reporters to look at the bank robber—including a woman, before whom he could not cover himself decently. They shot off flash powder and took pictures of him.

He shuddered. They were serious. They were going to hang him.

The second day they brought him a woman's dress. They guffawed when he put it on, but it covered more of him than the blanket did, and it was warmer.

What evil spirit governed his fate? How had he come to deserve the tribulations that—? God had tested Job and had not found him wanting. He, Maurie, had been tested in Louisiana and *had* been found wanting. He should have fought off John at the cost of his life. That was what the Lord had expected, and he had failed. Now . . .

The second night, he managed to sleep fitfully. Until about four in the morning, when he was wakened by the sound of a key turning in the lock. A dawn hanging. A lynch.

But no. It was Max Sand. He jerked Maurie to his feet and shoved him out into the sheriff's office, where the deputy who had tormented him lay facedown on the floor.

They rode out of town. No one bothered them. Houston was not unaccustomed to seeing women riding astride horses. The odd-looking woman riding with the bearded man was obviously a whore, being taken out to entertain. She'd earn her money. People who noticed them shrugged and shook their heads. Many of them laughed.

47

7

They rode hard. A posse would not be far behind, but Max seemed to know where he was going, to some place he had been before. He avoided everything that might have made traveling easier and stopping more comfortable: groves, streams, grassland. They sat down at last, under a high sun, in a dry creek bed, where two rattlers retreated as they rode in.

"How can I thank you?"

"You can't. But you don't have to. If you hadn't said hello to me and bought supper and all, they wouldn't have grabbed you."

"Where's Mike?"

"He was hurt. He ordered me to leave him behind and go on. Worst thing I ever did, but I did it. 'Cause I figured I had an obligation t' come back and he'p you."

"How'd you know they grabbed me?"

"We didn't run out of town all that fast. Wanted to get some he'p for Mike. Figured too we'd better bring you with us. I saw 'em grab you."

"Max . . . They say you shoved a red-hot poker in a man's eyes."

"I did it," said Max.

"My God!"

"That man," said Max, "was the last of the gang that tortured and murdered my father and mother. One of 'em carried a tabacca pouch made from my mother's tit, cut off her whilst she was still alive. Tanned and sewed up into a tabacca pouch."

"My God!"

"None of 'em died easy," said Max. "I shot the balls off one. I shoved a red-hot poker into the eyes of the last of 'em. I wisht they was all alive so I could kill 'em all again."

"What are you gonna do now, Max?"

"'Nough of this shit," said Max. "Got some money in a ranch. Gonna change m' name, shave off m' beard, and go to livin' honest. What *you* gonna do, Maurie?"

4

1

MAURIE DIDN'T SEE MAX AGAIN FOR MANY YEARS, until after Max had changed his name.

They parted with a handshake, at a railroad station in Missouri: two young men, each twenty-six years old. Max gave him a hundred dollars, from the proceeds of a year-old bank robbery, and rode off on a horse. Maurie boarded a train for Kansas City and began to work his way east and north.

For a while he was a grifter. It was all he knew how to do. In Missouri and Kansas, then across the river into Illinois and Indiana. For five years he struggled as a flimflam man, working every game he could devise. He sold fake insurance policies again—this time smart enough to scram while the scramming was good. He played cards in Kansas City, St. Louis, and Chicago. The players there weren't as dumb as the ones in Texas, and the profits were slim.

He had catalogs and order blanks printed and sold everything from railroad watches to basketballs, asking as little as ten percent in advance as "earnest money" or an "order-handling charge." He sold wholesale to stores and retail door-to-door, and when he had collected a few hundred dollars in cash he would slip away from his boardinghouse and catch a train.

His best flimflam was with automobiles. He would buy a new Chevrolet or Ford for four hundred dollars, drive it fifty or sixty miles to another country town, let it be known that he was a factory representative who could discount automobiles as much as forty percent, and sell it to some happy buyer for two hundred fifty dollars. Then he'd say he could sell a few more. Of course, he would have to collect down payments—after all, he had to buy the cars at the factory. Having collected maybe five hundred dollars, he would return to the dealer fifty or sixty miles away and buy another car. When he delivered that one to a happy buyer, his bona fides was established, and more down payments would come in. It was of course a pyramid scheme. He could continue collecting money, buying and delivering cars, and collecting more down payments until he judged the time had come to take his profits and scram.

The scheme was ruined in 1913, when an article warning of the scheme was syndicated and appeared in scores of small-town newspapers. Maurie decided the time had come to go home to Manhattan.

It was a strange experience. He had left home at sixteen and now came home fifteen years older and fifty years wiser, with scars on his back and purple circles around his ankles, marks of the Plaquemine prison, that he would carry the rest of his life. Odd. The first time he undressed with a girl and she saw them—"Maurie! You got *these?* You went down sout'! You shoulda never gone down sout'! Wha'd they do to you? You don't let your mother see, no?" And then she would give him the best sex she knew how, because he was the adventuresome man who had gone down south.

51

Word got around. Maurie Cohen was back from down south. Prob'ly carrying a fortune he'd taken off the rednecks. No? Well, the goyim could be bastards. Anyway, he was back, in a good suit, a sharp guy, a wise guy. Guys could use a man like Maurie.

A little fellow like him could not work as a legbreaker. But he was sharp. He had a head for figures. He was honest. Well . . . you could trust him. He was given a job as a numbers runner, then as a numbers book. He made money. He had everything a man could want: nice clothes, a comfortable apartment, a girl when he wanted her . . .

Some good years.

Then—

He had suffered nightmares. At last a dream. The Christians, in their smarts and beauty, imposed Prohibition on a nation that was going to drink, one way or another. A whole new business! Numbers was suddenly small potatoes. And Maurice Cohen was smart enough to see it.

In a small way at first. Then bigger and smarter. Smuggling the stuff in from ships or across the Canadian border was a fool's game. Make it here! You could make gin easy, and beer easier. It could be done by anybody. Of course, where there was real money there would always be thieves, guys that skimmed money off the take. To make money go where it was supposed to, you needed a trusty guy who could keep books—and cook them, too, when you wanted him to.

That was for Maurie. He had a head for figures.

He started in New York. But the Eye-tyes began to take over. Sicilians. Maurie looked around. He'd been around and knew the country. Guy like him would be valued anywhere. In 1922 Maurie went to Detroit to talk to a guy named Firetop—so known for his red hair. They made a deal, and Maurice Cohen became a member of the Purple Gang.

Prestige. Everybody had heard of the Purple Gang. In Detroit and Toledo, the guy who kept books for the Purple Gang was somebody. He was forty years old, and suddenly everybody wanted to know him. Guys wanted to know him. Broads wanted to know him.

He was the guy who toted the revenues and payouts. To pay him, they gave him a piece of a numbers book. The guy who worked it cheated. When Maurie reported that to Firetop, the guy disappeared into Lake St. Clair.

Maurie counted the shipments and the bucks. He never knew, or professed not to know, what happened to guys who shorted. He knew he didn't see them again. He was never tempted to count wrong. His reputation was that he never shorted. He cooked the books, sure, but he cooked them to rook other guys, never the Purple Gang.

Trouble was, it was small-time. He wore handsome suits. He wore spats over his shiny patent-leather shoes. His gray fedoras were of beaver felt. Wearing no more celluloid collars, he now wore silk collars and paid twenty-five cents apiece for them. He was shaved by a barber every morning. He had his hair trimmed twice a week. He lived in a comfortable apartment and listened to a six-tube console radio that worked on socket power and required no batteries. He smoked dime cigars and drank real Scotch smuggled over from Canada. He drove a 1926 Chevrolet.

Small-time. He could not afford to buy a house in the suburbs. He could not afford a new Cadillac or Packard, the kind other guys drove. He didn't take vacations in Florida or sail to Europe. He bought girls when he wanted them but didn't feel he could afford to keep one, not a classy one anyway.

The worst thing was, he took orders, and he knew where he'd stand if he made any kind of a mistake—dead at worst, on the street at least. They liked him. Sure. He was a good boy. An errand boy.

Oh, they'd sell him a piece of something, sure. But only for cash. When you bought a piece of the action, there was no such thing as time payments.

In 1927 they made him manager of a carpet joint on the road between Detroit and Toledo and just across the Ohio line—a roadhouse called The Clock, where a customer could buy a drink, gamble, and take a girl upstairs. It was called a carpet joint because it was fancy enough to have carpet on the floor. It attracted a high-class clientele, including Harry Daugherty and Will Hays, the late President Harding's attorney general and postmaster general. They came to The Clock because they were assured that Maurie Cohen, the manager, was an absolutely trustworthy guy. Hays was now the czar of the movies, responsible for the nation's morals. His sexual predilections were so bizarre that Maurie could never persuade a girl to see him twice, no matter what he paid.

Maurie made bigger money as manager of The Clock. He bought his Packard at last. But he was still an employee.

Toledo had a fine burlesque house downtown. Maurie liked it. Coming out of it one night, he happened to walk past a movie theater where a Western was playing. The star was a handsome cowboy named Nevada Smith. Even in poster artwork, the face looked familiar.

Maurie went inside and watched the picture. It was Max Sand! No question. Nevada Smith was Max Sand!

That night Maurie wrote him a letter. He was discreet. He didn't use the name Max Sand. He just said he wondered if Nevada Smith remembered his old friend Maurie Cohen.

2

Max remembered. Maurie received a note three or four weeks later, saying sure he remembered, and someday when he was in the area he'd stop by and say hello.

The man in the camel coat and the white homburg looked like a gangster. By his clothes. The resemblance ended there. He was tall and lean and tanned. He was Max Sand.

Maurie hurried across the room. "Max . . ." he said quietly as he took his hand. "Nevada Smith. Congratulations. You've done damned well!"

Nevada glanced around. "Looks like you're doin' okay yourself."

Maurie shrugged. "Well . . . C'mon. Have a drink. Have— What can I do for you?"

What Maurie could do for Nevada was not the question, it turned out. Before the evening was over, Maurie had told Nevada how dolefully precarious his position was and had put the touch on his old friend for money to buy a piece of The Clock.

"You need a stake," said Nevada dryly.

Maurie nodded.

"How much?"

Maurie shrugged.

Twenty thousand dollars was a lot of money in 1929. Maurie swore he would pay it back. It was enough to buy The Clock: all of it, not just a piece.

3

Maurie made payments to Nevada over the years, but it took him fifteen years to repay the twenty thousand dollars. Only two years after the loan was made, he repaid the favor—even if Max never knew.

Nevada met Maurie on the station platform. Maurie had been in Texas but never in California, and he found the sun blinding and the heat oppressive. Nevada led him, not into shade, but to a magnificent Duesenberg roadster. With the top off and the sun beating on their heads, they rode behind a chauffeur who drove them through palm-lined streets and up into barren hills studded with gorgeous mansions.

Nevada's house was not pretentious, yet was the home of a movie star.

His wife was there: a woman conspicuously overwhelmed by her circumstances and not really happy with them. She was almost as old as Nevada and was dark-skinned and pudgy, with a weathered face that said this luxurious life was new and troubling for her. She seemed not to know there was such a thing as a swimsuit and swam innocently nude in the pool behind the house, while Maurie and Nevada sat at poolside and talked about old times.

After dinner, when the woman was washing the dishes and going to bed, Nevada and Maurie sat in the living room over cigars and more whiskey and talked. Nevada told Maurie about a problem he faced.

"Y' remember what happened to Fatty Arbuckle?" Nevada asked.

"Charged with rape," said Maurie.

"Yeah. He wasn't guilty of it, but it ruint his career."

"Don't tell me that you—"

"Yeah," Nevada grunted. "I never even *seen* the girl. But her mother claims she's pregnant and says I'm the daddy. Worst part, she's just fifteen years old. Hell, even if they can't prove a thing, just the story gettin' out will prob'ly be the end of Nevada Smith."

"Sounds like extortion to me."

"Right. They're askin' fer money."

"That's a dirty shame, Max. What's her name?"

"Emily. Emily White. Her ma is Ruby White."

Maurie shook his head. "A dirty shame," he repeated.

The next morning Maurie made half a dozen telephone calls, putting the word out that the bookkeeper for the Purple Gang was in town and wanted to talk to somebody about a personal problem. Several men in Los Angeles were glad to do something for a representative of the Purple Gang.

Three days later Maurie was at lunch with Nevada at the Brown Derby and was called from their table to take a telephone call. His caller told him they had confirmed what they suspected, that Ruby White was using the threat of a paternity suit or even a statutory rape charge to extort money from Nevada Smith. She had threatened Francis X. Bushman the same way, and he had given her money to get rid of her.

"Want us to take care of it?" asked the man on the phone.

"I'd appreciate it."

"Consider it done," said the man.

The next morning's newspapers carried the story of a fatal accident. Ruby Smith, drinking and driving, had taken a curve too fast on the Coast Highway. Her Buick had crashed through a guard rail and rolled down a rocky slope and into the ocean. She and her daughter were killed.

Maurie didn't tell Max what he had done. If Max

guessed, he didn't mention it. The thing was done, there was nothing he could do about it, and it was not Max's way to do a lot of talking about what was done and couldn't be changed.

4

Saturdays were big times at The Clock. People came early and stayed late. A third of all the whiskey and beer sold in a week was sold on Saturday nights. The girls made most of their week's money on Saturday nights.

Just before midnight, Saturday, November 21, 1931, three men pushed their way into Maurie's office.

"You lyin', cheatin' Jew bum!" one of them yelled.

And then the beating began. He was too small to struggle against it. When the men left, he lay unconscious on the floor. His nose, jaw, and a cheekbone were broken. Also two ribs.

Six days passed before detectives could question him in the hospital.

"Okay, Cohen, who did it?"

Maurie shook his head. "Don' know," he muttered through his teeth. His jaw was wired shut.

"Th' hell you don't!"

Maurie shook his head again. "Huh-uh."

"Omertà, huh," the detective grunted. The cops were starting to talk in Italian terms. They spoke of the Black Hand and used the word *omertà,* meaning code of silence.

Maurie was able to smile faintly. *"Me? Omertà?"*

"You c'n learn their tricks," said the detective. "I guess you have."

Of course he knew the guys that beat him. What he didn't know was why.

He found out when Firetop came to see him. The big redheaded man sat down beside his bed, took his hand, and explained—

"It was a mistake," he said. "Somebody told us you were sellin' beer somebody else cooked. Not true, we know now. Too late, but we know now. We'll make it up to you some way, Maurie. We'll take care of you right."

Maurie nodded and smiled painfully. "'S okay," he muttered.

"And you've kept your mouth shut," said Firetop. Then he grinned and shook his head. "Bad choice of words, hey? But you didn't tell the cops who did it. We won't forget that, Maurie. That's somethin' we'll never forget. There'll always be guys that'll remember that. You'll always be taken care of."

What Firetop said was true. Maurice Cohen was from then on a favored man, the man who took a savage beating he didn't deserve and didn't squeal on the guys who did it to him. Firetop soon went away to serve a life sentence. The Purple Gang was broken up. But there were always guys who would remember. There would always be something for Maurie.

5

One thing they couldn't save him from. The Toledo detectives were furious. They knew who had beaten him. They had wanted those leg-breakers for a long time but could never make a case against them. Now they had beaten a man who could identify them, and he wouldn't do it.

On another Saturday night, January 23, 1932, The Clock was raided by state Prohibition agents. Maurie was taken out of his carpet joint in handcuffs and lodged in the Lucas County jail. The Clock had operated for years without a raid, but the Toledo detectives had demanded this raid. Selling liquor was against the law. Few were arrested anymore, since Prohibition was likely to be repealed soon, but it was a handy tool occasionally when somebody wanted to embarrass a politician or punish a guy like Maurice Cohen.

On an icy day in February, Maurie—again in handcuffs and trembling with fear—was led inside the high stone walls of the notorious Ohio Penitentiary. He had been only eighteen years old when he entered the Plaquemine prison camp: young enough and resilient enough to survive. Now he was fifty, and he was not certain he would live to the end of his three-year sentence.

As at Plaquemine, the first day was the worst. The warden himself described the intake process as a day that made grown men cry. Maurie would remember spending six or seven hours stark naked. Issuing clothes was the last step in the process, and the new inmates were herded naked from shower to barber to doctor to dentist to fingerprinting to mug shot to indoctrination lecture, with long waits at each station. Finally, in their uniforms, the new convicts were marched across the yard and into the bewildering labyrinth of the huge prison. They ate their first meal in the dining hall. They were marched to a cell block and assigned to a cell.

Maurie compared what he had to endure here to what he'd had to endure in the Louisiana camp more than thirty years ago. In some ways this confinement was easier, in other ways harder. He wore no leg irons, but the convicts were organized into companies and marched as companies from the cell blocks to the cafeteria, to work, to the cafeteria again, back to work, to the cafeteria again, and back to the cell block. Only with a written pass signed by a guard could a prisoner cross the yard alone on his way to the infirmary, the library, or the chapel.

At Maurie's age, no one wanted him for a "wife," so he was not assaulted. He was not the only Jew in the prison. In fact there were so many that a rabbi held services in the ecumenical prison chapel on Saturday mornings. His work assignment was the noisy little factory where the convicts made license plates. He sat at a bench six hours a day, stuffing license plates into brown envelopes.

He wore what the convicts called a hickory shirt, made from a fabric so coarse and rough that it must have been mattress ticking, oversized blue jeans that he had to roll up, a cap, and black shoes made inside the prison. The shirt must be buttoned to the collar; that was the rule. Except when locked in his cell, every man had to keep his cap set squarely on his head.

He lived in a cell meant for two men but housing four. From their stations and while walking their rounds, the guards could peer through the chain-link cell doors at all times; and, unlike the Louisiana guards, these did not leave the prisoners alone all night while they went off somewhere and slept. It was a rule that prisoners must not masturbate, and to be sure they didn't the rule required them to sleep with their hands outside their blankets. When a guard spotted a man with his hands under the blankets he would bang on the cell door with his baton and order him to get his hands out. One of the men in Maurie's cell was caught masturbating and spent ten days in solitary for it.

After a little time, Maurie knew he would survive, but he was not absolutely sure he wanted to. Weeks and months of his life passed in utter monotony, wasted and never to be recovered. He did not suffer from systematized cruelty but from constantly oppressive discipline, total want of privacy, and austerity so severe that it dispirited even men who had never known much of comfort or amenities.

Firetop arrived to begin his life sentence. Maurie saw him occasionally but could almost never find a chance to say a word to him, since they were not in the same company or the same cell block.

When he had served one year of his term, he appeared before the parole board. In the argot of the prison, the board "flopped" him—denied him parole. They thought of him as a gangster. Besides, the Toledo police recommended he be kept in prison till the end of his term.

That is why he was surprised when he was granted parole in 1934, with a year of his term remaining. The board reasoned that it was pointless to keep a man in prison for violating a law that had been repealed.

Maurice Cohen never reported to his parole officer. He went directly to Detroit. The Purple Gang was no more, but that didn't mean there was no gang. Maurie was welcomed home with a wild party, at which it was announced he was the new manager of a new carpet joint in Flint. He was Maurie, he was the guy who hadn't squealed and had even done time in the Ohio pen because he wouldn't squeal. There had to be something good for a guy like that.

Maurie had an announcement too. From now on, he told his friends, his name was Morris Chandler.

6

He was always glad to hear from Max. This time he was glad to have the chance to do him a favor.

They had seen each other from time to time over the years, as Chandler moved from managing the carpet joint in Flint to managing others in various parts of the country. For eight years he managed one in Saratoga Springs during the racing season, then moved to Fort Lauderdale and managed one there during the winter. Max visited both of them.

More and more, the Sicilians took over everything the gangs had operated. It made no difference to Chandler. If anything, the new managers had even more respect for a man who had kept his mouth shut. With them, *omertà* was a matter of honor, the essential quality of every man they trusted and accepted, an essential foundation stone of their organization. Morris Chandler would not become a "made man," would not be inducted into their society, but they accepted him as a man of honor and courage, whom they could trust.

He met many of them. Lucky Luciano, the greatest of them. Frank Costello. Albert Anastasia. Joe Profacci. Carlo Gambino. Frank Nitti. They weren't all Sicilians. Murray the Camel Humphries, in Chicago. Meyer Lansky. Bugsy Siegel.

Max didn't want to know them. He wouldn't come near one of Maurie's joints if he knew any of them were there.

5

THE RAIDERS

1

MORRIS CHANDLER ASSURED JONAS THAT EVERYTHING was being arranged: the telephones with scramblers, the relay through San Diego, new locks . . . everything. And he hoped Jonas and Nevada would be his guests for the show that evening.

Shortly they sat around a table in a glass-fronted box overlooking the stage. The glass tipped forward at an angle, so as to cast bright reflections on anyone looking up from the dining floor or the stage, rendering anyone inside invisible. Their table was covered with heavy white linen. It was set with heavy silver and crystal glasses. A bottle of bourbon and one of Scotch sat in the middle. A bottle of champagne sat in an ice bucket to one side.

A special bottle, label soaked off, sat at Chandler's place. He poured a little green liqueur from the bottle into a glass and added a touch of water. The clear liquid clouded. "Absinthe," he explained. "Illegal. I have to get it from Asia. Taste I acquired in New Orleans before it was banned. You're welcome to try it. It's said to damage the brain."

"I've tasted it," said Jonas, "and I'll have another taste. My grandmother made cookies with that taste: anise."

"Licorice," said Chandler.

"I'll pass it up," said Nevada.

The box was like the airport where they had landed: an accommodation for men who wanted to enjoy some of the pleasures of Las Vegas without being seen.

The first show opened a few minutes after they sat down in the box. It opened with energetic dancing by twenty chorus girls wearing brightly colored feathers. Gypsy Rose Lee followed, delivering a series of quick one-liners to the audience as she danced and stripped all but naked. As she took her bows and departed stage left, a spotlight focused on a man standing stage right, his arms folded, his chin dropped. "Well!" he said. He was Jack Benny, and he took the stage for a thirty-minute monologue. Gypsy came out to join him at the end.

"Uh, Miss Lee, I want to ask you. . . . Do you feel . . . I mean . . . *embarrassed* to be out here on the stage in front of all these people . . . *naked?*"

"No, Jack. Do you?"

The show closed with another appearance by the chorus girls.

Dinner was on the table. Having had steak at the airport, Jonas had ordered fish, which he ate with glasses of the champagne. He ate sparingly. He felt himself running down. Except for the brief sleep he got at Nevada's, he had been on the move without sleep for twenty hours. He was only forty-seven years old: too early for a man to begin losing his stamina.

"That's a fine show," said Jonas to Morris Chandler.

"Costs a fortune," said Chandler. "But let me tell you why places like this make money the old Western-style gambling joints never dreamed of. When we get people in here, we get 'em for *days*. They gamble. They swim in the pool. They gamble. They eat and drink. They gamble. They see a show. They gamble. They sleep a few hours in a very nice room and start the whole deal over. It's a *vacation*. And let me tell you, we take a whole lot more money off people who come for a vacation than we do off professional or compulsive gamblers who come in here and go nowhere but the tables. They're smart. They know how to play. They usually don't drop much. But the house builder from Milwaukee brings the little lady, settles into The Seven Voyages, and they do all the stuff. She plays the slots, he plays the tables, and they drop a bundle. And you know what else? They leave here feelin' good about it. They had a good time."

"Sounds good," said Jonas noncommittally.

"Let me tell you something else," said Chandler. "If the builder from Milwaukee loses too much, he may come around asking for credit. He wants to sign a note. At this point we ask him how much he's lost and how much he can afford to lose. We usually find out he brought with him all he can afford to lose. So we tell him no. Sometimes I've given a guy a couple hundred to get him and the little lady home."

"So next year he comes back," said Jonas.

"Besides which, I want him to tell all his friends back home what a swell bunch of guys we are."

"Short course in how to run a casino." Jonas laughed.

Though he hadn't intended to, he found himself liking this man, this curious combination of craft and calculation with ingenuous enthusiasm. He wondered where and how Chandler and Nevada had become friends. It had to go back long before anyone had so much as imagined The Seven Voyages. Nevada Smith did not extend his friendship readily. If he trusted a man, that should be a man anyone could trust.

"There are tricks to every trade," said Chandler.

"But what deal can we make about the top floor?"

"Happy to accommodate you, Jonas," said Chandler. "The top floor has two suites, each with a nice big living room, two bedrooms with bath, and a kitchenette. The elevators won't take anybody up there unless they have a key. Likewise, we keep the stairway door locked. Ordinarily, high rollers occupy those two suites, but from time to time we help out a man in a position like yours."

"Nevada says you can make special telephone arrangements."

"We got a telephone hookup that switches your calls through San Diego, which puzzles the hell out of anybody trying to trace. We've got scramblers available. Course you have to put a descrambler on the other end. The bottom line is, we're set up to give privacy to a man who wants privacy."

"What's the rent?" asked Jonas.

"Look at it this way," said Chandler. "Each of those suites rents for fifty dollars a night. That's fifteen hundred a month. Two of them is three thousand. We got expenses in the special telephone stuff and in keeping security guys around to make sure nobody tries to invade you. Frankly, Jonas, I usually get nine hundred a week or thirty-five hundred a month for those two suites, when I rent to a man in your situation."

"I'll pay you eight thousand a month," said Jonas. "Two months in advance, though I may not stay two months. The sixteen thousand is yours if I move out sooner."

Morris Chandler smiled and nodded. "Jonas, you are a gentleman and a scholar," he said.

2

Arrangements had to be made. Jonas realized he could not telephone Monica that night. What could he tell her? What she wanted to know was where he was and when he would come home. He hadn't promised he would be in touch within twenty-four hours. So he didn't call.

The suites were comfortable, furnished unimaginatively like most hotel rooms everywhere. The bar was stocked. In the living rooms, picture windows overlooked the pool, and someone who had lived in the suite Jonas chose for himself had equipped the place with a big telescope on a tripod, maybe for watching the girls around the pool, maybe for checking out who arrived in the parking lot.

Chandler had suggested he could send up a girl, but Jonas had declined for tonight. He took a final slug of bourbon and went to bed.

In the morning, Morris Chandler arrived not long after Jonas and Nevada had finished breakfast. Both of them ate big breakfasts: ham and eggs, fried potatoes, buttered toast, and coffee. Jonas poured coffee for Chandler.

"I can help you with some things, if you want," said Chandler. "To start with, you brought no luggage. Give me your sizes, and I'll send up some clothes. Also shaving stuff and so on. But something more important. Twice a week I send a plane to Mexico City to pick up high rollers and bring them in for a couple days' gaming. I send a man down there on each flight. He can post letters, send telegrams, and so on."

Jonas nodded. "I'd like to send two telegrams."

The first telegram from Mexico City was to Monica:

EVERYTHING IS OK STOP WILL BE IN TOUCH AGAIN IN A
FEW DAYS STOP MY LOVE TO YOU AND JO-ANN STOP

The second was to Philip Wallace, Attorney, Washington, D.C.:

TELL LA AND NEVADA NEW YORK OFFICES TO INSTALL
IMMEDIATELY ON MY PRIVATE LINES DESCRAMBLER
EQUIPMENT AS FOLLOWS STOP VERICOMM MODEL NUMBER ONE DASH FOUR TWO FOUR STOP THESE LINES TO
BE MONITORED BUSINESS HOURS STOP SUGGEST YOU
INSTALL SAME YOURSELF STOP EXPECT TO CALL NO
LATER THAN FRIDAY SO EQUIPMENT MUST BE IN PLACE
STOP

A shop downstairs delivered clothes chosen by
Morris Chandler, and Jonas sent the suit he had worn
from Bel Air down to the dry cleaner. His new clothes
were resort wear: light-colored slacks and golf shirts,
also after a couple of days for tailoring a royal-blue
jacket. Chandler sent up similar things for Nevada.
Nevada accepted them, knowing he could not venture
downstairs in the hotel in jeans and a buckskin shirt.

On Friday Jonas placed a telephone call to Phil
Wallace in Washington. Phil answered and could
understand him, so Jonas knew the descrambler was
in place.

"Somehow I guess," said Phil, "that you're not
really in Mexico City."

"You guess right. How much heat is on?"

"Well, you're not on the Ten Most Wanted List, but
if your whereabouts is discovered you'll be served
with the subpoena. A couple of senators are pissed.
Counsel for the committee is pissed."

"And the competitors who want my ass are pissed,"
said Jonas. "I don't give a damn."

"Monica is pissed," said Phil. "She called and demanded to know where you are. Demanded. She said she knew damned well you're not in Mexico City."

"Monica's not stupid."

"You didn't order a descrambler for her."

"The only reason would be to tell her where I am, and I don't want to do that, not yet anyway. I'm not sure she could hold out if they pressured her to talk."

"You got a problem there. Monica's not just a little pissed. She's *big* pissed. She's going to New York."

"Well, she's got her job in New York. She travels to New York—"

"She's taking Jo-Ann with her."

"Jo-Ann's in school. She—"

"She's taking her out of school, transferring her credits to some school in the East."

"I'll take care of the Monica problem. Don't worry about it."

"I'm not. I'm just telling you what she said."

"Okay. You want to know where I am?"

"If I need to know. Otherwise I don't. I've told people I don't know. I'd like to continue doing that."

"Do you mind passing along some orders?"

"Not at all."

Jonas stood looking down on the swimming pool, convinced now the man who had brought the telescope to the suite had brought it to do some plain and fancy girl watching. Two-piece bathing suits were in style, and some of the girls around the pool were spectacular. Looking at them made a man horny.

"Okay," he said to Phil. "I want some people to join me. I'd like to have Sheila." He meant his personal and private executive secretary, in the Los Angeles office. "But I'm afraid that, apart from Moni-

70

ca, she's the one person they might follow. Besides, she's got a child, and I can't ask her to leave it."

"Do you want her to know where you are?"

"No. I want her to communicate through you. As my lawyer, you have privileged communication with me. No. The guys I want to join me are Buzz Dalton from Inter-Continental, Clint McClintock from Cord Electronics, Bill Shaw from Cord Aircraft, and Len Douglas from Cord Explosives."

"I get you," said Phil. "Second-level men from each company. None of your top executives."

"Bright, knowledgeable young fellows," said Jonas. "None with family obligations that would prevent their spending some time with me. Tell them to bring along the paper about pending stuff. They'll know what that is."

"Okay, but where do they go?"

"Make notes," said Jonas. "They come one at a time. Dalton first, Shaw next, then McClintock, then Douglas. On Tuesdays and Thursdays at noon there's a flight from Mexico City to where I am. It does not go from the Benito Juarez International Airport. They'll have to get to the Tlalpan Airport. A sixteen-passenger De Havilland comes in about noon. Tell them to identify themselves to the agent that comes with the De Havilland. From that point they can relax. They'll be brought to me. Tell them to bring summer-weight clothes. They'll only need one suit. Do I have to tell them not to talk to the people they meet?"

"It sounds like you're settling in for a long stay," said Phil.

"Long enough to screw the bastards that are trying to screw me," said Jonas.

3

Jonas quickly grew bored with living in the suite. He could only call the offices that had installed the descramblers. He could think of a thousand other calls he wanted to make, and he gave orders to his people at the offices with descramblers to telephone this person and that, saying they had heard from him and he had ordered them to relay a message. It was not a satisfying way to do business.

On his fourth night in the suite, Morris Chandler offered to be host for dinner, which he would have room service bring up.

"What you need up here is a cute girl," he said to Jonas.

"What I need is an executive secretary," said Jonas.

Chandler laughed. "A horizontal secretary."

"No, seriously. A secretary. I can't bring in my executive secretary, and I need a woman who's competent and I can trust."

Chandler glanced at Nevada and shrugged. "If you say so," he said.

They ate lobster, which were flown in on ice and were kept live in a tank in the hotel. Chandler and Nevada talked a little about old times in New Orleans. Jonas guessed that was where they had met, in Storyville, in one of the celebrated old whorehouses. At least, both of them had been there in the early years of the century. Both remembered a whore who had always worn a black satin mask trimmed with lace and received her callers while reclining nude on a red plush settee. The rumor had been that she was the wife of a prominent New Orleans cotton broker.

They remembered musicians: a pianist named Ned

and a trumpet player named Charley. They spoke of something called *herb sainte*, which Jonas deduced was a fiery liquor as destructive of a man's mind as the wormwood-tainted absinthe the French used to make, which was now illegal in every country in the world. They laughed about how it had got them in trouble.

Abruptly Chandler broke off the reminiscences and spoke to Jonas. "You want an executive secretary? Trustworthy and competent, you said. How 'bout one that's honest and competent and you can trust—and would probably be glad to sleep with you, too?"

"They don't make 'em like that," said Jonas.

"Trust me," said Chandler. "I'll send somebody up for you to interview in the morning."

He did. She arrived at half past nine, and she was more of a surprise to him than Morris Chandler had been.

"Mr. Cord? My name is Mrs. Wyatt. Mr. Chandler sent me up to be interviewed as a possible executive secretary."

She was one of the most beautiful women he had ever seen, and Jonas formed a quick determination that he would take her to bed as soon as he possibly could. Golden-blond hair surrounded the perfect features of her face. She was flawless. He couldn't see anything wrong with her, unless maybe it was that her eyebrows were distinctly darker than her hair. She wore a putty-colored linen pullover and a tailored knee-length dark-gray skirt, white shoes with thin high heels, and smooth, sheer nylon stockings on long, sleek legs. She was no girl. She was probably thirty-two or -three. She wore on her face a look of worldliness, even of world-weariness, that suggested she had seen a lot and had a few things to regret.

"Come in, Mrs. Wyatt, and sit down," he said. "I just sent the table back down, but I can order us another pot of coffee if you'd like some."

"You needn't," she said.

"I think I will anyway. I could use some myself."

She sat down gracefully, crossing her legs below her knees the way girls in finishing schools were taught to do. Her skirt crept up a little, but she had it under control and showed no more leg than she wanted to.

Jonas picked up the telephone and ordered coffee, knowing a few small pastries would come with it.

"I'll be blunt, Mrs. Wyatt," he said. "Why did Morris Chandler recommend you?"

"He told me what your requirements are," she said plainly. "He judged I could meet them, and so do I."

"What is your experience?" he asked.

"I was a secretary with Boise-Cascade Corporation. The last four years I was there I was an executive secretary. Then I got married, and then I got divorced."

"Do you have any children?"

"No, sir. After my divorce, I worked again as an executive secretary, in the office of the state auditor of the State of California. I've had eleven years of secretarial experience, six of them as a confidential and private secretary to an executive."

"What are you doing in Las Vegas?"

"I'm stranded here," she said.

"How so?"

"I came here on a romantic trip with a friend. He wanted to gamble. So did I. I signed a chit to buy some chips. He promised me he'd pay my chit, just as soon as a check he'd given the hotel cleared. He lost everything he had with him, panicked, took off, and left me with an unpaid chit. I'm working it off as a waitress."

"How much is it?"

"Five hundred dollars. I've paid off sixty-five."

Jonas shook his head and picked up the telephone. He dialed Morris Chandler. "Morris, this is Jonas. Put the balance of Mrs. Wyatt's chit on my account."

"You hired her, then," said Chandler.

"We'll talk about that later."

He put down the phone and looked up to see her frowning at him, her chin high.

"That's how you do things, I imagine," she said. "Quick decisions. The only thing is, now I owe *you* four hundred and thirty-five dollars. That's how *I* do things."

Jonas grinned. "I guess I *have* to hire you, then. Otherwise, you can't pay me."

"Well . . . You're not a Las Vegas casino. You don't hold people prisoner until they pay off their chits. Do you? You don't break legs either, I imagine."

"You think Chandler would do that?" he asked.

She shrugged. "He's *your* friend."

"Do you know why I'm here?"

She nodded. "I also know if I told anybody you're here, I'd be lucky if all I wound up with is *two* broken legs."

"I don't do business that way, Mrs. Wyatt," said Jonas coldly.

"No. I don't suppose you do. But Chandler does. Why do you think he trusted me, telling me who was up here and sending me up?"

"Maybe I'm an innocent," he said.

"Maybe you are. Were you ever in Vegas when Bugsy Siegel was running the Flamingo?"

"No, as a matter of fact, I never was."

She nodded. "I was. I've always liked to come here. My husband brought me here and introduced me to gambling. Bugsy was dangerous. Bugsy killed people.

The town has changed since they got rid of Bugsy Siegel. They *had* to kill him. He was bad for business. But only because he was too public. It wasn't that he beat up on people and killed them—or had them killed—that got him his death sentence. It was that he did it too openly. When it's done now, it's done quietly."

Jonas shook his head. "I can't think Morris Chandler—" He stopped. What he had in mind was that he couldn't believe a man Nevada Smith trusted could be what she suggested.

"He doesn't make all the decisions here," she said. "He's a partner, not the sole owner." She sighed. "I'm being stupid. You want a secretary that won't blab everything she knows, and here I am doing it."

"You're not Chandler's confidential secretary," said Jonas.

"I won't kid you. I'd like to be yours. Uh . . . Chandler spoke of . . . other requirements."

Jonas smiled. "Well. Let's say what he mentioned isn't required. It would be appreciated."

She stared at him evenly for half a minute, a quizzical smile on her face. Her tongue flicked out between her lips. "Would you want me to live here?" she asked.

"I have two bedrooms."

She grinned. "Yeah. You have a certain reputation, Mr. Cord."

"The job is yours," he said. "I'll appreciate your calling me Mr. Cord when others are with us. When we're alone . . . Jonas."

"My name is Angie," she said.

6

1

ANGIE MOVED INTO THE SUITE THE AFTERNOON AFTER her interview. She slept in the second bedroom that night. The next night she slept with Jonas.

That the new executive secretary was an exceptionally attractive woman and lived in the suite with Mr. Cord came as no surprise to the four young executives who arrived in Las Vegas within the week. As Angie had said, Jonas had a certain reputation.

Making all the arrangements took some time, but by the end of his second week in Las Vegas Jonas was firmly in control of all his businesses. He called his companies on the scrambler telephones. The four young executives could go anywhere any time as couriers, flying the De Havilland junket flight to Mexico City and catching flights from there to anywhere Jonas wanted them to go.

He was not the subject of an FBI manhunt. He was just a missing witness in an investigation few in Congress or in the press thought was very important. Such newspapers as did run stories about his disappearance treated it as a joke on the Senate. One page-five headline read, CORD STRINGS OUT SENATE SNOOPS.

Another read, NOAH IN DE ARK, JONAS IN DE WHALE?

He could not even be held in contempt of Congress, since he had never received a subpoena.

Angie first saw the newspaper report that Monica had filed for divorce.

She and Jonas were sitting at breakfast, he following his lifelong habit of eating a hearty breakfast, she contenting herself with juice, coffee, and a Danish. She did not have any provocative nightgowns or peignoirs, and they slept nude. She came out to breakfast in her white nylon panties, he in his boxer shorts. He was reading *The New York Times,* she the *Los Angeles Times.*

"Oh, Jonas!"

"What?"

She handed over the newspaper, pointing at the story.

CORD DIVORCE

Mrs. Jonas Cord Files for Divorce

Mrs. Jonas Cord, née Monica Winthrop, has filed an action in Los Angeles Superior Court, asking for a divorce. Alleging adultery, cruelty, and abandonment, Mrs. Cord asks for a decree of divorce, child custody, division of California property, and alimony.

Mr. Cord's whereabouts are unknown. He left his Bel Air home shortly before United States marshals arrived to serve on him a summons to testify before a Senate subcommittee investigating airline operations and has not been seen since. He is believed to be living in the vicinity of Mexico City. Jerry Geisler, Mrs. Cord's attorney, said there would be no problem about obtaining jurisdiction over Mr. Cord, since under California law he can be served his summons by publication.

Jonas shrugged and handed the newspaper back to Angie. " 'Adultery, cruelty, and abandonment,' " he muttered. "She can't prove any one of them."

Angie put her hand on his. "I'll swear under oath that we've never slept together," she said.

He smiled wanly. "You won't have to do that, Angie. It's good of you—and loyal—but you won't have to do it. My lawyers will negotiate a settlement. Monica knows better than to demand too much. She'll be reasonable."

"Did you love her . . . ever?"

Jonas nodded. "Twice. I married her twice."

Angie frowned and nodded at the newspaper. "It's none of my business. I shouldn't ask you questions. But— It mentions child custody."

"Monica doesn't need to demand child custody. The girl will be eighteen years old soon. Anyway, I wouldn't demand she come to live with me. I want her to visit me—that is, if she wants to, but only if she wants to."

He glanced over the newspaper story again, frowning, then laid the paper aside. His lips were tight.

"I'm sorry, Jonas," Angie whispered.

"If you want to be sorry the marriage has broken up, okay, be sorry. If you want to be sorry for me, don't. If you want to be sorry for her, don't."

Angie blinked, squeezing tears from her eyes. "I shouldn't ask you personal questions," she said. "I'm happy to be with you, whatever the answers are."

He stood, walked behind her, lifted one of her breasts in each hand, and nuzzled her alongside the throat. "You ask me anything you want. If I don't want to answer, I won't."

Angie looked up and grinned. "Or lie," she said.
"Or lie," he agreed, chuckling.

2

Sure. Lying was an alternative. It was one he sometimes took. He did not want to know everything about
Angie. He put through some inquiries and found out
that the life story she had given him was not the truth.
He didn't condemn her for that. He could understand
why she didn't want to tell the truth. He was confident
that he could trust her. Nevada thought so, too, and
that counted for a lot.

Edgar Burns died of shrapnel wounds at Château-
Thierry on June 6, 1918, two weeks after his daughter
Angela was born and twenty-six years to the day
before her first husband would die on Omaha Beach.
Her young mother remarried, and Angie was twelve
years old before they told her about her real father. In
school she was Angie Damone. She never used the
name Burns.

Damone was a bootlegger, operating in Yonkers
and sanctioned by no less a figure than Arnold
Rothstein. When Rothstein was killed, Damone was
sanctioned by a don of the Castellamarese group, and
he continued to distill gin until the repeal of Prohibition. After Repeal, the don gave him a share of the
bookmaking in Yonkers. Angie grew up understanding that her family lived just as well as the families of
the lawyer, the dentist, and the real estate agent who
were their neighbors on a tree-lined residential street
in White Plains. Her father—stepfather, as she came
to understand—was in the import-export business.
So she believed. So the neighbors believed.

Angie was seventeen when Damone was arrested

and the newspapers revealed the true nature of his business. The charges were dropped, but Angie was so humiliated that she never went back to school. She asked Damone to give her a job with a bookie, but he adamantly refused. For a year she did nothing. She avoided her old friends and made a group of new ones among the unemployed and malcontented element of the young people of White Plains.

One of them was a young man named Jerome Latham. Considered handsome, he had a square face with a long, strong jaw, heavy-lidded eyes, and slicked-down hair usually covered with a snap-brim hat. He always had money to spend, and no one was sure how he got it, which lent him a dim aura of mystery and glamour. Angie fell in love with him; and, since she was by far the most beautiful girl he had ever seen, Jerry— She couldn't say Jerry fell in love with her. She was an ornament to him, or a trophy. But they became a pair. They were seen everywhere together. He spent money on her. He bought her clothes.

Her mother and stepfather did not like Jerry Latham. Damone called him a hoodlum, to which Angie replied angrily that Damone was an odd man to be calling another man a hoodlum. That exchange soured the relationship between her and her mother, as well as that between her and her stepfather. She went to Jerry and told him she wanted to live with him.

Jerry took her in. He lived in a room, just one room, but shortly he rented a small apartment, and in July of 1937, when she was nineteen years old, they married.

She learned how Jerry made the money he was never without. He was a distributor of counterfeit money. He bought the money from a counterfeiter in

New Rochelle, paying him eight dollars apiece for twenty-dollar bills. Then he traveled throughout the New York metropolitan area, making small purchases and tendering counterfeit twenties. In a typical transaction he would buy five dollars' worth of something, hand over a twenty, get fifteen in change, and make seven dollars profit. He would ride a bus, say to Paterson, New Jersey, pass half a dozen twenties in the course of an afternoon, and come home fifty dollars richer. He might make more if he could sell the merchandise he bought. Often he hocked it and never redeemed it.

He was never caught. The secret was that he wasn't greedy. In 1938 a family could live quite comfortably on a hundred fifty a month. He went out no more than once a week. Also, he kept careful track of where he went. He never returned to the same merchant, usually not even to the same block.

The ease with which her husband got money fascinated Angie. She suggested he let her try it. She went with him a few times, then went out on her own. She was useful to him. She could go back to stores where he had been, where he wouldn't return, and take the same business for another hit.

In February of 1940 something terrible happened. Treasury agents raided the New Rochelle print shop. Their counterfeiter went off to federal prison.

Jerry had to find a new racket. He began to loot mailboxes. She helped him. They poured bags of mail out on their kitchen table, sometimes finding cash, sometimes checks, sometimes money orders, occasionally a stock certificate or a bond. He was an artistic forger, too. When he found a good-sized check, made out to, say, Arthur Schultz, he would forge a driver's license in the name of Arthur Schultz, and use it as identification as he offered the check at a bank. If the check was made out to a woman, Angie cashed it.

The Selective Service law went into effect on September 10, 1940. Jerry Latham had one of the first numbers picked. Before the year ended, he was at Fort Dix, undergoing basic infantry training.

Angie was desperate. She had no real idea how to make a living, except by doing the kind of thing Jerry had done. On March 11, 1941, federal agents entered her apartment, arrested her, and seized more than four hundred pieces of mail. They found driver's license blanks and even a few counterfeit twenty-dollar bills. On June 20 she entered the federal reformatory for women at Alderson, West Virginia.

They brought the telegram to her cell. Sergeant Jerome Latham had been killed in action on June 6, 1944. She received her parole in September.

During her three years in prison she had learned to take shorthand and to type.

She never worked for Boise-Cascade or for the California state auditor. Her parole officer helped her obtain a job as secretary to the War Ration Board in White Plains. Before long she met the man who was to become her second husband, Ted Wyatt. He was exactly the kind of man Jerry Latham had been: a grifter whose specialty was counterfeit ration stamps. As a secretary to the board, she could learn what stamps would be authorized for use next month, which was useful information for a man who needed to know what stamps to print.

Her term of parole ended in September 1945. She married Ted Wyatt, and they set out for California, where both of them hoped to be free from the reputations they had made in the New York area. He did introduce her to gambling, as she had told Jonas. He took her to Reno, then to Las Vegas, and when casinos like the Flamingo and The Seven Voyages opened, they were familiar figures in the gaming rooms.

Wyatt lost money. Too much money. He disappeared. She was not sure if he'd been taken out in the desert and killed or if he had run. Either way he was gone, and she divorced him on the grounds of abandonment.

She got a job as a secretary in a Las Vegas automobile agency. She became the officer manager. Nights, she picked up extra money as a shill in the casinos. She was never a B-girl. Ten men a week propositioned her and offered everything from straight cash to European vacations, but she never accepted.

Two years ago Morris Chandler had offered her a job as *his* secretary, and she had left the automobile agency, for more money. What Chandler had done was send up his own secretary to become Jonas's. Of course she did not owe him five hundred dollars on a gambling chit. Chandler had been surprised when Jonas called and told him to put Mrs. Wyatt's account on his bill. He went along, amused. He did not suggest to her that she act as a spy. He only suggested, diffidently, that she might find out something it would be to their mutual benefit to know.

Morris Chandler did not suspect that she saw in this job with Jonas Cord a chance, not just to do something better with her life at long last, but to do it with a man any woman could be glad to be with.

3

One more thing about Angie pleased Jonas immensely. Over the years he had found he most appreciated women who would give him oral sex. It was not only that he enjoyed the act—which he most assuredly did—but he had found, too, that women who were willing to do it were bold and playful not just in bed but in their approach to life in general. They were the kind of women he most liked and was most ready to respect.

"Say, Angie," he whispered to her one night during their second week together. "You're great in bed, but—"

"But?"

"No, not 'but.' You're great. I wondered, though, if you . . . if you'd take me into your mouth."

She lifted herself up on one elbow. "Seriously? I don't know. I don't really know. I've never done it." She reached down and lifted his penis in her hand. "I could never get all that in. I'd gag."

"Getting it all in is not the point," he said.

"What *is* the point? How would I do it?"

"Like eating a lollipop," he said.

She laughed. "Like eating a lollipop! Well . . . Is it a big deal for you?"

He drew a deep breath. "I'd like it. I don't demand it."

She stared at his crotch for a few seconds. "Will you wash it first?"

"For sure."

"Well, then . . . I'll try."

She was telling the truth. She had never done it. She had heard it called ugly names, heard women who did it called ugly names. But— He was worth it.

When he came back from the bathroom he smelled of soap and of shaving lotion he had splashed on his upper body. He plumped up pillows and put them against the headboard of the bed, then sat and leaned back against them—and waited.

She took a moment to firm up her courage. She

smiled at him, then lowered her face, opened her mouth wide, and sucked his throbbing organ into her mouth. She held it there and massaged his puckered foreskin with the tip of her tongue. Then she pulled back, seized the thick stalk in her left hand, and began to lick it, taking long strokes from the base up to the tip. He whispered a suggestion that she lick what was below, too: his dark, wrinkled pouch the size of two fists. She did that for a moment and returned to it briefly now and again, but mostly she alternated between holding the upper half of his penis in her mouth, manipulating his foreskin with her tongue and lips, and pulling it out and licking its full length.

He began to gasp and moan. She was giving him ecstasy. She was surprised; she hadn't imagined a man would experience utter bliss under such ministration. So . . . He would love her for it. Well—not love. He would treasure her for it. She had heard women denounce it as debasing, abnegating. They might consider that she was in control of this, as she was never in control when a man was on top of her, pounding himself into her in his final stage. Of this, *she* was the manager and could bring him along or slow him down, as she wished. No way at all did she feel degraded.

She found nothing unpleasant about it, though she was nervous about his ejaculation, wondering what she would do with his fluid, wondering if it was nasty-tasting stuff. She worked to bring it, but it took some time, five or six minutes anyway. When the abrupt gush came, she discovered it had almost no taste at all. Certainly it was nothing offensive. The word for this was sucking, so she guessed she was supposed to suck when he climaxed, so she closed her lips around his shaft and drew the stuff from him. Some of it went down her throat. She swallowed. Some accumulated in her mouth. She swallowed that, too.

"Oh *god,* Angie!"

She smiled gently. Some of his ejaculate gleamed on her chin. "You like that, huh?" she whispered.

He reached for her and drew her into his arms.

4

Nevada and Angie gaped at Jonas. They laughed, and yet they knew he was serious.

Clint McClintock, on a trip to Los Angeles, had gone as ordered to a costume shop in Culver City and had come back with a number of items Jonas had specified. One was a gray, almost white toupee. Another was a pair of silver-framed eyeglasses, with ordinary glass, not lenses, in the round frames. Another was a can of wax an actor could mold by hand into the desired shape and then work into place in the mouth between gums and cheeks, shoving out the cheeks and making a man's face look fatter, even jowly.

Jonas had experimented for two hours with his disguise and was now showing it to Angie and Nevada. With a toothbrush he had worked gray-white from a jar into his eyebrows and into the bit of his hair that showed below the edge of the toupee. The spectacles were astride his nose. The wax in his mouth puffed out his cheeks.

"What th' hell is th' idea of that?" asked Nevada when he stopped laughing.

"I'm going down and have a look at the casino operation," said Jonas. "A lot of money is moving down there. I want to see how."

"Maurie'll *tell* you how."

"I want to *see* how."

He put on the suit he had worn on the flight from Bel Air: gray with a white pinstripe, double-breasted. He wore a white shirt and a flowered necktie, the kind that was in style that year.

"I'll go with you," said Angie.

Jonas considered her offer for a moment, then accepted it. She would complement his disguise, the more so since her face was known in the casino.

They went down in the private elevator and stepped out into the part of The Seven Voyages that Jonas had not yet seen. The casino floor was the hotel's reason for being. It was the focus of the entire operation, the source of the profit. Without the take from the casino floor, The Seven Voyages was a losing proposition.

Jonas had gambled in other casinos and understood something about the layout. The casino offered only fast-moving games: roulette, craps, blackjack, and chuck-a-luck. The players stood or sat around solid tables with green covers, under bright lights. Jonas had played in French casinos, where the players dressed in formal clothes. Here they could wear almost anything, though The Seven Voyages would not admit cowboys in jeans. The house men wore white shirts with black bow ties and black trousers— with no pockets. Girls in thigh-high ruffled skirts and net stockings carried trays among the tables, offering free drinks to players, trying to avoid giving any to people just wandering through. The air was blue with tobacco smoke.

The players stared and frowned at the tables or at their cards, and there was little conversation. When they talked at all, they talked quietly. No one cheered a win. No one groaned at a loss.

Morris Chandler wanted the casino in The Seven

Voyages to have the aspect of the casino at Monte Carlo, as much as practicable. Little was practicable, since he could not ask the players to wear evening clothes. But the croupiers at the roulette tables kept up a tradition by making two announcements in French. They called for the bets by saying, *"Faites vos jouets,"* and they closed the betting just before they spun the wheel by announcing, *"Rien va plus."*

Jonas understood that the games were scrupulously honest. The wheels were not weighted, the dice were not loaded, and the cards were not marked. The casino did not need to cheat to win. It could not lose, because it set the odds.

The roulette wheels, for example, had a zero and a double zero—an American innovation; European wheels had only the single zero. When the ball landed on zero or double zero, the house won. At the blackjack tables, the house kept the deal—and the small advantage of the dealer—even when the player had a blackjack. And so on. An individual player might win, might in fact win heavily, but every day, over the whole operation, the house inevitably won. Knowledgeable players understood that; but, with the chronic optimism of gamblers, they believed they could beat the odds. Gamblers who played any way but knowledgeably, rationally, and unemotionally invariably lost—and often heavily.

Two-way mirrors covered the ceiling of the casino. In a dark chamber above, supervisors prowled catwalks, observing the action below, looking for any possibility of skimming by the dealers and stick men. Though the house men could not have carried away the bulky chips in their tight pocketless clothes, sometimes one would cheat by shoving stacks of chips to confederates who had not actually won.

They watched also for cheating players. Cheating by players was all but impossible. They could not touch the wheels. The oversized house dice, especially made for The Seven Voyages, carried the casino logo etched into the surface, so players could not substitute their own dice for the house dice. Just about the only serious problem the house had was with card counters at the blackjack tables. Card counters were prodigies of memory who kept track of what cards had been dealt and improved their odds greatly. To discourage them, the games were played with two decks of cards. Still, some were good enough to count even two decks. There were few who could do it, and they were generally recognized. The casinos had a blacklist of them. When a house man saw a known counter, or when he suspected a new counter, that player was taken by the elbow and gently expelled from the casino. Strictly speaking, card counting was not illegal. All the casinos hated the card counters, though, and tried to keep them away from the games.

With Angie at his side, Jonas bought five hundred dollars' worth of chips. He played blackjack, the game where a smart player had the best chance, and in the course of an hour won a hundred twenty-five dollars. That was no big deal. When he cashed in, the cashier took no particular notice of him.

They walked through the hall where ranks of slot machines swallowed half dollars and silver dollars, spun, clunked to a stop, and did not pay. Slot-machine players were more emotional than the gamblers on the casino floor. When they won, they whooped and yelled—which was good for business. Some of the payouts were big, but they were infrequent. A twenty-five- or fifty-dollar payout was more common. It kept the players happy, kept them at the machines. The slots were pure profit. There was no risk the house would lose on them, even temporarily.

"The place is a license to print money," Jonas muttered to Angie as they returned to the top floor.

7

1

JONAS ADOPTED A NAME FOR THE GRAY-HAIRED JOWLY man who played blackjack: Al String. It was a play on the name Cord. He gambled night after night for a week in The Seven Voyages and lost eighteen hundred dollars. He moved from there to the Flamingo, where he played four nights and won three hundred. He moved on to some of the older howdy-pardner gaming rooms. Angie went with him every night. Nevada, dressed in a suit that would have looked right on a Texas oilman, complete with champagne-colored Stetson, went with him to the old places.

"I'm beginning to figure this thing out," Jonas said to Nevada and Angie one night when they sat down over a late supper in the suite. "The beauty of casino operations is that most of the money that passes through them is in cash. That's what attracts the kind of operators that are running this town. Think about it! Think of the opportunities."

"Like?" asked Nevada—though he was not so innocent that he didn't know what Jonas was about to say.

"The simplest element of it is tax evasion," said Jonas. "What part of the take do you guess they report? Fifty percent? Seventy-five percent? In those back rooms they count cash. How much of it slips out of the hotel without being accounted for?"

"There's more to it than that," said Angie. "The casinos are owned by partners, most of them back East. They fly out here on junkets and gamble. They fly home with briefcases full of cash, which is their share of the partnership profits. If the tax boys happen to find out about their cash, they say they had good luck and won a lot of money. They never admit they own a part of the casino and get a regular distribution of the profits. The cash they get is skimmed off the take every night."

Their late-night snack was club sandwiches. Angie and Nevada drank beer with theirs. Jonas drank bourbon. He had pulled off his wig and had of course pulled from his mouth the wax which for some odd reason made him thirsty.

"A lot of the partners can't afford to be identified as partners," Angie went on. "They have criminal records, and the State of Nevada would lift the casino license if it were known that they own shares. So they come out here and play the tables, go home with 'winnings,' and no one's the wiser . . . so they think."

"It's a stupid risk to take with businesses that could make a hell of a lot of money without skimming," said Jonas.

"There are partners they don't dare shove out," said Angie.

"You know a lot about this for a gal who's just a secretary," said Nevada.

"If you're around here awhile and watch, you see a lot of things," she said.

"I want to talk to Chandler," said Jonas.

2

Morris Chandler came up for lunch the next day. Angie was not asked to join Jonas and Nevada.

Chandler stood at the window for a while, looking down at the swimming pool. He put his eye to the telescope and peered at something, probably an exceptionally bare girl. Then he swept the telescope up and began to look at something else.

"You figured this out yet?" he asked Jonas.

"Well, I've looked at some of the bathing beauties, but—"

Chandler turned toward him and grinned slyly. "You're looking in the wrong direction. Take a look through it now."

Jonas put his eye to the tripod-mounted telescope and looked at what Chandler had focused on. He saw naked girls.

The penthouse atop the newest hotel had a terrace surrounded by potted shrubbery that shielded the girls from the view of everyone below. The top floor of The Seven Voyages had the only windows within a mile that were high enough to afford a view of the sunbathers. Several hundred yards separated the two hotels, and apparently the owners of the penthouse and their girls thought the distance was great enough to protect the girls' privacy. Morris Chandler had bought the astronomy-class telescope to give his fifth-floor high rollers a little something extra for their money.

"The girls work there," said Chandler. "That's their job: to sit around naked."

"Tricks of the trade," said Jonas. He returned to the table and their lunch. He sat down. "The first night I was here, you started to give me some basic lessons in the casino business. Nevada says you'd be willing to give me more."

"What do you want to know?" asked Chandler.

"How much do you skim?" asked Jonas.

Chandler's face stiffened. He hesitated for a moment, then asked, "What if I say we don't?"

"Say it."

Chandler glanced at Nevada, who was watching him gravely, interested in his answer. He took a deep breath and blew it out. "I give *you* lessons," he said. "You should give me. You know too much already."

"Well, I'm hardly a government spy," said Jonas. "Hardly an informer."

"What was strictly illegal a hundred years ago is absolutely legal now," said Chandler. "What was immoral fifty years ago is acceptable now. And some things that used to be legal and moral are illegal and immoral now. Some big American families built their fortunes doing things the keepers of the public morality don't tolerate today. Like importing slaves. Like keeping whorehouses. It's just a matter of time. What goes around, comes around. Now we got these crap politicians, like Kefauver, making hysterical accusations for whatever political profit they can get. It's—"

"Who owns The Seven Voyages, Morris?" Jonas interrupted.

"I own eighteen points," said Chandler. "On the record I own sixty-one points, but all except the eighteen I hold for men who don't want their names associated."

"Men whose names you can't afford to have associated with the operation," said Jonas.

"Have it your way. A point, you understand, is one percent."

"Does Lucky Luciano own any points, directly or indirectly?"

"Are you *kidding?* Luciano? No way."

"Frank Costello? Jimmy Blue Eyes?" Jonas asked. Chandler shook his head emphatically.

"Meyer Lansky?"

"No. Meyer doesn't own any points. But he has a consulting contract with us."

"What's he consult about?"

"The contract is in writing and has been looked at by Justice Department snoops. It says he advises us on how to do our accounting and keep the casino honest. Everyone acknowledges he'd know. He's run plenty of illegal joints in his day. The Justice Department found nothing wrong with the contract, nothing wrong with our hiring him as a consultant. I don't know if you understand this, but Meyer Lansky has *no* criminal record."

"In point of fact," said Jonas dryly, "he tells you how to skim."

"In point of fact," said Chandler, "he tells us how to distribute the profits."

"Officially a corporation owns The Seven Voyages," said Jonas. "Seven Voyages Corporation owns the gaming license. You own all the stock."

"You checked," said Chandler. "Okay. Officially, legally, I own everything," said Chandler. "I'm like Meyer Lansky in one respect. I'm clean. I have no criminal record. So I make a perfect front man."

Nevada grinned. "Why, Maurie has never even had a ticket for jaywalking."

"I'm not going to ask you who really owns the points," said Jonas. "But I am interested in one thing. What does it cost to put up a casino hotel in Las Vegas?"

Chandler sipped wine. "When we first came out here, say in 1946, there was a rule of thumb," he said. "To set up a decent-size hotel and casino, you spent one million dollars, max—including the price of the land. By the time Siegel and his partners got the Flamingo into operation, they had three million in it. It cost five and a half to open The Seven Voyages."

"What would happen if you didn't skim?" Jonas asked.

Chandler shook his head. "You couldn't pay off your investors. Banks would never have put up five and a half million dollars to build a casino hotel in Las Vegas. We had to have investors."

Jonas nodded. "If you *had* the five and a half million, you wouldn't need to sell points, and then you wouldn't need to skim. You could run strictly legal and make a good profit."

Chandler grinned. "You thinking of building a casino hotel, Jonas?"

Jonas lifted his eyebrows and shrugged. "Well . . . Suppose I offered package tours from LA and Frisco. Round-trip flight to Las Vegas, accommodations at a Cord hotel, with meals, at a fixed price. I—"

"Your people will fly in here, swim in your pool, eat your food, see your shows, and wouldn't gamble. Hell, they'll bring the kids."

"Okay. The price includes a chit, redeemable only in chips. Say a hundred dollars' worth. So they've paid for their gambling in advance."

"Smart guys will turn in their chits for chips, walk around the room, and come back and turn in their chips for cash."

"Junketeers can always do that," said Jonas. "The remedy is, you watch out for them. You don't let them do it to you twice. But the great majority will gamble with their chips, lose them, and buy some more. You get somebody hooked on casino gambling, they stay hooked. The junket is an investment."

Chandler laughed. "I see why you're a multimillionaire. I also see why you're holed up in The Seven Voyages ducking a subpoena."

When they had finished their lunch and conversation, Morris Chandler left the suite. Angie came in. Jonas's four young men, who had been working in the living room of Nevada's suite, came in.

Nevada stood with Chandler as he waited for the elevator.

"A word to the wise, Max," said Chandler quietly. "Your boy's awful sharp. *Too* sharp. I hope he has sense enough not to talk to other guys."

"Jonas has got brains he hasn't used yet," said Nevada.

"Well, tell him to use them. I like the guy. I don't want him to get hurt."

3

The telephone rang as Jonas, Angie, and Nevada sat together on a sofa and sipped bourbon as the sun set in the desert. She picked it up. "Morris Chandler," she said.

"Problem," said Chandler grimly. "Guess who just checked into the hotel? Mrs. Jonas Cord!"

"Damn," Jonas muttered.

"She had a reservation. My guys took it. They don't know you're here. I couldn't refuse to accommodate her. She's in a room on the fourth floor, right under you. How the hell did she find out you're here?"

"Uh . . . Maybe she didn't. Maybe she doesn't know."

"Even so, you can bet she's been tailed. If those subpoena hounds really want you, they'll be tailin' your wife. The way their minds work, they figure the divorce is just a cover."

"All right. We'll have to play it as smart as possible. My crowd has got to stay in their rooms, out of sight. She'd recognize any one of them."

"And so would the subpoena hounds, right?"

"Right. I'll get off the phone and get to each one of them."

4

Monica stripped and hurried into the shower. Alex followed her, dropping his clothes on the floor. In a moment he was under the shower with her, and they washed each other, running their soap-slick hands over each other's bodies, hardly able to finish and dry before their out-of-control carnal fervor overwhelmed them. They went half dry to the bed, and in a moment he was on her and rammed himself into her. Alex was like Jonas, she reflected for a moment—when he was aroused he was in a hurry. But he never failed to satisfy.

They lit cigarettes when they were finished and lay on the bed, satiated to exhaustion—never guessing that the management of the hotel on which Chandler's telescope focused had returned the favor, so that half a dozen men and women in the high-roller suite of that hotel had amused themselves immensely by watching Monica and Alex in their frenetic labors, through the window they had supposed was too high and remote to give anyone a look into their room.

"The casino's gonna lose money on us," said Monica. "I don't think I'll be able to spare five minutes after din-din before we come back up here and do it again."

"It's a great place, isn't it?" said Alex.

"How'd you know about it?"

"It's got a reputation as a place where people can go that want to be discreet."

"Well, we've been discreet. The reservation is in my name. The room is in my name. Your wife will never know."

5

The phone rang again. Morris Chandler. "It may be nothing but a coincidence," he said to Jonas. "She's got a man with her. No big stud, I'd guess. But not a bad-lookin' guy."

"Monica could always pick 'em," said Jonas.

"If it would help you, I can bug her room while they're down to dinner. They've just gone down."

"You mean I can listen to them when—"

"And we can tape it. Might be very useful when your lawyers sit down to discuss settlement with her."

"Do it, Morris. Wire it so I can listen up here, and we'll tape it, too."

When he put the phone down, Angie shook her head, smiled, and said, "You can be a real bastard, can't you?"

"You'll enjoy it," he said.

She grinned. "Yeah."

6

The voices and the other sounds came through as clearly as though the activity were taking place in the next room. Nevada went to his own suite, unsubtle in expressing his disapproval of what they were doing. Chandler remained, his cheeks drawn in between his

teeth, frowning. Angie listened soberly, and so did
Jonas, sipping bourbon.

—"Careful! Careful! Like . . . like that. Yeah!"

—(Laughing.) "I thought you told me you were a
virgin."

—"What the hell would you want with a virgin?"

—"I don't know. I never had one."

—"*Jesus Christ!* Somebody's at the door!"

—"Here. I'll wait in the bathroom."

The buzzer on the door had sounded clearly on the
speaker. It would be on the tape.

—"Who is it?"

—"United States marshals, Mrs. Cord."

—"What do you want?"

—"We're looking for Mr. Cord."

—"He's not here."

—"It will make everything a whole lot simpler if
you'll let us in."

—"For a minute. For just a minute."

No sounds came through for a moment, apparently
as she opened the door.

—"You're Mrs. Jonas Cord?"

—"Temporarily. The divorce is pending."

—"You say Mr. Cord is not here?"

—"No, he's not here."

—"There is a man here. You don't deny that, do
you?"

—"I don't deny anything."

—"Who's the man?"

—"It's none of your business. He's not Jonas
Cord."

—"If you'll let us make sure of that, it will make
everything a whole lot simpler."

Another moment of silence. Then the man's voice:

—"Okay, guys. I'm not Jonas Cord, okay?"

—"Nope. You're not Jonas Cord. Can we look in the bathroom to see if anybody else is there?"

—"Look in the closet and under the bed while you're at it, which will make everything a whole lot simpler, then get your asses out of my room."

—"Do you know where Mr. Cord is, ma'am?"

—"I don't know where he is. Furthermore, I don't give a damn."

A long silence, punctuated by the slamming of a door.

—"Shit. You've lost your erection."

7

In the morning, while Monica and Alex slept at last, Jonas and Angie ate breakfast, read the newspapers, and exchanged a few bland jokes about what they'd heard last night.

When they had finished eating, Jonas called in Bill Shaw and sent him off as a courier to Los Angeles, by way of the De Havilland junket flight to Mexico City. He sent the tape with Shaw, to deliver to the lawyer who would represent him in the divorce settlement negotiations. He wrote a note and enclosed it with the tape:

Use this as you see fit, not at all if you don't have to. Notice that the talk after the door buzzer eliminates all question about who we are hearing.

8

Ten days later Jonas called Morris Chandler to a meeting in the suite.

Three days before, Chandler had asked Nevada how much longer he thought Jonas would want to occupy the entire fifth floor of The Seven Voyages. The money Jonas was paying in rent was very generous, Chandler said, but he'd decided he had made a bad deal. The rent he would have received from high rollers who would otherwise have occupied those suites, plus what they would have lost in the casino, substantially exceeded Jonas's generous eight thousand a month. Besides, some high rollers had complained about not getting their usual deluxe suites.

When Chandler came into the suite, he found Nevada and Angie and Len Douglas with Jonas. The three men wore golf shirts and slacks—Nevada looking incongruous in his. Angie wore a raspberry-colored golf shirt and white slacks.

"You know everybody, Morris," Jonas said. "Coffee?"

"Yes, thank you," said Morris Chandler. He was not wearing one of his usual dark suits today but wore instead a cream-and-brown-checked jacket and dark-brown slacks. He was visibly nervous, as if he anticipated that the call for this meeting presaged something ominous.

"Take a look through the telescope," said Jonas. "I checked them five minutes ago, and they were up there."

Chandler sat down and put his coffee on the table.

"Nevada tells me I'm costing you more than I'm paying you," said Jonas.

Chandler nodded. "It's just a business fact, Jonas. Nothing personal. You've been fair. I'm sure you had no idea I'd come out short. *I* didn't."

"We'll take care of that one way or another," said Jonas. "I want to talk to you about something else."

"Still thinking of building a hotel of your own?" asked Chandler.

"I've got something better in mind," said Jonas. "I'm thinking of buying this one."

Chandler jerked up his chin and shook his head. "It's not for sale."

"It might be," said Jonas. "The men who own the points just might be interested, if they got the right offer."

"You don't even know who owns the points," said Chandler.

"Most of them, I do," said Jonas.

"How could you find out? How could you find out when the feds can't find out, when the State of Nevada can't find out?"

Jonas glanced at Nevada. Both men had amused gleams in their eyes. "I hired a consultant," said Jonas. "He doesn't know who he's working for, but he likes his fee."

"Who? Who would tell you?"

Jonas grinned. "Meyer Lansky," he said.

Morris Chandler got up and walked to the telescope. He leaned against the eyepiece and was silent for a full half minute as he seemed to be staring at the girls atop the neighboring penthouses but was actually taking the time to compose himself and think through the implications of what Jonas Cord was saying.

"They call Meyer the Chairman of the Board," said Jonas. "But money doesn't stick to him. It seems to have a way of flying from him. In spite of all his connections and all his smarts, he's not rich. He didn't jump for my offer. He's too smart for that. But he took it."

Chandler sat down. He glanced at his coffee cup but did not pick it up. "Do you mean to tell me you actually know—"

"Who owns the points," Jonas interrupted. "I do. With a few exceptions. And I know who'll sell. For the right money, I can pick up seventy-two points tomorrow. My consultant will help me buy seventy-two points. You've got eighteen that you'll sell me. That leaves just ten points out, and I figure you know who has them."

Chandler's face turned red, and his voice rose thinly. "I'll sell you mine? You think I'll sell you mine? What makes you think I'll sell you mine?"

"There's something in it for you, Maurie," said Nevada. "I said to Jonas, 'There has to be something in it for Maurie.' You stay. You manage. You get a share. Of stock. No points. There'll be no more points."

"I'm an easier guy to work for than the guys who have the points," said Jonas.

Chandler calmed down a bit. "What do you figure on paying for a point?" he asked.

"My accountant will tell me."

"Accountant! No accountant will ever figure out how a place like this works. No accountant will ever figure out what a point is worth."

"My accountant already knows," said Jonas. "Meyer Lansky."

"You put a hell of a lot of confidence in Lansky," said Chandler.

Jonas shrugged. "He's got no criminal record. He likes money. Better than just any old money is money paid by check, that he can report for taxes. Now, the way I want to do this, I'm going to buy your stock in Seven Voyages, Incorporated. You distribute the money to the points holders. You'll have a capital gain. I'll take care of that with a bonus I'll pay you for your services as manager of the hotel."

"What if some guys don't want to sell their points?"

"As soon as I take over, I'm stopping the skim," said Jonas. "Anyway, they're in no position to make noise. They're tax evaders at best. Besides, I'm going to pay a good price."

"Some guys you can't shove around," warned Chandler.

"Maurie, you're looking at one," said Nevada, nodding toward Jonas.

9

Four days later Jonas sat down on the couch, surrounded by files and papers that Angie had assembled for him, and began a long telephone conversation with Phil Wallace in Washington.

Angie listened. She was astonished by what she heard—and very pleased that Jonas trusted her so much as to discuss his businesses in great detail within her hearing.

The telephone was equipped with a squawk box, so she heard both halves of the conversation.

"I'm going to move out of Las Vegas. Once it's known that we're buying a casino-hotel here—"

"They'll be all over the place looking for you," interrupted the metallic voice of Wallace. "So, where you going? Mexico City?"

"Acapulco. Top floor of a hotel. Shaw has worked it out."

"Well, that brings up something. You have a friend in Mexico. In fact, you have a friend in Mexico who comes up to Las Vegas on junkets to The Seven Voyages. She's been in the hotel since you've been there."

"Who the hell are you talking about, Phil?"

"Sonja Batista."

Angie saw Jonas's face whiten. "Where'd you hear that name?" he demanded of Phil Wallace.

"It was in the files I inherited from McAllister. None of my business. Nothing to do with anything. But her name came up in a news story in *The Washington Post* Tuesday. The rumor from Cuba is that her uncle may take power again. Fulgencio Batista. You've heard the name?"

"Of course I've heard the name."

"He's connected, if you know the meaning of the word. He's got friends in the States who'd like him to take over in Havana."

"I know why," said Jonas. "But say why."

"He'll turn the country into a paradise for those people and their interests. Casinos. The world's greatest whorehouses. The works."

"Sonja," Jonas mused.

"Escalante," said Wallace. "She's married to a guy named Virgilio Diaz Escalante. He's got money from oil."

"Sonja," Jonas murmured. "Jesus Christ! Phil. Get me her address and phone number. Discreetly. Okay?"

10

Angie licked the last of his fluid off Jonas's penis. She rolled over on her back.

"You're not taking me with you, are you?" she asked. "To Mexico. You're leaving me here. What could be so important—?"

"There are better things for you in this world," he said.

"Name one," she whispered, on the verge of tears.

"We're forming a new corporation: Cord Hotels, Incorporated. Temporarily, the fifth floor of The Seven Voyages is corporate headquarters. Nevada Smith will be president of the new company. He's staying here to watch things for me. I'm making Morris Chandler a vice president. Nevada may trust Morris too much. I'm not sure, but I think he might. I want you to stay here, keep an eye on things, and report to me. I'll make arrangements for you to have a direct communications channel to me. I'd make you a vice president, too, but I can't. You know why I can't."

She closed her eyes and nodded. "Making me an officer would risk the gaming license. I have a criminal record."

"Right."

"How long have you known?"

He shrugged. "Pretty soon after you came here."

"You could have thrown me out."

"I don't want to throw you out. You can be valuable to me. Besides, I like you. I'll pay you twenty thousand a year."

"Jonas!"

"Plus bonuses. You'll earn it. Anyway, I won't be gone so long. I'll be back. The biggest thing is, I trust you. That's on instinct, mine and Nevada's. You already know more about my business than Monica ever did. I trust you, Angie. Don't let me down."

She bent forward and kissed his penis, then sucked it in between her lips and teeth. "When you trust a woman not to bite you," she muttered, "that's trusting her more than you do when you tell her about your business." She looked up and grinned playfully. Then she was solemn again. "I want to go with you, wherever you go. But—" She shrugged. "I know better. I know that can't be. So . . . You can trust me, boss. If for no other reason . . . because I love you."

8

1

Jonas had sent Bill Shaw ahead to make arrangements. Colonel William Shaw had come with Cord Aircraft immediately after his discharge from the Army Air Corps in 1946. He was a useful man to have on a staff. He had proved to be a capable administrator, a man not daunted by details. Besides, he had been a test pilot and was a skillful flyer and navigator. He had picked up a Beech Baron from Inter-Continental Airlines in Los Angeles and flown to Mexico. Since there was nothing unusual in a flight by Colonel Shaw from Los Angeles to Mexico City, the subpoena hounds had taken no notice.

Not so the newspaper stories telling that a new corporation, Cord Hotels, Incorporated, had bought The Seven Voyages casino-hotel in Las Vegas. Jonas had known the marshals would arrive with their subpoenas in hand as soon as that word got out. Shaw's mission to Mexico City and Acapulco had not been to afford Jonas a pleasure jaunt but to arrange a new hiding place.

Angie helped him to disguise himself as Al String. He left for the airport in one of the hotel's Cadillac limousines, in the company of a group of Mexican junketeers who had spent three days at The Seven

Voyages and had undoubtedly dropped several fortunes. At the airport, the limousines drew up to the De Havilland. The junketeers, plus Jonas, climbed the steps into the sixteen-passenger airplane, and shortly it took off.

2

When the plane had reached cruising altitude and was flying smooth and level, Jonas went to the head in the rear, waited his turn, and went inside. There he killed off Al String. The wig and the wax went in the trash. He used wet paper towels to scrub the silver-gray from his eyebrows and hair. When he returned to his seat he was not the man who had boarded the plane. He was the man whose name and picture appeared on his passport.

Returning to his seat, all but unnoticed by the Spanish-speaking junketeers, he took time to observe his fellow passengers.

Franklin D. Roosevelt had taught *norteamericanos* to be embarrassed by conspicuous consumption, but it did not embarrass Mexicans. Mexican businessmen wore gaudy gold jewelry: heavy rings with star sapphires, glittering diamonds, emeralds, also gold wristwatches set with gems, even gold chains hanging just inside their open collars. Their women wore furs, necklaces, bracelets, rings, anklets. They also wore— Jonas had heard this sworn to but could not confirm it—exquisitely jeweled but wholly non-functional chastity belts.

Their party continued on the plane. Two hostesses in short skirts served champagne and caviar to the roistering Mexicans.

It was inconceivable to Jonas that Sonja could have

become one of these shallow, talky, befurred, bejeweled women—or that she could have married one of these greasy gambling-junket men.

He shook his head at the offer of champagne. He asked for bourbon instead, and when the young woman brought it he turned and stared out the window. They had crossed the Mexican border by now. In the distance ahead and to the right he could see the Sierra Madre.

3

In early afternoon the De Havilland settled onto the runway at the Tlalpan Airport, a satellite airport for Mexico City. The Mexican officials at this airport recognized the De Havilland and knew who was aboard. None of them would suggest that these wealthy and influential citizens should identify themselves to immigration control or make a customs declaration. Those functions simply disappeared, and the junketeers—Jonas ignored and moving with the crowd—moved directly into the airport terminal building.

Bill Shaw was there waiting to drive him to La Plaza Real, where he would stay for a few days before he moved on to the top floor of a hotel in Acapulco.

Jonas sat down on the couch in the living room of his suite. Though the Mexican government would pretend not to know he was in the country, the hotel knew who he was; the suite was fragrant with fresh flowers, and the bar was equipped with champagne, brandy, and with the liquor it was understood that Señor Cord liked best: Tennessee sour mash bourbon.

"Communication is not all it might be," said Shaw. "When we get to Acapulco—"

"I can make local calls?"

"Oh, sure. It's the taps on the other end, in the States, that I'm worried about."

"We have a directory?" Jonas asked.

Shaw nodded and retrieved a telephone directory from a drawer in the Louis XV writing table where the telephone waited.

"Well, thanks, Bill. Suppose I see you later."

Sitting on the couch, sipping a small shot of whiskey, Jonas flipped through the fat Mexico City telephone directory, half expecting not to find the number he needed and to have to hire someone to locate—

But there it was: Escalante, Virgilio Diaz, listed at the address Phil Wallace had wired him.

He went to the writing table and dialed the number.

"¿Quién habla?"

"Do you speak English?"

"Momento, señor."

The moment was more than a moment, but eventually another voice came on the line. "I speak English."

"I am calling for Señora Sonja Escalante. I am Jonas Cord, from the States."

"The Señora is not at home at this time. Would you like to leave your number?"

He did. He was not willing to take the shower he wanted, for fear she would call and he would miss her. He drank some more whiskey. He walked around the room. He stared down from the windows at the bustling streets below. He wished he had asked how long she might be out, when he might expect her to call.

The telephone rang about five. "Señor Cord? *Momento*. Señora Escalante."

"Jonas?" A small voice. Familiar? He was not sure.

"Sonja? Do you remember me?"

"Remember you? What would you suppose, Jonas?"

Her English was as it had been: only faintly accented. The image of her that he had retained in his memory all these years was vivid; and he wondered if she was anything like that image anymore.

"I deeply regret . . ." His voice caught.

"What do you regret, Jonas?"

"That so many years have passed. That I didn't come looking for you."

"I wouldn't have received you," she said with a firmness in her voice that he had only rarely heard but still vividly remembered. "I have always known where you were. You might have had a little difficulty finding me, but I would have had none finding you. Your name is in the newspapers constantly."

"I'd like to see you, Sonja."

"It's all right now," she said. "You will be welcome for dinner tomorrow night. My husband knows about you and will be glad to meet you."

"I would like to meet your husband, Sonja. Might we, though, meet for the first time . . . alone?"

"Where?"

"In a public place. In a restaurant. It's your city. Tell me where."

"Harry's American Bar," she said. "I don't go there often. Make a reservation for nine tomorrow evening."

"I will. And I—I will be there at nine."

4

He was on time. She was on time. She recognized
him. He recognized her. He stood. She came to the
table, let him kiss her hand, and sat down.

The years had not changed her much. He had not
seen her for twenty-five years, but she was Sonja
Batista, just as he remembered her. She smiled. She'd
always had a beautiful smile. She'd always had a
strong, symmetrical, beautiful face.

Changed— Well, she did have a bit more flesh on
her face, softening the lines of her high cheekbones
and her firm jaw. Her face was incised with very fine
lines at the corners of her eyes and mouth but with no
others. If he could judge through her clothes, her
breasts were a little more generous than they had been
before. They had always been generous enough to win
his attention and admiration.

Unchanged— Her dark-brown hair framed her face
and fell to her shoulders, a little unruly as always.
When he met her, bobbed hair had been in fashion,
but Sonja had never bobbed hers. She had been too
proud of it. Her brown eyes confronted the world with
challenging skepticism, just as he remembered. He
remembered too and saw again a stalwart face that
did not flinch from reality.

"Twenty-five years," he said. He shook his head.
"It's unbelievable."

"I have followed your career," she said. "The
newspapers mention you often."

"But what of you, Sonja? I am embarrassed to have
to say I have not followed your life."

"That would have been difficult," she said. "I have
lived a very quiet, very private life, very different
from the way it was when you knew me."

"I told you to call me if you ever needed anything."

For an instant her warm smile turned mordant, but quickly it returned to the open, welcoming smile she had shown him since she sat down. "I never wanted anything from you, Jonas," she said. "I thought of calling you once and decided not to."

He glanced down at the huge diamond she wore on her ring finger. She wore a wedding band also.

She saw the glance and said, "I have been married for twenty-four years."

5

The chastity belts Jonas had heard rumored were in fact worn by a few very traditional, typically very wealthy Mexican women. Sonja wore one.

It could not have prevented her having sex with a man not her husband, if she wanted to. All it did was identify her as the wife of Virgilio Diaz Escalante y Sagaz and was more in the tradition of the name-embroidered silk ribbons some Islamic women wore around their waists in the Middle Ages than the iron belts some Frankish women were condemned to endure. It was exquisitely crafted, forbiddingly expensive, and entirely comfortable to wear. Two fine and flexible diamond-studded platinum bands circled her upper legs, another circled her hips, and a supposed shield joined these three bands. Nothing guarded her rear. She could easily have broken the thin metal and taken it off, and if she had, Virgilio would almost certainly not have suspected anything ill. On the other hand, if she didn't break it she could not have removed it; it was locked on her. Virgilio took it off when they had sex, or whenever else she asked him to.

She had worn it for more than twenty years and was proud her husband had never had to return it to the craftsman to be enlarged—as did most husbands who had fitted their wives with these belts.

The man sitting with her, Jonas Cord, could not have understood why she consented to wear the belt. Such a thing was beyond his *norteamericano* comprehension. A Yankee, he was deficient in the warm, sympathetic understanding, man for woman and woman for man, that so much characterized the Latin peoples. She had once admired his unsentimental Yankee practicality—and maybe did yet, a little—but she was glad her son had been reared in a different tradition.

Her family tradition could not have been more different from the Cord tradition. Her uncle was Colonel Fulgencio Batista y Zaldivar, once President—dictator—of Cuba and likely to be again. Jonas Cord could not begin to comprehend what that meant. When she met him, in 1925, not long before the death of his father, her uncle—her father's baby brother, much nearer her own age than her father's—was a fugitive, and so was her father. They would have been summarily shot if the then Cuban government could have laid hands on them.

She herself might have been shot. At the very least, if she had been caught in Cuba, she would have been—well, it would have been a painful experience. Her uncle's ambition and what he did in pursuit of it had interrupted her education and forced her to accompany her family into exile, first in Florida, then in Texas, finally in California.

When she met Jonas Cord she was nineteen years old. He was twenty-one. She had been educated in a convent and was confused and frightened, not just by the world but by this strange, bustling *yanqui* world into which she had been precipitated. She was so naive that she did not understand that *norteamericanos* did not apply the word Yankee to the residents of Florida, Texas, or California. It was all Yankee to her. The nuns had taught her English—but not the kind of English she heard spoken. They had taught her that America was a land of big men and big women.

The women . . . They dressed outlandishly in short skirts and tight bodices and were aggressively bold, the nuns had said. They painted their faces. They smoked little cigars. (The nuns didn't know about cigarettes.) They drank distilled liquors. Unmarried girls went abroad in the streets day and night, without *dueñas*. They went to theaters and to dance halls without escorts. Some of them drove automobiles. Some of them lived in flats they shared with other girls, without parents or brothers to supervise and protect them. As a result, American men had no respect for American women, and any woman's virtue was constantly at risk.

Arriving in the United States, she had found that what the nuns had taught her was true, mostly. Girls her age did indeed wear their skirts above their knees, and they cut their hair so short their ears were exposed. They smoked and drank like men. They lacked elementary grace and seemed to know little of common courtesies. Worst of all, in their country they were not strange; she was.

Her father and her uncle traveled, where she did not know; but they were not often at home. A Mexican family somehow involved in her uncle's plans to seize power in Cuba were glad to offer Sonja and her mother a place in their home in Los Angeles, and they lived there for two years.

The daughters of this family were thoroughly Americanized, and they urged Sonja to dress as they did, to bob her hair, and to learn to smoke cigarettes. The pressure to conform gradually overcame her resistance. Over a few months she became half Americanized. She would not bob her hair, but she began to wear short dresses, to smoke, and—very cautiously at first—to venture into the noisy, uninhibited society of young Americans. She was, she realized painfully, neither fish nor fowl. She was no longer the timid, convent-educated girl who had come to Los Angeles from Cuba; but neither had she become a hard-edged, giddy American. She was deeply curious about American ways and wanted to learn more about them and selectively adopt more of them, but she remained confused and embarrassed by the conspicuous difference between her and the young people around her.

Oddly, they did not attach any importance to the difference. Another American habit, it seemed, was to be welcoming and uncritical. They accepted her.

She met Jonas Cord at a party held aboard a yacht. It was an evening she had been looking forward to ever since she heard about it—to go aboard a *yacht* and mingle with people who could afford yachts. Jonas was a handsome young man, exceptionally virile as she saw him. His manifest virility, plus his air of self-confidence, set him apart from the other young men aboard the yacht that night. She had observed of other young American men that many of them were ambiguous about their masculinity. In their exuberant gaiety some of them were as giddy as girls. Also, many of them lacked confidence in themselves. More accurately, they lacked confidence in anything.

It seemed Jonas Cord had nothing he needed to prove. He knew who he was. He knew what he wanted. He looked around the partygoers on the rear deck of the yacht and walked directly to Sonja Batista. He asked her to dance. He offered a drink from his pocket flask. After an hour or so he suggested they leave the party and go for a drive.

He explained his car to her. It was a Bentley, imported from England, and the driver sat on the right. It was dark green, with nickel plating on the frame above the radiator and on its big lights and its wheel hubs. The windshield folded down, so the wind blew in your face. The hood was fastened down with a strong leather strap. The seats were upholstered in fine leather and had the odor of leather.

Sonja put her foot on a stirrup and climbed in. The frame of her seat folded around her in a sort of U, as did the body of the car, so she felt secure enough; but there were no doors, and if she leaned forward a little she could see the road rushing underneath. Jonas removed a delicate silk scarf from the glove box and helped her tie it around her head to control her hair. He handed her a pair of goggles to protect her eyes.

He drove her where she had never been: into the mountains north of Los Angeles, from where they had beautiful views of the lighted city and of the Pacific Ocean.

"I want to learn to fly an airplane," he told her. "So I can have a view like this of any city."

It seemed a glorious dream. "I would fly with you," she said. "I would not be afraid."

Then the question was Of what *would* she be afraid? Would she be afraid to allow him to kiss her? She was, but she allowed it.

From the moment of that kiss, Sonja ceased to think she was a virgin. She ceased to think she was pure. Not because he had violated her, of course—she was not so naive as to think he had. It was the way she had welcomed and enjoyed his kiss that had debased her. It was the fact that she wanted him to do it again that corrupted her.

He touched her breasts and her legs. She shook her head. She was frightened. He stopped, smiled, lit a cigarette, and offered it to her.

When they returned to the yacht, the party was still going. Hardly anyone had noticed they had been gone.

She *was* naive. She had no doubt he would want to see her again, that he would pursue her—court her, after the old-fashioned term. She expected probably he would propose marriage.

He did not. She didn't see him for several weeks. When she did see him, it was at another party, this one in the courtyard in the center of a block of small attached stucco houses. When he approached, she was standing by a fountain lighted with red and blue spotlights.

"Sonja! How nice to see you."

"Señor Cord . . ."

"I got that airplane we talked about," he said. "Are you ready to go flying?"

"I am not certain," she said. "Maybe I am afraid after all."

Jonas Cord was a perceptive man. He recognized hesitancy in this young woman who had been so forthcoming before. He understood why. "The world has changed for me, Sonja," he said. "That is why I did not call you again before now. You see . . . my father died suddenly."

"Oh, Jonas!" (She pronounced his name Hoe-nass, as she pronounced her own Sone-yah.) "If I have known . . . such sympathy I would have extended!"

"I knew you would. You are a wonderful girl, Sonja."

She knew he was bold. He was direct, in the *yanqui*

way. She had not guessed his boldness and directness would extend so far as the proposition he made before the evening was over.

They were in his car once again. He had kissed her again as he had done before, and she was aroused. She let him slip her dress off her shoulders and down around her waist. She allowed him to unhook her brassiere. He kissed her nipples, licking them and sucking them between his lips. She knew if he suggested it she would allow him the ultimate privilege. She wanted that and had ceased to fear it.

Instead— "Sonja. I inherited my father's business. Shortly before he died he committed our company to a major venture in a new product called plastics. I have to go to Germany for two months. Sonja . . . Would you come with me?"

6

She went. Her mother was appalled, but her father and uncle encouraged her to go. They knew who Jonas Cord was. They envisioned a perfect alliance: Cords and Batistas. Sonja would play the traditional female role: a marker in a game, her body would cement the alliance.

1925 was an important year. Jonas's father died. Jonas's stepmother sold him all her claim to the Cord estate, leaving Jonas in complete control of the Cord businesses. A man who seemed to be his dearest friend, named Nevada Smith, left Jonas and went off to run a Wild West show.

Calvin Coolidge was inaugurated President of the United States, for a full term in his own right. A squat, pockmarked, obviously brutal man who called himself Josef Stalin took control of Russia. An elderly retired field marshal by the name of Paul von Hindenburg was elected President of the German Republic. A man named Clarence Birdseye froze fish fillets so hard they were like small oak planks, in which condition they would last indefinitely and were tasty when thawed. Jonas took an interest in the process but decided not to invest in it. What interested Americans most that year was a spectacular courtroom trial that resulted in an odd little schoolteacher named Scopes being fined a hundred dollars for teaching Darwin's theory of evolution in a Tennessee school.

The two months in Germany was a dream. Jonas traveled first class. They crossed the Atlantic on the *Aquitania,* which had to be like living in the palace at Versailles; certainly no palace in Cuba was as elegantly appointed as the cabins, lounges, and dining rooms of the ship. They flew to Germany on a Dornier flying boat that lifted off from the Thames and landed in the harbor at Hamburg. In Berlin they took up residence in the Adlon Hotel, one of the city's finest.

Luxury and privilege did not come without its price. She was expected to give herself to Jonas without reservation. That was expected by her father and uncle as well as by Jonas. She gave herself to him without reservation: whatever he wanted, whatever he suggested. She never said no to him, not once. It was no high price. She had not imagined what rapture she would find in the most animal of human relationships.

Some of the Germans took him for a playboy. They were wrong. Jonas Cord was an astute, even a Machiavellian, businessman.

One of the Germans introduced him one evening to

a strange little man who walked with a limp, smiled too readily and too broadly, and spoke of a *Führer,* a man who would lead the German nation to glory. The little man's name was Dr. Josef Goebbels, and a week or so later he arranged for Jonas and Sonja to meet his *Führer,* an oddly charismatic man named Adolf Hitler. Neither Jonas nor Sonja thought much of the encounter at the time. They would later search their memories to try to reconstruct the conversations.

On the way home on the *Berengaria*—the former German liner *Imperator*—they discovered that the Prince of Wales was a fellow passenger. Everyone sought his company. Jonas did not. Perhaps it was as a consequence of his refusal to intrude on the privacy of the prince that he and Sonja were invited to dine at the prince's table the third night out. They found the personable, gracious Edward Albert Christian George Andrew Patrick David a far more memorable fellow than the two peculiar Germans. For years Sonja would talk about the evening when she dined with the Prince of Wales.

As they neared the end of their journey, Sonja began to wonder when Jonas would propose marriage. She felt sure he would. For more than two months they had lived together as though they were a married couple. She utterly failed to realize they were like a married couple in another way. He was becoming a little bored with her.

Aboard the *Berengaria* he openly courted the daughter of a Massachusetts banker—or, said more accurately, he tried to seduce her. Sonja was aware but failed to understand. It was not unusual for a married man to have his little flings on the side. That was understood and accepted both in Cuba and in *yanqui* land. She was troubled but not alarmed.

They reached Los Angeles. He took her home—that is to the home of the Mexican family and her mother—and left her there. He said he had to travel to Nevada and then to San Francisco and would call her when he was next in Los Angeles.

During the three weeks before he called she learned she was pregnant. She would not tell him on the phone and asked him to come to the house. He said he was only passing through and would be leaving for Texas in an hour or so. She did not see him until eleven days later, when he returned from Dallas. Then he took her to lunch.

All he wanted to talk about was what they had done in Germany. She could not endure his chatter and finally asked him, "Jonas, what of the future?"

"Future? What future?"

"Ours," she said simply.

He frowned. "I'm not sure . . . My god, you don't mean marriage!"

"We have been together as husband and wife."

Jonas shook his head. "You slept with me for two months. It was great. I appreciated it. I took you to Germany. We went first class. Did I ever mention marriage?"

"No."

"Well, then."

Her eyes filled with tears. "Then . . . the lovely traveling, the ships and all, were meant as . . . *payment?*"

Jonas smiled. "I wouldn't put it quite that way."

"The payment for the services of a *puta*," she said bitterly.

"Sonja! No."

She got up and walked out of the restaurant. He didn't follow her.

7

Her father and uncle were angry. Her father spoke of horsewhipping Jonas Cord, better yet of killing him. Her uncle demanded that she be married immediately, so quickly that her husband would believe the child she was carrying was his. He knew who she could marry: the son of Don Pedro Escalante. The Escalante family was not as rich as the Cords, but an alliance between the Escalantes and the Batistas could be mutually profitable. Fulgencio Batista traveled to Mexico and arranged the marriage.

Two days before the wedding Sonja contrived a private meeting with Virgilio in the garden of the hacienda near Córdoba. She told him she was pregnant. He was already in love with her.

8

"Twenty-five years," Sonja murmured. "And now for some reason you called. You didn't telephone me for sentimental reasons. I don't think you do anything much for sentimental reasons."

"Sonja, I—"

"You're being divorced again," she said with a thin smile. "So, are you going around looking up old girlfriends?"

Jonas shook his head.

"If you like kidneys," she said, "there is no place in Mexico where they do them better. Nowhere in this hemisphere, I should say." She shook her head. "You still do favor that foul *norteamericano* whiskey, don't you? Bourbon. Whiskey flavored with maple syrup. Anyway, you came to see me about what?"

"It can wait," said Jonas.

"You've bought a casino-hotel," she said. "You want to buy one—or build one—in Havana. Right? Uncle Fulgencio—"

"Maybe," he interrupted. "We can talk about it another time. Right now, I want to know about you. I am told your husband is a very wealthy man," said Jonas.

"No. But of a very old family," she said. "The Escalantes are hidalgos, if there is any such thing anymore."

"Do you live in Mexico City?" Jonas asked. "I mean, all year round."

"We have an apartment here, where we spend most of our time. Our chief residence, in theory, is a hacienda near Córdoba."

"Do you have children, Sonja?"

She frowned, as if the question distressed her. "Yes," she said. "I have two sons and two daughters. My elder daughter is married and has made me a grandmother."

"You're too young to be a grandmother."

"I was too young to be a mother when I first became one," she said. She opened her purse. "Here. Here is the business card of my elder son."

Jonas took the card and looked at it.

JONAS ENRIQUE RAUL CORD y BATISTA
Abogado y Jurisconsulto

GURZA y AROZA ABOGADOS

1535 Avenue Universidad

Jonas's lips parted. He blanched. For a long moment he stared at the card, and then he turned his eyes from the card to Sonja's face.

"Our son," she said quietly.

9

1

"BUT WHY? MY GOD, WHY DIDN'T YOU TELL ME?"

Sonja raised her glass and sipped champagne. "When you left me, you said the affair was over. You were most emphatic about it." She shrugged. "Need I tell you I was not feeling very positively toward you at that time, Jonas? Besides, I had my pride. I didn't want you thinking I was asking for an allowance."

"Allowance? I'd have been happy to send . . . to send money, to send presents. I'd have come to visit."

"I didn't want you interfering in his upbringing," she said bluntly, coldly.

"Meaning you didn't want him to be like me."

"I never had to worry about that. He isn't."

"Does he know—"

"He knows who his father is," she said. "He has read every news story about you. For a long time he was not sure if he liked you, if he ever wanted to meet you. I can tell you now that he would have sent a letter to your office before much longer. He wanted to be firmly established in his career before he contacted you. He didn't want you to think he asked anything of you."

"My god, he's twenty-five years old!"

128

"Almost twenty-six. He graduated from Harvard Law School with honors. His law firm is an international firm. Mexico does not allow American firms to open branch offices in our country. But there is a brotherly relationship between his firm and a prominent firm in New York. They exchange young lawyers for a year's training. Jonas will be spending next year in New York. He expected to see you during that year."

"Tell me more about him," said Jonas quietly.

"My husband and I saw to it that he had every advantage, a good education, foreign travel, exposure to the better things of life. He is perfectly bilingual. In fact, he is fluent in French and German also. He graduated from a private secondary school in 1943, when he was seventeen. He completed a year at Harvard before he enlisted in the United States Army."

"United States Army?"

"He is your son, Jonas. He is a citizen of the United States. He would have been drafted early in 1944. He was with A Company, Seventh Armored Infantry Battalion, and crossed the Remagen Bridge on March 7, 1945—one of the first hundred Americans across."

"Why did I never hear of him?"

"He enrolled at Harvard as Jonas Batista."

"Was he hurt in the war?"

"Yes. He was wounded twice, nearly killed the second time. He was awarded the Distinguished Service Cross. He was a lieutenant when he was wounded. They made him a captain then."

Jonas felt a burning weight in his stomach. A son . . . A war hero. A Mexican lawyer. He looked into Sonja's face and saw a look of unalloyed satisfaction she was making no effort to conceal.

"I have to meet him, Sonja. When can I meet him?"

She nodded toward the bar. "He is sitting there. He came here with me. He decided to have a look at you, whether I introduced you this evening or not."

She raised a beckoning hand, and a young man slipped off his seat at the bar and walked toward their table.

Jonas rose, not entirely steadily. He was like a man who'd been hit with a sucker punch: trying to regain his equilibrium and be ready for a new and harder blow.

Then abruptly the young man stood before him and extended his hand. "I am your son," he said simply.

The younger Jonas was taller than his father. His shoulders were broad, his hips narrow, and Jonas could guess he was solidly muscled and probably played some sport or other. It was his face, though, that was impressive. It was long and strong and open, with sharp, bright-blue eyes and a broad, expressive mouth. His hair was blond. He didn't look like either of his parents. He looked like the sort of young man found among the officers of British guards regiments. He had been staring from the bar long enough to have satisfied his curiosity, and now he showed no sign of emotion, none of any kind.

Jonas had feared his voice would fail. He was right; it did. He was hoarse and whispery as he said, "I would have contacted you a long time ago, if I had known of you."

His son smiled—but only a measured smile, a polite smile, not a friendly one. "Perhaps it is better that we did not meet until now," he said quietly.

Jonas ran his hand across his eyes, wiping tears. "Well . . . in any case, I am so very pleased . . . so very, very pleased."

"As am I," said the younger Jonas blandly.

2

Never in his life did the young Jonas suppose he was the son of Virgilio Diaz Escalante. From the time when he became aware of such things, he understood that another man was his father. He was invited to call his mother's husband *Padre,* and he did; but he knew what it meant that his younger brother's name was Virgilio Pedro Escalante y Batista while his own name was Jonas Enrique Raul Cord y Batista.

He was baptized Cord y Batista. The family never deceived anyone about his origin. But the word *bastardo* was never used about him. That would have incurred the wrath of Don Pedro Escalante, and Don Pedro was a hidalgo whose wrath no one wanted to incur. Don Pedro, it was well known, was the father of several children outside his marriage. It was extremely unusual for a woman of good family to bear an illegitimate child and acknowledge it; but in this case the man involved had been a man of wealth and position, and the child had probably been conceived in a first-class cabin on a luxury liner, or if not there then in Berlin's finest hotel. The circumstances made it all acceptable to Don Pedro. His daughter-in-law had not succumbed to any cheap adventurer but to a man like himself, like his son Virgilio. And if Virgilio did not object, why should he?

The boy was always intensely curious about the man who was the origin of his names Jonas and Cord. *Madre* was never reticent about it. She told him that his father Jonas Cord was a wealthy American businessman. They had loved each other for a time, she said. Unfortunately, differences between them were very great, and they had not been able to marry.

What really mattered, she told the young Jonas

often, was that she loved him, *Padre* loved him, and *Abuelo*—Grandfather—loved him, which was very important. As the family grew, he was always older brother. His brothers and sisters knew he was different, but they, too, had been reared to understand the difference didn't matter.

His brothers and sisters, when they were old enough to understand, watched Jonas struggling over the Sunday edition of *The New York Times,* which came in every Thursday's mail. Sometimes his mother marked stories and told him to be sure to read them. They were stories about Jonas Cord.

Padre was often away from the hacienda on business. *Abuelo* stayed at home. From the time Jonas learned to talk, his mother spoke to him sometimes in Spanish, sometimes in English, and his grandfather did the same. Jonas Cord, they told him, was a *norteamericano,* and he must learn to speak his father's language, not just as it was spoken by educated Mexicans but as it was spoken by the *yanquis* themselves. When *norteamericanos* came to the hacienda, for whatever reason, they were asked to talk with the boy, to let him study their accents.

Abuelo became his grandson's closest friend. He told him who Sonja's family was. To many Mexicans, Fulgencio Batista was only an upstart colonel and maybe worse. But Don Pedro Escalante, though he was a hidalgo, had secretly sent money to Pancho Villa. And now he was secretly giving money to his daughter-in-law's uncle.

He was catholic in his political predilections but not Catholic in his religious ones. Little Jonas was baptized by a priest, but he was not reared a Catholic. His father was not a Catholic, so Grandfather deemed it would be inappropriate someday to present a devout Catholic son to a non-Catholic father—and he had no doubt the family would someday present the son to the father.

Grandfather sent the boy to the grammar school in Córdoba. Boys there knew he was a bastard and not only that but the son of a *yanqui,* but they dared not torment the grandson of the hidalgo. One did and suffered a broken nose for his effrontery.

Abuelo carried a pistol on his hip. He taught his grandson to shoot, and when Jonas was only eight years old he gave him a .22-caliber seven-shot Harrington & Richards revolver. Jonas practiced with it, under the careful tutelage of the old man, and he became accurate, so accurate that his targets were spent shotgun shells set up on a sawhorse to be fired on from twenty meters.

One of the boy's proudest moments came when he was nine years old. His little sister Maria was a toddler. She had been in the kitchen, where the cook had given her a slice of pie, and she wandered out through the back door, across the dooryard and beyond. Shortly Jonas heard the cook scream. He was in his room reading, and before he ran out to see what was wrong he grabbed his revolver. He had an instinct that if some sort of danger was threatening, a gun might be useful.

He ran into the dooryard. The cook stood flushed, trembling, terrified, pointing at the little girl. Maria sat on the ground, ten meters beyond the dooryard fence. She too was frightened. Not two meters from her a coiled rattlesnake buzzed its warning. She had wandered near it when it was shedding its skin and was in a foul, aggressive mood. Whether or not it would strike was uncertain, but it might if she moved. It almost certainly would if anyone else came near.

Jonas closed his left hand around his right wrist and took steady aim on the rattlesnake. Its head was as big as four of the shotgun shells that were his usual targets. Still, this was no easy shot. He held his breath, which he did not usually do when he was shooting. He fired. The .22 slug split the head of the rattler, and it writhed and thrashed as the boy rushed up and grabbed his little sister to drag her away from it.

He was a hero. It was a fine thing to be a hero. He enjoyed it.

3

The next year, 1936, he did not return to the grammar school in Córdoba. Instead, he and his mother went to live in Mexico City, in a flat maintained by Virgilio Escalante for his convenience in his frequent visits to the capital. The family had used its considerable political and economic influence to secure a place for Jonas at La Escuela Diplomatica, an international school for the children of diplomats. There he would study with Europeans and improve his English and learn French and German.

He learned something else: that Mexico was not one of the world's great nations, not in wealth, not in military might, not in cultural achievement and influence. No. The Estados Unidos to the north was all these things. Mexico was not. Mexico was a respectable nation but not a leader of the world. At the grammar school in Córdoba the teachers had taught otherwise.

His mother smiled when he asked her about this. The nuns had never taught her, she said, that Cuba was one of the great nations. They had taught her that Spain was the greatest nation of the world, with the world's supreme culture, admired and envied by everyone. The poor silly women had believed it, she said. And the teachers at Córdoba had believed what they taught.

At La Escuela Diplomatica it meant nothing that he was the illegitimate son of Jonas Cord, nothing that he was the grandson of Don Pedro Escalante. No one there had ever heard of either of them. He was Jonas Enrique Raul Cord y Batista, and all that counted was that his family had enough money to pay his tuition—that and the fact that he was bright enough to meet the challenge of a singularly demanding school.

During his first year at the school he lived at home in the Escalante apartment. In 1938, when he was twelve and no longer in the grammar-school department, he moved into the boys' dormitory.

The boys lived two to a room. His roommate was Maurice Raynal, a boy one year older than he was, who was supposed to act as a sort of mentor in the realities of school life. Maurice was the son of the naval attaché at the French embassy. Though a year older, he was no bigger than Jonas, who was tall and muscular with a man's voice, no longer a child in any sense.

Maurice's Spanish and English were heavily accented, as for that matter was his German. The teachers were constantly at him about it. The teachers asked Jonas to help him. They suggested that the two boys speak only English and Spanish in their room. Jonas was happy to do that, especially the English. The more he spoke English, the better.

Maurice complained that Jonas did not speak English the same as their English teacher. Eventually he understood. *"Ah, Jonas, c'est Americain! Ce n'est pas Anglais! Vous parlez Americain!"*

Jonas could not have been happier. He was not English. His father was not English. He wanted to speak his father's language, and his father spoke American.

Maurice was the source of a problem, and also of an education. He took off his clothes when they were alone in their room and the door was bolted. He walked around naked. Jonas never did. Usually when he did it, Maurice had an erection. Jonas was mature enough to know what that was.

And then one evening Maurice lifted his penis in his hand and asked, *"Dites-moi, mon ami. Est le votre si grand?"*

Jonas glanced casually at the stiff organ. *"Oui,"* he said. *"Plus grand."*

"Vraiment? Me montrez."

Jonas considered for a moment, then stood and unbuttoned his pants and pulled out his own penis. *"Voilà,"* he said. *"Assez grand?"*

Maurice grinned and nodded. *"C'est beau."*

Jonas stuffed his back in, buttoned his pants, and turned his attention to a problem in plane geometry.

He had supposed what Maurice had in mind was a competition. That was not what Maurice had in mind at all. The next evening he asked Jonas if he ever had wet dreams. Jonas admitted that he did.

Maurice spoke English. "A pleasure, no? But you need not wait for that pleasure. You can make it happen."

That was an interesting idea. Jonas had guessed as much but had not experimented.

Maurice saw he was interested. "I will show you how," he said solemnly, and he proceeded to masturbate, casting his ejaculate into a handkerchief. "See? Shall I do it for you?"

"I will do it for myself," said Jonas.

"Do. Let's see how much time you need."

Aroused, Jonas did what Maurice suggested, wetting his own handkerchief.

"It is good, no?" Maurice asked. "It is better when we do it for each other—at the same time."

The next evening Jonas consented. The two boys stretched out naked on Maurice's narrow bed. They rubbed their penises together until both of them were on the verge of their orgasms; then, cued by Maurice's urgent cry, they grabbed at each other and finished with their hands.

What followed was inevitable. He would learn not long afterward that there were ugly names for boys who did what he and Maurice did, and he never did it again, but he would never hate the memory of Maurice Raynal.

4

During the summer of 1939 many embassies called their staffs home. Maurice Raynal wrote Jonas a letter from Paris, saying he would not be returning to *La Escuela* for the fall term. His father had been called home and was serving as first officer aboard a French cruiser.

Jonas wrote Maurice that he would not return to the school either. His mother and stepfather and grandfather had anticipated what would happen: that the school would lose three-quarters of its European students and would replace them with students who would not have been admitted before, from Latin American nations. It would make the school provincial—exactly what they did not want. His family had enrolled him in a school in the United States, Culver Military Academy in Indiana. Maurice should write him there, he said.

Jonas never heard from or of Maurice Raynal again.

Culver Military Academy was a difficult school, and not one that he liked. He was lonely there. The climate was cold. The *norteamericanos* were cold. He found it difficult to make friends. He learned to introduce himself simply as Jonas Cord, a name that sounded *yanqui* and saved him from the contempt most of the boys felt for Mexicans. A few knew the name Jonas Cord. They did not guess, fortunately, that he was an illegitimate son. He wore a uniform and learned to stand at attention and march. He did well academically. If he won any reputation at all, it was for his marksmanship. He won medals on the rifle range. Even so, he did not like Culver and did not enjoy his three years there.

The school had, just the same, a major impact on his life. His English became more American. He studied more of science and mathematics, less of languages, and so made up a deficiency in his education. He acquired a lasting distaste for military organization and discipline, yet a credential in them that would serve him well.

He learned that the relationship he'd had with Maurice was held in sneering abhorrence by Americans, who made crude jokes about it in foul language.

He graduated in June 1943. His mother and grandfather traveled all the way from Mexico to be present. On their way home on the train, his mother beamed as she announced what would be next in his life.

"We are very pleased, son. You have been admitted to Harvard!" Then her smile faded. "Of course . . . Next year you will be of the age when every young American can be called to military service."

5

In the fall of 1942, Cambridge, Massachusetts, was an austere place. Most of the upperclassmen were gone. The few who remained had obvious physical infirmities. Jonas had no basis for comparison, but he sensed that two things were missing from Harvard College that year: first, the effervescence of youth and optimism, and, second, a confident sense of permanence that must have been traditional.

Instead, the college was gloomy and tentative. The institution and everyone associated with it were feeling their way, confident that Harvard would endure, yet not quite sure how, confident they would personally survive the war, while conscious that not all of them would.

His classes were not difficult. He was enrolled in an English class, which was really a class in English literature; a mathematics class, where the subject was calculus; a class in the history of Europe beginning with the Renaissance; a class in French, advanced; and a philosophy class, in which the entire first semester was devoted to the study of Plato's *Republic*. Except for the last, his courses covered nothing he had not studied before. When he took his first exams, the college decided it had a prodigy.

He was also required to take a class in physical education, and in order to avoid the strange American games of football and basketball, he concentrated on swimming and learned to play tennis. His coaches were pleased, though they knew they would have him for only one year.

The swimming coach had great difficulty finding boys willing to compete in the butterfly. It was, guys said, a "hairshirt" way to swim. To Jonas, who had first learned to swim at Culver, all the competitive strokes but freestyle seemed unnatural, no one any more so than any other. When the coach asked him to swim the butterfly, he agreed. Within a few weeks he was the freshman butterfly man. He won the intra-mural competition, then won a war-diminished inter-mural competition. He sent his blue ribbons to Córdoba.

He received two letters a week from his mother, one a month from his grandfather, an occasional letter from his stepfather, and one occasionally from his half brothers and sisters, usually writing together. He wrote to his mother in English, the other letters in Spanish. His roommate marveled over his ability to write easily in two languages. In truth, Jonas could have written in French or German almost as easily.

6

His roommate's name was Jerome Rabin, a Jew from Brooklyn and the first Jew he had ever met. Jerry was in the same situation as Jonas. He would be draft-eligible early in 1944.

They talked about it. "I'm going to apply for a naval officer's commission," said Jerry. "What they call the ninety-day-wonder program. Ninety days after I enlist I'll be an ensign. But, say, do you have to go at all? You're Mexican."

"I am a citizen of the United States," Jonas said soberly. "My father is a citizen, which makes me a citizen. It is important to me to keep my citizenship."

"They can't take it away from you," said Jerry.

"But I don't want to be known later in life as one who evaded his military obligation. That could become a great impediment."

"You've thought this through," Jerry remarked dryly.

"And discussed it with my mother and my step-father and my grandfather."

"With your father?"

"I've never met him."

"I'm sorry," said Jerry. "I shouldn't have asked. I didn't mean to pry."

"I am not offended."

"Well— Let's change the subject," said Jerry. "Since both of us will be going away next year, we have only this year to get our wicks dipped."

"I . . . don't understand."

Jerry Rabin grinned. He was a lighthearted boy who would later confide to Jonas that when they first met he found his roommate formidably solemn. He was not as tall as Jonas and was slight of build. His features were delicate. Girls envied his dark eyes. He had a Mediterranean complexion.

He opened a drawer in one of the two small desks in the room and pulled out a quart bottle and two small glasses. He poured and handed one glass to Jonas. "A shot of rye," he said. "It will put us in a better mood to plan our campaign."

Jonas sipped cautiously. It was his first taste of distilled spirits. He had drunk wine with dinner since he was ten years old, but his stepfather and grandfather had never invited him to share in their after-dinner brandy—nor, for that matter, to smoke cigars with them. The rye whiskey tasted terrible. He swallowed it with difficulty.

"Your English is perfect," said Jerry. "Apparently, though, somebody neglected to tell you a few words. Do you know what 'fuck' means?"

Jonas nodded. "Yes." His attention was focused on the rye remaining in his glass. He did not want to seem unappreciative; neither did he want Jerry to guess this was his first taste of whiskey.

"Have you ever done it?"

"No."

"Well, neither have I, and wouldn't it be a tragedy if we went off to war, maybe even got killed, and hadn't ever done it? That's why we've got to plan a campaign to get girls up to this room. And, incidentally, getting your wick dipped is a politer way of saying fuck. We have all kinds of ways to avoid using the word. Don't ever use it. You'll shock the eyeteeth out of people. We say"—he raised his voice a register and spoke through pursed lips—"we say, 'have sexual intercourse.' We say, 'make love.' We say, 'go to bed.' Or we say, 'get our rocks off.' Anything to avoid saying 'fuck.'"

Jonas grinned. "I've been denied an essential element of my education," he said—although it wasn't true, because he had heard much talk of this kind at Culver. He tipped his glass and finished his drink. "I will be grateful to you for more instruction."

Jerry refilled their shot glasses. "What's between our legs is a penis. Isn't that a terrible word? Guys call it 'cock' or 'peter' or 'dick.' What girls have is a vagina, another terrible clinical word. Guys call it a 'cunt,' chiefly. But don't ever use any of these words, the polite ones or the other ones, to girls. They'll go ga-ga. In fact, don't talk about these things at all. Except to guys."

Jonas laughed. "We have all these funny words and can't use them."

"Anyway," said Jerry, "we're virgins. I don't know about you, but I intend to remedy that as soon as I can."

"Why didn't you remedy it before?"

"The family. The neighborhood. Why didn't you?"

"The same, I suppose. Actually, I don't even know very many girls."

"Well, tell me, what did you put down on your card as your religion?"

"I wrote nothing. It was optional."

Jerry clapped his hand to his forehead in mock grief. "Why couldn't you have put down Catholic? Then you'd have been invited to a church and a Catholic youth club, where you could have met not only girls but naive girls."

Jonas shrugged. He had begun to learn something of what rye whiskey did to a person.

"*Girls,* Jonas! Nooky. Poontang. Don't you enjoy seeing their tight little asses twitch when they walk?"

"Well . . . I haven't watched . . . that much."

"*Start* watching! Start looking. Look at asses. Look at boobs. Concentrate on the job at hand, which is get our wicks dipped before we have to go into uniform."

7

When Jerry learned that Jonas could not go home for Christmas break—the journey was too far, and wartime restrictions on transportation might have made it impossible—he invited Jonas to come home with him. Jonas accepted the invitation, went home with Jerry Rabin, and lived for two weeks with a Jewish family in Brooklyn. It was a rewarding experience. He even learned a bit of another language: Yiddish.

Neither Jonas nor Jerry had by then gotten his wick dipped. They remained virgins. But at Jerry's prompting Jonas had begun to look more closely at girls: appreciatively, speculatively. Ironically, he looked that way at Jerry's sister, Susan. He noticed the size of her breasts. He studied the way her backside twitched when she walked. He studied that so closely he realized he had to be careful not to be so obvious. Lying in his bed in the guest room, he fantasized a faint knock on the door, then Susan coming in, undressing, slipping into his bed. In real fact, he would not have touched her. She was his friend's sister! But he found the fantasy delicious.

8

Spring break came, and they hadn't hauled their ashes.

It occurred to Jonas that they were too obvious. Girls they met knew what they wanted. The girls didn't want the same thing.

Finally, in April, Jerry succeeded in persuading two girls to visit the dorm room. They were not supposed to be there, so they had to climb up a fire escape, enter the dorm through a window, and slip along the hall to the boys' room—which process alone had discouraged several girls from accepting an invitation.

They were town girls. That is to say, they lived in Cambridge. One was still in high school. The other had graduated and worked as a waitress. Both lived with their parents and had to be home by eleven.

Neither was exquisitely beautiful. Helen was dark-haired, brown-eyed, and chubby. Ruth was blond and thinner. Her face was marred by pimples—only two that evening, but the marks of others remained on her cheeks.

None of these four young people had any doubt why the two girls had come to visit the two boys in their dormitory room. Only two questions remained: Which girl would be intimate with which boy, and what were the terms of this visit?

The two girls, it turned out, expected to be paid five dollars apiece. Jerry shook his head firmly. Maybe two, he said.

Jonas seized Jerry by the sleeve of his gray tweed jacket and shoved him out into the hall. "Listen, goddammit," he said. "Didn't you ever read *Innocents Abroad* by Mark Twain?"

"What's that got to do with——"

"All their lives the 'pilgrims' had dreamed of going for a boat ride on the Sea of Galilee. When the boatmen asked for eight dollars, they offered four, and the boatmen rowed away. Those 'pilgrims' never did get to sail on the Sea of Galilee. Because of four dollars divided among eight men. I'm going to give one of those girls five dollars and get my wick dipped. I suggest you give five to the other one."

Jonas strode back into the room and handed a five-dollar bill to Helen, the dark, chubby one. For his decisiveness he got his choice. Jerry would later complain of that, but for now he grudgingly counted out five one-dollar bills to Ruth.

Once again decisive, Jonas led Helen to the maroon-plush-upholstered sofa that was the center-piece of the living room. His eyes shooting annoyance, Jerry took Ruth into the bedroom.

Helen undressed, directly without diffidence or hesitation. When she was naked, she helped Jonas undress. "Y' know," she said, "I bet this here's your first time."

"Not really," he said.

She lifted his penis in her hand. "Well," she said. "Y' got what it takes, anyway. Y' ready?"

"Sure." He didn't know the term foreplay but had supposed there would be something before the act. But he didn't want her to suppose he didn't know what to do. "Sure. Let's do it."

She opened her purse and took out a Coin-Pak. Stripping the foil off, she pulled out the rubber and stretched it on her fingers. "Not circumcised," she muttered. "Bet y' friend is. Anyway, y' want it skinned back?"

"No."

She rolled the condom onto his erect penis. Then she lay on her back and spread her legs. "C'mon."

It was purely mechanical. Yet the satiation was so complete that it exhausted him. When he was finished and dropped his weight on her hips, Helen tousled his hair and patted his back: the first sign from her of anything like affection. He became conscious that his skin and hers were wet and their sweat was mingling. Their odors mingled. It had not occurred to him until then to kiss her, and she had not offered herself to be kissed, but he kissed her now and felt her tongue coming between his lips and into his mouth.

When Jerry and Ruth came out of the bedroom, Jonas was on his back under Helen, he was in her, and she was moaning quietly as she rotated her hips. His eyes were closed. So were hers. They were not aware that the other couple stood gaping, watching them.

"Well, Jee-zuss Christ!" said Ruth.

10

1

HE RETURNED TO CAMBRIDGE IN THE FALL OF 1943. IN February 1944 he registered for the draft, using as his address the dormitory where he had lived the past year with Jerry Rabin. Then he enlisted in the United States Army.

The first thing the army did was give him a new name. The army was no-nonsense about names. Everybody had a first name, a middle initial, and a last name. The sergeant who handled the matter took his first name as Jonas, his middle initial as E. (for Enrique), and his last name as Batista. What "Cord y" meant, he didn't know and didn't care. So far as the United States Army was concerned, Jonas Enrique Raul Cord y Batista was Private Jonas E. Batista.

Within a few days his name was changed even further. The guys in his outfit didn't like the name Jonas. It sounded too much like the guy that was swallowed by the whale, one man said. Or like Judas, which was a jinx. Anyway, he didn't look like a Jonas. They tried calling him Joe, but there were too many Joes. Batista? So, okay, he was Bat. The nickname stuck. Bat. Men called him Bat who had no idea his last name was Batista.

Two weeks after he arrived at Fort Dix he was summoned to the office of a Captain Barker.

"Where you from, Batista?"

"Cambridge, Mass, sir."

"Graduate of Culver."

"Yes, sir."

"Fluent in German. And French."

"Yes, sir."

"Shit, Private. The army's got better things for you to do than basic infantryman. I'm transferring you. The army's got ninety-day wonders, not just the navy."

2

"Captain's looking for you, Lieutenant. He's in the beer hall up the street."

First Lieutenant Jonas E. Batista nodded at Sergeant David Amory and walked off toward the beer hall, a hundred yards up the street. He had just finished interrogating three German civilians, without learning anything he needed to report to Captain Grimes. A cold drizzle had been falling all morning, and he walked on slippery cobblestones.

"Hey, Bat." Another lieutenant, named Duffy, came across the street. "Grimes is calling in the platoon leaders."

"Yeah. I just got the word."

"What's up, ya know?"

"Change of orders," said Bat.

"How ya know?"

"Hell, there's *always* a change of orders."

Duffy was an older man, almost thirty. He was in fact older than Captain Grimes. Bat was the youngest platoon leader in the company. He was the youngest first lieutenant in the battalion. He had six months of combat experience and had suffered a flesh wound in the left armpit in Belgium—wound enough to merit a Purple Heart. He had killed a German soldier—that is, killed him one-on-one, not just by directing platoon fire. Still almost a year short of his twentieth birthday, Bat had acquired the reputation of a tough, effective, aggressive infantry officer.

Inside the beer hall, Captain Grimes sat at one of the heavy oaken tables. Four big steins of beer stood on the table, one for himself and one for each of his three platoon leaders. A map was spread on the table.

"Okay, guys," said the captain. "Everything's changed." He put a finger on the symbol for a village on the Rhine. "That's where we're going. Remagen. The Krauts haven't blown up the Ludendorff Bridge yet. There just might be a chance, just a chance, to capture that bridge before it goes boom. Our orders are to bust ass into Remagen as fast as we can. We're gonna outrun the tank companies, 'cause the roads are shitty. If we run into light resistance, we bypass it if we can. Other infantry companies are moving. Whoever gets to the bridge first gets the honor of going across."

"And of getting our asses blown into the river when the demolition charges go off," said Sergeant Cline, leader of the third platoon. Cline had the most experience of them all, more than the rest of them combined, and he was a battle-weary cynic.

"Blown into history," said Captain Grimes sarcastically. "That's the way it is. Ride as far as you can, but you'll have to go into the village on foot. Now move!"

Bat took one great gulp of beer, then trotted down the street to where his platoon sat around their vehicles: a truck and a halftrack. He ordered his men into the truck and halftrack, and they set off. Half an hour later they dismounted and advanced through a vineyard on foot. They reached a small grove of trees, hurried through it, and emerged to a spectacular view.

The Rhine lay below. A smooth paved highway ran along the west side of the river. The village was directly below them, dominated by a beautiful centuries-old church. And there was the bridge. It stood. Men and vehicles were streaming across.

Bat used a pair of binoculars from the halftrack and stared at the bridge. "Those are Krauts," he said. "Retreating. Okay. Let's move down. C'mon."

He led his platoon down the hill. He did not take time to look for a road or path. They just walked down, through terraced vineyards. Other units were moving. Something like twenty halftracks were advancing on the highway. The Germans on the bridge began to run. Only a few of them stopped to fire at the Americans.

"They're running away!" one man yelled. "They're not going to defend it!"

"Don't kid yourself," grunted Sergeant Dave Amory.

As Bat's platoon reached the bottom of the hill and the first houses of the village, sniper fire from the windows caught one man in the leg. He was Corporal Prizio, the son of a farmer from upstate New York. He screamed and fell. Bat ordered heavy fire on the houses and then knelt beside Prizio. He would survive. How well he would walk in future was another question.

The platoon moved forward. Their burst of automatic fire, especially that from the BARs, had shattered the windows of the nearest houses and knocked big jagged holes in the stucco on their rear walls. No more sniper fire. First squad, led by Sergeant Amory, kicked down the back door of the nearest house and charged in. Second squad entered another house.

Bat ordered two men to carry Prizio forward and into the first house. First squad spread out through the house and found a German family cowering in the cellar.

"Heraus!" Bat screamed. *"Heraus! Schnell!"*

The Germans came up from their cellar: an elderly woman and two teenaged girls. Bat spoke German to them. "One of you fired on my soldiers and wounded that one. Lawfully, I can shoot all of you. If I decide to shoot you, I will allow my men to take such pleasure of you as they may wish before we shoot you. I offer you one chance to survive. You care for my wounded man. I will return for him—or one of us will. If he has not survived, or if he has been mistreated, you will die, and this house will be burned to the ground."

The women swore they had not fired a shot. It had been done by a *Volkstürmer*—an overage militiaman—who had run when the Americans fired on the house. Bat left Prizio with sulfa and morphine, also with a carbine and a grenade.

The platoon assembled and advanced toward the river and the bridge. Other Americans were in the streets. They could hear the roar of tank engines.

The Ludendorff Bridge was a railway bridge. The Germans had planked over its tracks so tanks and trucks could cross. And it stood there, crossing the sullen gray and swift Rhine. At the far end it debouched at the foot of a stone escarpment. Whoever crossed it would have a hard fight to get beyond it.

As Bat and his platoon stood staring at the bridge, Captain Grimes came to them. "We go across," he said.

A moment later an explosion lifted the bridge and filled the air with smoke and dust. Bat shook his head, then shrugged. Well ... they were relieved of the crossing. The honor would not be theirs. They had arrived a few minutes too late.

But as the air cleared they could see the bridge again, still intact. The explosion had blown open a trench that would temporarily block tanks from crossing, but nothing but German small-arms fire blocked the infantry. Other units ventured onto the bridge. Enemy machine guns in stone guard towers opened fire. American infantrymen moved against it, peppering the towers with steel and lead. Engineers went over the railings and began to cut wires, disarming charges.

Emotions never to be experienced otherwise in life govern the combat soldier. Bat's ran strong, wholly in control of him. He was relieved not to be first across the bridge, but he was torn with anger that other platoons were rushing forward while his stood and stared. From the corner of his eye he saw Captain Grimes returning to give the order. He would not wait.

"Go, for Christ sake! What're we waitin' for? Move! Move! Move!"

He ran ahead of his platoon. He didn't have to glance back to see if they were following him. His men, some of them old enough to be his father, respected him or were afraid of him. They wouldn't let him go across alone. They dreaded what he would do to a man who proved afraid to follow him.

Maybe they dreaded more what their fellow soldiers would think of them.

Bat ran forward. He jumped over the bodies of Americans who had fallen to defensive fire, then over bodies of Germans caught in the sudden onslaught. Tanks on the river highway had zeroed in on the defense towers at the eastern end of the bridge. The white smoke and red fire of phosphorous shells enveloped the entire east end of the bridge. He could hear the agonized screams of German soldiers with phosphorus burning on their skin.

Slugs ricocheted off the steel around him. Ahead he saw a man fall. Drizzle and sweat in his eyes obscured his vision. The air was chilly, but he sweated nevertheless. Time, too, was obscure. He ran for less than a minute, but it seemed as if he were running for ten minutes. His eyes were dimmed, but he saw the situation as if it were engraved on a bright crystal. The danger was the explosive charges under the bridge.

"Hey, Mac! Hey, Mac!"

The man was yelling at *him*. A man over the side.

"Hey, Mac! Look! See the cable? Can you hit it?"

Bat saw what the man was yelling about: a cable about half the thickness of a man's wrist, running from somewhere to the east and under the bridge—to an explosive charge, without any doubt at all.

"Shoot the son of a bitch! Break that son of a bitch!"

Bat nodded. The carbine he was carrying was not the war's most accurate weapon, but he braced himself on the bridge rail and took aim. His first shot missed. A little high. He adjusted. His second slug severed the cable. It hung in shreds. He fired again. And again. The two ends separated and fell apart.

"Hey, Mac—"

He had stood still too long. It made him a target. He felt the shock in a lower right rib, then the burning pain. He was aware of nothing after he felt Sergeant Amory dragging him into the shelter of a steel girder.

3

In that, on the 7th day of March 1945, First Lieutenant Jonas E. Batista, while leading his platoon across the Ludendorff Bridge in the face of heavy enemy fire in the best practice of infantry leadership, did stop and, exposing himself as a target, did by accurate fire from his weapon break an electric cable that connected heavy explosive charges to the enemy's source of electric power, thereby preventing detonation of such charges, but subjecting Lieutenant Batista to severe and life-threatening wounds; and

In that First Lieutenant Jonas E. Batista did conduct himself in the face of an armed enemy with extraordinary courage and gallantry in the finest tradition of the Armed Services of the United States,

NOW THEREFORE it is ordered that Lieutenant Jonas E. Batista be awarded and he hereby is awarded THE DISTINGUISHED SERVICE CROSS.

He was also promoted to captain. He was hospitalized first in Antwerp and then in Paris, finally at Walter Reed in Washington. He was at home for Christmas, at the hacienda outside Córdoba.

While he was away his grandfather had died. The hacienda seemed empty without him. Virgilio Escalante now invited him to share cigars and brandy after dinner. He took him into the town and treated him to the ministrations of the finest young *puta* Córdoba could offer. Bat accepted the gift. He returned to see the girl several times. She became a teacher for him.

At the end of his leave he went back to Walter Reed Hospital. The war was over, and he would be discharged as soon as the hospital granted him its final release. He took some time to inquire of Corporal Prizio. The young man had survived and was at home on a farm not far from Watkins Glen. He inquired of Jerry Rabin and learned that Ensign Jerome Rabin had been killed in the Battle of the Coral Sea. Captain—now Major—Grimes was in Japan, a professional soldier staying in the army. Sergeant Dave Amory was at home in Boston.

Bat applied to Harvard, to return and begin the rest of his education in the fall term of 1946.

The fall term began six months later. He had nothing to do for six months. He bought a car: a 1938 Cadillac. He drove up to Watkins Glen and visited Corporal Prizio. After that he drove on to Cambridge and began to look for a place to live. The returning GIs did not want to live in college dorms, and he didn't either. He began to look for an apartment.

He remembered that Sergeant Dave Amory lived in Boston. He called him, and they met for beer and sandwiches at a Cambridge pub.

He didn't raise the subject immediately, but after they'd finished a beer Bat said to Dave, "You saved my life."

"I did like hell," said Dave. "You were down. They wouldn't have wasted ammunition on you."

"Well then, they might have wasted it on you, while you exposed your ass running out there to get me."

Dave shook his head. "I had to run someplace. The other option was run on across the bridge, toward where the firing was hotter. Taking a minute to drag you behind a girder may have saved *my* life."

Dave Amory was as tall as Bat, and he was a great deal bulkier. His shoulders were broader than Bat's, his body was more solid, and his arms and legs were thicker. His broad, long-jawed face was more often solemn than jocular, but he had a submerged sense of humor that emerged in eccentric comments on just about anything. He was two years older than Bat and would begin his senior year in the fall. After that he would go to law school.

"What are you doing this summer, Dave?"

"Nothing. I'm drawing my fifty-two twenty. Sit around the VFW hall and soak up beer. I figure I'm entitled to a little time off before I pick myself up again."

Bat frowned at him. He lifted his chin. "You bored?" he asked.

Dave tipped his head to one side and drew one corner of his lower lip back between his teeth. He hesitated for a moment, then said, "Yeah. I guess I am. You know what it is."

"I sure do. It was a fuckin' nightmare, Dave, but nothing ever gets a man's juices flowing as strong. I doubt anything ever will. We have to admit it. God grant we never find anything again in our lives that—Well, it sure as hell wasn't boring. I wonder if everything for the rest of our lives will be boring . . . by comparison."

"Are you absolutely sure you want to come back to Harvard?" Dave asked.

"No. But I've got to do something, and I don't know what else to do. Besides . . . I don't want to disappoint my mother."

Dave chuckled. "As good a reason as any," he said. "What are you, Lieutenant? Twenty-one?"

"Not quite, but please don't call me Lieutenant."

"What you doing about boredom?" Dave asked. "Gettin' laid any?"

"When I was at home last winter, my stepfather set me up with a pretty little whore. I had a wonderful time with her, but—" He shrugged.

Dave nodded.

"When I was here in '42 and '43, my freshman roommate couldn't think of anything but what he called getting his wick dipped. He said he didn't want to die a virgin. Well, he . . . didn't. He died, but he wasn't a virgin. God, what enthusiasm we had for it! My first. It wasn't very good, I know now, but—"

"It'll never be quite as good again," said Dave. "In another sense. When the mystery is gone out of a thing—"

"I was terrified of being shot," Bat interrupted. "Then I was hit. I got hit twice, you know. It's not the biggest thing in my life. It would have been if I'd been killed. It would have been if I'd been crippled."

"You had a punctured lung, didn't you? I saw the blood running out of your mouth."

"Lung was full of rib fragments," said Bat. "The Germans made good ammunition. The slugs went through cleanly. But not the bone fragments. Let's talk about something else."

"You looking for a roommate?" asked Dave.

"Sure."

"You have a car. So have I. That means we can look for a place outside Cambridge. Maybe Lexington. We can get more space for less money, and it'll only be a five- or six-mile drive."

"Deal," said Bat.

"Before we can live together, though, I've got to have the answer to a question. The story in the outfit used to be that you were a mysterious guy. We weren't even sure what your name is."

Bat faced Dave with a wry smile. "My name is Jonas Enrique Raul Cord y Batista."

"Cord! Jonas . . . Jonas Cord!"

"My father. And my great-uncle is Fulgencio Batista."

"And you use the name Batista, not Cord?"

"Accident. Batista is the last name on the string, so people tend to call me Batista."

"Which would you rather?"

"I don't care."

"What does your father think?"

"I've never met him."

"Good enough. That was the last question."

They agreed to drive to Lexington the next day. That afternoon they rented the second floor of a big old white frame house. It was furnished, but they told the landlady they would rather store her furniture and buy new. They furnished their apartment—living room, two bedrooms, kitchen, and bath—and moved in.

4

Bat thought about contacting his father. Jonas Cord was constantly in the news. In the hospital in Antwerp, Bat had read newspaper stories about how his father had crashed a huge flying boat in the Pacific off San Diego and lost seventeen million dollars. Then, when Bat was in the hospital in Paris, a story appeared saying his father had remarried. Odd, he had remarried his ex-wife. Another news account said he was going to manufacture television sets, devices that would receive pictures the way radio received voices and music; and he was quoted as saying that millions of American families would own television sets within the next ten years. A busy man. He might not want to meet a son he didn't know he had.

In any case, Bat didn't want to meet him while he

was a student. When he was somebody—doctor, lawyer, merchant, chief—maybe he would confront this peripatetic tycoon. He would confront him when he was established, and his father could not suppose he had come to beg for something. Putting the matter more simply, Bat didn't want to meet his father until he could, if he chose to, tell him to go to hell.

11

1

"Toni, Toni, Toni, Toni . . . I *love* you, Antonia Maxim. Will you marry me?"

Antonia Maxim—she pronounced her name Ahn-toe-NEE-a—glanced up into his eyes, a playful expression on her face. "You didn't even have to ask, Bat. You *know* I'll marry you. You know I love you. I've proved it, haven't I? It's been a whirlwind courtship, but you have to know I love you."

It was a sunny Saturday afternoon, in the fall, when many Harvardians and Radcliffe girls had gone to the football game. Dave had gone to the stadium—more as an accommodation to his friends than because he was interested in the game—so Bat and Toni were alone in the bright, spacious, comfortable living room of the second-floor apartment in the house at Lexington.

He was naked. She had learned not to stare at the ugly purplish scar where a German bullet had crashed through his lower right ribs and nearly killed him—or at the lesser white scar in his left armpit, the mark of a flesh wound. She knew she was welcome to stare at what hung between his legs: oversized, at least in her experience, and straight and powerful. He was tanned. He had spent the summer before—that is, the summer of 1947—at home in Mexico and had spent a great deal of time in the sun, playing tennis and lounging around a pool. He was a trim, sleekly muscled man, not lacking in self-confidence.

She was naked, too, except for a pair of white rayon panties. Antonia was exquisitely beautiful. Her hair was dark-brown, her eyes big and brown, her mouth narrow but her lips fleshy, and her face was stretched over well-defined cheekbones and a firm jawline. She carried no extra flesh, except perhaps for her breasts, which were large and firm and tipped with big rosy nipples. Her panties covered a commodious shiny-pink cleft, with which he had become profoundly intimate.

He had learned of Toni that she was comfortable exposing to him her legs and hips and belly and breasts and was never in any hurry to cover them but that she was not comfortable exposing her crotch and would not pull down her panties until absolutely necessary.

Right now she did not need to have her panties down.

She ran her tongue around his scrotum, then up the length of his penis to the tip. He drew a deep breath and let it out in a low moan.

"You really like that, don't you?" she asked, grinning.

"I had to teach you how," he said, squeezing her shoulder affectionately.

"Well . . . if somebody had asked me two months ago if I'd *ever* do it, I'd have told them hell no, and you're crazy if you think I will."

"That's about what you said when I suggested it."

He had suggested it because they were in bed together and had just discovered they had no condoms; the package was empty. She had shaken her head indignantly. "You mean you want me to *fellate* you?" she had sneered. "What do you think I am?" Even so, she had lowered her head and impulsively, also a little sullenly, kissed his penis. The next afternoon, after they had coupled, she had pulled off his condom, wiped him with Kleenex, and kissed him again. Then very tentatively she had licked him— including his foreskin which again gleamed with his fluid. She had looked up at him, frowned, then quickly and decisively opened her mouth and shoved half his length into her mouth. She had held it there for ten seconds or so before she pulled away. "Just what you always wanted," she had said. "Your own personal fellatrix."

A week had passed before she actually brought him to an orgasm in her mouth.

Now—comfortable with it, and practiced—she worked rhythmically with her tongue and lips. She had her own way of doing it: without vigor, without bobbing her head up and down, without using her hands, using only her mouth, expertly finding his most sensitive nerves and flicking her tongue over them, drawing the shaft in and sucking on it to tighten her wet caressing lips. "Don't you dare come," she said. "It's too soon."

"I'll try not to spoil your fun," he said.

She murmured a small laugh. "It *is* fun . . . sort of," she said. "But you—you love it, don't you?"

Bat put both hands on her head, gently caressing. "What I love is you, Toni," he said solemnly.

She pulled her head back and held his penis between her hands. "I love you too, Bat. You know how much I love you."

She was in her senior year at Radcliffe, he in his junior year at Harvard. They had met in a psychology class about six weeks ago. She was the same age as Bat, but she was a mature woman with mature ideas about what she liked and what she wanted.

2

Antonia did not remember when there hadn't been a boat. Her memories of the 1930s were of days of sunshine, many of them spent on the blue water. She remembered nothing of the Depression, but she remembered that there had always been a boat hanging from the davits or tied at the canalside dock behind their home in Fort Lauderdale. The first one she remembered was a nineteen-foot utility fisherman, powered by a gasoline engine. She remembered always wanting to go fishing, insisting she must not be left behind, then growing bored and a little sick and sometimes frightened as her father and mother fished. They would not let her take off her life jacket, ever. She remembered the humiliation of having to squat over a jar to pee, since the boat had no head.

She remembered the day when the alligator waddled out of the canal behind their house and snapped up her cocker spaniel puppy. Her father had come running from the house with a baseball bat—and also a pistol—but by the time he reached the shrieking Toni the gator had dragged the puppy into the water. That, after all, was how it killed the dog; it drowned it.

She remembered her mother and father driving her to the rail at the bow of the boat while they landed a lunging, snapping shark on the stern deck. Her father had brained the shark repeatedly with his baseball bat, but even after it was quiet it was still dangerous, they said; and Toni had to cling to the bow in terror that it would come to life and do to her parents what the gator had done to her dog.

She learned to swim before she was three. They had a pool behind the house. Sometimes you had to drive off the big birds before you could use the pool. Her mother bought chicken necks and hand-fed them to herons and pelicans, with the result that the Maxim family had more birds than other people had, which did not endear them to their neighbors. Her father built a chain-link fence around the backyard, so no more gators could come, and Toni's next puppy thrived. She called her Pupp'l, and so the dog remained, even when she was old—Pupp'l.

The next boat was a forty-one-foot offshore twin-diesel fishing cruiser, which they called *Maxim's*. On *Maxim's* they could stay at sea an entire weekend. Toni loved that boat. It had a galley and a head, and when she was tired she could nap in her own bunk. The fisherman who hooked a big one would shift into the rotating fighting chair in the cockpit and sometimes fight a fish for more than an hour. That was exciting.

Even Pupp'l went to sea. It was Toni's duty to clean up after her.

Toni was eleven when she caught her first big fish, a four-foot mackerel, and thirteen when she caught her first sailfish. The sailfish was mounted in the den.

Dr. Jean Paul Maxim was a handsome, personable man, a psychiatrist. Toni observed early that a psychiatrist made a lot of money, that Dr. and Mrs. Maxim were well off, even among people who lived along the Fort Lauderdale canals. It was much later before she figured out what a psychiatrist did to make that money. Later she would tell that and add a quip that she still didn't understand it.

Her mother, Blanche Maxim, was a formidable

woman with sun-tanned skin and sun-bleached hair, cold pale-blue eyes, and large prominent teeth.

Toni did not go to the public schools. Her parents sent her to a girls' school called Seaview Academy. In her high school years she became an editor of the school newspaper and yearbook, a member of the drama club, and president of *Le Cercle Français*. She played basketball and tennis.

In at least one way, Antonia was an odd girl at Seaview. Her parents remained married. She was one of few girls who had both parents at home. Then that oddity evaporated. She had heard the arguments around the house. But she was surprised when, at fourteen, she found herself being interviewed by a kindly blue-haired woman with great thick eyeglasses, who asked her whether she wanted to live with her mother or her father.

What Toni wanted— Later, when she thought of it from a more mature perspective, she recalled a child's brutal cynicism. What she wanted was to continue to sleep in her own room, with Pupp'l, to swim in her own pool, and to go cruising on *Maxim's*. That meant living with her father, and that is what she chose.

She had no sense of guilt about her choice; and later, when she might have thought that way, she understood that in fact her mother had been relieved. Blanche had had a ten-month affair with a Miami lawyer before Dr. Maxim found out. The lawyer, as Toni would learn in the course of visits with her mother, was contemptuous of psychiatry and offshore fishing. His own tastes, which her mother now proclaimed were her own as well, ran to golf and tennis.

Within a year Dr. Maxim married another tall, tanned, sun-bleached blonde named Morgana, who admired his boat and said she loved his daughter and his daughter's dog. She seemed sincere. She extended herself to become a friend to Antonia, and Toni accepted her. The exchange of mothers, after the initial shock and curiosity, was not painful.

3

When Antonia was fifteen years old, her years of innocence, the simplicity of loving Pupp'l, swimming in a backyard pool, and fishing off *Maxim's,* going to school at Seaview, and beginning to take an interest in boys, with nothing more troubling to worry about than the mysteries of trigonometry, came to an abrupt end—on December 7, 1941.

She had been interested in the war, of course— enough interested to have thumbtacked a *National Geographic* map of Europe on her bedroom wall and to push in red and white pins to mark the advances and retreats of armies. But it had all been remote, thousands of miles away. Within a few days of December 7, *Maxim's* was lifted from the water and trucked to a warehouse, where it would remain for— a term she learned to hate—"the duration." Worse— On a night in January she woke to the sound of a distant rumble and a dull red glow on the eastern horizon. A tanker had been torpedoed by a German U-boat, not twenty miles off the coast, in waters the Maxims had fished twenty weekends a year. It was too easy to say the war had come home. It had come into their very yard.

The beaches were closed. National Guard soldiers patrolled them day and night, stretching barbed wire and building barricades against raids by Nazi commandos. Fort Lauderdale was certain to be bombed or attacked by submarine-borne commandos, and the town had to be prepared. Her father was summoned to a hospital, where he trained as a member of a Civil Defense medical emergency team. Her stepmother practiced as an emergency telephone operator at the Civil Defense communications center. When they went to these training exercises, Antonia was left alone in the house—as she would be if a raid happened. What was more, she was left behind heavily curtained windows—blackout curtains—and could not see what was happening outside. She switched off all the lights in the house and climbed through a trapdoor onto the roof, where many nights she sat alert and worried. Twice more she saw ships blow up off the beach.

Everything in life was in suspension for "the duration." She did not resent it. She was a patriotic American. Yet— Yet she realized she was losing an important part of her life. It was a little enough sacrifice, but it was real. For instance, her father had promised her he would buy a new car when she was sixteen and would give her his old Plymouth station wagon. Now he could not buy a new car, or buy enough gasoline to drive this one much.

She was introduced to sex about the same time, that is, when she was a little short of seventeen. Two boys somehow had accumulated enough gas to take two girls out into the Everglades in a big old dark-blue Packard. They parked, and the couples took turns walking along the road and looking at the flowers and wildlife, leaving the back seat of the car to the other couple. Half an hour, each couple promised the other. Toni was intoxicated by the feelings the experienced young man could induce in her, and she went further with him than she had intended.

Then she decided he had taken unfair advantage of her and would not see him again. She developed an affection for another boy, and for a few weeks they were intimate on the couch in her family living room—assured of their privacy by the despised black-out curtains. Twice they even did it on the roof while Piper Cubs checking the completeness of the Florida Atlantic Coast blackout flew overhead not more than two hundred feet above them. The darkened houses that did not silhouette ships for German submarines leaked no light to afford the pilots a clue as to what was happening on that roof.

4

In May 1944 she graduated from Seaview Academy, first in her class.

Her mother wanted her to go to Rollins College; her father's first choice was Emory University; and her stepmother urged her to apply to Radcliffe. She applied to all three, and others, and she was accepted at every college she applied to. She chose Radcliffe.

The photos she sent with her applications showed that she was an exceptionally pretty girl. She had by then lost the baby fat around her face. She wore her hair in a loose, careless style that obviously took only an occasional whip or two of the brush to control it. She was pretty but no contrived glamour puss.

The second Mrs. Maxim was active in Democratic politics. She was a delegate to the Democratic National Convention in 1944. She saw to it that Antonia met as many as possible of the prominent Democrats who came to south Florida, and so Antonia was introduced to Senator Harry Truman, the peppery little man running for Vice President with President Roosevelt. He said he had a daughter her age—in fact, Margaret Truman was two years older than Antonia

Maxim—and told her he hoped she would be as loyal a Democrat as his daughter was.

In the fall of 1944 she arrived in Cambridge, Massachusetts, and within no more than a day she developed a troubling, even frightening sense that she was hopelessly narrow and provincial, inexperienced, naive, and ill educated. After a month or so she amended her initial pessimistic judgment and decided she was provincial and inexperienced, not narrow or naive or ill educated. Before the semester ended she realized she was not provincial either, no more provincial anyway than the other girls in the college. No one, she observed, was more provincial than New Yorkers, followed by New Englanders. She learned that she could compete very handily with them.

Only when they spoke of their travels was she at a disadvantage. She had never seen Paris or London, or even Texas or California, but they had and could talk with brittle gaiety about this hotel and that restaurant and about how they hoped these places would survive the war. When they told stories of how they abandoned their virginity, Toni conveniently forgot the back seat of the Packard and said she had given up hers on a flat roof during a blackout, with low-flying planes buzzing overhead. None of them topped that story.

She was an excellent student. She majored in history, with minors in political science and languages. Her mother wrote her a letter suggesting she make an appointment with a Boston cosmetician recommended by a friend and have herself done over. She was so beautiful, her mother said, that she should make the most of herself and consider a career in modeling and maybe even acting.

She made few male friends. The boys who hadn't been in service were . . . well, boys. Many of the returned GIs were married. Others were moody, and some were aggressive. She dated two of them and allowed one to be intimate, but they drifted apart, finding no great attraction in each other.

Her stepmother arranged to meet her in Washington during the spring break of her junior year, to take her around and introduce her to senators and congressmen. She also took her to the offices of *The Washington Post,* where she introduced her to the publisher and editors. In their hotel room, Morgana and Toni talked about what she would do after she graduated. Was there a marriage in sight? No. Was she interested in government? Yes. Did she like Washington? Yes. Well then—maybe she could come to Washington as a congressional aide. Morgana would inquire around.

5

For the fall semester of her senior year she enrolled in a class at Harvard in abnormal psychology, just to round out her education, just because it was something she thought she ought to know something about. It was an eight-o'clock class, and people came in carrying paper cups of coffee, smoking their first morning cigarettes. Toni put her coffee on the writing arm of her chair and snapped her Zippo to light a cigarette. She was wearing blue jeans rolled up to mid-calf and a man's white shirt, tail out and collar open, also brown-and-white saddle shoes with white cotton socks. Of the eight young women in the class, only two were dressed otherwise than in this uniform.

By his first words the professor announced that

smoking would be allowed in his classroom only so long as the weather permitted them to keep the windows open. After that, no smoking would be the rule.

"Why wait till then?" asked a voice from behind Toni.

She turned around and saw a tall, handsome man, looking at her with intimidating bright-blue eyes. He too wore a white shirt, but his shirttail was tucked into khaki corduroy pants. She had meant to look at him defiantly, maybe even to blow smoke in his face; but she decided not to. They stared at each other with eyes equally steady. He was smiling faintly, very faintly.

"I like the idea, Mr.—"

"Batista."

"Oh, yes. Mr. Batista. I like your idea, but I guess we'll stick with my original plan, to postpone the onset of nicotine fits."

Toni had heard of Jonas Cord y Batista, who was nicknamed Bat. He was known in Cambridge. The story about him was that he was an illegitimate son of the rapacious tycoon Jonas Cord and was somehow related to the former and perhaps future president of Cuba, Fulgencio Batista. He was of course one of the returning GIs, and the rest of the story about him said that he had been wounded and decorated. He had been in Cambridge for a whole year, but this was the first time she had seen him.

She stopped outside the classroom later and said to him, "I hope my smoke didn't drift up your nose."

"I hope my suggestion didn't spoil your pleasure," he said dryly.

She grinned. "I'm Antonia Maxim, and I'm usually called Toni."

"I'm usually called Bat," he said. "Because a lot of

people are uneasy with my name—which is Jonas. Do you have a nine-o'clock?"

"No."

"Neither do I. Let's go across the street and have some doughnuts."

Two nights later he took her to dinner and a movie.

Two months later word circulated among her friends and his that Toni Maxim and Bat Batista were in love and planned to be married. Some noted scornfully that she had stopped smoking and wearing blue jeans with her shirttail out.

When his mother, Señora Sonja Escalante, came to Boston for one of the only two visits she would make to the States to see her son while he was at Harvard, she stayed at the Copley; and Toni Maxim was her guest for dinner two of the five nights she was in town.

6

Some of her friends could not imagine Toni could fall in love with Jonas Cord y Batista. Oh yes, he was handsome, and apparently he was rich, but he was a queer duck. He took courses that had no apparent aim—lots of history and government, some economics, chemistry, physics, psychology, philosophy, literature, and art. He was seen on the Yard during the day, sometimes in the library at night, but he lived as far away as Lexington, as though he made a conscious effort not to associate himself with the college any more than necessary. He didn't seem to care about much of anything—about anything, that is, that other people cared about. He didn't go to football games. He didn't go down to the river to watch the rowing. It was as if he went out of his way to make it clear he was not in awe of Harvard and didn't think himself privileged to have been admitted.

Toni shrugged at this talk. So? A lot of the returning GIs were like that. They had seen too much, experienced too much, to go rah-rah at football games. So far as being admitted to the college was concerned, Bat was an outstanding student. So far as she was concerned, if he was privileged to be at Harvard, Harvard was privileged to have him.

She had met his mother but not his father. He told her, finally, that *he'd* never met his father and wasn't sure he wanted to. Mexico City and Córdoba were too far away for him to go home often. He had gone last summer, but would not go home for Christmas. He accepted her family's invitation to spend Christmas with them in Florida.

Dr. Maxim was not pleased to have his daughter talking about marrying the illegitimate son of Jonas Cord but was reconciled to the idea after he watched Bat land a big tarpon. The young man had fished from a boat out of Vera Cruz and was experienced and skilled at fighting a big fish. What was more, he passed a test put to him by Dr. Maxim—he backed *Maxim's* smoothly into its slip, steering with its twin screws more than its rudder. The doctor was prepared to accept him after watching him do that.

Morgana liked him better after several evenings of dinner and after-dinner conversation. When he said he thought President Truman might be reelected— and backed his judgment with reasons—she decided she liked him very well indeed.

When Toni and Bat caught the train to return to Boston, the Maxims did not comment on the obvious fact that they would be sharing a roomette. They were in fact traveling as Mr. and Mrs. J. Batista, as their luggage tags indicated—because railroads in 1947 would not allow an unmarried couple to share a roomette.

"They like you," Toni said as she waved at her parents through the window.

"I tried," he said.

"Well, they do like you," she said. "They do. They've bought the idea of our marriage. Not one hundred percent, but . . . no parents ever accept one hundred percent the marriage of a son or daughter to some stranger they did not choose. Of course"—she grinned wickedly—"if they knew I go down on you, they'd kill you."

"We should just go ahead and marry," he said. "Then we could live together."

"Soon . . ." she whispered, glancing one more time at her parents on the platform as the train pulled away. "We have to let them give me a wedding."

Toni could not move in with him in his apartment in Lexington, but she spent hours there almost every day. She spent as little time as possible in her college living quarters—only from 1 A.M. to dawn, as the rules demanded. She kept most of her clothes in Lexington, most of her books, and her two portable typewriters.

She had two portable typewriters because she had one that typed Greek characters. During her senior year she wrote a thesis for a class in public ethics, in Greek. She won the award for the best senior thesis of the year. The title was Δεμοκρατια εσχατη τυραννις, a quotation from Plato that translates "Democracy passes into despotism."

Bat was proud of her. Dave made him prouder by marveling over her Greek typewriter and her Greek thesis. Dave encouraged Bat to go to law school, and Toni joined in that. It would be a fine career for him. Besides, he needed focus. He had been thinking of law school anyway. His mother, too, urged it. He applied for the fall class in 1948 and was admitted.

So far as Bat was concerned, everything was settled.

7

'We can buy a house," he said to Toni one afternoon in the spring. "Or lease an apartment in Boston." He grinned. "We can't go on living with Dave. I'm going to accelerate law school, go all summer and so on, and graduate six months earlier. Then—New York. Or would you rather live in Connecticut?"

"Bat . . . What about my thing in Washington? I told you it's almost certain I'm going to be appointed an aide to Senator Spessard Holland."

He stiffened. "You mean, even if we are married, you—"

She nodded. "Of course. It's what I've wanted to do. I've planned for it, studied for it. Washington is where a person may be able to make a difference."

"What about children?" he asked.

"I don't want to have any children for a while. I want to see what I can *do*. Then . . . There'll be time. I'm only twenty-two."

"The perfect time for children," he said.

"I didn't say I want to wait ten or fifteen years. But I didn't come to college to learn to be a housewife. That's what my mother and my stepmother are. There are more important things in this world than shopping for groceries and doing laundry and playing golf. An arrangement can be worked out, Bat. An element of it is that I'm not going to have children for a few years."

"And that's that," he said, his voice rising to a testy

sneer. He got up and walked across the room. "That's the way it's gonna be, huh? *You've* decided."

"There is nothing we can't discuss," said Toni.

"Except that our marriage would be subordinate to your *'career,'*" he scoffed.

"Oh? Well . . . hasn't your father's marriage—and his affairs—always been subordinate to his?"

"No. I'm not that contemptible *norteamericano* asshole!"

"Really? Tell me how you're going to be different."

"My . . . 'father'— That man whose biology is in me, and nothing else? All right. From what I know of him, all his life he has subordinated everything to his career—his love for my mother, his love for his wife, his home, his friendships . . . everything. *Time* says he has a daughter who never saw him until she was fourteen years old. He has a son who hasn't seen him yet. He wouldn't marry my mother. He married another woman, then walked away from her, and she divorced him . . . and then he married her again. I love you, and—"

"I love you, Bat," she interrupted. "But I'm a person too. If we are going to marry, we'll have to work out something that recognizes that."

"I *do* recognize it."

"Then don't ask me to move into a house or apartment in Massachusetts and be there waiting for you every evening when you come home, with a roast in the oven. I'm going to Washington. I *am* going to Washington."

He sighed. "I guess we'd better put off marrying. For a while. Till I graduate from Harvard Law. Till you . . . do whatever it is you think you have to do."

"If I didn't love you so goddamned much, I'd tell you to go to hell," she muttered. "I ought to. If I didn't love you, I would."

"I love you, too," he said.

Toni nodded. "So maybe it will work out some way. Listen, I have to be in Washington on June sixteenth. I'm going to be down there all alone, missing you so much. Come down that weekend. Promise me you'll come down that weekend."

"Sure. I'll try," he said.

She understood that meant he wouldn't. And he didn't.

12

1

BAT? WHY BAT? BECAUSE YOU'VE USED THE NAME Batista?"

Jonas and Bat were together in Bat's Porsche 356. Bat had told him that moving into a hotel floor in Acapulco was foolish, that he could live in a comfortable house in a good neighborhood here in Mexico City, for a fifth of the cost. Besides, privacy and security and communications would be easier from the city than from Acapulco.

Jonas had accepted the idea. It seemed to him that his chances of establishing a good relationship with his newfound son would be improved if he accepted the boy's suggestion about something important.

Using his contacts in the local real estate industry, Bat had found a place he thought suitable. He was driving Jonas out to have a look at it.

"I didn't make a choice of names," said Bat. "Here in Mexico I am thought of as Cord. In the States, where they don't understand the Spanish tradition of using both parents' names, I am thought of as Batista because it's the last name in the string."

Jonas sat as far as he could to the right in the somewhat cramped little car, so he could study this son of his. He found the boy bland. No, that was not right. He found him enigmatic. His life seemed to have left no mark whatever on him, and he stared at the road and the traffic ahead of them with the innocence of a young man who'd had no experiences in this world at all. Jonas looked for the mark of a soldier who had been grievously wounded, and he didn't see it. He looked for the curiosity, or maybe the resentment, an illegitimate son might feel toward the father who had abandoned his mother—and he didn't see that, either.

"You understand, I didn't know your mother was pregnant."

Bat glanced at him. "Would it have made any difference?" he asked.

"Yes— Yes, *goddammit,* it would have. It sure as hell would have made a difference."

"I'm glad to hear it," said Bat dryly. Neither the hard raised voice or the "goddammit" had penetrated his calm. He whipped the little car in and out in the heavy traffic.

Jonas changed the subject. "You know why I'm in Mexico, of course."

"Yes. I read the newspapers."

"I'm not a fugitive from justice," said Jonas.

"Maybe from injustice," said Bat.

"It's political."

"That's how I read it," said Bat.

Jonas nodded. "You understand about it, then?"

"I'm sure I don't have all the information. From what I know—"

"I'm probably pretty much what my reputation says I am," Jonas interrupted. "But I'm not a goddamn crook. I really am not."

"You don't have to convince me," said Bat dryly.

For a minute or so Jonas stared at the road. Then he said, "I treated your mother ill. I'm glad to see she's happy. She would not have been with me. You know? You know enough about me to understand that. Don't you?"

"Don't try to justify yourself," said Bat without taking his eyes off the traffic. "You don't need to. And if you did need to, you couldn't. She made up her mind about you a long time ago. Even now, you contacted her only because you think she might have some influence you can use, with her uncle."

"You've got your mind pretty well made up," said Jonas. "I couldn't justify myself with you, either. The fact I didn't know you existed makes no difference."

Bat glanced at his father. "Exactly," he said.

Jonas leaned against the right-hand door of the car and scowled at his son. The boy was more of a Cord than he had suspected.

"Changing the subject, I do have to . . . hide."

"Why?" asked Bat. "Officially, the Mexican government doesn't know you're here. Unofficially, it won't acknowledge it. That can be arranged for very little money. Besides, I sense the American government has become bored with the chase. There have been editorials saying the government surely has something better to do than hound you. What did those editorials cost you, incidentally?"

"Jonas . . . Bat. You know too fuckin' much."

Bat smiled at last. "A man can get along in this world knowing nothing. Or he can get along—maybe no better—trying to know everything."

Jonas stared at his son and nodded. "Like I said, you know too much. I didn't buy any editorials. I just fed those papers information."

"It would have been more direct to buy them," said Bat.

"So you're cynical, too."

"Cynical is another word for realistic."

Jonas grinned. "You inherited something from me—and from your grandfather. You—you wouldn't mind using the name Cord?"

"Here in Mexico, I am Cord. It is only in the States that they have that confused."

"And everyone knows you're my son?"

"Everyone."

Jonas closed his eyes for a moment. "Everyone but me. I didn't know I had a son. Are . . . are you married?"

"No."

"Have a girl? A prospect?"

"Maybe. Not really, I guess. I thought I did, but she's a career woman."

"Meaning what?"

"I asked her to marry me, and she accepted. Then she was appointed an aide to a United States senator and went to Washington. Three years ago. I've seen her a couple of times since."

"I'm glad to hear there's *some* way in which you're a damned fool."

"Meaning what?"

"Either you were a fool to ask her to marry you in the first place, or you were a fool to resent her wanting a career of her own. Which was it?"

"It's personal," said Bat glumly.

"Fathers and sons tend to discuss personal things with each other," said Jonas.

"I wouldn't know about that."

"Neither would I," said Jonas. "My father never talked about anything personal with me, except to raise hell with me about something or other. It was only after he died that somebody told me he once said he loved me."

Bat took his eyes off the road and looked at Jonas. He frowned and shook his head.

"If I'd known I had a son—"

"You didn't ask."

"I didn't guess."

"It may be just as well," said Bat. "I'm not sure I could have coped with you."

"But you can now, hmm?" Jonas asked.

Bat smiled. "Well . . . We'll see."

"Are you going to handle this business with the Mexican government for me? I mean, letting me stay in the country and so on."

"I'm a very new lawyer. My firm can handle it."

"All right. You've brought in a client. I'll have a variety of legal problems for your firm. But understand something. Anything that's personal and confidential, I want *you* to handle it. You have a stake in it, you know."

"What's that mean?"

"You're my *heir,* you damned fool. What did you think?"

"Heir?" Bat asked, tossing up his chin. "I learned in law school that you can't refuse a legacy, so that you have to pay inheritance taxes even if you don't want the inheritance. You have to accept the inheritance and pay the taxes out of it, before you can get rid of it. But don't do me any favors until I decide if I want them."

2

Mexico City was a city of startling contrasts. Downtown, high-rise office buildings rose above broad avenues. Out a little, people lived in what had to be the world's most squalid slums. The villa Bat had found was located in as pleasant a suburban neighborhood as Jonas had ever seen.

The house had a red tile roof above ocher stucco walls. In the Mediterranean style, it faced the street and its neighbors with windowless walls. All the windows opened on its central courtyard, affording views of a green pool inhabited by large goldfish that swam placidly among lily pads. The goldfish were so tame you could reach down in the water and pick one up. Chameleons scampered among the shrubs, wary of the sharp-eyed birds that watched them from branches and occasionally swooped down and caught one. The rooms were all large, with dark wood floors and white plaster walls. The furniture was heavy, most of it upholstered with leather of various colors, from black to coffee-with-cream tan. The villa suited Jonas very well.

A man and wife worked as household staff: the woman as cook, maid, and laundress, her husband as gardener and houseman. They lived in a suite of rooms at the rear of the house.

Bill Shaw stayed with him and occupied a room on the south side. He had brought Jonas's telephone scrambler, and they attached it to the house line. Jonas called for Angie, and she came down.

Bat came to see him nearly every day, so often that Jonas began to wonder if he came to see him or to see Angie. The young man was not subtle about his admiration for his father's woman. He stared at her legs. It amused her, and she would allow her skirt to creep up. When she noticed him staring at her breasts, she would shrug and thrust them forward. Their little game amused Jonas at first, then ceased to amuse him.

Bat suggested they go to a bullfight on Sunday

afternoon. "It's not one of my favorite spectacles, but everybody should see it once."

He bought them good seats in the shade, where they were surrounded by happy aficionados. A noisier and more exuberant crowd sat in the sun on the opposite side. The spectacle was, as Bat had said, something everyone should see once, for the color and the horses and the brassy music, if not for the killing of bulls.

Angie sat between Jonas and Bat, drawing honest stares. She wore a white dress and a white picture hat. She sat with her legs crossed at the ankles, the way finishing schools taught; and no one, especially not Bat, guessed that *her* finishing school had been a women's reformatory. She studied her program for some time, then turned to Bat and said, "I hope the score is matadors seven, bulls one. I think the bulls should be entitled to win occasionally."

After the first fight, a group of American tourists got up and left. One of the women had fainted—or pretended to—when the bull's blood gushed from its neck. One of the men, wearing a panama hat, a light-blue suit, and white shoes, proclaimed indignantly that bullfighting was no sport and was brutality practiced to entertain brutes.

"¿Qué quiere usted decir?" Bat asked innocently: What do you mean? He judged his group looked *norteamericano,* too, and he wanted the angry Mexicans seated around them to think they weren't. The tourist in the panama hat shot him a hard look as he bustled by. Bat turned to the Mexicans sitting around them, turned up his palms, turned down the corners of his mouth, and shrugged. The people laughed.

In the second fight, Angie got her wish. The matador was gored and thrown. The bulls did win occasionally.

"It's no secret that I'm in Mexico City," Jonas said

to Bat as they waited for the third fight. "Someone knew how to find me."

"Who?" Bat asked.

"A man by the name of Luis Basurto. Ever hear of him?"

"I've heard of him," said Bat. "What's he want?"

Their conversation was interrupted by the cry of a boy selling chewing gum and candy. *"¡Chicle! ¡Chocolate!"*—Cheek-leh, Choco-lawt-eh.

"He wants to interest me in investing in a Mexican hotel deal."

Bat shook his head. "Basurto is a crook."

"That simple?"

"That simple. Are you interested in investing in a Mexican hotel?"

"Well, I bought The Seven Voyages," said Jonas. "I'm going to make it pay, too. I'm looking for at least one more."

"There's no legal gambling in Mexico."

"Well, that's what—"

"¡Chicle! ¡Chocolate!"

"—that's what Basurto says he can take care of."

"I expect he can," said Bat dryly. "But it would be damned risky. What would happen is, you'd invest in the hotel and pay him a fee to do whatever he does to get officials to look the other way; and then as time went by he'd up the fee and up it again, claiming the locals were demanding more. He'd take a percentage off you. If you didn't pay him what he wanted, he'd have you raided. He'd have you closed down. That's the way he works. He invests nothing, but he takes a percentage."

"I imagine there are ways of handling him," said Jonas.

"He'd have you at a disadvantage. This is his turf, you know. Anyway, why buy into trouble?"

"Well, he's coming out to see me. What do I say to him?"

"Say, 'This is my son Jonas Enrique Raul Cord y Batista, a lawyer with the firm of Gurza y Aroza. That firm will be advising me.' Basurto won't even make the proposition. He'll just pass the time of day and say he's pleased to have met you. And good-bye."

"¡Chicle! ¡Chocolate!"

"There will be others besides Basurto," said Bat. "Some of them entirely legitimate. They will invite you to invest."

"Do you want to vet them for me?" asked Jonas.

"I'll be happy to."

3

After a week, Angie returned to Las Vegas. After she was gone, Sonja called, asking Jonas to come to Córdoba and spend a weekend at the hacienda. Bat would drive him. Jonas agreed, and on Friday afternoon Bat picked him up in the Porsche. He gave him an exciting ride, at speeds sometimes greater than 160 kilometers per hour.

The hacienda was actually some distance to the east of Córdoba. It was situated on a mountainside, and on clear days a very distant view of the Gulf of Mexico could be seen from the windows.

Sonja was the chatelaine of the hacienda, mistress over an extended family and a dozen servants. The mountain land had once been a working sheep and cattle ranch. In years past, Sonja explained, the family had sold the land cheap and on good terms to tenant farmers and farm laborers who now worked all but about fifty hectares of land immediately adjacent to the house. The family kept the house as a home, but the income to maintain it came from oil and other investments.

She showed Jonas the thickness of the outer walls: a meter and more. The dining room had once been a chapel. A pantry had once been an arsenal. The swimming pool had been dug out of the rocky land that had once been a courtyard enclosed by high walls, now torn down, and the well that supplied the pool with water had been inside those walls.

"The place was built to sustain a siege," she said. "Once in fact it was attacked by Zapatistas." She smiled. "And the people inside surrendered."

She gave him the bedroom suite that Fulgencio Batista used when he came to visit—which he occasionally did. Emiliano Zapata had slept two nights in that same room.

She introduced Jonas to one of Bat's half brothers and one of his half sisters. The others were away: the boy in school in France and the girl living with her husband in the States.

The half sister, whose name was Rafaela, told Jonas how Bat had saved her life by shooting a rattlesnake with a pistol.

"You lived in a handsome home," Jonas said to Bat as they stood on a stone terrace looking at the distant sea.

"I didn't live here long," said Bat. "I went away to school."

Over dinner, Jonas stared at Sonja as much as he could without being noticed. He was sure what he had said to Bat had been right: that she was living a better life than he would have given her. Still, he couldn't help reflect on what might have been. He might have lived his own life very differently if he'd known she

HAROLD ROBBINS

was carrying his child and had married her. On the
other hand, he might have resented her, as men tend
to do when they marry women they have made
pregnant without intending to.

He remembered her bright wonder as they crossed
the Atlantic twice on the big liners. He remembered
her gratitude. Painfully, he remembered the hurt he'd
dealt her when he left her. He had been simply unable
to believe she was as innocent as she was.

A rationalization. He *had* known.

Now here she was, still beautiful, and now sophisticated and dignified.

She'd brought the boy up wonderfully. It was going
to be a pleasure to introduce him to Nevada Smith.

In the Old World tradition, the women left the table
after dinner, and the men remained for coffee, brandy, and cigars—Bat and Jonas and Virgilio Escalante.
Virgilio and Bat wore white suits. Jonas didn't have
one and wore a summer-weight tan suit.

"The price of oil is down," Bat said to Virgilio.

"It will come back," said Virgilio.

"When the price of oil goes down," Bat said to
Jonas, "they don't pump as much. Which means that
not only do they get less per barrel but they don't sell
as many barrels. It makes income fluctuate wildly."

"I never invested in oil," said Jonas. "It has always
impressed me as a business in which a fool and his
money are soon parted." He nodded at Virgilio
Escalante and added, "I mean, señor, it is a business where a man should not venture unless he is
knowledgeable about that business."

Virgilio smiled. He was a graying, compact man
who could, so far as appearance was concerned, have
been a native of the United States or any country in
Europe. "I understood your meaning," he said.

"I've never invested in uranium either," said Jonas. "For the same reason. It's a legitimate business in which some men are making fortunes. But for those who don't know what they're doing—" He shook his head.

"You've invested in a casino-hotel," said Bat.

"I have an experienced, knowledgeable consultant on my payroll."

"When I was last in the States," said Bat, "I saw Cord television sets in the stores."

"We're not as successful in the field as RCA or General Electric," said Jonas, "but I think we can compete with Philco, Zenith, Magnavox, DuMont, Emerson, Sylvania, and the like."

"I am hoping to see television broadcasting in Mexico before too much longer," said Virgilio. "I am afraid the broadcasting will be government-controlled, however. It is in most countries."

4

They had no bourbon in the house, so Jonas carried half a bottle of brandy to his room. He took a bath, stretched out on his bed, and looked through an English-language book he had found in the library. *Main Street* by Sinclair Lewis. He'd heard about it for many years but had never read it. He'd never had the time. Starting it now, he didn't find it terribly interesting and was about to put it aside when someone knocked on his bedroom door.

God! Not Sonja. Surely not . . .

No, not Sonja. When he opened the door he found Virgilio standing there.

"May I come in?"

"Of course."

Two chairs faced the small fireplace, and the two men sat down. Jonas had undressed for bed. He hadn't brought a robe, so he'd pulled on his pants before he went to the door. Virgilio was still wearing the white suit he'd worn at dinner.

"I hope you will forgive the intrusion," said Virgilio. "I hope even more you will forgive the reason for it."

Jonas nodded. "Would you like some brandy?"

"No, thank you. I . . . I am most embarrassed about what I am about to say. After dinner, when Bat spoke of the price of oil and the wide fluctuations we experience in oil income, he was not prompted by me, but he was explaining something that I would otherwise have had to explain."

Jonas knew what was coming. He was about to be touched for a loan.

"Even the past few months' diminished income would have been entirely sufficient . . . but for one thing. I have been very foolish in Las Vegas. I am heavily indebted to the casinos, which of course expect payment. I need time. When the price of oil recovers, which it will, I shall be in a position to pay in full, with reasonable interest. For the moment—" He turned up the palms of his hands.

"How much do you owe?" asked Jonas.

"More than a quarter of a million dollars," said Virgilio glumly. "I owe the Flamingo a hundred ten thousand. I owe The Seven Voyages a hundred sixty-five thousand. Imagine my surprise and embarrassment when I learned that you own The Seven Voyages."

"You gamble badly," said Jonas. "Do you have other expensive habits?"

"No," said Virgilio humbly. "I am loyal to my wife—I mean, as loyal as any man; I have ventured but have never kept another woman. Like any man. No significant money."

Jonas was distressed that the man would bare himself this way. He demeaned himself, confessing his peccadilloes to a man who was almost a stranger to him. "You have what we call a cash-flow problem," he said to Virgilio.

"I believe that is the term."

Jonas's mind worked fast. This man had reared his son for him—and reared him well. He decided.

"One sixty-five at my hotel, one ten at the Flamingo, you say. Don't worry about it. I'll take care of it."

"A loan," said Virgilio.

"We can talk about it again sometime when the cash is flowing. In the meantime, don't even think about it. I'll take care of it."

5

From the villa in Mexico City, Jonas telephoned Morris Chandler on Tuesday, using the scrambler telephone.

"What are we carrying on the books in the name of Virgilio Escalante?" he asked.

"We don't have books for that kind of thing," said Morris.

"Then I'm sure you've got it in your head, Morris—that kind of money."

"Hundred sixty-five," said Morris.

"Write it off," said Jonas.

Morris Chandler said nothing for a long moment, then said, "Well, you own the place."

"Right. Now, I understand that Senõr Escalante owes a hundred ten at the Flamingo. Call and offer them fifty for it."

"They won't go for it."

"See if they do."

"Okay," Morris sighed. "You're the boss."

"Let me ask you something," said Jonas. "How much are we carrying for our Mexican junketeers?"

"Oh, I'd say another five hundred thousand. More than that, actually."

"And how much do we make from them in a year?"

"Offhand—"

"Enough to justify flying a plane back and forth from Mexico City twice a week, right? Enough to justify rooms, meals, drinks, gifts, right? Well then, it's enough to invest a hundred sixty in one of their high rollers. It's *business*, my friend, business."

6

When Bat came to the villa on Friday evening, Angie was there again. She had come down on the Thursday junket flight and would return to Las Vegas on Tuesday.

From the moment when Bat walked into the living room, Jonas saw that his son was angry. Dressed in a gray suit of some shiny material, with a narrow black necktie, Bat looked more Mexican than Jonas had ever seen him. He didn't sit down and spoke to Angie.

"I hope you won't be offended, Angie, but I would like to speak with my father alone . . . for a few minutes."

Angie rose, nodded, and quietly left the room.

"Why?" asked Jonas.

Bat stepped over to the chair where his father was

sitting. He reached into the inside pocket of his jacket and pulled out an envelope. He handed the envelope to Jonas. "There," he said. "There's twenty-five thousand in cash. That's all I could raise for the moment. The balance is represented by a note for two hundred fifty thousand. I'll pay as soon as I can. With interest."

Jonas didn't open the envelope. He thrust it toward Bat, who stepped back and didn't take it.

"May I ask what the hell this is for?"

Bat glared. "Virgilio . . . *Padre* . . . put a touch on you for his Las Vegas gambling losses. It was a despicable thing to do. I'm not sure you didn't do something worse, though. You gave it to him."

"I made him a loan."

"Do you have a note?"

"No. A deal like that doesn't need a note. It's a deal between gentlemen."

"Virgilio is no gentleman," said Bat. "His father, the man I called *Abuelo*—grandfather—would have horsewhipped him for asking money from you, from *you* of all people! And you gave it to him! 'A deal between gentlemen.' Bullshit!"

Jonas flared. "Who the hell are you to talk to me that way?"

"I want a straight answer to a straight question."

"Let me hear your straight question," Jonas muttered, his face glowering and red.

"The two seventy-five thousand cleared accounts between you and Virgilio, didn't it? It wiped the books clean. He married my mother, knowing she was pregnant by you. He brought me up in his household and treated me as if I were his son. He paid my tuition—well, part of it. Most of that was paid with Batista money, and we know how that is earned. But you and Virgilio. You're even, aren't you? My straight question is Can you tell me you didn't think of it that way? You hand over two seventy-five thousand and you feel no more obligation to Virgilio Escalante. Isn't that the way you figured?"

Jonas shook his head. "In the first place," he said, "you know nothing about casino gambling if you think high rollers like Virgilio have to pay a hundred cents on the dollar. I bought his markers from the Flamingo for fifty thousand. Morris Chandler would have sold him his markers at my hotel for a hundred ten or a hundred twenty. Your note is more than a hundred thousand too rich."

"That's not a straight answer to my straight question," Bat snapped angrily. "What the hell's the difference how much you paid? You paid him off! *Didn't you?*"

"If you've made up your mind to that, why should I even answer?"

Bat stiffened as he drew a deep breath. He stood for a full quarter of a minute breathing heavily. "Because," he said hoarsely between clenched teeth. "Because— All right. If you give me your word on it, I will believe you. I have no choice."

Jonas smiled, almost imperceptibly. So— His son. Formidable. He had backed his father—not just his father but Jonas Cord—into a corner.

Almost. "I will give you my word on a condition," said Jonas.

"Which is?"

"Which is that you take this money and this note back. Virgilio will repay me. If he doesn't, it's a business risk *I* took, for reasons that are sufficient for me—and which have nothing to do with you."

Bat nodded. "All right," he muttered. He reached for and accepted the envelope.

Jonas looked up and met Bat's eyes with his. "I did

not pay off Virgilio Escalante for what he did for your mother, for you, or for me."

"What choice do I have, but to believe you? I used to think I didn't want to meet you until I was in a position to tell you to go to hell. So now I'm in that position."

"Are you telling me to go to hell?" asked Jonas.

Bat shrugged scornfully. "What's the difference?"

13

1

IN THE LAW FIRM OF WILSON, CLARK & YORK THERE WAS no Wilson and no York. There was a Clark: the great-grandson of Depew Clark. The founders were all long since dead, none of them having lived past 1930. The custom was to keep their names on the firm letter-head, giving the dates of their lives to solve any possible ethical problem that might arise if someone was naive enough to believe his law business might be handled by one of the founders.

The firm's twenty-nine active partners were listed in a column down the left margin of the letterhead. A column down the right margin listed the associates. One of these was Jonas E. Cord.

He was spending a year in the offices of Wilson, Clark & York by reason of the agreement between that firm and Gurza y Aroza in Mexico City to exchange junior associates for one-year terms. Two Wilson, Clark & York lawyers were in Mexico City. Two Gurza y Aroza *abogados* were in New York.

The fall crop of associates were traditionally wel-comed at a cocktail party held at the Harvard Club. There they met all the partners and all the more senior associates and were welcomed into the fraterni-ty of the firm. The partners kept keen eyes on their new associates. They wanted to see how much the boys would drink and how drunk they got. In point of fact, the test didn't work, and everybody knew it didn't. Among the senior associates there was invariably someone disloyal enough to warn the new associates, so the boys drank sparingly. Usually it was the partners who got drunk.

Occasionally, lawyers from other firms came to the party. They came to see how well Wilson, Clark & York had done with its recruiting, but they were welcome.

Dave Amory came. "Bat!" he exclaimed as he strode across the threadbare carpet that was an element of the dignity and cachet of the Harvard Club and seized Bat's hand. "I heard these pettifoggers had got you. Welcome to New York!"

"Bat?" asked one of the firm's junior partners.

"Well, you aren't going to call him *Jonas,* for Christ's sake," said Dave. "Bat and I go back a long way. He was my platoon leader during the late unpleasantness."

"Dave saved my life," said Bat solemnly.

"Bull," said Dave. "If I had anything to do with it, it was only because he was fool enough to run across the Ludendorff Bridge as if it were the Brooklyn Bridge."

"I was in the Pacific," said the junior partner. "Anyway, we're glad to have another name for this guy, also to know we've got a genuine hero in the office."

"Hero— Oh, come on!" Bat complained. "Dave, you've got a big mouth."

A little later, as Bat and Dave stood at a window looking down on the street, Dave said, "Take the opportunity while you're in New York and get yourself admitted to the New York bar."

"I'm already admitted," said Bat. "I took the New York bar exam before I went back to Mexico."

"Good. Get all the admissions you can. And, hey, it's none of my business, but have you seen your father yet?"

Bat nodded. "He has an apartment in the Waldorf Towers, would you believe? I met him in Mexico, actually. He's not in town very often, but when he was here, a week or so ago, he invited me to dinner at '21.'"

"How 'bout Toni?"

Bat drew a breath and sighed. "I suppose I ought to go down to Washington and see her."

"When did you see her last?"

"Well, it's been . . . a year."

Dave shook his head. "Maybe you better stay away from her. After all that time, she's probably made other arrangements."

2

Toni had cheered herself hoarse, but when she sat down over a Scotch and soda later with Nick Gargagliano she shook her head and sighed and admitted, "We don't have a chance."

They had driven from Washington to Baltimore to be present at a campaign rally for Adlai Stevenson. She couldn't think of a man in public life that she admired more, but she knew he would not be elected President of the United States.

"It's not *that* bad," said Nick, who was always the optimist.

"Not? It's worse. The great war hero is going to be elected President—and that slimy little creature from

California will be elected with him. There's not a goddamned thing we can do to stop it."

Nick had ordered a plate of steamers and a mug of beer. Toni didn't feel like eating and was sipping Scotch and glancing around for the waiter who would bring her another one. She had started smoking again since she didn't see Bat anymore, and she inhaled the thick smoke from a Chesterfield.

They sat side by side in a high-backed wooden booth painted with shiny red enamel, facing a table painted the same way but blackened with dozens of cigarette burns. They had privacy, and Nick was casually fondling her left breast. She allowed this. She allowed more, though she had never done with him some of the things she had done with Bat.

Nicholas Gargagliano was assistant to the director of the Bureau of Apprenticeship and Training, Department of Labor. He was an exceptionally handsome man, with dark curly hair, a long jaw with the blue shadow of a beard always showing, active brown eyes, and a puckish smile. He was about forty years old and came from a county in southern Oklahoma known as an Italian enclave where wonderful red wine was somehow made, to the amazement of the Oklahomans.

"I just can't believe the voters would trust the country to those people," said Nick.

"Neither can my stepmother," said Toni. "But we have to face it."

"Toni . . . I won't have a job if it happens. I think I can stay in Washington, though. I've talked with Reuther. I think there'll be a job for me with the United Auto Workers. I've got no promise, but I do have encouragement. I'm going to drive out to Oklahoma next week. I'll be back in two weeks. I was hoping you'd come with me. I'd like to introduce you to my family."

Toni stared at the table, smiled, and shook her head. "I'll be spending a lot of time in Florida between now and November. My senator is on the ballot, after all."

"Besides, I'm getting ahead of things, huh?"

"Nick, I didn't say that. I simply said I have obligations."

"Well— Yeah, sure. Of course. Obligations."

They didn't go back to Washington that night. They spent the night in a motel on the highway between Baltimore and Washington. She had to change clothes before she could go to the office, so Nick dropped her at her apartment, very early in the morning.

She went in. The two young women with whom she shared the apartment were asleep. She took a shower and stretched out on her bed in her panties and bra, thinking she might doze a little but not meaning to go to sleep. She did though.

"Hey, kiddo!"

She came awake and glanced at the clock. Oh, my god, it was after eight! Time to get moving.

"You had a call last night. You know a guy in New York by the name of Bat something? He wants you to call him. I left his number on the back cover of the phone book, the number in a heavy square. Okay?"

3

Bat's call to Toni had been prompted by an invitation from his father. It had been made over dinner in Jonas's apartment in the Waldorf Towers.

"I haven't yet congratulated you on the way you got the Senate subpoenas quashed," said Bat.

"Months ago," said Jonas.

"When we had dinner before, I knew they had been withdrawn, but I didn't know how you did it."

"Phil Wallace is a good lawyer," said Jonas, "but in all modesty, the way we got the Senate politicians off our back was *my* idea."

"A triple-damages anti-trust action," said Bat, nodding.

"Right. I figured all along that the senators didn't care about gate positions for Inter-Continental Airlines. The problem was that certain senators were in the back pockets of certain airline executives. Hell, I've got a couple on the string myself. So I had Phil and his co-counsel dig around a little, looking for evidence of collusion on the part of three airline companies. They found enough to justify the suit. I don't know if we would have won, but for the next three or four years we'd have been dropping subpoena after subpoena on them and digging through their files. Besides, their attorney fees—"

"What about your own attorney fees?"

"I don't pay fees," said Jonas. "I pay retainers. Phil Wallace and his partners get a flat one million dollars a year from me, whether they do any work for me or not—though I always have plenty of work for them. I've got other firms on smaller retainers, like Wilson, Clark and York and Gurza y Aroza. Besides which, I've got a dozen staff lawyers on my payroll. The anti-trust suit wouldn't have increased my legal costs much."

"Anyway, you scared them off," said Bat.

"Anyway, I scared them off. They asked the senators to drop the investigation, which the senators were glad to do."

"Everybody in the office talks about it," said Bat. "With a certain amount of— Awe, I guess I'd call it."

"I guess you're entitled to congratulations yourself, in a sense," said Jonas. "Your great-uncle is President of Cuba again."

"I'd like it better if he'd been elected," said Bat. "It was a military coup d'état, or as the Germans would call it, a putsch. He'll loot the country."

"That's the way things are done in Latin America, isn't it?" Jonas asked.

"All too often," said Bat.

They were served at the table by a tall, spare black man named Robair. Jonas had explained earlier that Robair had been houseman to the first Jonas, so had served the family for something like forty years. Now, as Robair was pouring wine, Jonas remarked that he knew more about the Cords than the Cords knew about themselves.

"No man is a hero to his valet," said Bat.

"Lord Chesterfield," said Jonas.

"Excuse me, Mr. Jonas," said Robair. "Actually, that was written in a letter by a Frenchwoman named Madame Cornuel. *'Il n'y a point de héros pour les valets de chambre.'*"

"Damn! My *valet de chambre* is better educated than I am."

"No, Mr. Jonas," said Robair with a faint smile. "I've just made a point of studying my trade."

They sat at the table after dinner. Jonas sipped bourbon. Bat sipped Courvoisier brandy.

"I've got several things I want to talk to you about," Jonas said. "First, and simplest, why don't you move into this apartment? I'm only here two or three nights a month and sometimes not that much. It's here, available to you."

"I couldn't afford to keep it clean," said Bat.

"Look. I leased it because Monica wanted it, because she spent so much time in New York. She asked for it in the divorce, but she didn't get it. I keep suites in hotels in Chicago and Los Angeles, so when I come to a city I'll find things the way I want them. Like, I've got my own telephone scramblers on the phones in all these places. I've got safes with papers locked inside—with combinations only I know." He shrugged. "I've got my brand of bourbon. I've got clothes. You don't have to clean the place. It *is* cleaned. You can save whatever you're paying. Besides"—he grinned—"think of what impression you'll make on a broad if you ask her to shack up and this is the shack."

Jonas and Monica had not put much of a mark on the apartment, Bat reflected. Likely they had bought the furniture from the previous occupant. The apartment was handsome but impersonal.

"Well?"

"Let me think about it," said Bat.

"Your gratitude is overwhelming," said Jonas sarcastically.

"I— Well, all right. And thanks." He didn't want to be beholden to his father, didn't want to be drawn within his orbit either, but it was true he could use the money he would save. Wilson, Clark & York didn't pay generously, and he didn't want to have to ask his mother to send him money. "I do appreciate it."

Jonas lifted his glass, looked at the remaining bourbon for a moment, then put it down. "Which brings up the next thing I want to talk to you about. Are you going to Córdoba for Christmas?"

"I don't think so."

"Well, I have a proposition. Come out to the home place, the ranch in Nevada. I'd like for you to see where we come from. I want you to meet Nevada Smith. Uh . . . I was wondering about that girl. Suppose you could talk her into coming, too?"

"I don't know. I doubt it."

"Her senator will be reelected. She's been working her ass off and is entitled to a vacation. Also, she isn't committed to anybody else."

"How do you know about her? *What the hell have you done?*"

"Easy, son, easy. Phil Wallace knows Senator Holland. To use an expression you seem to favor, we asked straight questions and got straight answers."

"I don't remember that I even told you her name. She's none of your business."

Jonas smiled. "I plead guilty to a little snooping. She's a fine girl. You could hardly do better. Well— Okay, it's none of my business. But I'd like for you to spend a few days with me in Nevada, and Toni Maxim is invited too, if you want to ask her."

Bat hesitated for a moment, then said, "I'll think about it."

"About both parts of the invitation?"

"Well, I accept for myself. Whether or not I invite Toni is what I'll think about."

4

Christmas Eve. Toni had never before felt such an energy on such an occasion. The Cords. They made an electricity. The vigor of these people and the tension among them was unique in her experience.

Standing in the living room of the ranch house, Toni wondered where Jonas Cord really did live, since it was apparent he did not live here. She had seen the apartment in the Waldorf Towers twice since November, and it was apparent he did not live there. The places where he was supposed to live were too tidy, too sleek; they looked like hotel suites. He had an office in the Towers apartment and one here, and in those she could see some mark of the man; but she saw none in the living rooms, dining rooms, and bedrooms.

The decor was too resolutely Western, saying this was not really a Western home lived in by a man of the desert and mountains, but was the simulacrum of a ranch house, its furnishings assembled to make the effect.

Only one item said something. Sitting on the crude mantel above the huge smoke-stained fieldstone fireplace was a small framed photograph, a snapshot actually, of a grim, solid man in his fifties or sixties. He wore a no-nonsense expression, glaring disapprovingly at the world but not at the photographer. He wore a dark three-piece suit, not very well tailored and not well cared for, plus a gray hat set squarely on his head. He sat at a rolltop desk in a wooden swivel chair. If you knew what you were looking for in the picture, or used a magnifying glass, you could identify a bottle of bourbon on the desk. On a table at his side were two candlestick telephones. That was Jonas Cord the First.

She sipped Scotch and spoke to Bat and his half sister Jo-Ann. "Your father is not what I imagined he would be."

She had seen pictures of Jonas Cord, so his appearance was no surprise. What she had not seen in his newspaper and magazine pictures was that he swaggered. Yet . . . he carried it off well, and it was not offensive. A man who had achieved what he had achieved had to be engaging; an ugly, aggressive man could not have won the kind of success he had won, could not have enticed all the women he was said to have seduced. He was aggressive, beyond doubt, but besides that he was easily, naturally charismatic.

"Our father is no end of surprises," said Jo-Ann acerbically.

Bat hadn't been able to take his eyes off his half sister, from the moment they arrived. Toni could have become jealous, except that she understood his fascination had its origin and motive strictly in curiosity. She knew Bat was struggling to read Jo-Ann. The girl had reason to resent him, but if she did she concealed it.

Jo-Ann was about eighteen years old, as Toni understood it; and she was extraordinarily beautiful. She was a student at Smith College. From her father she had inherited poise and self-confidence, obviously. What she had inherited from her mother would be difficult for Toni to guess, since she had never met Monica Cord. She could guess that an element of it was a sense of style, since Jo-Ann wore a cherry-red cocktail dress with bold décolletage and a flared skirt that was shorter than this year's styles dictated.

"For example," said Jo-Ann, continuing her response to Toni's comment that Jonas was not what she had expected, "look at the dish he's brought with him. I don't know what made me think he wouldn't bring his new girlfriend to this party. But I didn't. I didn't think he'd have the nerve. Jesus! Look at her!"

Toni had decided that Angie Wyatt was the most beautiful woman at the party, in her thirties and older than Toni or Jo-Ann. If she was not the most beautiful, she was the most self-possessed—conspicuously pleased with herself and with her place in life. She worked for Jonas Cord and slept with him, too, as Bat had confided. She was handsomely dressed, from the spike-heeled shoes that tightened the muscles in her sleek legs, to the tight cream-white silk brocade dress that clung to her figure, to the emerald necklace—likely a gift from Jonas—that hung around her neck.

Jo-Ann spoke to Bat. "Make a point of getting to know Nevada Smith. Nevada knows more about the Cord family than anybody, including Jonas himself. If he chooses to talk to you, he'll give you plenty of ammunition to use when you have to deal with our father."

"Ammunition?" Bat asked. "Will I need ammunition?"

"The way I see it," said Jo-Ann, "you have three choices: to let him run your life the way he runs everybody else's, to back away from him and go your own way, or to fight him. Nevada knows his weaknesses . . . but probably won't tell you."

Nevada Smith fascinated Toni even more than Jonas did. As a little girl she had gone to as many of his movies as she could. He was everything anyone might have expected of him: the tall, rawboned, sun-wrinkled Westerner, probably seventy years old. He dressed like the movie cowboy he had been—more like William Boyd as Hopalong Cassidy than like one of the singing cowboys.

Smith was a neighbor, with a ranch of his own not far away. The connection between him and the Cords was greater than that, but what it was was not apparent. Bat himself didn't know what it was.

Bat had explained who Robair was. Tonight he was a guest. He had come to Nevada from New York two days ahead of everyone else and had decorated the house for Christmas. A tree, which reached the ceiling, was strung with popcorn and hung with dried fruits and simple paper ornaments, no silvered glass balls, no colored lights. Complimented on it, Robair said that Nevada had helped him. It was amusing to think of those two old men solemnly stringing popcorn.

They sat down for dinner. A pair of ranch hands in white jackets served awkwardly.

When the wine was poured, Jonas rose and offered a toast. "To my daughter and my newfound son." He nodded at Nevada and Robair. "To old friends." He nodded at Toni and Angie. "And new. I'm happy we're all together."

After dinner the evening turned painful for Toni. Not knowing who would be there, she had come with small presents for Bat and his father but none for anyone else. Jo-Ann was in the same situation. So, for that matter, was Angie, though she seemed comfortable with it.

It was embarrassing to receive gifts from the hands of people you had just met—particularly such gifts as they were. Nevada Smith gave her a .30-30 Winchester lever-action carbine, telling her he would take her out and teach her to shoot before she left Nevada. The old man's innocence in giving such a gift was endearing and at the same time ominous—in that it meant he expected she would be spending a lot of time in Nevada.

Robair gave her a pair of tight, tapered blue jeans, a blue-and-white-checked wool shirt, and a Stetson hat: riding clothes. This, too, assumed she was not just a one-time guest.

Jonas Cord gave her a pair of handmade snakeskin Western boots. And a bracelet set with rubies and diamonds. For a moment she was tempted to say no, she couldn't accept it.

Bat gave her a silver and turquoise squash-blossom necklace.

Her father and stepmother, apart from disliking her being in Nevada and not in Florida for Christmas, had warned her that going out there implied a commitment. Apparently the Cords thought so, too. She was being treated like a Cord.

Jonas gave Bat a Porsche automobile, saying he ought to have one in the States, since he drove so well. He gave another one to Jo-Ann, telling her Bat would teach her to drive it. He gave a third one to Angie. They were identical, and they carried Nevada license plates: CORD ONE, CORD TWO, CORD THREE.

Toni had brought "the basic little black dress," this one of silk satin, supported by spaghetti straps, with a skirt ending exactly at her knees. The heavy silver squash-blossom necklace would be incongruous with the dress, but Bat wanted her to put it on. His father wanted her to wear his gift, too: the jeweled bracelet. She went to their room—and it was *their* room, not hers alone: another manifestation of the assumption behind her invitation—to leave the little string of cultivated pearls and don her extravagant new jewelry.

Bat followed her to the room.

"Bat . . . You and your father are more alike than I could have dreamed."

"What do you mean?"

"You arrange things. So that people can hardly back away from them. He is manipulative. And so are you."

"We can talk later," he said.

5

"I am not your fiancée, Bat," she said when they were in bed, a little after midnight. "Your father has made an assumption. Have you?"

"No. I've been reminded how much I love you."

"But your father assumes—"

"Yes, he assumes we are going to marry. He also told me I was a fool not to accept the idea you should have a career of your own."

"He did?"

"I grew up in a different tradition," said Bat. "I am an American in all but the basic things: family and so on. I'm learning."

She put her hand to his crotch and fondled his erect penis. "I've missed you, Bat," she said softly. "If we— Are you going to be in New York? That is, New York and Mexico City?"

"I'm not certain," he said. "I think my father is going to offer me a retainer as attorney for some part of the family business."

"My god, you can't take it!"

"That's what I've thought. Give me *your* reasons."

"Your father is a fine man, Bat. He's not what I expected. But he's like a— What is he like? What can I say? Everything that comes within his reach becomes *his*. If you go to work for him, you'll belong to him."

"But I'm his son. If he and I can get along together, I could inherit—"

"Forget what you'll inherit! Think about what you can be and what you can build on your own. Think what you will give your own children, not what you'll get from him!"

"Toni, he's not exactly what you think."

"Okay, he's a great warm-hearted, generous spirit—and he'll *crush* you. You've got ability of your own, Bat. You don't need him."

"Maybe he needs me."

"Sure he does. The question is, do you need him?"

"I can cope with him," said Bat grimly. "I know more about him than you do, and I can cope with the son of a bitch."

"You'd better read the history," she said. "The fields are strewn with the corpses of people who thought they could cope with your father and grandfather. What a horrible cliché! But there's truth in it. You can't cope with him. Nobody ever did."

"Maybe you underestimate me," said Bat somberly.

"If you let him drag you into his business, it will be a lifelong fight," she said. "And you'll lose."

"Maybe not. If you'll help me—"

"I'll help you, Bat. I love you."

"Then we can marry?"

"Not yet. Being married to you will be a full-time job, and I'm not finished with my other job yet."

"Toni, goddammit—"

"Patience, Bat. Besides . . . Let's don't waste a night in bed arguing. I've got something better in mind."

6

They didn't have a night to waste. At six on Christmas morning they were wakened by a knock on the door. Robair had come to tell Bat his father wanted to see him.

The usual heavy Cord breakfast was not yet on the dining table, but a small table in Jonas's office was set with a breakfast of sausage, scrambled eggs, toast, and coffee. Already, this early in the morning, Jonas had a bottle at hand and was sipping bourbon. He wore a heavy gray turtleneck sweater and blue jeans.

"Before the girl's up, before anybody else is up," he said to Bat, "I want to talk to you alone."

"You summoned me out of a warm bed with a warm body," said Bat ruefully.

"There are more important things. I've got something I want to talk with you about. As we might put it . . . your future. I hear you're a good lawyer. You've got a promising career ahead of you. On the other hand, you're an heir. In due time you will inherit . . . probably half of my estate."

"I never expected anything like that," said Bat. "I'm surprised even now that you should say it."

"Who else is going to get it? What do you think of your half sister? Jo-Ann's a smart girl. But her talents, if I'm any judge, lie more toward the artistic. Her mother has encouraged her in that. Anyhow, she can't take over the business after I'm gone or have got too old to run it anymore."

"I wouldn't underestimate her," said Bat.

"When I was twenty-five years old and my father died suddenly, I came into possession of the whole shebang. One minute I was a careless kid having a good time. The next minute I was one of the wealthiest young men in America—but also one saddled with a heavy and complex burden. I could have lost it all. Almost did. The various Cord businesses, what some people call the Cord empire, are worth ten times and more what they were worth when my father died. People say I did it by being tough, not by being smart."

"The word about you is that you're both tough and smart. That's what I've always heard about you," said Bat.

"Yeah? Well, you've also heard that I'm a ruthless, rapacious son of a bitch. Right?"

Bat nodded. "I've heard that."

"Okay. Well, I've done something, too; I've *built* something. But where does it all go if what happened to my father happens to me? And of course it's gonna happen, eventually. What I need is a son to take over the way I did."

Bat frowned. *"My god,* what are you saying?"

"What's it sound like? I want you to come into the business. If you're not interested in it, everything's going to wind up in the hands of somebody not named Cord, somebody that's got nothing of me in him and nothing of my father. No Cord genes. Lawyers, accountants . . . pencil pushers."

"I want to practice law a few years at least. Long enough to prove I can do it."

"I won't say no to that. But we may not have all the time in the world. I'm forty-eight years old. I'm coming into— What do they call it? The hurricane years. I'm reminded all the time that I don't take very good care of myself. Anyway, if you came into the business, you could be a lawyer at first. Corporate law. Anti-trust. Securities. Tax problems. It will take time to learn what you'd need to know if . . . Well, if—"

"I'll have to think about it."

"You do that. I'm offering you a *goddamned world,* and you'll 'think about it.' Okay. I won't offer a second time. I won't shove it down your throat. But you better make a pretty careful appraisal of what you're accepting or rejecting . . . a pretty thorough goddamned appraisal."

"I'll keep it in mind," said Bat. He wondered what Toni would say to *this.*

7

Using the excuse that he wanted to drive his new Porsche, Bat drove into town and placed a call from a pay telephone in a gasoline station. On the way, he told Toni what Jonas had said. She was predictably appalled. Toni sat impatiently in the car, waiting while he made his call. She knew who he was calling: his mother in Mexico City.

They spoke Spanish, so the man in the station would not understand. Virgilio picked up an extension phone and listened. Bat told his mother what Jonas was offering.

"I knew from the day you met him that you would give up your career in law and take employment with your father," said Sonja gravely.

"It is an immense opportunity," said Virgilio Escalante. "You may become one of the wealthiest and most powerful men on the continent."

"But you must be realistic about your father," said Sonja. "He is not a modest man. He is not an honest man. Don't forget that he had a motive for telephoning me. He wanted to make a connection with Uncle Fulgencio."

"I can see my father's faults," said Bat. "Among them is that he is not very well educated and has a limited perspective."

"Don't underestimate him. Above all, you must always remember that he is capable of lying," she said.

"So am I," said Bat.

"But you must be able to tell the difference, to know when he is and when he isn't. And let me ask you this: Do you have any personal feeling toward him at all?"

Bat drew a breath and blew it out. "I suppose so," he said without conviction. "I can't ignore the genes, can I? Not entirely. No. They're in me. Which means I can out-Jonas Jonas. Maybe. He never had to contend with the likes of me before: a man who's got the same stuff in him as he's got in him."

"'Out-Jonas Jonas,'" she repeated quietly. "Do you really think you can?"

"Why not?"

14

1

JO-ANN WAS ANGRY AND RESENTFUL. LIFE HAD CRAPPED on her. For fourteen years her father had refused even to acknowledge she was his daughter. Then he had. There had been a few halfway good years. Then he'd walked away from her and her mother to duck a subpoena, and the next thing they knew he had acquired a grown son.

On Christmas night she lay alone in bed. The next room was shared by her newfound half brother and his girlfriend, and Jo-Ann could hear their exuberant coupling—humping was the word that came to her mind. In the master bedroom her father was no doubt doing the same with *his* girlfriend.

Jo-Ann could see the attraction this Angie had for her father. The woman was of course a great deal younger than her mother, and she was superficially glamorous, with a hard edge to her that spoke "hooker" to the girl. If Angie wasn't that, she was something like. Jo-Ann could see it on her face.

She did not hate her father for divorcing her mother once, then getting himself divorced by her, and now bedding with this Angie. Monica had never slept alone. Two nights after Jonas left the house in Bel Air another man—What was his name? Alex—had slept in Monica's bed.

Without even letting her finish her year at Pepperdine, her mother had moved them to New York, so she could be closer to her work and closer to the men she had known for years and now once more was free to welcome to her bedroom. Jo-Ann was able to transfer some credits to Smith, but she had an anomalous status there and could not be sure exactly when she would graduate.

Monica had meant to live in the Cord apartment in the Waldorf Towers, but after she and Jo-Ann had stayed there only a week the lawyers informed them they would have to get out. The lease did not belong to Mr. Cord but to Cord Explosives, which was not a party to the divorce suit. Mrs. Cord could raise her cash settlement demands, since she was not going to get the apartment, but she could not remain there. Besides, Mr. Cord's attorneys had come up with some embarrassing evidence. So, out again. They moved into a furnished apartment on East Fifty-ninth Street.

That was one of the problems. They had moved too much. Sometimes they had tried to follow after her grandfather, whose name was Winthrop. She remembered that old man: a nauseating drunk. He had done only one good thing—he had died saving her father's life. The good thing he'd done was die; saving her father's life had been extra.

The brother. The newfound brother. Her father was ecstatic to have found a third Jonas, even if he did call himself Bat. He was what *she* wasn't and could never be: a male. Her father was not subtle about what he had in mind. This son who had dropped on him like something from heaven was going to be his heir-in-chief and the next head of the family business.

She had never imagined she would be the head. Her

mother had explained to her that, although she would probably inherit most of the Cord stock, her father would arrange a voting trust or something of the kind so that she would not be able to control the business, not even to exercise much influence over it.

In her naiveté she had speculated on how her father might react if she married well—well, that is, in terms of a young man with demonstrated intelligence and maybe an MBA from Harvard. Would he take *him* into the business and confide in him? When she dated, she appraised young men in terms of how her father might react to them. So . . . She need not worry about that anymore. She would date for fun now. She'd find herself a stud and have a good time.

She would not go on sleeping alone, either. Nobody else did. This house tonight was a goddamned whorehouse! As she pressed fingers into herself and tried to find some relief, she was glad she had hit the Scotch and brandy bottles every chance she got. For the time being bottles were damned important to her. At least she would go to sleep. At least she could go to sleep . . .

2

Nevada understood her feelings, and maybe he was the only one who did. Nevada understood more than most people—and more certainly than either her father or her mother. She was glad she'd had a chance to talk with him. Glad and . . . then for a different reason, not glad.

The family hadn't even flown out here together. Her flight had landed at San Francisco, where Nevada met her at the airport. An Inter-Continental Airlines company plane, a Beech Baron, had flown them to the ranch landing strip. She had been the first to arrive. The Beech went back to pick up her new brother and his girlfriend, and she had been alone at the ranch with Nevada.

They'd had horses saddled and had gone out to ride across the sandy, rocky countryside.

"You always was a natural in the saddle. Shame your parents decided to move you to California."

"I think I could have been happy here."

"Uhmm. That mean you're not, where you are?"

"I might be. But who knows how long I'll be there before I'm packed up and sent somewhere else? There's nothing permanent, Nevada."

"Don't feel like you got no roots down," he said.

Jo-Ann shrugged. She frowned at a coyote limping across the ground in front of them. It had been bitten by a rattlesnake apparently and was dying. Nevada pulled a .30-30 Winchester from its scabbard on his saddle, took aim, and put the creature out of its misery.

"I'm shoved this way and the other," she said. "Obviously, I've got nothing of my own. I'm so— Nevada, I'm so goddamned *dependent!*"

"Who ain't, your age? Of course me, I had to go out younger. But that was another time, another place. You're the daughter of Jonas and Monica. You gotta get your education and be smart and sophisticated-like. Who's not dependent at that time of life?"

"Do you believe that man he found in Mexico is really his son?" she asked.

"I expect he is," said Nevada. "I remember the girl. Sonja Batista. First thing he had to do after he sudden-like inherited everything was go to Germany to see how they made plastics, since that was what his daddy had bought into. He took Sonja Batista with him. I was surprised when he didn't marry her. Pretty thing, she was. All this was before he met your mother."

"That wouldn't have made any difference. They never really loved each other. She was a piece of ass. He was a cock. That's all either of them ever wanted."

"Young lady," said Nevada sternly, "you shouldn't use them kind of words. Anyhow, you're wrong. I don't know what happened, but they did love each other. At least twice. Once when they made you. Once when they got together again. I didn't see the first part. I saw the second. You got a point if you wanta say they're not the kind of folks that fall in love in the romantic way. But don't put 'em down, Jo-Ann. Love ain't always a lifetime thing."

Jo-Ann loved the kind of country they were riding across. They were five miles from the house. It smelled good: big and fresh and dry. The horses spooked occasionally. Living things skittered in the low dry brush to either side of them. They came across the track left by a sidewinder. That would spook a horse. The mountains rising in the distance were more beautiful for their promise from miles away than they were when you reached them.

"Nevada . . ."

"Uh?"

"I'm a virgin."

"I'd sort of hope you was, at your age."

Jo-Ann shook her head. "My mother wasn't when she was eighteen. My father—"

"Prob'ly was when he was eighteen," Nevada interrupted. "Th' old man wasn't for foolin' around. 'Course . . . your father made up for it pretty quick, when he got the chanct. Uh— Come to think of it, once he started to drive a car . . ."

"Nevada . . . I'm very uncomfortable."

The lanky old man shook his head. "Honey, you ain't got no idea what uncomfortable *is.*"

"I'd like a man I trust to— It could be you, Nevada."

"Missy! Don't you never say nothin' like that ag'in! *Jeezuss Christ!* I don't ever wanta hear nothin' like that ag'in. I won't tell your father, but—"

Jo-Ann sobbed. "But you can see!"

He shook his head. "I can't see."

"Somebody I trust. That was the point."

"I could be— I could be your grandfather. Grandfather? Hell, I could be your *great*-grandfather."

"Forgive me?" She sniffed.

"Sure. But look, sis. When you're eighteen it looks like that's got to be the most wonderful thing in the whole world. It ain't. It's good, but it's not the best thing in the world. You gotta learn to live with it, like you do with everything else."

"I heard my father say one time that you were the smartest man he'd ever met when it came to . . . life."

Nevada shook his head. "Maybe that's because he's done some dumb things in that department. It could be that was what killed his daddy, findin' out that Junior had done it dumb again and was going to have to pay hush money."

"Blackmail?"

Nevada shrugged. "Whatever they called it. Oh, hell, it didn't kill him. He died of bourbon and hot temper and maybe of tryin' to keep up with the young woman he'd married to keep your father from marryin' her."

"Rina?"

"You've heard of her. Your daddy wanted to marry her. He was set on it. Your granddaddy married her and carried her off to Europe on a honeymoon."

"What a family! No wonder I'm crazy."

"You're not crazy, honey." He chuckled. "Maybe you're a Cord, though."

Jo-Ann reined her horse to a stop. "Sex," she said. "If you won't teach me, tell me something, anyway. It ruins lives."

Nevada reined his horse around and sat facing the beautiful dark-haired girl in the tight blue jeans and wool shirt. "Blue-eyes lives," he said. "My daddy was a buffalo hunter. My ma was a Kiowa. The Kiowa were noble people that knowed how to live. A Kiowa man never dreamt dreams about doin' it. He didn't have to; he *did* it. A Kiowa woman never worried about it. She didn't have to; she *did* it. The Kiowa wouldn't-a cared about *pictures* of people doin' it. What good was that? They wouldn't-a read in books about people doin' it. What good was that? They didn't make up stories about it, or make laws about it, or suppose the Great Unknowable cared how and when they done it. If children come and nobody could figure out exactly whose they was, that didn't make no difference; children belonged to the tribe, and all of 'em was taken care of. You understand?"

"Do it with whoever I want to?"

"Not quite that. Do it with whoever'll take responsibility, the way the tribe did. Responsibility. That there's the point. An ugly word with the white man. And forget all the hoodoo-voodoo. This thing we're talkin' about, it's mine, it's your'n, it's his'n, it's her'n. It's nobody else's but. And it's not worth moanin' and groanin' and worryin' and hurryin' about. Live, little girl! Pee when you have to and fuck when you want to. But you wouldn't pee on the street in public, so don't fuck where and when it ain't right—and not with the wrong man. That's all the rules they is about it."

Jo-Ann smiled and started her horse back toward

the house. "Thank you, Nevada," she said. "My father was right about one thing. You are the smartest man about life either one of us has ever met."

3

She had known yesterday afternoon that she and Nevada would be returning to the house alone—alone, that is, but for Robair and the ranch hands who worked around the place. The plane bringing her new half brother and the woman from Washington wouldn't arrive before midnight.

She had continued to wish Nevada would consent to come to her bed, but she'd known he wouldn't, and she'd known better than to mention it again.

A hundred yards from the house, Jo-Ann reined her horse to a stop again. She yawned. "Would you believe I got out of bed this morning in New York?" she said. "Are you having dinner with me, Nevada?"

"I wasn't countin' on it, but you are alone, huh? Gonna eat early?"

She nodded. "Surprise Robair," she said.

"Not much surprises that man. Anyway, sure, tell him to set two places."

The dinner was what she'd asked for because she knew it was what the ranch kitchen most easily afforded—besides which she did not want to invade the food stocked for the Christmas Eve party. She and Nevada sat facing each other across the table, over steaks and potatoes, salads, and a bottle of red wine. Neither had changed clothes since their ride. Nevada actually wore buckskins. Jo-Ann wished he would wear them tomorrow night but knew he wouldn't. She would like to show up at the party in her jeans and wool shirt—and knew she wouldn't.

"If I asked him," she said, "I think my father might let me come and live here. My mother would hate it, but—"

"You'd be lonesome out here," said Nevada. "Tomorrow this house is gonna be full of folks. It isn't that way most of the time."

"You'd come and see me, wouldn't you? It's only a short drive. And I could come and see you."

"You can't count on me," he said.

"What? We've always counted on you. My grandfather, my father—"

"Not much longer," said Nevada.

"Nevada . . . ?"

He smiled. "A man ain't forever, y' know. I'm seventy years old."

"Kiowa men live to be ninety."

He shook his head. "Not this Kiowa. I tell you because you talk about countin' on this ol' man, like the Cords have always counted on me. If you tell your father what I'm goin' to tell you, then you ain't my friend. But the Great Unknowable has started callin' fer Nevada. Fer Max. That's my real name, y' know: Max Sand. I sit on my porch and look at the country. The country's callin' me. I kin hear it in the wind."

"What are you saying, Nevada?" Jo-Ann asked, alarmed.

"Promise me you won't tell."

"I promise."

Nevada stared for a moment at the bite of rare beef on his fork. "By god, that's good," he said. "There ain't nothin' better to eat than a real good piece of beef. We didn't have it in the old days, you know. This comes off a *fat* steer, one that couldn't a lived on the range grass. We—"

"Nevada. You're changing the subject."

He sighed loudly. "Man doesn't know how long he's got. But they's signs. Mine don't read good."

Jo-Ann put down her knife and fork. "You can't read life and death from owl feathers," she said. "Or anything like that."

"Don't be so sure. But that don't make no difference. That's not what I'm readin'. I've started rottin' away inside. I can feel it, and I can smell it. When a man don't smell good—"

"Nevada! Have you seen a doctor?"

He nodded. "Cancer."

"Oh, my god! But you *must* tell my father! There are wonderful hospitals where—"

"You gave me your word you wouldn't tell him."

4

She had exacted from Robair a promise to wake her when her new half brother arrived. He did. She had not been asleep, really. What Nevada had told her, the cancer, had intruded on every sleep fantasy and jarred her awake. It was nearly one o'clock. She dressed in tight blue jeans and the blue-and-white wool shirt she had worn in the afternoon and at dinner. She brushed out her hair and put on a little lipstick.

They were in the living room waiting for her, standing before the fireplace where Robair had kept the fire going.

Jonas the Third stepped toward her, smiling broadly, his hand reaching for hers. "Jo-Ann! I've been looking forward to meeting you and am only sorry it didn't happen sooner. Let me introduce Antonia Maxim."

He was not what she expected, not in any way. Having heard he had been born and reared in Mexico, she had expected a swarthy, dark-haired man with a Spanish accent. This tall, handsome man was blond. He looked nothing like their father. He spoke perfect American English and yet not like their father's. She could detect no family resemblance at all.

The woman he had brought with him was beautiful. "Call me Toni" were her first words, and she reached out with both her hands and took both of Jo-Ann's.

Jo-Ann was polite to Toni, but her eyes fastened on Bat. She had wanted to dislike him, had decided to dislike him. But how could a woman—how could *anyone*—dislike a man with laughing eyes that drew you in and invited you to share whatever was making them laugh? Her half brother was naturally, gracefully magnetic, even more so than her father was.

"We've wakened you in the middle of the night," said Jonas the Third. "And we've been up since dawn. What time do we meet for breakfast, Jo-Ann?"

"Oh, let's be late. When our father is here, he'll be at the table by six-thirty, eating bacon and eggs and potatoes and God knows what. The Christmas Eve party is at seven and will go on well after midnight, but plan on being up at dawn again on Christmas Day. I don't have to tell you that his schedule will be our schedule."

5

On Christmas afternoon, Nevada took Toni out to teach her to fire her Winchester. Bat and Jo-Ann came along.

The weather was raw. The sky was pale, and snow

threatened. Except for Nevada, they wore coats from the ranch house closets: sheepskin that cut the wind.

Watching the old man, after what he had told her two days ago, was painful for Jo-Ann. That Nevada Smith was mortal had never occurred to her. And he walked and talked like a man who expected to live to be a hundred. He put wine and liquor bottles on fence posts. He talked quietly with Toni, telling her how to hold her rifle and aim; then he stood back and let her try.

She shattered three bottles with her first three shots, missing only the fourth.

"Know why y' done?" Nevada asked her.

Toni shook her head.

"Locked y' elbow. Keep 'er loose, Miss Toni. Nothin' stiff, nothin' locked. Easy . . . easy . . ."

She missed twice in knocking down his bottles. Now he set up beer cans, half as big. She needed eight shots to knock down five of them.

"Got a natural talent for it," he said. "Let's let Jo-Ann try."

Jo-Ann shot about as well as Toni.

"How 'bout you, Bat?"

"I'm better with a pistol," said Bat. "Happen to have brought one out from the house. What I like to shoot at is empty shotgun shells, but I couldn't find any. But I found a bunch of bottle corks."

Nevada shrugged as Bat walked forward and set up wine corks on the fence posts.

Five corks. Six shots.

Nevada grinned. "Y' ever decide y' bored bein' a lawyer, I kin prob'ly git y' a job in a Wild West show."

Jo-Ann tried to hide her feelings. Her new half brother was too goddamned good! Give him a blackboard and chalk, he'd probably square the circle.

6

She had one more chance to talk with Nevada. She didn't know it, but it would be the last time. They went riding, alone.

"What do you think of my new brother?" she asked.

"Y' dad's lucky to find him," said Nevada blandly.

"Bullshit. What do you think of him?"

"He's gonna be a handful," said Nevada, staring at the mountains and not turning his eyes toward her. "You know somethin'? He's a Cord. Your old man's figured that one out. I ain't sure he likes it much."

Jo-Ann smiled and nodded. "He'd have liked to have a son he could—"

"What *his* father wanted," Nevada interrupted. "A boy who'd take orders. Well, they didn't neither of them git that kind of son. This new boy has got somethin' of his gran'dad in him. Jonas sees it. That's hard for him to take. Could be this boy's got the old man's tough and your dad's smarts. Could be."

"Shuts me out of everything, doesn't it, Nevada?"

"Wouldn't think of it that way. I'd make my peace with the new man, if I was you. Looks to me like an honest sort of fella. He ain' gonna take on your dad right off, but them two's gonna go nose to nose. I'm not ready to place my bet."

7

Jo-Ann broke her word to Nevada, and three weeks later he was admitted to the Sloan-Kettering Institute in New York City.

Jonas was with him and stayed at the hospital through ten days of tests, going to the Waldorf Towers only at night. Monica came to visit Nevada. Robair came. Morris Chandler. Angie. Bat, who had known Nevada only for a little while but had impressed him favorably. And Jo-Ann, and he forgave her.

The prognosis was not good. The doctors talked of radiation therapy and chemotherapy—and six months, maximum.

Nevada said no to all of it. "Y' cain't fight nature" was the way he put it. "Anyways, why should y'? Who knows what's next? Y' fight it off, maybe y' just postponin' somethin' awful good. In all my life I only took stock in one writer. Mark Twain said he warn't afraid of where he was goin'. He'd been there before, and it didn't hurt."

A Cord company plane flew Nevada back to his ranch. He sat in his old rocker on the porch, in his buckskins, sheepskin coat, and a stained old hat; and he stared at the desert and the mountains. He told Jonas to go on about his business. He promised to call if he felt the end was near. Meantime, he would just sit and wait. He was content just to wait.

Jonas knew Nevada would never call. He promised to come back to see him, but he left him with a sense he would never see him again.

8

When Nevada died, Jonas called Jo-Ann.

That afternoon she left Northampton in the black Porsche he had given her for Christmas, bearing the Nevada license plate CORD TWO. She drove to New York in three hours. And having reached the city she was not sure why she had come or what she would do. She had driven mindlessly, probably assuming she would go to the apartment on Fifty-ninth Street. Then she realized she would face a mother who would demand to know why she had left Northampton—or a mother so absorbed in whatever man was there with her that she would hardly notice that her daughter had come home. She drove past the apartment and did not stop.

She put the Porsche in a garage on Fifty-seventh Street and had dinner in a Hungarian restaurant she had learned to appreciate. When she came out and retrieved the car, it was after ten o'clock and she had to face it that she could not drive back to Northampton that night and could not cruise through the streets of Manhattan in an expensive sports car much longer. She had drunk a whole bottle of rich red Hungarian wine. A sense of urgency, not panic but approaching it, seized her.

She drove into the garage at the Waldorf Towers.

"Miss?"

She showed the garage attendant her key to the Cord apartment. She didn't know what her mother had done with hers, but Jo-Ann had never surrendered her key. The man glanced at the license plate on the Porsche and opened her door. She got out, and he drove the car down into the garage.

The key gave her access to the elevator, too. She went up. At the door she pressed the bell button before she used the key. No one responded, so she unlocked the door and entered the apartment.

When Bat came home a little before midnight he found Jo-Ann sitting on a couch in the living room. She was smoking a cigarette and had taken off her dress and her stockings and garter belt and shoes. She sat in a white silk slip.

"It's a *family* apartment," she said.

He nodded. "Of course. The garage man told me you were here. I'm glad to see you."

Jo-Ann nodded. A bottle of Scotch sat on the coffee table before her. The ice in her glass had long since melted, and she had been sipping Chivas Regal neat. "Nevada died," she said.

"I heard. Our father called from California. I didn't know the man as well as you did, but I understand what a great loss it is."

Jo-Ann picked up her glass and drank the little that was left of the warm whiskey. "I feel as if I'd lost a father. He was more of a father to me than Jonas ever was."

"I understand," said Bat. He sat down on the couch, at the opposite end.

"I don't think you do, but it's all right."

"I know something of the family history," said Bat. "You grew up in odd circumstances, too. Did you have anybody to talk to?"

"My mother," he said. "My grandfather."

"Lucky you," she said despondently. She crushed her cigarette. "Jonas is nobody's father, you know."

"He's a great man."

Her eyes narrowed as she glanced at him. "Do you think so? Or is that a Cord employee talking? Congratulations on your job, anyway."

He got up and went to the bar to get a glass. "A little more Scotch?" he asked.

"A spl^sh."

He brought back two glasses, both with ice. As he poured, he glanced at her and said, "I wish we'd known each other sooner. I have two other little sisters: Rafaela and Mercedes. I was away from home during most of the years when they were growing up."

"Do you love them?" Jo-Ann asked.

Bat nodded. "Of course."

Jo-Ann scooted across the couch to sit close to him.

She reached for his hand. "You and I would have loved each other."

"Yes."

"Still can," she said.

He squeezed her hand. "Of course."

"Nevada gave me some advice," she said softly. "He told me to give my love to a man I could trust. A man who would accept responsibility for the consequences."

"That was good advice."

She lifted his hand and kissed it. "Nevada and I weren't talking about the kind of love you're thinking about."

"Jo-Ann . . . ?"

"A man I can trust," she said simply, directly. Then her voice rose, and she said, "I'm a *virgin,* goddammit!"

Bat frowned. "You've had too much to drink."

Jo-Ann snatched up her glass and drank the Scotch he had poured. "Drunk! You think I'm drunk. No. Let me tell you what I am. I'm Jonas Cord's daughter. I'm the granddaughter of another Jonas Cord. When I heard about you, I wondered if you were a Cord at all, or some kind of fraud. There was never a Cord by the name who'd turn down a shot of whiskey or a piece of virgin pussy!"

She grabbed at the hem of her slip and pulled it up and over her head. She was wearing panties but no bra.

"Jo-Ann," he murmured.

"C'mon, big brother. You a Cord, or you not?"

"My sister—"

"My brother. So what the shit? You're the man I can trust, if you've got the guts. Brother and sister. We're gonna love each other—brother and sister, for the rest of our lives. If I can't trust my brother, who can I trust? I need your help, big brother. Besides the fucking I need from you right now, I need a standard to compare with."

"Our father—"

"Jonas will *laugh* if he finds out, which he doesn't have to. He'd do it himself if he were here. Only I wouldn't let him. *Him,* I wouldn't trust. Hey, brother! Look at me! Toni have nicer tits than these?"

For a moment Bat closed his eyes. "Oh, Christ," he muttered.

"You wouldn't know maybe, but Nevada Smith was a great man," said Jo-Ann. "Greater than our father and grandfather in some ways. He said something to me—I wrote it down when I got back to my room, and I think I've got it exactly the way he said it. He said, 'This thing we're talkin' about, it's mine, it's your'n, it's his'n, it's her'n. It's nobody else's but. And it's not worth moanin' and groanin' and worryin' and hurryin' about. Live, little girl! Pee when you have to and fuck when you want to.' *You bastard,* I want to!"

" 'Bastard.' You used the wrong word, little sister. Okay, I'll fuck you outta your mind!"

Jo-Ann grinned. "Promise? Promise it's going to be everything I've ever heard about!"

9

Everything she'd ever heard about.

Jo-Ann had seen pictures but had never seen a male organ before. He guided her hand to it and let her examine it with her fingers before he brought it near her. She satisfied her curiosity She had been told it would be hard, but it wasn't hard; it was just stiff. She had been told it would be cold. She had been told it would be hot. It was neither. She curled her hand around it and squeezed it gently. A drop of gleaming moisture appeared on the rosebud of its tip. She pinched the drop off between her thumb and finger and tested it. It was slippery.

"Life," he said quietly.

They lay on his bed. She wanted to be kissed more before he entered her, so she rolled on her side and pressed her mouth to his. He responded forcefully. They kissed so hard she could taste blood from her lips. Then he turned gentle and pushed his tongue into her mouth. She had heard of this but had not imagined the lazy delight she would find in it. They lay side by side for a long time, their tongues caressing each other. She held his penis in her hand, and he stroked her wet private place with one long finger.

Until his patience ran out. Then he pushed her over on her back and rose to straddle her. For a moment she was afraid. For a moment she was sorry she had brought herself to this point. Then it was too late for fear, too late for regret.

He was tough and he was tender. He was gentle and he was rough. He hurt her and he soothed her. He subdued her and he exalted her. She shrieked and writhed under his unrelenting deep strokes: from pain and pleasure so intermixed she could not separate them. And when he finished and withdrew, she was hurt, she was exhausted, she was drenched with sweat; she was submerged in warmth and wonder.

For sure she would never again live without it.

"Big brother," she whispered, playfully mimicking a girl child.

"Hmm?"

"How soon can we do it again?"

"In a few minutes," he said. "Then never again after tonight."

15

1

FOUR MONTHS AFTER THE DEATH OF NEVADA SMITH—
that is, in late summer 1953—Bat flew to Havana.
Jonas sent him. It was the first time Bat would be
working alone, without his father's close supervision.

Fulgencio Batista had sent Jonas an invitation to
come to Havana, delivered as a personal message by
the Cuban consul-general in New York. Batista hoped
Jonas Cord would invest money in Cuba: specifically
in building a casino-hotel. Jonas had replied that he
could not come anytime soon but would send his son,
Jonas Enrique Raul Cord y Batista.

They sat down over dinner in the presidential
palace. Batista pronounced himself overjoyed to
make the acquaintance at last of his niece's son.

"We've met before, of course," he said, speaking
Spanish. "I came to Córdoba. You were but a child."

"I remember," said Bat.

"I came again. You were in Europe fighting the
war."

Fulgencio Batista was fifty-two years old that year, a
compact man who still carried himself as the army
officer he had been. He appeared to be of Spanish-
Indian extraction: swarthy of complexion, with dark
eyes and brushed-back hair held in place with a

235

fragrant oil. He wore a cream-colored single-breasted suit, a pearl-gray shirt, and a red-and-blue tie in a bold pattern. On his left hand he wore a massive gold ring.

They talked for a while about nothing consequential. Then Batista explained why he had invited the Cords to come to Cuba.

"It is too bad that neither you nor your father has ever come here before," he said. "This country is poor, but this island is beautiful. The climate is better than Miami's. The beaches are extraordinary. The fishing is superb. The flight is short and easy. The Cuban people are hospitable. No nation in the world offers more beautiful—or complaisant—women. I have determined to build our economy by making Cuba attractive to tourists. Anyone who invests merely two hundred thousand dollars in a hotel or motel can have a gaming license. Cord Hotels, Incorporated, wants to build a casino-hotel in Las Vegas. Why not build it here?"

"The *Saturday Evening Post* article—" Bat started to say. He referred to an article published in that magazine in the spring, exposing dishonest practices in Cuban casinos.

"But you do not know what we did," Batista interrupted. "I turned the army against the card sharps. Military intelligence was given the task of identifying them. Many were Americans. We arrested them and deported them. The Cubans were released from jail with a warning they would return to jail and stay there if they ever went near a casino again. Now we play by new rules. The razzle-dazzle games— eight-dice games and all that—are forbidden. We know we cannot attract the clientele we want if we allow cheating."

"It's hard to control," said Bat.

"I've hired an expert," said Batista. "You know him. Meyer Lansky."

"I've never met him," said Bat. "My father knows him."

"A really profitable gaming operation," said Batista, "can only operate if the people who play can have confidence in it. That's what Lansky knows: what the rules should be and how to enforce the rules. Strictly."

"That's what we're doing in Las Vegas," said Bat. "Playing by the rules. Including the tax laws."

"I want to make Cuba the Monte Carlo of the Caribbean," said Batista. "Most Americans don't want to take the time or spend the money to fly to the Mediterranean, but here—a short flight from their shores—we can provide everything Monte Carlo offers and more."

2

Bat accepted Great-Uncle Fulgencio's offer of "a really superior girl" for the night and woke exhausted and hungry when the telephone rang and the hotel operator said a Mr. Lansky would like to see him. Five minutes later Meyer Lansky was at the door. Wearing a white terry-cloth robe, Bat welcomed him in.

The word about Lansky was that he was a small man. He was: a solemn little man, prematurely aged as Bat judged him. His temples were gray, his face was marked with liver spots, and his eyes looked weary. He had an extraordinarily big nose. He bore the marks, too, of a heavy smoker. He wore a dark-blue suit that looked a little too large for him, a white shirt, and a bow tie.

"I wasn't expecting you," Bat said.

"I can come back another time," said Lansky.

"No. Sit down. You'll have to forgive me, though. There's a girl in the bathroom, and breakfast is on its way up. She'll be out of the suite in five minutes. I ordered for two. Can you use some breakfast?"

"Just the coffee," said Lansky.

"I'm told it's a Cord family trait to be hungry in the morning," said Bat. "I'm only gradually picking up on Cord family traits. Anyway, I'm glad you're here. We have some things to talk about."

Lansky sat down in a leather-upholstered chair facing the couch where Bat would sit and take his breakfast off the coffee table. "The President," he said, "made you a pitch about building a casino-hotel here."

"Right."

"If he can make it work, what he's talking about, there's a ton of money to be scooped up in Cuba."

"The country isn't stable," said Bat.

"Once there's a big American investment, certain people will lend their talents to make it stable," said Lansky.

Bat shook his head. "I wish you hadn't mentioned it."

"I've got nothing to do with that," said Lansky. "You'll have nothing to do with it. It'll happen just the same, and the President will accept the help he gets."

"We'll all be tarred with the same brush," said Bat.

"Would you refuse to take profits from oil because John D. Rockefeller was a robber baron?" asked Lansky.

"You're a consultant to President Batista. You're a consultant to us. Is there a conflict of interests?" Bat asked.

Lansky shrugged. "Find one," he said. "My job for

the President is to make gaming profitable in Cuba—
by making it honest. That's what your father asked
me to do for The Seven Voyages. That and to avoid a
tax prosecution by stopping the skimming. There's
money to be made in Cuba. I wish I had enough to
build a casino of my own."

"I'd be reluctant to make a long-term investment in
Cuba," said Bat. "And I know my father would be
reluctant. It would take ten years to recover the
money it would take to build a hotel. Cuban govern-
ments don't last that long. You may be confident in
the staying power of my great-uncle, but I am
skeptical."

Lansky pursed his fleshy lips and frowned. He lit
another cigarette. "You don't have to build a hotel to
have a casino," he said.

"I know. If you invest two hundred thousand,
they'll give you a gaming license. Surely you have two
hundred thousand, Mr. Lansky."

"My money is tied up in a place called the Montmartre Club," said Lansky. "Ask around about it."

"I already have," said Bat. "You attract the high
rollers because they know the Montmartre is run to
the Meyer Lansky standards. Serious gamblers
respect you and your club."

"But they leave my tables to go get something to
eat, to see a show, to get laid. I can't afford to build a
big swimming pool for their wives to lie around while
they play. Look, Mr. Cord—"

"Call me Bat."

"Okay. And call me Meyer. You know the origin
of the name Meyer? It comes from the name of a
rabbi called Mei-or, meaning 'the bringer of light.'
I was born Meier Suchowljanski. When we arrived in
New York forty years ago, my father changed me

from Meier to Meyer and changed us all from Suchowljanski to Lansky."

Bat smiled. "I am Jonas Enrique Raul Cord y Batista," he said.

"Anyway, Bat, I have an idea. I'd like to install a casino in a hotel like the Floresta—which is a *hotel*, with pool and shops and all that. I could attract the serious gamblers the way I do at the Montmartre. I'd also get the tourists, who'd know they were playing honest games."

"The way the new Vegas hotels work," said Bat.

"Exactly. Ben Siegel saw the connection. The difference is that Havana is a tropical paradise, not a dusty desert town. What's more important, Chicago and everything east of it are a lot closer to Havana than they are to Las Vegas."

"Are you making a proposition, Meyer?"

"A million dollars will build a gaming room and a show room on the Floresta," said Lansky. "It's a more modest operation, but the investment can be recovered in four years, maybe less."

"The President wants Cord Hotels, Incorporated, to build a casino-hotel."

"Tell him you want to test the waters by investing in the Floresta," said Lansky. "If that's a winning proposition, you'll do something more. I can assure you he'll welcome an investment of one million."

"I want to see the Floresta," said Bat. "I'll want to talk to President Batista."

3

"How much of a commitment did you make to him?" Jonas asked.

They sat over lunch at the Four Seasons. Bat had

returned from Mexico and was reporting to his father on his talks with Fulgencio Batista and Meyer Lansky.

"I made no commitment," said Bat. "I had no authority to make a commitment."

"But you think it may not be a bad deal?"

"It may not. The Floresta is known for quiet, sumptuous rooms, good food, and an interesting swimming pool set partly in living rock and surrounded with flowering shrubs and palms. Americans stay there. They come back to it as a refuge after a night in the gaudy, flashy places. Lansky means to keep it that way. The casino and show room would be in a separate wing. He wants to do higher-quality shows than are done at most of the Havana clubs. And of course the gambling will be honest."

"Do you trust Lansky?"

Jonas lifted his glass and took a sip of Jack Daniel's Black Label. It impressed Bat as a strange thing to be drinking with the famous Four Seasons crab cakes, but that was not the only strange habit his father had.

"No, and I don't trust Great-Uncle Fulgencio either. But let me tell you something about Meyer Lansky. In this country his reputation is that he's a gangster and nothing but. You know—'the Chairman of the Board.' He—"

"It's exaggerated," said Jonas.

"When the government wanted the cooperation of Lucky Luciano in 1942, they used Lansky as the go-between," said Bat.

"I doubt that."

Bat shrugged. "You can look it up. *I* did."

"Did your homework, huh?"

"In the States," Bat continued, "Lansky is known as a gangster. In Cuba he's thought of as a businessman. And not just by Fulgencio Batista."

"He couldn't get a Nevada gaming license," said

Jonas. "But for all his reputation, he has no criminal record. In his entire life he's spent only three months in jail."

"He couldn't be a silent partner in the Floresta," said Bat. "It would be his reputation that would attract the high rollers."

"We wouldn't buy the hotel, I assume," said Jonas.

"No. We'd build the wing for the casino and show room. The owners of the hotel would lease the wing to us. But we'd pay no cash for the lease for, say, fifty months, until we got our investment back."

"Who owns the Floresta?" asked Jonas.

Bat grinned. "A real estate group in Havana. But if this deal goes through, ten percent of it will be owned by my Great-Uncle Fulgencio."

"Insurance?" asked Jonas.

"Whatever you want to call it. I'm glad I went to Cuba. It was worth the trip to meet Lansky. He told me something we are going to have to think about."

"What?"

"Our friend Morris Chandler has been talking to some pretty rough characters. For one, Jimmy Hoffa went to Vegas and met with him."

"I know," said Jonas. "Angie saw him and called me."

"That's not the half of it," said Bat. "Lansky says he's been in touch with men like Murray the Camel in Chicago and Anthony Provenzano in New Jersey. If he's working for us, why would he contact people like that?"

"Because Nevada Smith is dead," said Jonas. He put down a gulp of whiskey. "That's why."

"Meaning?"

"He and Nevada were close. Besides, I think Nevada had something on him. With Nevada gone—

Chandler resented my taking over The Seven Voyages. He doesn't like the way I make him run it. I'd guess he wants to muscle us out."

"Buy us out?"

Jonas shook his head. "Muscle us out. Your assignment is to get out to Las Vegas and take over the hotel. The Cuban thing is a sideshow. Where I want you is Las Vegas."

Bat nodded as he lifted a forkful of crab cake to his mouth. "Las Vegas? What am I going to be doing in Las Vegas?"

"As of today you're a vice president of Cord Hotels," he said. "The corporate headquarters is the fifth floor of The Seven Voyages."

Bat shook his head. "Wait a minute. Our deal is that I learn the business, the *overall* business, not just the hotel business. In New York or Los Angeles."

"I ran the overall business from the fifth floor of The Seven Voyages for months," said Jonas.

"But—"

"What do you think I'm doing? Sending you into exile? We'll be in touch every day."

"About the hotel business."

"Right now, about the hotel business chiefly. Jesus Christ, you've got to start somewhere! Right now, that's where I *need* you. I'm running a *business*. You're my son, and I want you with me. But you've got to go where I need you. Learn the business? Okay, learn the hotel business first. Then— Well, each piece in time."

Bat shook his head. "This isn't the deal we made. Las Vegas, for Christ's sake?"

"As a vice president of Cord Hotels, Incorporated, your salary will be a hundred thousand," said Jonas as he lifted his glass to sip bourbon.

"You can be very persuasive," said Bat. "Said another way, you have ways of getting what you want out of people."

4

Bat arrived in Las Vegas on an Inter-Continental corporate Beech flown from Los Angeles. From the moment he saw the town, he didn't much like it. It was what Meyer Lansky had called it: a dusty desert town. Only Lansky hadn't added that it was a *pretentious* dusty desert town. Without Nevada's laws allowing casino gambling, it would be nothing.

Though he hadn't said so to anyone, he hadn't much cared for the Cord ranch either, or for the land around it. As somebody in the army had put it, "Y' seen one boondocks, y' seen 'em all."

The ranch house was in distinct contrast to the hacienda house near Córdoba. The hacienda house had style. The ranch house had fashion. Las Vegas had neither. The Seven Voyages was a plastic dump.

"I'll take over the top floor, all of it, for the company headquarters," Bat said to Chandler within five minutes after they met.

"I explained to your father, that'll cost money," said Chandler.

"I may need part of the fourth floor, too," said Bat.

Chandler shrugged. "You're the boss."

"I'm glad you understand that. Angie will be my father's personal and confidential assistant when he's in town, mine when he's not. The rest of my personal staff will be coming in from Los Angeles and Mexico City."

"Whatever you say, boss."

"Don't call me boss."

"What do you want me to call you?" Chandler asked.

"Until we know each other a little better, you can call me Mr. Cord," said Bat. Then he grinned and walked over to where Chandler was sitting and slapped him on the shoulder. "I figure we'll know each other better in about fifteen minutes, and then you can call me Bat."

As soon as Chandler was out of the suite and on the private elevator, Bat turned to Angie and said, "I'm hot. I want to go swimming. You have a bathing suit handy?"

"Uh . . . Sure. In my room."

"See you at the pool in ten minutes," said Bat.

She appeared in a white two-piece swimsuit and white high-heel shoes. Swimsuits that exposed the navel and a little below were just beginning to appear in the States and were being called bikinis, and Angie attracted stares as she crossed the pool deck and sat down beside Bat at an umbrella table.

"You are a luscious woman," he told her. "If you didn't have a relationship with my father—"

"If I didn't have a relationship with your father, I'd be glad to have one with you," she said soberly. "Let's understand, though, what that relationship is. I love your father. I don't suppose he loves me, at least not the way I love him, but I do love him; I don't just sleep with him."

He put a hand on hers. "I asked you to meet me down here because we have to establish some new rules. I've hired a company in Los Angeles to come here and sweep the hotel for hidden microphones and the like. Until that's done, no business talk in the offices or rooms. Also, none on the telephones until I have new lines installed."

"Someone said you're tougher than your father."

"Not at all. Not a question of tough. Question of realistic. When you called my father and told him Hoffa had been here, he was grateful. I have to wonder if Chandler doesn't know you made that call."

"If he did?"

"It puts you on his shit list," said Bat.

"I'm on it anyway."

"It's something more than just personal," Bat said. "Las Vegas is immensely attractive to organized crime, and they're moving in more and more. In times past, guys were making money by skimming the casino take. Now it's something more. Have you heard of the term money laundering?"

"I've heard of it," said Angie.

"A lot of secret money from a variety of rackets is laundered in Las Vegas. Some of it is being laundered in Cuba now. Money laundering makes casinos all the more important to the rackets."

Angie nodded. "You know I did time in a federal pokey, don't you?"

"I do know that, Angie. If my father doesn't worry about it—which obviously he doesn't—then I don't either. So far as I am concerned, we can forget all about it."

"Thank you, Bat," she said softly. "Anyway, I learned more about this kind of thing than I wanted to know."

"Anyway," said Bat, "we are going to have to watch out."

"Bat . . . they are dangerous," she said solemnly.

5

When Bat's bug sweepers worked the fourth and fifth floors of The Seven Voyages they did find hidden microphones. Several of them were hidden in the telephones. Others were behind pictures, in the bases of lamps, in the upholstery of chairs, and in the box springs of beds. The telephones were tapped, as he had expected. The bug sweepers killed all the bugs and removed all the taps. They left devices that would detect new ones. Bat contracted with them to return at irregular intervals to sweep again.

He said nothing to Chandler about the bugs and taps, and Chandler said nothing to him. It was remotely possible—*very* remotely possible—that Morris Chandler didn't know. Bat considered having Chandler's office swept but decided not to.

He settled into the fifth-floor suite his father had occupied two years before. Toni flew out from Washington to spend a week with him. She disliked Las Vegas as much as he did.

"It's about as *cheap* a place as I've ever seen."

"Actually, it's one of the most expensive places I've ever seen."

"How long will you be here, Bat?"

"Only as long as I have to be."

He saw Morris Chandler every day, but in October Chandler asked for an appointment and came up to talk with him.

"A couple of guys coming in from the East want to meet with you."

Bat shrugged. "I'll meet with just about anybody. Who do you have in mind?"

"A couple of men with money to invest," said Chandler.

"Do you want to tell me who they are?"

"Mr. David Beck and Mr. James Hoffa," said Chandler. "Mr. Beck is the president of—"

"Dave Beck is president of the International Teamsters. Jimmy Hoffa is his bag man. I know who you mean."

"The union has hundreds of millions of dollars in its pension fund," said Chandler. "It is looking for investments. Knowing that you and your father want to build another casino-hotel in Las Vegas—"

"They want to be partners," said Bat. "Not likely. I'll meet with them. But partnership . . . Not likely."

Bat called New York, and four days later, Jonas arrived. The next day, Beck and Hoffa arrived and were taken up to the fifth floor.

Bat had no difficulty in seeing Jimmy Hoffa for what he was and would have recognized him for it if he had read nothing about him. He'd met the type in the army: scrappy, cocky little street bullies. Some of them had smarts, too. Hoffa did. Hoffa was a street tough, and he was short-tempered and quick with his fists, but he was shrewd. Dave Beck was something else: a fat thug, a straw-hatted waddling hunk of grease.

Morris Chandler treated them with oily respect. He introduced them to Bat and suggested which chairs they might like. He had already ordered a cart of liquor and snacks.

Little time was wasted on small talk. Beck came to the point.

"Your company is operating what is probably the most profitable hotel-casino in town," he said, speaking directly to Jonas. "We understand you want to build another one and maybe a third one. Obviously you have expertise. You have the connections that get the gaming licenses. We have capital. The Central States Pension Fund is looking for secure investments with more than conservative return. Some of your money . . . And some of ours . . . Some of your savvy . . . And some of ours . . ."

"I control my businesses," said Jonas.

"I control my union," said Beck. "Like, you've never had any problem with drivers refusing to back trucks up to your docks because they don't exactly meet safety standards. Inter-Continental Airlines has some real problems with non-standard loading docks, but we've never made an issue of it. You see what I mean? One hand washes the other."

"One hand washes the other," Jonas agreed. "Before we could do business, though, you'd have to wash your hands."

"What the hell's that mean?" barked Hoffa.

"To start with, Tony Pro," said Jonas.

"Whatta ya mean by that?"

"Tony Provenzano," said Jonas. "He may be a great guy, but I don't want to do business with him. There are others."

"Are you gonna tell me who I can associate with?" asked Beck angrily.

"Not at all. But I'm gonna tell you who *I'll* associate with."

Beck looked at Chandler. "I don't think Mr. Cord has been listening."

"Why bother?" asked Bat.

They stood, and Hoffa strode up to Bat. "Who the hell are you, *sonny?"* he asked, his saliva spraying.

"I'll tell you who I'm not," said Bat. "I'm not a cheap little street punk. That's who I'm not."

Hoffa danced like a boxer and threw a punch. It glanced off Bat's left cheek, stinging but not hurting. Hoffa danced some more, his fists up, ready to try again. Bat smiled faintly and kicked him sharply on the shin. Hoffa yelled and was distracted for the instant it took Bat to drive a fist hard into his solar plexus. Stunned, Hoffa dropped his hands, and Bat flattened his nose with a left jab, then broke his front teeth with a right cross.

"Open the door, Chandler!" Bat yelled. When Chandler hesitated, Bat yelled again.

Chandler opened the door. Bat grabbed the reeling Hoffa by the nape of the neck and seat of the pants and threw him into the hall. Hoffa rolled across the floor and against the elevator doors.

Dave Beck, crimson-faced, shrieked at Jonas, "You'll regret this till the day you die!"

Jonas snapped a punch against his nose, splattering blood. "That's just a sample of what you'll get if you try calling a strike on me, you sleazy tub of lard," he said. "You get out of town. I don't want to see you here again."

16

1

TONI SOMETIMES FORGOT ABOUT THE TIME ZONES AND phoned Bat as soon as she arrived at her office. Her calls woke him.

"Can you keep a secret?" she asked at six-fifteen in the morning.

"Yeah . . . Yeah, sure. What you got in mind, honey?"

"Is this phone line clear?"

"Clear. Clear. What you got in mind?"

"A federal grand jury has returned a secret indictment. It will be announced this afternoon. They've charged Dave Beck under enough specifications to keep him behind bars for the rest of his life!"

"What about Hoffa?"

"Not Hoffa. But the whole damned gang will be tied up in knots, trying to keep their boss out of the slammer. I don't think you have to worry about them for a while, Bat. That is . . . until Beck is gone and Hoffa takes over."

"Well, thanks. I guess there's nothing like having a girlfriend in the Senate."

"That's something else, Bat. In the spring I'll have been a Senate aide four years. I'm leaving. I've given the senator my resignation."

"And . . . ?"

"I'm going to work for *The Washington Post*. As a political reporter."

"I see."

"For a while, Bat. For a while."

"Okay."

"Bat, I—"

"I couldn't ask you to come and live in Vegas," he interrupted. "You hate it more than I do."

"Bat . . . We're not yet thirty years old! There's *time!*"

"Sure, babe. When will I see you?"

"If you don't come East in the next month, I'll come out there. Deal?"

"Deal," he grunted. He turned over and went back to sleep.

2

During her spring break in 1954, Jo-Ann flew to Las Vegas. She said she would like to drive her Porsche, and she didn't care if she ever went back to Smith College, but Jonas, Monica, and Bat all discouraged her from that plan and insisted she fly.

"You bastard," she said. "Oops! Sorry, Bat. I mean, you son of a— Well, that's not so good either. Why in hell did you have me put in a suite on the second floor, when . . ."

They were standing in the living room of the suite he used as an office, embracing, kissing. "Little sister," he said. "Get this straight. We are not going to sleep together." He ran a hand through her silky dark hair and down her cheek. "I'm not saying I wouldn't like to. But I told you the one time was all the times, and that's the way it's got to be. You're my *sister,* goddammit!"

"Pretty good piece of pussy, too, aren't I?"

Her warm young body, bound up in nylon and rubber bra and panty girdle, was firm and pointy and all but irresistible. But he resisted it. "Ruin your life, ruin mine," he said. "I'm *glad* we were together once, but we can't do it anymore."

"Coward."

"Jo-Ann . . . You drink too much."

"I'm the daughter of Jonas and Monica. If that didn't make a girl drink, what would?"

He sighed. "We'll talk about that later. I've got an agent and his girl dancer coming in for an audition. Why don't you sit down and watch?"

"Audition?"

"For the show. In the show room downstairs. I've started booking the shows myself. You know how it is. I was supposed to be a company lawyer. Instead I find myself managing a hotel."

"What about Chandler?"

"Chandler does his job. Booking talent isn't part of it. I took that away from him. Relax. Sit down and have a light Scotch. An agent named Sam Stein is bringing up a dancer named Margit Little. The girl is going to show us what she can do."

Sam Stein was a small man, wearing a faultlessly tailored gray double-breasted suit. He was bald, and his face was cherubic and looked as if it had been drawn in sharp, unshaded lines by a skillful cartoonist.

As he had promised, Margit Little was cute. Her big round blue eyes spoke wondering innocence. Her light-brown hair was tied down tight. She was probably nineteen years old, maybe only eighteen.

"Margit has real talent," said Stein. "I don't want for her just a place in the chorus. She should be a featured dancer. She can sing a little also, nothing too challenging. She has brought a record. You have a player?"

Bat had a high-fidelity record player in the suite. He put the seven-inch record the girl offered on the turntable. She removed her skirt and shoes to dance, and danced barefoot in black leotards cut high on her hips. Her first number was classical, akin to ballet. When she was finished she asked Bat to turn the record over, and she danced then to a fast, rhythmic jazz number.

When she finished and bent over to retrieve her skirt and shoes, Stein rubbed his hands together. "She has talent, yes?"

"She has talent, yes," Bat agreed.

"When did you become a judge of talent, big brother?" asked Jo-Ann.

Bat smiled at the little girl and said, "You don't have to be a judge to know talent when you see it." He turned and spoke to Stein. "I'd like to have her in a show, Mr. Stein. My only problem is, I'm not sure where I put her. She can't dance in the bar. I can only use singers there. In the show room I've got a revue. I can't slot her into it, I don't think."

"I have a bigger proposition for you, Mr. Cord," said Stein. "Your revue has been running a long time. Have you thought about a new production?"

"Proposition," said Bat.

"Glenda Grayson," said Stein. "And Margit. An unforgettable show."

3

Brother, sister, and Sam Stein sat at a table in The Roman Circus in Los Angeles watching a loud and colorful production number on the big stage. A brash blonde wearing a rhinestone-studded pink dress was energetically belting out a song, dancing at the same time. She was Glenda Grayson.

"Jonas won't like her," said Jo-Ann flatly. "She's too frenetic. She bounces around too much."

"He's given me authority—"

"Which he'll withdraw in a moment, if he wants to," she said. "Don't count on him to give you a free hand. There are guys lying bleeding on the floor who thought they had a free hand from our father."

Bat did not respond. He turned his attention to Glenda Grayson.

The show ended. The lights came up. Bat reached for the bottle of Johnnie Walker Black and poured for himself and Jo-Ann. He and his father shared a habit: They poured for others without asking if they wanted any more.

Sam Stein had overheard the exchange between brother and sister. "I also represent Doug Howell," he said. "He's looking for somebody to produce a series of Westerns, hour-long shows probably. He wants to do realistic Westerns—no singing, no guitars, no comic sidekick, no embroidered shirts. Actually, he's thinking of shows along the lines of the old Nevada Smith films."

"There are a lot of Westerns on television already," said Bat.

"The American public never tires of them," said Stein. "The archetypal American morality play."

Bat frowned and shook his head. "What you say may well be right—I mean, that there may be room for another Western. But I don't think I'll want to produce it."

"Oh?"

"My chief interest in getting back into film production—that is, videotape production—is to utilize the facility we already own. Cord Studios. We've got soundstages there that we've been renting to other people. I want to use them myself."

Jo-Ann listened to her brother and was surprised. He didn't talk about what his father might want, or even what "we" might want, but about what "I" want. She wondered if his father knew that was how he expressed himself. Big brother was taking a big risk. God knew how his father would react if word got to him that his son talked this way.

"I can understand that, Mr. Cord," said Stein. "But—"

Bat interrupted. "If I make Westerns, a lot of the shooting will have to be on outdoor locations, which means I'll be losing the economy of using an asset we already own. No, Mr. Stein, I think our first ventures into television production will be sitcoms or variety shows, where we can shoot on our soundstages and not have to go out. That's why I came here to see Glenda Grayson."

Stein drew a deep breath. "Well, how did you like Glenda? I'm sorry you don't like her, Miss Cord."

"I'd like to meet her," said Bat.

"She has to do another show," said Stein. "After that she'll be totally exhausted. I'll go back and speak to her. She might meet with you for five minutes tonight. Tomorrow . . . maybe for lunch."

4

Sam was wrong. Glenda Grayson came to their table after her second show, sat down, and accepted a Scotch from Bat. They could not talk, though. People in the nightclub came to their table to say they had enjoyed her performance or to ask for her autograph.

"Let's go up to my suite," she said. "We can have a drink there without all this."

"Aren't you tired?" asked Sam.

"I want to talk to this man," said Glenda. "After all, he came all the way to Los Angeles to see me. I'll see you at lunch, Sam."

Jo-Ann was insightful enough to understand that she was being dismissed, too.

In her suite, Glenda poured Scotch for Bat and poured a shot of vodka into a large glass of orange juice. She was not wearing a costume from her act, just a rather ordinary white blouse and a black skirt.

"You are supposed to be totally exhausted," said Bat.

"I am," she said. "You might not believe this, Bat, but I lose two or three pounds during an evening. Then I gain it back the next day. It's loss of fluid, mostly. I *sweat*. Then I drink a quart of orange juice and—"

Glenda Grayson was a slender blonde with a good figure and an extraordinarily expressive face. Jo-Ann had called her performance on the stage frenetic, which it had been, and now, being alone with her, Bat saw that the woman was incapable of relaxation. She was possessed by a sort of irrepressible tension that perhaps released her only when she was asleep. It was difficult to think she was comfortable, or ever could be.

Her performance on the nightclub stage had been dynamic, as she danced, sang, and delivered comic one-liners in rapid-fire succession. When she began a line with her catch phrase "Y' wouldn' b'*lieve* it," her audiences began to laugh before she told them what it was they wouldn't believe.

She used no coarse language in her act. Her comedy did not rely on titillating or scatological references, but a heady eroticism was never far beneath the surface, meticulously contrived to achieve the maximum effect from subtlety. She was good at that. She changed costumes twice during each performance. The final costume was a form-fitting red dress that was fastened up the back with Velcro and could be torn off in one movement. At the end she tore it off and sang and danced in a red corselette with garters holding up dark stockings. People seeing her act for the first time felt sure she would tear off the corselette, too, and stand revealed at the end either naked or in something sensationally brief. But she didn't.

She was thirty-two years old and had been a star nightclub performer for thirteen years. She had appeared on network television a score of times, always as a guest on someone else's variety hour or talk show. She'd wanted a special of her own but had never had one. She had wanted a movie of her own but had never had one. Her name was known to nearly everyone—but at a level well below that of superstar. She was one of the top fifty performers in the United States, maybe, but certainly not one of the top ten.

"You like the act?" she asked Bat. She was not accustomed to having to ask the question, but he had not said anything.

"Oh, sure. You've got a lot of talent. I've just been wondering how it can be packaged for a television series—assuming it can be packaged."

"Cord Television?"

"No. Cord Productions."

"What are you thinking about?"

"I'm thinking about a weekly show. The *Glenda Grayson Show*. But I'm thinking about how to do it. You can't repeat the act once a week. Even if you could stand the strain, we couldn't come up with enough material to let you do a forty-minute performance once a week. You've got a great act. But you can't do it time and again, time and again, week after week."

She nodded. "I don't repackage at intervals," she said. "If you see my shtick a month from now, you'll see it's different. Next month, more different. By the time I get back to The Roman Circus for next year's show, it will be *all* different. Different songs, different dancing, new costumes—but all worked in gradually over the course of the year. That's how I work. I may try something different tomorrow night, just to see how it works. If it bombs, I fix it or drop it. That's the great thing about club acts. You can tinker with them. TV—" She shrugged. "You go on the air with a bit and it falls flat, *you've* fallen flat. You don't have a chance to fix it. Tough damned medium, TV."

She poured more orange juice into her glass, without adding vodka.

"Does Sam make your decisions?" he asked.

"Sam finds opportunities," she said. "I choose. I make my own career decisions."

"Would you be interested in trying to work something out?" he asked. "A weekly show. The *Glenda Grayson Show*."

"Sure."

"Then I work with you. Or Sam?"

"With me. *And* Sam. He's a great guy. I'm not

gonna shut him out. But he's the business side of things. We make a deal, he'll negotiate the contract."

Bat reached across the table and took her hand in his. "We could come up with something real great, you and I," he said quietly.

Glenda put her other hand to her face and used a finger to wipe the corners of her eyes. "Hey," she whispered. "Careful. I'm a sucker for handsome *shkotzim.* I've made a fool of myself more than once."

"Shkotzim?"

She grinned and closed her hand around his. "Guys that're not Jewish," she said.

"Glenda . . ."

He rose and walked around the little table to stand behind her. He put a hand on her curly blond hair and found it stiff. He realized he was touching hairspray. Throughout her energetic performance her hair remained in place because of spray lacquer.

"Another word," she said. "Shiksa. It doesn't just mean non-Jewish girl, like you may think. My family calls me shiksa. It means a Jewish girl who tries to act like a gentile. They *spit* the word."

"Glenda . . ." He ran his hand along her cheek.

She turned and looked up at him, smiling tearfully. "My real name is Golda Graustein. But why do I tell you this? You didn't ask for an education in the peculiarities of my background and family. I'm sorry, Bat."

He bent down and kissed her forehead. "If it helps you at all, any way at all, then *tell me,"* he said.

"Are you going to stay with me tonight?" she asked abruptly.

Bat nodded. He was surprised but was not going to pass up the opportunity.

"You don't know what you're getting into," she

said. "Glenda falls in love. Glenda makes a fool of herself."

"So do I," he said.

She stood and began taking off her clothes. Besides the blouse and skirt she was wearing a bra and panties, garter belt and stockings. In a minute she was naked. She had a beautiful body, oddly white as if she never exposed it to the sun. She had no swimsuit marks. The contrast between her bright pink nipples and the white skin of her breasts was fascinating.

"C'mon, baby," she said. "I wanta see you, too."

Glenda grew visibly excited as Bat stripped. She winced when she saw the bullet-wound scar on his chest, but her eyes stayed on it only an instant before they dropped to his loins as he pulled down his shorts.

"Oh, marvelous!" she whispered. "Not mutilated. Not circumcised. My uncle is a *mohel*. He cuts little boys. I hate it. Bring it to me, Bat! Oh, God, I want it!"

She dropped to the floor, rolled on her back, and spread her legs for him. She brought to lovemaking the same energy and frenzy she brought to performing on stage, and she ascended to levels of rapture he had never seen a woman attain before. They coupled twice on the floor before she would consent to interrupt long enough for him to carry her to the bedroom and put her down on the bed. No other woman had ever exhausted him, but when finally Glenda Grayson grew heavy-lidded and soft of voice he was glad.

"C'n we put it in the contract that you'll give me nights like this at least three times a week?" she asked.

"I'm not sure I could handle it," said Bat.

"What an admission!" She laughed. They were her last words before she fell asleep.

5

A week later Jonas arrived in Las Vegas, flown in from the airstrip at Cord Explosives. Bat met him at the airport.

"What's this crap about making a television show?" Jonas asked as soon as they were on the road.

"I've got a good idea," said Bat.

"Yeah? Well, when did I say I want to make a television show? I suppose you mean to use my money?"

"It's a business proposition," said Bat. "A good business proposition. One we're going to need."

"Need?"

"We're beginning to lose money on the manufacture of television sets," said Bat. "The little makers are going to be squeezed out. That's why I think we should go into producing."

"Why should we be squeezed out?" Jonas asked. "The Cord sets are quality."

"Research and development costs are going to go out of sight," said Bat. "Are you aware of this thing called the transistor that they developed at Bell Labs? In a few years, the only tube in a television set will be the picture tube."

"What good will that do?" asked Jonas. "Sure, they've got pocket radios, which is all very well and good, but a TV set has to be big enough for its picture tube."

"How often does a Cord set have to be serviced?" Bat asked. "Servicing television sets is a minor industry. Day or night, somebody will come in a little truck and fix your TV. And what are they fixing? Tubes. Ninety-nine percent of all service calls are tube-replacement calls. Tubes fail."

"Transistors don't?"

"Occasionally. But not regularly, like tubes. And they're cheaper, too. I've read some technical papers on this. In a few years tube sets will not be competitive. Not only that, the sets of the future will receive color broadcasts. Aside from that, the Japanese are coming in. Ever hear of a company called Sony?"

"I've heard of Sony. You paint a goddamned gloomy picture, for a guy just now sticking his toes in the water."

"Not gloomy. Television will be bigger than ever. That's why I recommend we go into the production of shows—and maybe get out of the production of sets."

"So you got this broad you want to use as a star. What you think she can do?"

"A combination situation comedy and variety show," said Bat. "She's a performer more than an actress: a singer, dancer, and comedienne. But she can act, particularly comic acting. The situation comedy would be based on the idea that Glenda has a weekly television variety hour, featuring herself as principal performer. But we show her at home, too, with a husband and children; and we show in a comic way the difficulties she has combining the roles of wife and mother and performer."

"That's a cliché," Jonas observed.

"Name a successful television show that isn't. They're all cliché-ridden, and they're all predictable. Originality is poison on TV. Let's say we open each show with Glenda singing a song, then do the situation comedy, and close with a production number. I think it'll work."

"It'll work if somebody, namely me, puts in a pisspot full of money."

"Not all that much. We can build the New York apartment into one soundstage, the theater where she does the variety show into another. We don't have to do any location shooting. Talent costs will be reasonably high. We've got one young little dancer I want to use on the show. She's a newcomer, so she'll be cheap. Her name is Margit Little. She's going to be a star one day, and we'll have her under contract."

Jonas sighed heavily. "You're way outa line. When did I tell you to get me into a new business?" Jonas asked.

"If all you want me for is to run errands for businesses you've already got going, then take my resignation," said Bat. "Your father checked out and left you to run things your way. You put Cord Explosives into businesses he would never have approved of: airplanes, movies. Or maybe he would have approved, when he saw the money they could make. I don't think you'd have stayed with him if all he'd let you do is make dynamite. You—"

"You assume a lot," Jonas snapped.

"All right, forget what I assume about you and my grandfather. I'm telling you I won't stick if I'm shot down every time I come up with an idea. Even you can't turn me into an errand boy. *Capisce?*"

Jonas raised his chin high. "I'd have more confidence in your judgment if you weren't screwin' this woman you want to make your star."

"What do you want, a virgin?"

"Uhmmm," muttered Jonas nodding. "She a good piece?"

"Fantastic."

"Maybe *I* should give her a try."

Bat shook his head. "She isn't a whore we can pass back and forth."

"Will she do a nude audition?"

"She's a star," said Bat. "Already. Without us."

"Shit."

6

Glenda squeezed Bat's hand when he opened the door and admitted her to the suite. She let his father see no other sign of her affection.

She had dressed for this meeting with the redoubtable Jonas Cord: in a tight black knit dress that looked modest enough but strikingly displayed her figure.

"Bat has told me what kind of show he proposes you do," said Jonas. "I assume you know what you're doing, Miss Grayson. I assume Bat will hire people who know what *they're* doing. It seems to me, though, that you're taking on a damned heavy burden by trying to do this show every week—or by trying to do thirty-nine of them a season. Bat hasn't had any experience in show business, but I have, and I think it's too much. If I'm funding this deal, I want to do it every other week—twenty shows a season, not thirty-nine. Apart from saving you from burning yourself out, that'll make it possible to build a little more quality into each show."

"I think that's a good suggestion, Mr. Cord," said Glenda.

"I haven't accepted the idea, you understand," said Jonas. "Bat's still working at selling me."

"Yes, I understand," she said.

"Then I have a question," said Jonas. "Is this show something you really want to do? Do you feel a real commitment to it?"

"Mr. Cord," she said, "I've been a hoofer and singer more than half my life. It's all I've ever wanted to do. My family still doesn't like it, but it's all I ever wanted to do. To have my own television show, with my name on it— Well, that's the top. That's everything I ever dreamed of. Of course . . . it has to be a success. I'll work my ass off for it, Mr. Cord."

"Well . . . let's see how much you're committed. What I'd like to see is an audition. A *nude* audition, like a dance number in the altogether. Okay?"

Glenda turned to Bat, stricken, her eyes wide.

"No way," said Bat coldly. "No . . . fuckin' . . . way. Cut the crap, Jonas."

Jonas flushed deep red, and the veins in his neck stood out. But he said nothing. He dismissed Bat and Glenda with a toss of his hand.

7

"Well . . . I suppose that's that," said Glenda as they waited for the elevator. "Maybe I should have done it."

"No. We'll produce the show."

"What makes you think he'll go along?" she asked.

"He knows what's gonna happen if he doesn't— which is that he's gonna lose a vice president."

"And a son?" she asked. "I still say, maybe I should have done it. Maybe I should go back in there and do it now."

"No," said Bat firmly.

"You trying to save my feelings or my dignity?" Glenda asked. "You should know my dignity doesn't amount to much. Golda Graustein did some undignified things scrambling to become Glenda Grayson."

17

1

S_{HIKSA!}"

The first time she heard the word spat, it was not
directed at her but toward her Aunt Lela, her mother's
younger sister. That would have been— Oh, she had
been seven or eight years old. Aunt Lela had been
twenty-six or twenty-seven at the time.

The occasion was that Lela had broken the Shabbat
that morning. While the men of the house were at
worship, Lela had discovered that someone had forgotten to buy the extra bag of bagels that should have
been in the house because they had four guests. Lela
had slipped out of the house, first carefully covering
her head with a scarf, as a modest Jewish girl did
before she went out on the street. She had walked
eight blocks to the market run by goyim on Eighty-
seventh Street in Ozone Park. There she had made a
purchase. She had touched money on the Shabbat.
Someone saw, and someone brought the word to
Rabbi Mordecai Graustein.

"Shiksa!"

It was not Lela's first transgression. She had broken
the law before. What the family held most against her,
though, was that Lela had reached the age of twenty-
six or -seven and was not yet a wife and mother.

Nor was she finished with offending. When she was twenty-eight she would marry a young man from New Jersey and move with him to a town there. He was a member of a Reform congregation. They reared three sons in Reform Judaism. Rabbi Graustein forbade his wife ever to see those children, or ever again to speak to her sister. (She did see them, as he probably suspected, but husband and wife avoided confrontation by pretending she obeyed his injunction.)

Rabbi Mordecai Graustein was the father of Golda Graustein—Glenda Grayson. He was a formidable man. If not for her certainty that he loved her, little Golda would have been afraid of him. He was a bigger man than most: broad-shouldered, bulky inside his long black coats. He wore starched white shirts with collars buttoned tightly to his throat, without neckties. His beard usually covered his throat in any event. He wore his black hats set squarely on his head. He was a respected man in his Queens neighborhood. Many people spoke of him as holy. Men came to the house seeking the benefit of his wisdom and learning. Men came to him to hear him elucidate the law. Worried men came to the house to hear his opinion of the frightful things happening in Middle Europe.

Golda listened respectfully sometimes, and one day she heard him rule that the law proscribed the making of fire on the Shabbat and therefore light switches should not be moved on that day. Flipping a switch caused fire to appear inside an electric light bulb, he reasoned; therefore the switches should be set before the Shabbat and not touched until the Shabbat was over. A yeshiva student gravely but humbly argued the question, and the rabbi patiently overwhelmed his argument with citations to holy books.

The student then asked if it was lawful to allow a gentile servant to turn lights on and off during the

Shabbat. The rabbi pondered for a moment and ruled that it was.

Golda learned to speak and read Hebrew and Yiddish. That was a necessity for her brothers but not for her, and that she took the trouble to learn earned her a measure of respect not earned by her sisters. She learned many things besides: to speak quietly and carry herself modestly, to light the Shabbat candles at the proper hour, to make the proper responses as her father led the family prayers, to keep the meat dishware separate from the milk dishware, not even to wash them at the same time.

She always knew—she couldn't remember when she had not been aware of it—that she and her family were very much like most of their neighbors and very different from other neighbors. The men who came to see her father dressed exactly as he did. They wore beards as he did and kept their heads covered, if not by hats then by yarmulkes. The women, too, dressed much alike, very modestly, and covered their heads before they left their houses. They shopped only in selected stores, where things suitable for their use were sold. They shared a body of special knowledge, and they shared customs and traditions that seemed foreordained and inescapable.

Yet, she knew from an early age that not everyone lived as her family did. She learned, too, very soon, that some people hated her people. Her brother Elihu came home one day from school when he was nine, bloody and bruised. He had been set upon by other boys and beaten. *"Irländers,"* her father had grumbled. *"Italianers. Katholisch. Sturmabteilungers."* It never happened again, but Golda heard them yell sometimes—"Jew-boy! Kikey!"

She understood why those boys hated her brother. They were jealous of him because he was far brighter than they were and had a much better future ahead. He might become a rabbi like her father or a diamond merchant like her Uncle Isaac, while *they* were headed for toil on assembly lines in factories or greasy labor in automobile repair shops.

If they could get even such jobs. The Great Depression, which touched her family little, reduced many of their families to penury. Envy was the source of their hatred. Those whom G-d did not favor hated those whom He did. Throughout history, it had always been so, her father explained.

2

When she was seven her family took her to a street fair, and there for the first time she saw people dancing. *Dancing!* They moved their bodies, especially their legs, in rhythm to music and laughed and shouted in happy exuberance. The men danced first, then the women. Golda was ecstatic. She tried to do the steps. Her mother had to restrain her from trying to mimic the men's dancing, which would have been unseemly; but when the women danced she allowed the little girl to try the steps.

Golda could dance. Before her first experience with it was over she discovered something even more exhilarating than the dancing itself: that it made her the focus of attention. People close to her turned away from the women's dance to watch the little girl. That very first time she responded to them by mugging— grinning and rolling her eyes—and discovered they liked that, too.

Dancing was not a transgression. It should be done decorously, with appropriate modesty, but to enjoy it, even conspicuously enjoy it, did not offend. Nothing in the law, her father said, forbade people from enjoying themselves. Indeed, he had no objection to her mother enrolling her in a dance class, where she studied ballet. Her only problem with that was that her father judged tutus immodest and insisted she must dance in a knee-length skirt. But he never came to the dancing classes. He only supposed she would wear a tutu. He never dreamed that what she really wore was tights—leotards.

In this little friction over what she would wear in her dancing classes, Golda for the first time felt a tinge of resentment about separateness. She was the only girl in her classes asked by her family not to wear what the others wore; and if she had done it, it would have embarrassed her, not to say humiliated her. She didn't want to be different. She didn't want to be identified as someone unusual, peculiar.

She wondered then why her father dressed eccentrically, why she was supposed to keep her head covered outside the house, why they were obsessed about keeping the meat and milk apart, why their family and nearby friendly families were so different from all the other people she saw as she rode the bus to her dancing classes. She ventured to ask her mother, not her father, and was told that they obeyed the law and followed tradition, which was what G-d wanted them to do.

G-d wants us to do, G-d tells us to do. (They never broke the law that forbade them spelling out the name of the Deity, and in Golda's mind, God was G-d.) What G-d wanted seemed to justify everything.

She rode to and from her dancing classes with a girl who said she believed in God but believed very differently.

"Why is it," she asked this girl on the bus one day,

"that God tells you to do one thing and tells us to do something else?"

The girl shrugged. " 'The Lord moves in mysterious ways His wonders to perform,' " she said. "We are God's children. Blessed be the name of the Lord."

By the time she was fourteen, Golda Graustein was very secretly, but very definitely, a skeptic.

3

When she was fifteen she was introduced to the young man Rabbi Graustein had tentatively decided would be her husband. His name was Nathan. He was a student at the yeshiva, preparing himself for the rabbinate. He was eighteen years old.

Nathan was a slight young man, timid in the presence of the lordly Rabbi Mordecai Graustein, and respectful toward the rabbi's daughter. He was only an inch or so taller than Golda and probably weighed less than twenty pounds more. She disliked the redness of his full lips. She disliked the straggly patches of whiskers that grew here and there on his cheeks and jaw—which he might have shaved, she thought, until he could grow a manly beard. She disliked his totally practical little round silver-rimmed eyeglasses. He wore a calf-length black coat, wore his white shirt buttoned up and without a necktie, and wore his black hat set precisely square on his head—all like her father, only on Nathan these things did not lend dignity. Above all, she disliked his bland sincerity.

He had been in their house four times before he spoke a word to her. Then he said, quietly, bluntly, "Our fathers have chosen us for each other."

"Perhaps," she said noncommittally. "But that's a long time from now."

"Yes," he said. "I must continue to study."

Neither of her parents saw her first dance recital. For six months she had been working with Mrs. Shapiro, her dance teacher, to develop a routine. Her mother didn't know and probably would not have told Rabbi Graustein if she had.

The recital was given in the recreation hall of a temple in Hempstead, Long Island. When Golda mentioned that it was being presented in a Jewish temple, her father frowned but did not ask what kind of house G-d had that included a recreation hall. To the Graustein family, Hempstead sounded like a distant place, certainly one they could not reach conveniently, and they accepted the assurance that the young dance students would be transported there on a bus and returned by nine o'clock in the evening. In fact, that was the only negative reaction they had to the recital—that the bus had returned at 9:46.

They did not see their daughter perform. She was sixteen. She had ripened into a leggy, busty young woman. Some of the dancers in the recital were tap dancers, some essayed ballet. Golda Graustein came on the stage in bright-red hip-high leotards glittering with spangles, wearing a red spangled top hat and net stockings, and carrying a stick. She did a solo piece. She danced, and she sang, and twice she dropped in a one-liner—her own, not authorized by Mrs. Shapiro. She mugged. She rolled her eyes. Her enthusiasm was infectious. The audience stood to applaud and called her back three times.

"I will be a dancer. I will be an entertainer," she told her mother in the quiet of her bedroom that night.

"Your father has chosen a husband for you."

Golda's answer was simple. "No."

It was the first time he called her a shiksa.

He would no longer pay Mrs. Shapiro to teach her. Mrs. Shapiro taught her anyway. He wouldn't give her bus fare to go to her classes. She walked, until Mrs. Shapiro found out and gave her bus fare.

Naomi Shapiro had danced on Broadway in the 1920s and early '30s, without much success; and when her figure began to thicken they had discontinued hiring her.

"They will break your heart, darling," she told Golda. "You must think. You must think—"

Golda was eighteen. "I must think of the alternative," she said. "Marriage to a pale, pimply . . . unmanly—"

"I can arrange an audition. You see what you will have to compete with, then you will know."

4

Before this audition, Golda lost her virginity. More accurately said, she did not lose it; she got rid of it, something she had ceased to prize. She gave it away in a darkened rehearsal room at Mrs. Shapiro's studio, to a dancer two years older than she was: a muscular, handsome, manly youth, everything Nathan was not.

Doing this, she made her first great mistake about love. Innocent, she did not understand that a man could do to her what that young dancer did—unless he loved her. Oh, maybe not loved her in the great romantic way they heard sung about on records and radio, but cared for her at least. How could he have struggled with her through the ritual of passion without caring for her?

But he had. He was a nice Jewish boy, too. He thrust his big fat organ into her and caused her pain and pleasure and afterward treated her as a nuisance he didn't want to tolerate anymore.

A week later Mrs. Shapiro accompanied her to her first audition. It was, of course, a revelation. Golda discovered that she was only one of thousands—tens of thousands?—of girls who were dedicated to dancing and yearned for a place in the chorus lines of Broadway shows. She was seen at all only because someone felt he owed a favor to Naomi Shapiro.

She did not make the first cut.

As they stood on the street outside the theater in the rain looking for a cab to take them to the subway station—Golda depressed, wearing a scarf over her head, a too-short raincoat, saddle oxfords, and bobby sox, everything unstylish—a man walked up to them.

"Hi, Naomi," he said. "Disappointed?"

"I'm not," said Mrs. Shapiro. "I warned her. I suppose Golda is. Golda Graustein, meet Ernie Levin."

Golda looked at this man. He was maybe fifty years old. He wore a pork-pie rain hat and a black raincoat. He was not as tall as she was. His face looked squashed down, as if the jaws of a vise had been tightened on his skull and jaw, but an irrepressible smile shaped his eyes and mouth.

"Nice to meet ya, Miss Graustein. The first thing to do is change that name. The next thing— What are you, Hassidic? The next thing is to toss away the scarf, get your eyebrows plucked, get your hair cut, and learn to wear makeup."

"Ernie is an agent," said Mrs. Shapiro without enthusiasm.

"I was back there," said Ernie Levin. "I saw the audition. I can get ya work, kid. I can place her in the Catskills this summer, Naomi. Next fall, off Broadway maybe. Forget the chorus line, Golda. You got a shtick. That's why you'll never make it in the chorus line. You'd pull too much attention. What they want is uniformity. It's grunt work anyway. How old are ya?"

The family schism followed.

"You will do no such thing. You will marry Nathan before the summer is over and settle down to a proper and honorable life."

"No, Papa. I will not marry Nathan. I do not want to marry him. I don't love him."

"He is a good young man. He will be a rabbi. You will be the wife of a rabbi. Every girl wants to be the wife of a rabbi. You will share in the respect and honor that will be accorded him. The matter is settled, Golda. I have promised you to him. I will hear nothing to the contrary."

"I know a little of the law myself, Papa. You can't force me to marry Nathan. What is more, I am seventeen years old and will soon be eighteen. I can leave your home."

"SHIKSA!"

5

She worked that summer—the last summer when the world was at peace—at two borscht-belt hotels. To her disgust and shame, she discovered that she was expected to wait tables at lunch as well as to perform on the stage, two shows each evening. Ernie Levin told her not to worry, that was the way you broke in. He told her she was getting experience. He pointed out to her that she was allowed to work solo, to dance and sing, to crack jokes, and most of all to learn her trade.

A comedian was the star of each show, and she

worked behind five of them that summer. There were other singers and other dancers, but what Levin told her was true, that she had a small lead role in each show and was allowed to polish her shtick.

She wore leotards and net stockings, sometimes a top hat, and sometimes she used a cane. Levin urged her to study her audiences, to see how they reacted to what she did. It was essential, he insisted, that she develop a rapport with audiences. She must not just offer a prepared shtick, like merchandise on the counter of a store: take it or leave it. She must learn to respond to the audience's reaction, changing not just tomorrow night but right now if she saw she was not carrying the audience with her. The worst mistake of all, he told her, was to resent an audience that did not seem to like her, and to defy it. The customer is always right, he said.

She wrote to her mother that she lived in the waitresses' dormitory and that she ate kosher. She wrote that they did not perform on the Shabbat. What she did not write was that she no longer covered her head whenever she went outside. She did not write that she had given herself to one of the comedians. She did not write that once again she had misunderstood the quality and nature of a man's attentions and had annoyed him by falling in love.

When she returned to New York she was pregnant.

Resourceful Ernie Levin moved her into a flat with another client of his and arranged for her to have an abortion. It was not done by a back-alley abortionist but by a White Plains gynecologist. The doctor was a woman, and she was competent and sympathetic. Even so, the operation was painful, and it left Golda feeling she had committed an unpardonable sin.

"You have two choices, my child," Ernie had told her. "You can go home to your family, since after all you must have a home and support for you and your child; or you can abort the pregnancy. I have work for you. I can book you into clubs. God forbid, I should ever *urge* a young woman to have an abortion, but I want you to know what your options are."

"I have no options," Golda had said tearfully.

"I have a word of advice," said Ernie. "Do not be so ready to give your person to a young man. You are naive. You must be less trusting."

The doctor who performed the abortion gave her more specific counseling about birth control.

Ernie took her to a tiny comedy club in Lower Manhattan, where she auditioned for the owner—who had been told she was twenty-one. He wanted a different act. She could dance a little, okay, and she could sing a little, okay; but he wanted more jokes. It was, after all, a *comedy* club. And the songs— He wanted bawdy songs. And no bra under the leotard, okay? If she bounced around a little, the audience would love it.

In his office Ernie rehearsed her with a string of jokes. He bought some, stole others. Some were coarse, some weren't.

Golda used them all, and the audience liked them. Ernie got her permissions to use several songs from what were called party records. She got wild applause when she danced and sang, "Bounce your boobies."

It was a tough grind. The club didn't open until nine o'clock, and it closed at three in the morning, by which time she had done four shows. But the owner renewed her contract three times, and she performed there for a month.

Her last night someone yelled from the audience, "Hey, Golda! Where'll you be next?"

"Yellow Calf," she said. Ernie had already arranged her next booking.

"See ya there!" yelled the man in the audience.

6

Clubs announced new shows by running little block ads in the tabloid papers, and before the winter was over those little ads were promising a performance by the hilarious dancing comedienne Golda Graustein.

She polished her act. Comedy-club audiences were far tougher than the audiences in Catskill hotels. They were unforgiving. They didn't see her as a kid trying to please them but as part of a show they'd paid good money to see. They demanded earthy humor, filled with sexual innuendo. Sometimes insinuation wasn't enough for them; they wanted their comedy literally raunchy. Golda had to be taught, and Ernie Levin was her teacher. He began to buy jokes for her. A young writer fed her lines for ten dollars apiece. One night she got a huge laugh from a parody on the song "I'm Forever Blowing Bubbles," including the line "I suck like an Electrolux," and later she blushed when she found out what it meant.

What she was doing was not what she had meant to do and be when she was first inspired to dance and sing. But she had to make a living.

Eighteen years old, Golda had to make a living. She was allowed to visit her family home in Queens, but never to eat a meal there, never to stay overnight. Her father absented himself from the house if he knew she was coming. He declared she degraded the family name and left word that he would appreciate it if she would call herself something else.

Ernie Levin said she would probably do better if she did change her name. So . . . Glenda Grayson.

18

1

ERNIE . . . OH, ERNIE, ERNIE!"

Glenda wept over the pallid figure lying in the
wooden coffin. Ernie Levin. At Forty-eighth and
Broadway he had toppled off the curb and fallen on
his face on the rainy street. His signature pork-pie
rain hat had rolled out into the street and was run
over by a cab. He'd been hustling a deal, always
hustling. His heart quit. Just quit. He was fifty-five
years old.

"What'm I ever gonna do without him?" Glenda
asked quietly, of no one in particular.

Gib Dugan put his arm gently around her waist.
"The Irish do these things better," he said.

"Meaning . . . ?"

"A wake," he said. "We could all be drunk."

"I'd like to be drunk," she said, "but I have to work
tonight. And so do you."

In two years, thanks to Ernie, she had moved
uptown in more ways than one. She was working in a
club called Dingo's in the Bronx, where she was part
of a fully produced show with live music, a chorus
line of six dancers, a comedian, and Glenda Grayson.
She was the headliner. Her name was outside.

Her act had matured. She danced. She perched on a

piano, crossed her handsome legs, and sang. Her comedy was no longer just one-liners but a monologue that included touching lines about the way her family scorned her.

"Hey, you remember Jack Benny's great line? His father had wanted him to be a rabbi, not a comedian. But he said to him, 'Anyway, whatever you do, don't change your name, Benjamin.' What'd my father the rabbi say to me? 'Golda, as a favor to your family . . . *change your name! Please!'* "

Gib Dugan was one of the three male dancers in the chorus line, which meant he was not good enough to dance on Broadway. He was a big muscular good-looking guy, though; and, in Glenda's term, "hung like a horse." He satisfied her. She told herself she had learned enough to allow a guy to get in her pants but not to allow any guy, especially a goyish guy, to get into her head. Still, she had to admit she would be sorry if she lost this one.

"One or two won't hurt anything," he said. "C'mon. Ernie was a great guy, but—"

"No buts, Gib. We have to work." She glanced a final time at the corpse of her mentor. "Ernie . . . How'm I gonna get jobs without him?"

They worked two shows, and when they went home to her flat in Brooklyn, she was again tearful. Performing exhausted her, and while she was in the shower, Gib poured her a heavy Scotch over ice and handed it past the curtain. She drank while the water was still pouring over her and managed to relax.

She sat then in her living room, naked except for the towel that soon fell down, with the Scotch almost exhausted. He put in two more ice cubes and poured her some more.

"Ernie," she whispered tearfully.

"There was a limit to Ernie, Glenda," Gib said.

"There was a limit to his vision. You can do better than anything he could ever get you."

"C'mon. Meaning what?"

"You gotta get out of New York, baby. You've done all you can do here. Look at it. Things are changing. The hotels have quiet lounges. They want a gal who can play the piano and sing—but not so loud it interferes with the business talk over the tables. Clubs. There are fewer and fewer every year. The ones that survive have gone over to strippers. You wanta work with stripteasers? You wanta take off your clothes on stage?"

"So what the shit am I supposed to do?"

"Gotta get out of town," said Gib. "The Poconos. Miami Beach. Texas. L.A."

Glenda tossed back her Scotch. "Yeah, sure. I got an offer to make some party records."

"No," he said firmly.

"What do you mean, no?"

"That won't do your reputation any good. You got a name as a club act. You—"

She put her hand on his crotch. "Don't gimme advice," she said. "Gimme what you got better of."

"Sure. In a minute. But be serious, Glenda. You gotta get a new agent. Hey. Let *me* make a couple of calls. I know some people. Maybe I can get you something out of town."

2

"Maybe it was G-d's will," said her mother.

"God? The man was my *friend.*"

"You thought so. And what about this *shegetz* you are seeing now? Is *he* your friend? The *Katholischer?*"

"He is my friend."

They sat together in her family's living room on a Thursday afternoon. Rabbi Mordecai Graustein was, as always when his daughter visited, absent. Glenda stared at the crocheted antimacassars on the chairs, which had seemed so natural, inevitable in fact, when she was a girl and looked so antiquated now. She had come to the house in a cab, her head uncovered—without in fact bringing anything *to* cover it. That year shorter skirts were in fashion—it was women's patriotic duty to save fabric—and hers crept back above her knees when she sat. She was out of place in her own home.

"It is not too late for you, Golda," her mother said. "It is never too late for hope, always too early for despair."

"Which means what, Mother?"

"You did not marry Nathan. You should have married Nathan. He is a fine educated young rabbi, with a reputation that will one day rival your father's. And he married a girl who knew how to respect him. But there is another. This young man came late to his studies, but he is devout in them. He is rich! His father died and left him more than two hundred thousand dollars, which is what allows him to leave business and take up his studies. He wants only a devoted wife. Your father is sure you could win him."

"I have no interest in winning him," said Glenda.

Her mother lowered her chin to her chest. "We try to save you, Golda. Even your father, who will not see you, prays constantly for you."

"For me to become what?" Glenda asked coldly.

"Do something then for your mother. Answer me this question—Are you happy?"

Glenda drew a deep breath. "I cannot say I am happy. I am not unhappy, but—"

"Then. If you will not try to earn the respect of this

fine young man, then do something else for me. You remember Mrs. Gruenwald—the Gruenwald family? They had the delicatessen on—"

"I remember them, Mother."

"Mrs. Gruenwald's son, Saul, is a doctor. He helps people who are unhappy. Go see him, Golda. He is what they call a psychiatrist."

3

"It was done to you before you could prevent it," Glenda said to Dr. Saul Grünwald. (He used the form Grünwald, rather than Gruenwald.) She held his limp penis in her hand. "I prefer the ones that *aren't* cut, though. Gib's isn't."

"What's better about it?" the psychiatrist asked, unable to conceal a touch of indignation.

"Why tell you, since there's nothing you can do about it?" Glenda asked with a grin. "You can't have it put back. If you'd had a choice, though, I'd suggest you should have said no."

"Are you in love with the *shegetz?*"

"I'll tell you this. I will never fall in love with anyone who uses the word *shegetz*. Or nigger. Or kike."

Dr. Saul Grünwald was thirty-five years old and almost wholly bald. His brown eyes were beady. His solemnity had not forsaken him even when he was astride her. "Forgive," he said. "Old habits die hard."

"No, they don't," she said disdainfully.

Dr. Grünwald, who had been putting his clothes back on during this dialogue, frowned and glanced around the room. "The question we are addressing," he said, "is whether or not you are happy."

"I am for the moment," she said. "Since you just

screwed me good. How will I feel at midnight to-night?"

"You must not depend on that."

"Only for occasional therapy? For which I pay?"

"Golda, you are a prisoner of your resentments. Beginning with resentment of your father—"

"Have I no right to resent? I think I do."

"If I were you, I would put aside the goy and try to make peace with my father."

"Who speaks through you?" she asked. "Freud or Moses? Is it also your advice that I marry a rabbinical student and settle down to a quiet life of housekeeping and childbearing?"

"You would not have come to me," he said, "if you were happy. If you were satisfied with yourself and with your life, you would not have sought out a psychiatrist. I know, your mother sent you to me. But you would not have come if you hadn't felt you needed help."

"Make peace with my father . . . It could only be on his terms."

"What do you want, Golda? What do you want more than anything else?"

"I want a contract to do five weeks in a first-class out-of-town club."

4

In December 1942, when Glenda was just twenty years old, she worked in a strip club for the first time, in Miami. Gib Dugan, in spite of his having spoken scornfully about working with strippers, had made the deal for her and talked her into taking it. The contract was for two weeks at five hundred dollars a week, far more than she had ever made before.

Gib had promoted her to Mel Schmidt, the club owner, by promising him her borscht-belt humor would delight the Jews who still came to Miami in December in spite of the difficulties of wartime travel. It would delight GIs on leave, too, he had promised.

The owner bought Gib's idea, but he was adamant that she must appear in a costume appropriate to the club—meaning very little costume at all. She had signed a contract that specifically said she would work in "abbreviated costume, such as is worn by other performers at Casa Pantera." Gib had argued to Schmidt and to Glenda that a borscht-belt singer-dancer-comedienne working in strip-club deshabille would be a "dynamite attraction." Schmidt was so much convinced that he was advertising Glenda Grayson in the newspapers.

They traveled to Florida by train, standing much of the time. Glenda had never been farther from New York City than the Catskills, and she was fascinated by the country outside the train. Though she had expected it, she was astonished to step out into eighty-degree weather in December. They arrived in Miami early in the morning and checked into a hotel to get some sleep before they went to the club.

Casa Pantera turned out to be a squat concrete-block building on Biscayne Boulevard. A gaudy sign advertised striptease, promising BUSTY BLONDES! BOMBASTIC BRUNETTES! GORGEOUS GALS THE WAY YOU WANT TO SEE 'EM!

Posters hung behind glass in the entrance porch. Attached to them were photographs of the featured performers, with names like Eve Eden, Chesty Boone, Rusty Beaver, and Hope Diamond—all of these young women naked except for tiny bras and beaded G-strings. Glenda gasped. She had not imagined that the "abbreviated costume" she had contracted to wear would be *this* abbreviated.

Gig had mailed a photo of Glenda—in a leotard and net stockings. Her poster said, "Direct from New York and the Catskills, the sensational dancing, singing comedienne Glenda Grayson! See Glenda Grayson as you have never seen her!"

Her costumes were leotards, mostly. The corselette she sometimes wore consisted of a bra and girdle, in one piece. When they arrived at the club, she realized she had nothing suitable with her. For the first time in her life she was unprepared for a performance.

They sat down in Mel Schmidt's office, and she confessed she had no abbreviated costume with her and would have to arrange something during the afternoon.

"Hey, kid," Schmidt said. "No problem. Long dark stockings, a black garter belt, black G-string. That's always good. That always goes over big. It's sexy. Understand, our gals can only take off as much as the cops allow at this particular time. Right now, the G-string has got to cover all your hair, and you can't pull it down and show anything. But they do allow bare tits, so you've got to be bare-titted at the end of your act. My crowds will boo you if you aren't."

He called in the stripteaser called Chesty Boone—a woman of some thirty-five years with a spectacular figure—and told her to help Glenda get an outfit. Chesty said there was a little shop downtown called Stage Undies. She'd go with Glenda if she wanted her to.

"Do that," said Schmidt. "You can show her what she needs."

In her dressing room that evening Glenda fought back tears as she pulled up over her legs a pair of net stockings and clipped them to her black garter belt. A little triangle of black satin covered her pubic area—and she'd had to use a razor and scissors and trim back her hair so that none of it would show. She wore two bras: one an ordinary black brassiere, the other one a contrivance of sheer black rayon and thin black strings that covered her breasts but did not conceal them. Over all this she wore a black lace-trimmed teddy.

In a men's shop she had also found a black fedora, which she wore tilted forward on her head to throw a shadow over her face.

"Now, there's what I call *style*," Mel, the owner, exulted when he stopped in a few minutes before she was to go on stage. "You got style, real style."

When he had left, Glenda leaned against the door and closed her eyes. "I haven't got any choice, do I?" she whispered to Gib. "Without the thousand bucks Mel is gonna pay us, we can't even get back to New York."

"Don't even think of chickening out, baby," he said. "But you got no idea how beautiful you look. Think of how you're gonna look on that stage!"

"I'll look naked, is how I'll look."

The show went on at nine o'clock. The owner acted as master of ceremonies, braving his way through a line of brash chatter that was not original and not very funny. He introduced four strippers, then Glenda, then the featured stripper. A pianist, a guitarist, and a drummer, fully amplified, furnished the music.

Her half hour on the stage was an ordeal. The crowd liked her but began to yell, "Take it off! Take it off!" before she was out there five minutes. She took off the teddy, and they cheered and whistled. They settled down then to listen to her jokes and songs. But the necessity of stopping to take things off upset her timing, and her horror at having to appear before all these people with her breasts naked destroyed the natural exuberance that was essential to her routine. She was doubly miserable, for having to appear on stage all but naked and for failing to meet her own standards for a performance.

But the audience didn't seem to know. When she gave them the line "Golda, for the sake of your family, *change your name! Please!*" some people stood up to applaud. She had not guessed that her shameful nudity would make the line even more poignant.

Even so, they yelled for her to take off the bra, then to take off the little sheer bra. She did that at the very last moment, but they applauded so much she had to go out and take a bow bare-breasted.

For the midnight show, she saved the change-your-name line for last and left the stage to a standing ovation.

Mel loved her. He offered her another four weeks, and so she stayed through January.

"Let me give you a word of advice," he said over dinner her last night at Casa Pantera. "You're a great attraction. You're very classy. But you oughta work up an act that's not quite so . . . so *New Yorkish,* if you know what I mean. You got smarts. You work up a new act, an' we can make a contract for six weeks next winter."

By the time she brought her new act back to Florida, Casa Pantera could no longer afford her. In 1943 she worked a roadhouse club outside Camden, New Jersey, then a downtown club in Newark, then a club in Philadelphia and a club in Boston. From Boston she went to Raleigh, North Carolina, and from there to Covington, Kentucky, where in the summer of 1944, for six weeks and for the only time in her career, she lowered her G-string at the end of her act and exposed herself completely. From there she went to a club in Chicago, and her career began to find a new direction.

In the Chicago club she worked in front of a jazz band and wore a halter or bra of sheer dark material that didn't conceal her breasts entirely but stayed in place throughout the show. For the G-strings she substituted sheer black panties with opaque crotches. The stockings and garter belt displayed her shapely legs to good advantage, and the chiaroscuro contrast of dark sheer hose and white skin was dramatic. So was the contrast of her long blond hair falling from under the brim of the black hat. Those contrasts became her trademark.

Gradually she made her act less "New Yorkish." She knew what Mel had meant. He hadn't been subtle. Except in New York, the people who would turn out for a performance by Glenda Grayson would not want Jewish humor. They accepted it gladly from male comedians, less gladly from women, not well at all from a scantily dressed, effervescent singer-dancer.

She began to experiment too with taking a drink or three before she went on stage. She found it didn't hurt anything—at least, she thought it didn't.

Gib had photographs taken of her. She refused to pose bare-breasted, and the black-and-white eight-by-tens he distributed showed her in one of the more modest of her costumes: with an opaque bra and panties. Occasionally she got a mention in a newspaper. He reproduced her clippings and sent them out with the photos.

In Chicago in 1945 she omitted the teddy and

added a pinstriped black jacket to her costume. Only when she unbuttoned it were her breasts bared, if they were bared at all. A Chicago columnist wrote, "A saucy, interesting young performer, who really doesn't need to expose herself to win enthusiasm and affection from club audiences. Come back again, Glenda Grayson."

She never showed her breasts again. What was more, she had decided the garter belt, stockings, and hat costume was brazen and inelegant. It imposed a limit.

"The tits got you the good jobs, baby," Gib argued. "Don't be so damned determined to put 'em away. Without the tits, you could still be working the Catskills summers, waiting tables at noon and getting paid five percent of what you've been making. The guy at Casa Pantera was right about the garter-belt outfit, too. With your skin, it's sensational."

The night of September 20, 1946, a man knocked on the door of her dressing room. She let him in, and he introduced himself.

"My name is Sam Stein," he said. "Here is my card."

SAMUEL L. STEIN
Talent Agency
Los Angeles   New York   London

She met with him for lunch the next day. Gib Dugan came with her.

The little man with the bald head and tiny face was blunt and specific. "I can book you into a club in Dallas," he said. "For sure. Three weeks. A thousand a week. After that I've got a place in Houston in mind. And after that New Orleans. By the time you do those three you should be ready for Los Angeles. Get your act really straightened out and tuned up, I can book you into just about any club in the country."

"Just what needs to be 'straightened out'?" Gib asked, almost indignant.

"In the first place, we put clothes on her," said Sam Stein. "A girl with her talent doesn't need to run around half naked. That's in the first place."

"What else?" Glenda asked.

"Your funny-girl stuff is too bland. No bite in it. It sparks once in a while, but I have a sense you're holding something back. It's too Hollywoodish. Your bio says you worked the comedy clubs in New York. You didn't work them with this kind of stuff."

"I used to have a tough little monologue," said Glenda.

"I'd like to hear it," said Sam. "Could we go up to my suite?"

"She was difficult to book with that act," said Gib.

"Are you her agent?"

"Well, not formally. I've been helping her with bookings."

"Then suppose you let *me* worry about where I can book her with what kind of act."

In the Dallas club, two months later, Glenda came on stage in a tight white dress glittering with spangles. She delivered a few sharp lines of monologue, then carried her microphone around the stage as she sang. "I Got Rhythm" from *Girl Crazy*. "I Got Plenty o' Nuttin'" from *Porgy and Bess*. "The Lady Is a Tramp" from *Babes in Arms*. "Can't Help Lovin' Dat Man" from *Show Boat*. And from *Anything Goes*, "Blow, Gabriel, Blow" and the title song.

Tossing the microphone to the piano player, who usually deftly caught it, she snatched off her dress and draped it over the piano, revealing a spangled red leotard in which she danced to "Slaughter on Tenth Avenue" from *On Your Toes*. Winded, she climbed on a stool and did her monologue, using the line "Golda, for the sake of your family *change your name! Please!"* She finished with a spirited, energetic reprise of "Anything Goes."

Sam Stein had secured all the permissions she needed to use this music. He brought her records and let her hear how the stars of the shows had done the songs. The first-night audience loved her. The club owners loved her. But the next morning Sam called her to his suite, and they went to work. He pulled a song and substituted another. He pulled lines from her monologue and suggested replacements.

He changed the costume. When she unzipped and stepped out of the dress the second night, she was wearing a simple black dance leotard and dark sheer stockings held up by blood-red garters. Her upper legs were bare, once again taking advantage of the dramatic contrast between her white skin and the dark fabrics of her costume. Also, Sam had recalled the black hat. She picked it up off the piano and set it on her blond head.

The owners would have extended her contract for an additional three weeks, but she was already under contract to the club in Houston. She did three weeks there and went on to New Orleans, as Sam had promised.

"I only got one more problem, Glenda," he said to her over lunch in New Orleans. He gestured with his hand, indicating the tipping back of a bottle, with a clucking of his tongue to suggest the liquor chugging out.

"I got nerves, Sam," she said.

"You're *supposed* to have nerves. You can't do what you do without nerves. When do you suppose you stop having nerves? When you get to be a number-one star? No. I can tell you. You'll always have nerves. It goes with the territory."

"You weren't at your best last Wednesday night in Houston," said Gib. "In fact, you were a hell of a lot off your best."

"Oh, fuck off!" she snapped at Gib. "What'm I supposed to do?" she asked Sam. "Go on the wagon?"

Sam shook his head. "Airplane pilots have a rule," he said. "I think it's 'Eight hours bottle to throttle.' Let's say four. Or five. Then have enough to help you come down after the night's shows. Have a drink or two at lunch. But—"

"All *right,*" she interrupted. "Do it right, Glenda. So you guys can make money off me."

5

"Sam . . . ?"

"Glenda."

"Come help me, Sam. You're the only friend I've got. Gib bugged out. Not only that . . . He stole my lucky hat!"

Sam took her home.

"So, Rabbi Graustein," he said to her father. "You are a holy man. Wiser than God. Hmm?"

"You are a *shegetz,*" said Rabbi Mordecai Graustein.

Sam shrugged. "And you are a klutz. None of us are perfect."

"I obey the Law," said the rabbi stiffly.

"Where does the Law tell you to throw away a daughter?" Sam asked. "Why should a daughter honor a father when the father does not honor her? Golda is a fine young woman. For every man, woman, and child who has heard of you, a thousand have heard of her. And soon it will be more."

"Is this a value?" asked Rabbi Graustein. "Being widely heard of?"

"I wish she were *my* daughter," said Sam.

Glenda smiled shyly. "You're not old enough, Sam," she said.

Rabbi Mordecai Graustein glared at his daughter. By her little smile, her little joke, she had trivialized the conversation, trivialized *him*. "So," he said curtly. He stood.

"Uriel Acosta," said Glenda to her father, "was made to lie down across the doorway of the Amsterdam synagogue, and all the men of the congregation stepped over him as they walked out. If you think you can do that to me, you are the klutz Sam says you are."

19

1

BAT TOOK TIME OFF FROM THE PROBLEMS OF PRODUC-
ing and selling the first Glenda Grayson show to fly
to Northampton, Massachusetts, for Jo-Ann's graduation.

He met Monica Cord for the first time. She came to
Northampton in the company of a syndicated political cartoonist named Bill Toller, whose work appeared in more than a hundred newspapers. Like
Norman Rockwell he sometimes drew himself and so
had fashioned his own image: that of a broad-
shouldered, heavy-set man in a cardigan sweater,
sitting over his drafting table, smoking a pipe, and
peering at blank paper with an expression of comic
frustration. In person he was a better-looking man
than his self-caricature. He did smoke a pipe and had
one in his pocket as he sat beside Monica at the
graduation ceremony.

Anticipating the appearance of Bill Toller at the
graduation—and not to be compelled to face his ex-
wife in the company of a man while he was alone—
Jonas brought Angie. She drew stares and comments
as always.

Bat called Toni Maxim in Washington and asked
her to come to Northampton. His father liked Toni.
So did Jo-Ann, he thought. If he had shown up in

Northampton with Glenda Grayson, he would have made tension and a scandal. Anyway, he wanted to keep his relationship with Toni, and inviting her to be with him on an important family occasion made up for half a dozen occasions when he might have seen her and didn't. Toni was the right choice for this weekend.

Jonas took note. "Well. Back to this one. Which one counts?"

"Monogamy is not a Cord family tradition," Bat said curtly.

Even so, the weekend and the Monday commencement were one prolonged confrontation.

Monica seemed interested in only one thing about this son Jonas had suddenly discovered: Was he really producing a television show starring Glenda Grayson of all people? As a magazine editor, she was interested in that. She was also interested in seeing Jonas get laughed at—an interest she was unable to conceal.

Bill Toller was conspicuously out of place and embarrassed. He spent his time trying to find someone who would talk with him and settled finally on Toni. She could talk politics with him and so became a refuge for him.

Monica was annoyed that Jonas had brought Angie. Jonas was glad she was annoyed. Angie was amused.

2

Jonas told Bat to come to his suite for breakfast at 6:30 on commencement morning. Alone.

"We'll have two breakfasts," said Jonas when Bat sat down at the wheeled table loaded with eggs, bacon, pancakes, fruit, and coffee—also with a bottle of bourbon from which Jonas was sipping sparingly. "The whole crowd is getting together at eight."

Bat nodded. He took note that Angie had not come out of the bedroom.

"That girl you've brought with you is first rate," said Jonas. "Toni is first class, in every way I can see and I imagine in some others that only you know about."

"She's very special," said Bat solemnly.

"So, when you gonna marry her?"

"That's none of your business, really; but what would you say if I told you she's not sure she wants to marry a son of Jonas Cord?"

"She doesn't like me?"

"Oh, she likes you fine," said Bat. "But she's not sure she wants a husband whose father dominates his life."

"*I dominate your life?* I thought you'd declared independence of me, pretty goddamned emphatically. Look. You want out? You want to go back to practicing law? Why not? You're supposed to be good at it."

Bat nodded. "I've thought about it."

"Don't forget something," said Jonas. "You picked up the Jonas Cord way of living pretty damned fast, and you seem to thrive on it. Putting aside some of your expense accounts, do you figure a young lawyer would be humping a big nightclub star . . . on the q.t., besides the girl he's supposed—"

"I've made no commitment to Toni. She's made none to me."

"Well, that's too friggin' bad. Anyway— Never mind. This television show. Nobody wants it. No sponsor. Right?"

"We don't know yet."

"Well, when you gonna know?"

"I'm working on it."

"So far, you haven't got a sponsor. Could that be because you don't know fuck about how to build a successful television show? I've dumped more than a million—"

"You dumped seventeen million into the Pacific Ocean off San Diego in 1945," said Bat. "Could that be because you didn't know fuck about how to build an airplane?"

Jonas's face stiffened and reddened for a moment. Then he relaxed and smiled. "You son of a— Look, I want you to make a success of whatever you try. You think I don't?"

Bat hesitated, then said, "You think it's easy being a son of Jonas Cord?"

"No. Don't forget, I was . . . the son of the old man. Maybe I'm gaining a new appreciation of my father. It's not easy to be the father of a Jonas Cord either."

"Okay," said Bat. "Nothing good is achieved easy."

Jonas tossed back a gulp of bourbon. "Right. But take a word from me. You say Glenda is no hooker. Well, she's not far from it. Take it easy, mister. Be careful about her."

"Then send her to you, huh?"

3

Over breakfast and for the rest of the commencement weekend, Bat gave his attention to his little sister. The occasion should have been hers, but she seemed lost in the tangle of antagonisms that dominated the group. He watched her drinking. On what should have been a happy day for her, she wasn't happy, and she was anesthetizing herself with Scotch.

"Where are you going after commencement?" he asked her.

"I am supposed to go to Monica's apartment in New York," she said.

"Use our apartment in the Waldorf Towers," said Bat. "Our father is there only a night or so every two weeks, and I'm there not much more."

"I hear you rented a handsome beach house in California," she said. "Could I move in with you there for a while? I promise to behave."

Bat glanced toward Toni. "How good are you at keeping a secret?" he asked quietly. "You'll *have* to behave. I'm not living there alone."

4

Glenda loved the beach house, though she did not love the beach. Her white skin did not tan. It burned. Exposed to the sun, it turned bright red and peeled. Anyway, she didn't want to tan. Her white skin was a part of her persona. She even stayed off the deck when it was hot with sunlight. She wore a bikini around the house, only because she knew Bat liked it.

On a Sunday evening they sat on the deck, in the faint purple-orange light of a sun that had already disappeared below the Pacific horizon. They had Scotches and some cheese with crackers.

"I've got to fly back to Las Vegas tomorrow," said Bat.

"Again?"

"It *is* my business, you know. The Seven Voyages."

"Your business is being the producer of our show,"

said Glenda. "Sam's having trouble selling it. We may have to do some reshooting."

"I'm president of Cord Hotels," said Bat. "We bought land south of Flamingo Road. My father is flying in tomorrow. We're meeting with the architect."

"A second Cord hotel," she mused. "What will you call it?"

"Well, since our airline is Inter-Continental, we may call the hotel InterContinental—with a capital C in the middle."

"Plus you own the place in Cuba."

"Not really. We lease the casino and show room in the Floresta. We have nothing to do with the hotel operation."

"Bat—" She stared out to sea, abruptly shook her head, and didn't finish what she had started to say.

"What's the matter, baby?"

She turned her face toward him. "Bat. Be careful. There are some rough types in Las Vegas."

"That's something else I've got to look into. Our man Chandler seems to have too many friends among those rough types."

"Why don't you get rid of him?" she asked.

"We keep him busy, which gives him less opportunity to make mischief. If we turned him loose, he could become a full-time troublemaker."

5

They heard the door open, then heard the voice of Jo-Ann: too enthusiastic and slurring her words.

"Where are you guys? Out on the deck?"

Glenda pulled on a terry-cloth beach coat to cover her swimsuit. Bat turned around and knocked on the glass door, to indicate that was in fact where they were: out on the deck.

Jo-Ann was not alone. Ben Parrish was with her. Bat rued the day he had introduced her to Ben. He could not have imagined she would develop a hasty and intemperate infatuation for the man. He'd done it because Ben was a mature man and broadly knowledgeable about the things in Los Angeles and Hollywood that would most interest Jo-Ann. He had expected Ben to introduce her to some people in the film community and give her a good time.

Glenda had rued the introduction from the moment she heard of it. "My god, Bat! You don't *know* the man. He's a Hollywood hustler."

"I thought he was an agent. That's how I met him. He tried to interest me in a game show. In fact, I *am* interested in it."

"You don't know the other element of his reputation," Glenda had said. "He's got the biggest schlong in California. Girls will do anything even to get a look at it."

"You've seen it?"

Glenda had grinned. "No, lover, I haven't. But I've heard about it plenty."

There could be no discounting the man's charm. Ben was a squarish man: broad of shoulders, with a big solid head set on a short neck. His eyes were pale blue. He was deeply tanned. Though he was only a year or so older than Bat, his hair had begun to turn gray, and he had apparently hastened and completed the process by having chemicals applied to it. It was almost white, smooth and handsome. His square open face did not suggest the hustler Glenda said he was. To the contrary, it suggested a man who could not tell a lie.

Ben and Jo-Ann had spent the afternoon at a pool party. Jo-Ann wore a white terry beach coat like Glenda's. It was open, showing a tiny black bikini. She was drunk. Ben wore damp maroon trunks and a white polo shirt.

As soon as they were on the deck, Ben lit cigarettes for himself and Jo-Ann. They smoked only on the deck. It was a concession to Bat's pronounced dislike of cigarette smoke.

Everyone understood that Ben would stay the night. He had been doing that, several nights a week.

"We were gonna order in some dinner," said Bat. "You going to join us?"

"On a condition," said Ben. "On me. I buy. What would you guys like? Mexican? Chinese?"

"Chinee," said Jo-Ann. "With an order of fwied pickled . . . *cockwoaches.*"

"Fried pickled cockroaches it is," said Ben. "How about a nice bottle of champagne to go with that?"

"That'll make me burp," said Jo-Ann. "How 'bout just reg'lar white wine?"

Ben nodded. "I'll go and make the calls."

"I'll go with you," said Jo-Ann.

"You sit down," said Bat. "I want to talk to you."

Ben's face darkened for an instant as he heard Bat give his sister a direct order, but he turned and went in the house without a word. Glenda got up and went in after him.

"Little sister, you're drunk," Bat said. "I'm not your father, but—"

"Good. That's settled," said Jo-Ann. "I don't have a father. Don't try to play like you are my father."

She reached for the bottle of Scotch, but he jerked it away from her. "Our father is not that bad," he said. "Maybe the problem is you don't have any basis for comparison." She turned her face away from him and directed her attention to the sunset colors slowly fading on the ocean. He went on. "When I introduced you to Ben, I didn't expect you to start sleeping with him."

"You should appreciate him," she said dully. "You jerked the bottle away. Last night he slapped me and poured my drink in the toilet."

"He slapped you? Here? In this house? Last night?"

She nodded and glanced at him. "I had it coming."

"I doubt it," said Bat grimly.

"Don't interfere, big brother. He did it because he cares."

"Or so he says."

She shook her head. "He didn't say it. But why else? What difference to him if I get schnocked? Unless—"

"Do you think nobody else cares about you?"

"Nevada did," she said quietly. "I guess maybe you do, in your way. Jonas? Monica?" She shook her head.

"You're too ready to feel sorry for yourself," said Bat. "You're twenty-one years old. Our father has settled a generous allowance on you—"

"Generous? Is it?"

"It's as much as I'm paid as a salary," said Bat. "It's exactly the same."

"Well, tell me something, big brother. Would you accept an allowance from Jonas? He made you vice president of Cord Hotels, then president. You're supposed to *earn* your money. Would you accept it otherwise?"

Bat stared hard at her for a moment, before he understood and could respond. "All right. No, I wouldn't."

"Well, I have to. He won't make *me* a president of anything. So I have to take his charity."

"He's a generous man, and he loves you."

"If you think so. On both scores. I don't think he's capable of either generosity or love."

"You're wrong. Anyway . . . You want a job? Is that the point?"

"I want somebody to think I could *do* a job," she said.

"I'll see what I can do. Now. Ben Parrish—"

"Why did you introduce me to him?" Jo-Ann asked.

"I thought—"

"If I marry him, you and Jonas both can go to hell."

6

Three hours later Bat and Glenda lay in bed together. Her hair was not sprayed and spread softly over his shoulder. She was in a sleepy, dreamy mood.

"Jo-Ann . . . and Ben Parrish," she said quietly. "I can't believe it."

"It was the Scotch talking," he said. "She couldn't be thinking of marrying him."

"She had some more. Wine and Scotch. And *he* wasn't in good shape when they went to bed."

"Be lucky if they don't decide to go swimming in the purple dawn and drown."

"Water's too cold to drown in," said Glenda. "When he wades out deep enough for the water to reach his balls, he'll run back to the beach."

When the bedroom was dark, as it was now, Bat touched the switch that drew back the drapes. From the bed they could see the ocean and tonight could see stars in an unusually clear sky, and could see the odd luminescence of the breaking waves.

Glenda sighed. "The ocean is beautiful," she said. "But I can remember being afraid of it. When I was twenty years old I lived in an apartment with a girlfriend, on Nineteenth Avenue in Bensonhurst. I was working clubs, and I'd come home at night, and out there, just a little distance away, was the ocean. And out there . . . Who could tell? Fifty or sixty feet below the surface and only a mile away, maybe a Nazi submarine. Maybe a whole wolf pack of them. An armed force . . . of the people who wanted to kill you. I suppose it wasn't realistic. But the Nazis weren't so far away, you see. And if you were a Jew—"

Bat interrupted her with a kiss. "Honey baby," he said softly. "If any Nazis come ashore— There's a pistol in the nightstand."

She sighed again, a noisy exhalation. "You protect Golda?" she asked in the voice of a child.

He brushed back her soft blond hair and kissed her again. "Of course I will, honey baby," he whispered.

"Uhmm . . . You don't want to call me Golda, do you?"

"I think of you as Glenda."

"Golda Graustein. And Golda Graustein loves Bat Cord. It promises disaster. Golda Graustein, the daughter of Rabbi Mordecai Graustein, is in love with the son of Jonas Cord, the grandson of Jonas Cord. Love has never brought me anything but . . . ill fortune. It's never brought me anything but hurt. I'm hesitant to confess it, for fear it will drive you away."

"Golda—"

"No. You must call me something else. Not Glenda, either. I'm somebody else! Call me *Christy!* What could be more Christian?"

"Who asked you to be a Christian?"

"But—"

"No, Golda. I don't ask you to be anything but what you are. Hell, I'm what I am, and some people

think that's not so great. Golda . . . Golda . . . Hey, I
love you, Golda. You love me— Well . . . I love you,
too. C'mere . . . Christy, my achin' ass!"

7

Sponsorship and a network spot were the first big
problems for the *Glenda Grayson Show*. Cord Productions filmed a pilot program on the Cord soundstages
in March 1955, using the format and plot Bat had
suggested to his father when he first told him about
the idea.

Plot— A *Glenda Grayson Show* is in rehearsal in a
Broadway studio. The guest star is to be Danny Kaye,
but three days before the broadcast he is taken to the
hospital for an emergency appendectomy. Glenda's
predicament comes to the attention of her fellow
nightclub performer Liberace, who rushes in to help
her. At home Glenda faces a personal crisis in the life
of her daughter Tess, played by Margit Little. Tess's
prom date has announced he has been grounded for
knocking a fender off his father's car. Glenda's call to
the angry father doesn't help. Glenda consoles Tess by
letting her do something she has always wanted to
do—appear on the *Glenda Grayson Show*. Tess
dances a solo number to the music of Liberace, then
joins her mother to dance in the finale. The date calls
to tell Tess his father saw her on television and is so
impressed by the idea of his son going to the prom
with a television star that he has relented.

"A catalog of venerable showbiz clichés," Jonas
grunted. "Probably be a big success."

Glenda appeared in a variation on her signature
costume, that is in a black body stocking under a lace-

trimmed black corselette, with the black fedora atilt over her forehead. On that show she used for the last time her line *"Change your name, Golda. Please!"* It was worn out now, and she would not use it again.

Sam Stein took a print of the show to New York and offered it to a score of prospective sponsors. They liked it, but— Combining situation comedy with a variety show was a bold idea, and they were not sure audiences would like it. Glenda Grayson was too . . . Well, *sophisticated* for television audiences. ("Y' know, this gets beamed into people's *living rooms.*") Her costume looked too much like underwear, even though the body stocking covered everything. Anyway, no one had ever appeared on television in a body stocking. Margit Little's leotards rode too high on her hips. One of the lines suggested she had been *intimate* with this boy she was dating. Some of Glenda's lines *could* be understood two ways. Too many shows were set in New York. Would people buy a refrigerator Glenda Grayson recommended—any more than they would buy one Sophie Tucker recommended? American housewives would not identify with Glenda Grayson.

And so on.

Without a sponsor, none of the networks could commit a time slot. When Bat returned to California from Northampton, Sam had not yet found a sponsor.

8

Jonas picked up a bottle of bourbon from the rolltop desk in his office—his father's office—in the Cord Explosives plant. He poured into a shot glass, then handed the bottle and a glass to Bat. Bat took a splash, no more; he did not share his grandfather's and father's taste for bourbon.

"We could back off, take the loss, and forget it," Jonas said. He flipped over the pages on which Bat had brought him the numbers. "I've lost more than this on dumb ideas."

"It's not a dumb idea," said Bat.

"Depends on how you define a dumb idea. If an idea is supposed to make money and then can't, it's a dumb idea—by one definition, anyway. The other definition is, it's too damned *good* an idea, too good for the market. I don't know which this is, Bat. Maybe you misjudged it. The fact that you're screwin' the star hasn't influenced your judgment, has it?"

"Absolutely not."

"Okay. I take your word on it. But be damned sure it doesn't."

"Liberace is a good showman, whatever else you may think of him. He judged it was a good idea."

"Yeah, but he's been paid for his role. He doesn't have anything invested."

"Danny Kaye agreed to allow his name to be used on the first show," said Bat. "He's agreed to appear on a future show, if there is a future show."

"Another guy with nothing invested," said Jonas. "So what are you going to do?"

Bat shook his head. "I don't know," he admitted.

"Okay. I know. Your old man, who plunked seventeen million into the Pacific, as you politely reminded me, will bail you out."

"I can't ask *you* to pour more money into it."

"You can't? The hell you can't! If you believe in the project you can ask for more money. If you don't believe in it any more than that, then by God I don't believe in it either. Which is it?"

309

Bat stiffened. "I believe in it," he said. "But I don't know what we can do. If—"

"*I* know what we can do," said Jonas.

9

ABC broadcast *Cord Television Presents: The Glenda Grayson Show* for the first time in August 1955 as a summer special, filling a time slot that would be filled in the autumn by a returning variety show.

The notices were encouraging:

—"Miss Grayson's exuberant review was a happy relief from bland television variety shows." *The New York Times*.

—"The youthful cast, led by Glenda Grayson herself, went all out to offer an hour of exciting entertainment." *Newsweek*.

—"Nothing can rescue television's so-called 'situation comedies' from their hackneyed, overworked clichés, and *The Glenda Grayson Special* did not accomplish that impossible task. The variety segment of her show is something else again. Television variety may never be the same. Treacle is out! Sophistication is in! Or so we may hope."

The second show aired two weeks later, with Danny Kaye as guest. It drew twenty-two percent of the viewing audience.

A church in Mississippi published a "protest resolution," complaining that Glenda Grayson was indecent and a threat to the nation's morality. "What does it say to our young people when they see this woman cavorting on their television screens in clothing decent women wear *under* their clothing?" A few editorials laughed at that and won the show more public notice.

A third show was broadcast as a special in November. Two more specials were broadcast in the spring season 1956. The ratings were not spectacular but were not disastrous either. The network decided it had a time slot for the show.

For the 1956–57 season, ABC slotted the show at nine o'clock on alternate Wednesday evenings. American Motors came aboard as a co-sponsor, so the show was no longer *Cord Television Presents* but *The Glenda Grayson Show.*

10

The sun rose late in winter, so only a little gray light had entered the bedroom when the telephone rang. Glenda woke and stared at the ceiling as Bat took the call.

It was from Angie, calling from the Waldorf Towers apartment in New York.

"Your father has been taken to the hospital. I don't know if it was a stroke or a heart attack, but he was unconscious when they put him in the emergency-squad ambulance. I'm leaving here now to go to the hospital. I can't reach Jo-Ann. Try to do that, will you, Bat? Then I think you'd better come here."

Reaching Jo-Ann was a matter of knocking on her bedroom door. An hour and a half later the two of them were aboard a plane on their way to New York.

Jonas was in a cardiac unit at Columbia Presbyterian Hospital. Bat and Jo-Ann were allowed five minutes with him but found him so heavily sedated he could not talk. They found Angie waiting in a solarium. She said the cardiologist would talk with them and went to a telephone to call him. The doctor joined them in a coffee shop.

"He'll make it," the doctor said, "but he's lost about a third of his heart capacity. He'll have to take it easy from now on."

Bat smiled. "What chance do you think there is he will ever slow down?"

Angie shook her head. "He dictated a letter to you. He did it when he began to feel the symptoms and after I'd called an ambulance. I borrowed a typewriter here in the hospital and typed it out. It isn't signed, but it's what he wants, and I think you will be justified in acting on it."

The letter read:

It appears likely that I will be some time recovering from the flu. You will have to take on some additional responsibility for a while. That being the case, increase your salary to $125,000. Take it from Cord Explosives.

I authorize you to act as my surrogate in all corporate matters for such time as may be necessary. Don't overlook Cord Explosives or Cord Plastics. They are more secure sources of revenue than the airline, the hotels, or TV production.

You may require some assistance. See if you can get your friend David Amory to leave his firm and become full-time counsel to us—that is, if you want him. Having a lawyer you trust is very important.

You'll have to tend to business for a while. Consider living in New York. I urge you to come here alone. You know what I mean.

Give me complete reports as often as you can, as soon as I am able to receive them.

As Bat read the letter, he lowered his chin slowly to his chest, and his eyes flooded with tears.

11

Not until two days later was Jonas able to communicate in anything but an incoherent mumble. He smiled on Jo-Ann and Angie and thanked them for their concern, then said he wanted to talk with Bat alone, about business.

Bat drew a chair up to the bed. "I'm sorry about this," he said. "The doctor says you're going to be okay."

"Cut the shit and listen to me," said Jonas. "Lean over this way, so I don't have to yell. Now listen. Morris Chandler is talking to guys he shouldn't be talking to. Carlo Vulcano, Pietro Gibellina, and John Stefano."

"How do you know?"

"When I was living on the fifth floor, Chandler hooked me into his private telephone system. I didn't trust him, so I had my people rewire the whole system, unbeknownst to him. He routes his calls through a telephone drop in San Diego, so FBI types tapping those guys' phones won't figure it out they're talking to a hotel in Vegas. Of course, they never use names. They talk in codes. Chandler's code name is Maurie. Nevada called him that, so it's got some kind of meaning."

"What do you think they're doing?"

"They want to block us from putting up the Inter-Continental Vegas. They don't want the competition. They want to use the casinos their way, and we're an embarrassment to them."

"What do you think they'll do?"

"Give us trouble getting building permits. See if

they can arrange some strikes. Who knows? I don't think they'll try violence. Do you carry a gun?"

Bat shook his head.

"Well, I have for many years, on and off. I suggest you think about it."

"What do you think they'll do?"

20

1

THE SECOND WEEK AFTER JONAS SUFFERED HIS HEART attack, Sonja flew to New York. Bat met her at Kennedy Airport and took her to the apartment in the Waldorf Towers. She went the next day to visit Jonas at Columbia Presbyterian Hospital.

Bat offered to drive her, but she insisted she would take a cab. She wanted to do some shopping, too, and would meet him for lunch at the 21 Club at one-fifteen. Her first cab driver, a Puerto Rican, took a sympathetic interest in her when she spoke Spanish to him and suggested she remove a diamond ring and an emerald bracelet she was wearing and carry them in her purse. She thanked him for his advice and did what he said. He could not have guessed she was wearing a jeweled platinum belt worth more than the combined value of the ring and bracelet, plus his taxicab.

Jonas was grateful to her for coming. He was sitting up now, propped up by pillows and the mechanical bed. He was thinner already and looked a bit fragile. He had a better color, just the same. Maybe that was because this was the first time since his hospitalization after the crash of *The Centurion* that he had gone twelve whole days without a drink.

He was in a mood to speak earnestly, driven undoubtedly by his brush with mortality. "Do you have any idea how grateful I am to you for rearing our son to be the man he is?" he asked her. "Here I am, out of it. Bat is a godsend for me. Who else could I trust to take responsibility for everything?"

"You have a loyal staff," she said.

"They are not Cords," said Jonas with a tone of finality in his voice that suggested that was a complete answer.

"He *is*," she said. "I can see that."

"But Sonja . . . He doesn't like me. Why doesn't he like me?"

"Because the two of you are of a piece," she said sharply. "Both of you ought to see that."

"Christ, I've offered him the *world!* I've given him . . ." He stopped, shrugged.

Sonja nodded and did not comment. She was trying to assess the damage this man had sustained. Her memories of him were—first, of the twenty-one-year-old stud she had accompanied to Europe: handsome, muscular, filled with optimism and enthusiasm; and, second, the matured and self-confident entrepreneur she had met for the second time four years ago. He was fifty-two years old now, young to have suffered a heart attack. It was apparent that he knew it. He had planned at least twenty more vigorous years, without limitations, and now he had to reassess his plans.

"I would like to ask a favor of you," he said.

"Of course," said Sonja.

"Your Uncle Fulgencio knows my name. On Bat's recommendation, I have invested money in a casino in Havana. I depend on a man your uncle also knows to keep the operation honest."

"Meyer Lansky," she said.

"You know— Well . . . It would be in everyone's best interest—Uncle Fulgencio's, Bat's, and mine—if your uncle were to look sympathetically on an application Meyer Lansky will be making for a license to open a casino-hotel in Havana. He will adhere to the customs, if you follow my meaning."

"He will pay my uncle such bribes as are customary," Sonja said dryly.

"Whatever is customary," said Jonas.

"Will you have money in this?"

"Bat will make that judgment," said Jonas.

"You're letting Bat make judgments? That's something new, isn't it?"

Jonas shrugged weakly. "What else can I do? Anyway, he's smart. He's a Cord . . . and a Batista, of course."

"Do you want a word of advice?" she asked.

"Why not?"

"Invest a little more in your relationship with your son. It will pay a better return than any other investment you ever made."

"I *do*. I let him have his head on that television show. I put money where I shouldn't have put it. We'll be damned lucky if we break even on it."

"I'm not talking about money, Jonas. Investing money is your whole life. It's what you *do*, and you do it well. What you don't do is invest *yourself*. You don't commit yourself. Do you love our son?"

"Of course I do."

"Then why don't you tell him?"

"He's never said anything of the kind—" He stopped abruptly, and for a moment Sonja thought he'd felt a hard twinge in his chest. "—to me . . ." His voice trailed off, and Sonja was alarmed.

"Jonas?"

317

"It isn't easy. My father died without ever having said he loved me. He never heard it from me either. He died, and we never . . . told . . . each other. That was a huge mistake, Sonja, a horrible mistake. My god, am I making it again?"

"You have pride, Jonas. So has Bat. I could wish you were not so very much alike."

2

Sonja surprised Bat at "21" by ordering steak tartare. "They know how to do it here," she said.

"You've been here before, then."

"Did you suppose I had never been to New York before?" she asked with an amused smile.

Of course she had been in New York before. He should have remembered that. She had been in Europe, too, and not just when his father took her there. She had been in Cuba and most of the countries of Latin America. She had decorated two rooms in the hacienda outside Córdoba with pre-Columbian artifacts from Peru. Hanging in her own bedroom, instead of the crucifix that hung in the bedrooms of most dutiful wives, was a print by Picasso and a Calder mobile. She was no longer the innocent girl his father remembered. In fact, she was not the placid, compliant woman he thought he remembered as his mother. He should have thought before of being proud of her.

At age fifty, she was a memorably striking woman, who drew glances from men at nearby tables. His father had a taste for women who were beautiful when they were young and then aged well. Though he found it difficult to like Monica much, he could see why his father had married her twice. And the latest of them,

Angie, was a fit successor to the two others he knew about.

His mother had ordered an appetizer of caviar, with Stolichnaya vodka so cold that it was not absolutely liquid but had begun to change consistency to something thicker. He had never tried it but had duplicated her order and found it surprisingly good.

"Your father tells me you are having an affair with Glenda Grayson."

"That's true."

"She's older than you are."

"She's a wonderful woman. The world has not always been kind to her."

Sonja shook her head. "That is a very bad reason to fall in love with a woman."

"She's very outgoing, very loving."

"Worse reasons," said Sonja. But then she smiled. "I thought you meant to marry the little girl from Florida."

"She wants a career."

"And Glenda Grayson does not? If you should decide to marry her, which God forbid, would she give up her career and become a wife?"

"Things haven't come to that state yet," said Bat.

Sonja glanced around the room, as if to make sure their fellow diners could not overhear their conversation. "I need to talk with you about something. How much money have you and your father committed to Cuba?"

Bat, too, glanced around before he answered. He leaned a little toward his mother and said, "A little over a million dollars. In the Floresta casino."

"What about the hotel being built by Meyer Lansky? Don't you have money in that?"

"So far, we don't have any money in that. Lansky has secured financing through others. He'd like for us to buy out one of his partners. It would give him more respectability."

"Your father asked me to contact our Uncle Fulgencio and ask him to be certain Lansky gets all the necessary licenses and permissions."

"That might be helpful," said Bat. "Lansky has a good relationship with Uncle Fulgencio, but I'm not sure it's good enough."

Sonja took a sip of the icy vodka. "I will fly to Havana on my way back to Mexico," she said. "I am going to tell you something, however. I'll put in a good word for your friend Lansky. I strongly advise you, even so, not to invest any more money in Cuba."

"Why?"

"You'll lose it."

Bat touched his mouth with one finger. "You take seriously the—"

She nodded. "The whole thing is a house of cards. Our uncle may be dead in a year. If he's lucky, he'll be in exile. He is not bright. He steals too much. Cuba looks brilliantly prosperous. It isn't. A few miles from those beautiful new casino-hotels, people live in squalor. The rebels in the mountains are growing stronger. More of them all the time. And they're getting weapons from the Soviet Union. Our uncle's regime—" She shrugged. "He was driven from power before. It can happen again. It *will* happen again."

"Meyer Lansky has committed every dime he has to his hotel."

"He will lose it."

"The new regime, whatever it is, will need the casino-hotels just as much as the present regime does," said Bat. "And they can't run them themselves."

"The British thought the Egyptians couldn't run the Suez Canal," she said. "Anyway, they will close the casinos. Those people in the mountains are Communists. They don't want the tourist trade."

"You paint a gloomy picture," said Bat.

"It's a gloomy situation," said his mother.

Bat watched the waiter stir raw eggs and herbs into the raw ground beef. He wished he had ordered steak tartare.

"Tell me about your father," she said.

Bat sighed. "It's difficult to know what to say. One day he's a thoughtless egomaniacal tyrant, scornful of anything I suggest; the next day he promotes me and increases my compensation. You know— He's clever as hell. Little by little, he's drawn me within his orbit. It's a game. When he gets me to where I'm seriously thinking of chucking the whole thing, he makes a concession. He doesn't make them short of that. The longer I stay, the more difficult it is to tell him to go to hell and walk out."

"Do you have any personal feeling for him at all?" she asked.

"Uh . . . Well, he can be— He's a *man*. I don't know if you can understand what I mean by that."

"Do you think he has any personal feeling for you?"

Bat shrugged, then nodded. "Yes. I know he does. But do you know why? He's afraid. And what's he afraid of? Not of dying, not any more than any other man is afraid of dying. No, what Jonas is afraid of is that he'll die and everything he's spent his life building will fall into the hands of strangers. He thinks of himself as a king, and he wants the kingdom to survive him in the hands of— In the hands of a son."

"And that's all it amounts to, you think?"

"I don't know," he admitted quietly.

"You may be right," she said. "I'd think about it if I were you. There is something about you that is very much like him. You are a very generous man, except of yourself. You don't *give* of yourself. You're afraid to commit yourself. *That's* your Cord inheritance. That's an inheritance you've already got. You don't have to wait for him to die to inherit that."

3

Invitations to attend the grand opening of Meyer Lansky's Riviera Hotel were sent to Jonas and Bat. Jonas was not sufficiently recovered to make the flight from New York to Havana; but Bat flew from Los Angeles, taking Glenda with him, explaining to curious reporters—and through them to Toni—that his star might do a show at the Riviera between television seasons.

The Riviera was the paradigm of new casino-hotels. It was a turquoise-colored high-rise building in the shape of a curved Y, and every room had a view of the sea. Inside, it was more gaudy than tasteful; the effect was in fact overwhelming; guests were submerged in bright modernistic decor. The casino was in a golden dome outside the hotel.

Meyer Lansky personally welcomed Bat and Glenda. He escorted them to their suite, where he handed them tickets to the grand opening show in the Copa Room and told them they would be seated at his table.

They dressed for dinner: Bat in black tie, Glenda in a black gown glittering with gold sequins. They left their room early enough so they could look around a little before they went to the Copa Room. Bat was especially interested in seeing what the casino looked like. He liked what he saw. Jackets and ties were required of men. About half the players wore black tie. The big room was quiet except for the hushed calls of the croupiers and dealers. It was obvious that big money was at stake on the tables.

When they left the casino, Bat and Glenda stepped outside for a breath of the gentle tropical air, warm and heavy with moisture and the odors of tropical flowers. The strident beat of cacophonous Latin music drifted to the Riviera from a club not far away. Then suddenly a jarring sound came to their ears: the sharp, harsh crack of gunfire, followed by the signature rip of an automatic weapon. The firing lasted about ten seconds, then the night was quiet again except for the persistent music.

"What do you suppose that was?" Glenda asked.

"The *policía* are gun-happy," said Bat. "They're nervous."

They went to the Copa Room. Meyer Lansky was at his table. He introduced Glenda and Bat to the man who would be their dinner companion, Vincent "Jimmy Blue Eyes" Alo. Bat knew that Jimmy Blue Eyes was a partner in the Riviera. He was not the man Meyer Lansky hoped the Cords would buy out.

It was Lansky's theory that a good casino had to have a good kitchen. His official position in the hotel was director of food-service operations; and though that was only a front, he did take a personal interest in the kitchen, the preparation of food, and the way it was served.

President Fulgencio Batista arrived. He paused on his way to his table to salute Meyer Lansky, and when he saw Bat he came across the room with his hand outstretched. "*¡Sobrino!*" he said—nephew. "*¡Jonas Enrique Raul! ¡Bienvenida!*"

"*¿Puedo presentar a la Señorita Glenda Grayson?*" said Bat.

"Es una muchacha bonita," said Batista—She is a beautiful girl. Then with a sly smile he asked, *"¿Es ella su hija?"*—Is she your daughter?

Glenda understood nothing of the exchange and looked puzzled.

"I am very pleased to meet you, Miss Grayson," said Batista in English. "I know your name well. We receive American television in Havana. You would do well, Meyer, to book Miss Grayson to star in a show here in the Riviera."

"Yes. I mean to discuss just that with her this evening," said Lansky.

The star of the opening show was Ginger Rogers. Lansky told them that Abbott and Costello would play the Copa Room soon. Other major stars were being booked. He would indeed like to arrange an appearance by Glenda Grayson.

When the show was over, Glenda said she would be happy to put her agent in contact with Meyer Lansky. She said she had never seen a nightclub show so elaborately and expensively staged.

4

Lansky was ebullient when he accompanied Bat and Glenda to their suite after the show. They were trailed by waiters wheeling carts laden with champagne on ice, caviar, lobster salad, coffee, and Danish. Billy Blue Eyes Alo came, too, attracted by Glenda even though he knew he did not dare touch her.

"You see?" he said to Bat. "It is how a casino should be run."

Bat nodded. "And you'd like for us to put some money in it, hmm?"

Lansky grinned. "Only if you see in it the very great

likelihood of very great profit. I'm asking you to invest, not to shoot money into a speculation."

"Meyer . . ." said Bat. "Let's step out on the balcony. I'd like to talk with you alone."

From the balcony, twenty floors above the street, they had a view of the Straits of Florida—"You can almost see across," said Lansky—and of a part of Havana. The city was alive. President Batista had put out an invitation for everyone in the world to come to Havana; there was no limit to what they could enjoy there—the most honest casinos, the most luxurious tropical hotels, the most spectacular shows, the finest food, the youngest but most wanton whores, music, dancing, everything to amuse and arouse. (In one show room a man called The Giant laid out twelve silver dollars edge-to-edge on a table, then laid his penis on them to demonstrate that he could cover all twelve.) From the balcony, the vitality of the city's nightlife was evident. At midnight, traffic was heavy, as music floated up on the warm, scented air, as did the sound of laughter, somehow carried over a long distance.

"Meyer—"

And then they heard a random burst of gunfire, just as Bat and Glenda had heard it earlier.

"Do you know what that is, Meyer?"

"The police," said Lansky. "They're too quick to use their guns, but they fire in the air almost always."

Bat shook his head. "No," he said somberly. "That is the sound of war. Civil war. The rebels from the mountains. You are going to hear a great deal more of it."

Lansky turned his eyes away from Bat and out across the city. "Batista will take care of that. When he turns the army loose—"

"The army is already loose, and they can't stop it."

Lansky drew a deep breath. "You are saying you won't invest here."

"More than that," said Bat. "I am advising you to save what you can and get out."

"You have to be crazy. Everything I have in this world is tied up in the Riviera. Look at it! The world's finest casino-hotel . . . *The world's finest!*"

"Meyer, I know I can trust you," said Bat. "You can guess the source of my information. My suggestion to you is to bail out as much as you can."

Lansky shook his head. "No. No," he said. "I'm a professional gambler. I should have known better than to bet everything on one throw, but I did. I have to believe you're wrong."

"Fine," said Bat. "I hope I am, too."

"You've spoiled my evening," said Lansky dolefully.

5

As soon as Meyer Lansky and Jimmy Blue Eyes Alo left the suite, Bat turned off the lights and pulled back the drapes. Moonlight off the ocean, plus the warm orangish glow of the city, gave the room plenty of light for anything but reading.

As he stood for a brief moment looking at the ocean, he felt Glenda pressing against him from behind. He reached back, touched her, and was not surprised to feel that she was already naked. As he turned, she grinned impishly and handed him two lengths of coarse hempen rope.

"Where'd that come from?" he asked, laughing.

"I packed it, of course," she said.

"All right. Turn around."

She turned and offered her hands behind her back.

He tied her wrists together with tight hard knots. He tied the second length of rope around her chest, just under her breasts, to pinion her arms at her sides. She went into the bedroom and sat down on the bed. "Hurry," she murmured as he began to undress.

The rope had been her idea. At first, he had been reluctant to bind her, especially to pull the ropes and knots so tight she could not possibly escape, but she insisted that he must bind her not just symbolically but rigorously. He had to admit the effect was powerfully erotic, stimulating to both of them.

With her hands bound behind her, she could not lie on her back. So they coupled the way she enjoyed better than any other: she atop him and astride, her hips writhing. She loved doing it that way, whether she was bound or not. It put him in her deeper than any other way, and it made possible a greater variety of movements. Twice she lost her balance and started to topple off him. With her hands and arms bound she couldn't stop herself. Expecting this, because it had happened many times before, he reached up quickly to brace her. Each time she laughed.

She closed her eyes and wore a contented smile as she worked. She gasped and moaned, and he knew she had reached a climax. Then she reached a second one and maybe a third; he wasn't sure.

"Ready to come, lover?" she asked finally.

"Any time," he said.

He put his hands on her hips to steady her, and she began more vigorous thrusts, forcing him deeper and deeper into her and squeezing him almost painfully. His orgasm was powerful, enervating.

She lifted herself, then rose and walked out to the living room. Bat remained on the bed, satiated and exhausted. From where he lay he watched Glenda use an elbow to shove the sliding glass door open. She

stepped out onto the balcony and stood staring mood-
ily at the ocean—confident apparently that no one
could see her, though he was not so sure. Maybe the
idea that she could be seen occurred to her, because
she turned abruptly and hurried back into the room.

"Bat—"

"What, baby?" he asked, still not rising.

She came to stand in the bedroom door. "What's
going to become of us?"

"What do you have in mind?"

"For god's sake, if I have to tell you—"

"I don't know, Glenda," he interrupted. He rolled
off the bed and stepped toward her, meaning to untie
her.

She turned and walked back to the open sliding
door. "There's nothing for us, is there? In the long
run." She stared out over the moonlit sea. "I mean,
anything permanent. We fuck. We fuck good. But
that's all there is. Right? We say we love each other,
but—"

"Glenda—"

"You wouldn't want me to bear a child for you,
would you?"

"Are you telling me you're pregnant?" he asked.

"No. I've never been pregnant. I'm not going to get
pregnant. I can't afford to be pregnant. I don't want to
carry a bastard."

"My mother did."

"Oh, I'm sorry, Bat. Bad choice of words. I am
truly sorry. But—"

He began to untie her.

"The whole deal," she said quietly, "is that we
don't have any future. The biggest reason is, your
father—"

"My father has nothing to do with—"

"No? Your father doesn't like me. Oh, I'm fine as a

cash cow, but he wouldn't want his son to marry one."

"My father doesn't control my personal life!"

"The hell he doesn't."

6

The smell of cigar smoke wakened them. Bat woke first, but before he said a word, Glenda woke, too. Cigar smoke. Coming in through the air-conditioning vents? No. It was fresh and pungent. Someone was in the suite.

Actually, someone was in the bedroom. Bat first spotted the point of fire on the tip of the cigar. Then he saw the man, first as a shadow and then, as his eyes focused, distinctly.

Bat almost never suffered nightmares, and when he did there were just two. In the first he was running across the Ludendorff Bridge and was hit in the lower chest. In the second he awoke to find an intruder staring at him. This was that one, but it was no dream; it was real.

The man was sitting on a chair facing their bed. He was dressed in an open-collared pleated white shirt and nondescript trousers. An automatic pistol in its holster hung from a wide web belt. The man himself was anything but prepossessing. He wore a scraggly dark beard, as if he were not old enough to grow a solid beard but had let whiskers grow out where they would. He puffed with an air of thoughtfulness on his oversized cigar.

"You have not to worry, *señor, señorita,*" he said. "I come to do you no harm." His English was Spanish-accented.

"Then why are you here?" Bat asked as he drew

himself up in bed. He spoke Spanish. "And who are you?"

"I am nobody, *señor*. That is the point. And that is why I am here."

"You'll have to explain that."

"You are Señor Jonas Enrique Raul Cord y Batista," the man said. "The *señorita* is Glenda Grayson, the famous American television star. 'Cord y Batista.' You are the grand-nephew of our dictator. You have come to Havana to gather facts and to advise your father whether or not your family should invest more money in Cuba and in the Batista regime."

"You know a great deal," said Bat.

The man nodded. "It is essential to know everything," he said. "That is how wars are won."

"But—"

The man raised his hand. "The purpose of my visit is to demonstrate to you how very shaky the Batista regime is. You know we kidnapped a famous American racing driver?"

"Yes."

"And we released him unharmed. Our only purpose was to demonstrate to the world that this corrupt regime cannot protect Americans who come to Cuba."

"So, are we kidnapped?"

"No, no. We simply wanted you to see that the vaunted Batista secret police cannot even surround you with protection in a luxury suite in the Riviera Hotel. We have no interest in harming you, certainly not to murder you. But I could have done it, you see."

"It is your . . . recommendation, then, that we not invest in this hotel," said Bat.

"That is my suggestion, Señor Cord. If you do,

you will not be in danger. But you will lose your money."

"Suppose you take control of the country," said Bat. "This hotel will still be an important asset. Surely—"

"Batista has attempted to turn Cuba into the whorehouse of the Western Hemisphere," said the man, raising his voice. "Every kind of criminal is welcomed to Havana. The dignity of the nation and of its people has been sacrificed. We will restore our national honor, even at the sacrifice of the money these places bring."

"You are Marxists," said Bat.

"Our struggle is the people's struggle," the man said.

"Well . . . You have delivered your message. Now?"

The man rose from the chair. He shrugged. "You are right. I leave now. I— Oh. Incidentally, feel free to call hotel security as soon as I am out the door. They will not catch me, and that will be additional evidence of what I have been telling you."

Bat shook his head. "You are an interesting man, Señor . . . ?"

"Guevara," the man said. "Ernesto Guevara. I am more often known as Che Guevara."

21

1

WHEN JONAS WAS RELEASED FROM THE HOSPITAL HE went to the apartment in the Waldorf Towers. After two weeks there he called for an Inter-Continental plane and flew to the ranch in Nevada. He stayed there a week, then moved again into the fifth-floor suite at The Seven Voyages. Angie was with him all the time.

When Bat arrived, Jonas sat in the living room of the suite, surrounded by heaps of files. Clint McClintock and Bill Shaw were with him. Shaw, the former test pilot for the Air Force, had flown him from New York and had a Beech Baron waiting at the airport to take Jonas anywhere he wanted to go.

"You're looking good," Bat said to his father. "Like you're making a fast recovery."

Jonas looked comfortable in a dark-blue polo shirt and khaki slacks. "I'm drinkin' a little, again. Fuckin' a little, again," he said. "They want to keep me on a short leash." He shook his head. "Rather chuck it."

"I think you have other alternatives," said Bat.

"Well, anyway, sit down. What did you tell Lansky?"

"I told him no. My mother put the word in with the President, to help him get his licenses. I'm not at all sure he needed help, but he got it. But I said no to investing any more money in Cuba. My mother thinks her uncle is riding for a fall, and from what I observed in Havana I have to agree with her."

"Lansky's been trying to reach me on the phone, so I figured you'd said no to him."

"He wants you to overrule me."

Jonas nodded. "You've bet your ass on this one, my boy. You may have said no to a damned profitable venture. But I'm not going to overrule you."

"Why not, if you want to?"

Jonas ignored that. "On the whole," he said, "I like the architect's design for the InterContinental Vegas Hotel. But I don't think you've got the slot-machine arcade placed right. The people who play the slots are small-timers. We don't want them walking around in the casino just to gawk. Put the arcade near an outside door, so they can come in and play the slots without even entering the rest of the hotel. Also, the plan shows the arcade with windows. No windows, none in the casino, none in the arcade. The idea is for players to forget what time it is, which they won't do if they see the light changing outside."

"Okay," said Bat.

"I've been going over a lot of stuff," Jonas went on. "I see you haven't restructured the business. I wondered if I might come back and find my name wasn't on the letterhead anymore."

"Oh, sure," said Bat.

"You really think we ought to quit making TV sets? You never give up on that, do you?"

"I've given you my reasons."

"Yeah. Well, you've got me by the short hairs. Okay. Phase it out. *Your* job. *Phase* us out, so we don't look like we've been beat. Also, you're saying we ought to quit making airplanes."

"You're a pilot," said Bat. "Would you fly a Cord 50?"

"It's a good little plane. For a trainer."

"So's a Piper," said Bat. "So's a Cessna 150. And the Beech. Look at the sales numbers."

"What do you want me to do, give up Inter-Continental Airlines, too?"

"Hell, no. Inter-Continental is competitive. It holds its market share very nicely on its routes. It's a prestige property. Maybe someday we'll want to sell it. If we do, we'll get a big piece of cash for it—or a strong position in the stock of the buyer airline."

"Why would you ever want to sell it, for Christ's sake? Am I going to have *anything* left?"

"The airline business is going the way of automobile manufacturing," said Bat. "The trend is to fewer and fewer companies. Only the really big operators will be able to survive. But that's years down the pike."

"I can hear the wheels going around in your head," said Jonas. "Okay. So no Cord TVs, no Cord airplanes. But *phase* them out, not too fast. We don't want it to look like we gave up on something or were forced out. What else?"

"I think we ought to consolidate Cord Explosives and Cord Plastics. They're the same kind of business: chemicals. I don't see the point in keeping two sets of management on the payroll, two sets of accountants, two sets of lawyers, and so on."

"I'm damned if you're not telling me I haven't run things very efficiently!"

"I'm not telling you that," said Bat. "It's for you to decide if you have or haven't. I do have another suggestion, though. Cord Explosives. I think there's some disadvantage in calling the parent company of all the other enterprises by the name Explosives. In some quarters it brings a negative reaction. I suggest we give it a new name: Cord Explosives Division of Cord Enterprises. Then Cord Plastics and Cord Productions and Cord Hotels are also divisions of Cord Enterprises."

"You didn't restructure, but you were sure as hell thinking about it," said Jonas ruefully.

"Also," said Bat, "I recommend we call Cord Enterprises CE and design a distinctive company logo for it. General Electric is GE, International Business Machines is IBM, Trans World Airlines is TWA, and so forth."

"My father is spinning in his grave," said Jonas.

"If he were alive, he'd do things like this," said Bat.

"If he were alive he'd be in a rest home," said Jonas.

"They're not such big changes. They don't threaten your control."

"Okay, then," said Jonas. "Make your changes. I'll make you vice president and a director of this CE, which will be the parent company, as you say. I want frequent and detailed reports. I'm going to stay here and run Cord Hotels myself. I'm going to see to it that the InterContinental Vegas gets built. Also, I'm going to ride herd on that son of a bitch Chandler. He's getting a little independent."

"He keeps bad company," said Bat.

"Doesn't he? Listen, is your lawyer friend Amory coming aboard? We'll need a corporate lawyer to make these changes."

"What about Phil Wallace?"

"Phil Wallace is my personal attorney, though he's handled a lot of company business. Dave Amory will be general counsel to Cord Enterprises. That is, he will if you think he's good enough."

"He's good enough."

"Then that's settled. He should be in New York, which is where you should be. Why'd you take our TV star with you to Havana? She that good a lay?"

"She and I—"

"Yeah. But if she's around too much when things are happening, she'll get to know too much about our business. I don't want her to know anything. From a lifetime's experience, I tell you: Keep your business life and your sex life separate. Okay?"

"What if I told you I might marry her?"

"I'd think you'd lost your mind," Jonas said, total scorn in his voice. "Like your sister. She says she might marry that bum Parrish. I tried to talk her into going into a drying-out clinic, and she won't do it. Hey! I can't cover all these bases. Use the kind of smarts in your personal life that you do in business."

"What Jo-Ann needs is a job," said Bat. "She doesn't want to live on an allowance. She needs responsibility . . . and purpose. I'd like to give her a job with Cord Productions, say in advertising or maybe public relations."

"No," said Jonas. "Not if she marries Parrish. Not until she dries out."

Bat shrugged. "You're the boss," he said.

Jonas looked away from Bat for a moment, stared at the window where the telescope still stood on its tripod. "Don't you even *think* of marrying that bitch," he said. "You've told me not to meddle in your personal life, but a man's judgment about his personal affairs reflects on his judgment in business affairs. Are you telling me you're *infatuated* with Glenda Grayson?"

"You asked if she's a good lay. I'm gonna tell you, she's a *hell* of a lay."

"Let me tell *you* something," said Jonas. "In my

time I've humped a lot of women. I've had children by two of them, just two. And let me tell you, neither of them was a woman I'd have had to be ashamed of. Your mother is a fine woman. Monica is, too, in her way. If you married Glenda Grayson, or if she became the mother of a child by you, you'd be *ashamed* of her sooner or later, embarrassed to have your business associates and your personal friends meet her. She was a goddamned stripteaser, Bat! She's *coarse!"*

"Okay, okay. You've made your point," Bat muttered resentfully.

"Anyway, how could you do anything like that to the smart, beautiful little girl in Washington? Use your fuckin' brains, Bat!"

2

"You know what he said to me? 'You're the boss.' I just make the boy vice president of the main company, and when he disagrees about something, he just shrugs at me and says, 'You're the boss.'"

"Why does that offend you?" asked Angie.

Jonas was supposed to take an hour's rest in the afternoon. The doctor said that meant taking off his clothes and going to bed. Usually, Angie joined him. Usually, she could distract him from the racing thoughts that monopolized his mind and denied him the rest he was supposed to be getting. Right now she lay beside him, gently massaging his penis and scrotum, hoping he might relax and maybe even go to sleep.

"I don't know," he said in a voice that suggested maybe he was beginning to relax. "Damnit, I—I didn't think he'd get hostile if I overruled him on something. My god, I'd accepted all kinds of big changes he wanted to make; and when I said no to one thing, to just one goddamned thing, he shrugged me off, telling me I'm the boss. *Of course* I'm the boss. What the hell did he think?"

"Maybe it was because it was about a personal thing, his newfound sister."

"I want the boy to be a success. I want him to be ready to take over when the time comes. But *not yet.*"

"Just how big a success do you want him to be?" asked Angie.

"What do you mean?"

"I'm going to suggest how big," she said. "Big—but not quite as big as you. Right?"

Jonas kept silent for a quarter of a minute. "You're like Bat," he said then. "You're too damned smart for your own good."

3

"I was warned," said Bat to Glenda. "People told me I'd become his errand boy."

"Damned highly paid errand boy, I'd say," Glenda commented.

They were in bed at the beach house.

"I'm like a dog on a leash. I can run out a certain distance; and then, whenever he wants to, he jerks me back. I won't be your producer anymore, incidentally. He dropped that one on me this afternoon."

"You won't? Who will be?"

"I don't know yet. I don't know if it's my call or his. I'll be executive producer but I won't be in charge of day-to-day operations. I'm going to have to spend a lot more time in New York."

"In other words, I won't be seeing you so much anymore."

"I'll come to LA as often as I can. And you can come to New York."

"Not until a season of shows is in the can," she said.

"Well, I'll get out here. Often. It's just that we won't be together every day."

"Every *night,*" she said quietly. "You won't need the beach house anymore. I can—"

"Of course I need the beach house. *We* need the beach house."

"So the old man's going to have his way, after all," she said dully.

"What makes you say that?"

"You've got to go to New York. I've got to stay in California. He seems to be arranging things so as to keep us apart."

"I'm my own man," said Bat grimly.

"Sure you are," she sneered.

4

The *Wall Street Journal* published the story of the reorganization of what it, like many other newspapers, chose to call the Cord Empire.

NEW "CEO" CORD EMPIRE

Jonas E. R. Cord, the son of Jonas Cord II, has been assigned broad responsibilities in the restructured Cord conglomerate.

While the thirty-one-year-old Jonas Cord III is obviously being groomed to succeed his formidable father and grandfather at the head of the Cord

Empire, it is apparent that the real reins of power remain in the hands of the fifty-three-year-old father, who has retained his positions as chairman of the board and chief executive officer of what is now to be called CE—this in addition to owning a majority of the common stock.

Toni Maxim, although she was a political reporter and not a business reporter, covered the story for *The Washington Post*, writing in part:

The third Jonas Cord—Jonas Enrique Raul Cord y Batista—is anything but the All-American Boy. He is his father's illegitimate son and was born and reared in Mexico. He was educated in the States, though—at Culver Military Academy, Harvard, and Harvard Law. His education was interrupted by a stint in the United States Army, during which he was awarded the Distinguished Service Cross and two Purple Hearts.

He continues a family tradition begun by his grandfather and father, in that he is a ladies' man of note. He is frequently seen with nightclub and television star Glenda Grayson and recently took her with him on a visit to Cuba, where he inspected a Cord investment in a gambling casino and renewed his acquaintance with his great-uncle, Cuban dictator Fulgencio Batista.

When Toni came to New York, Bat showed her the wire he had received from his father.

I HAD SUPPOSED THIS GIRL WAS OUR FRIEND. SHE KNOWS TOO MUCH AND SHE TALKS TOO MUCH. REMEMBER WHAT I SAID ABOUT TELLING YOUR WOMEN ABOUT YOUR BUSINESS.

She sat across from him at his desk in the Chrysler Building. His desk was a big table, actually, and behind it, instead of a credenza, sat two handsome rolltop desks. It was in Bat's nature to live with clutter on his desk but also to like to hide the clutter by closing the rolltops. The teletype machine his father used to send him messages from Las Vegas stood in a corner. It was chattering away now, printing some query or complaint from Jonas. He seemed not even to notice it. When it stopped he didn't get up to see what message had arrived.

Toni was more beautiful than ever. At thirty-one, she had gained no weight; she was if anything maybe slightly thinner than before. Her heavy breasts swelled provocatively under the white silk of her blouse. He hadn't touched them for a very long time. The thought made him draw a deep, tense breath.

"I didn't mean to offend your father," said Toni. She said it with a sly little smile that contradicted her words.

"His heart attack has made him more curmudgeonly," said Bat. "The doctor warned me it might."

"Brush with death," she said.

"Something more than that. Something about the blood supply to the brain."

"I didn't stop by to talk about your father," she said. "I'll be interviewing the mayor this afternoon and wondered if you would like to meet for dinner."

"You bet," said Bat. He flipped a page on his calendar. "I'll cancel a couple of things."

"Fine. Where shall I meet you?"

"Where are you staying?" he asked.

"At the Algonquin."

"There's a fine dining room in the hotel. But, uh . . . why are you staying in a hotel? You know, I've got the place in the Waldorf Towers."

"How would Glenda react to my bunking in with you?" she asked.

"It's none of her business," said Bat.

"That's right—any more than it's any of mine that you've been sleeping with her. I mean, if we only see each other once every few months, I can't expect you to be celibate in the meantime. And, for that matter, you can't expect me to be either."

"Now that I'm on the East Coast we can see each other a lot more often," he said.

Toni nodded. "I'd like that. I still care for you, you know."

"Well, I care for you, too. We—"

"Let's don't get into a deep discussion," she interrupted. "I'll come to the apartment. When will you be there?"

He opened the center drawer in one of the rolltop desks and handed her a key. "Come as soon as you can," he said. "If I'm not yet there you can let yourself in. Keep the key. You don't ever need to go to a hotel in New York."

5

It was like it had always been when he was with her. On nights after long separations, they did not sleep at all. He would drop away from her exhausted, then quickly recover under her ministrations and return for something more. She denied him nothing. He denied her nothing. Twice they went in the bathroom and showered together, to rinse off their sweat and other fluids. Afterward they returned to the bed, straightened the tangled sheets, and gave themselves to each other again.

At four in the morning the telephone rang. Bat

hesitated but then answered it, knowing that nothing but something urgent would generate a call on his unlisted number at that hour.

"Jesus Christ!" Toni muttered.

"It's my father," Bat whispered. "Calling from Las Vegas."

"You heard from your sister?" his father asked.

"No. Should I have?"

"You can't guess where she is!"

Jonas was excited. *Too* excited. "Where is she?" he asked quietly, trying to communicate calm.

"She's in *jail*, for Christ's sake!"

"Where? And why?"

"Los Angeles. For drunken driving. She was in some kind of little accident, nobody hurt, thank God, but they hauled her in and gave her the test, and she didn't pass."

"What do you want me to do?"

"I don't know. Go to LA and see what you can do about it."

"I'll call you from Los Angeles," said Bat.

6

Jo-Ann, her face flushed and her eyes puffy from crying, sat behind a screen of wire mesh. She wore the gray cotton uniform of Sybil Brand Institute, the Los Angeles County women's jail.

"It's just three days," said Bat. "That's the mandatory minimum sentence for operating under the influence, and there was no getting you out of it. So . . . Thursday, Friday, and Saturday."

"So goddamned *humiliating*," she sobbed.

"We've posted a bond that allows you to drive, though your license is technically under suspension for one year. You don't know how lucky you are. You might have killed yourself. Or someone else."

"I might have been better off."

"Forget that kind of talk."

"Have you talked to Ben?" she asked.

"Yes."

"He hasn't come to see me."

"He can't. You're allowed to see family members and lawyers, no one else. We could get an exception, but you'll be out of here before it would come through."

"I don't want him to see me in here anyway."

"Now, I've got something else to tell you. I've checked you into the Sunset Hills Clinic. I'll pick you up when you're released and take you there."

"A drying-out clinic," said Jo-Ann despondently. "I don't . . . want to go there. I'll be locked up as much as I am here."

"If you don't go, our father will cut off your allowance."

She sobbed. "The goddamned allowance! Always the goddamned allowance! I have to do what he says, no matter what, to keep the goddamned allowance! And you have to do whatever he says to keep your goddamned job. You think you're independent of him? No more than I am, big brother. Nobody's independent of Jonas. How long do I have to stay in that place?"

"At the end of the month they'll evaluate your case."

She blew a loud sigh. "You drink. *He* drinks. Why do I have to be warehoused in a psycho ward because I drink?"

"I don't have to tell you why. You know why."

"And when I get out, how different is anything going to be?"

"When you get out, I'm going to give you a job with Cord Productions."

"He won't let you."

"I'm going to do it whether he likes it or not."

7

Glenda sat down on the bed in the room Ben Parrish had rented in the Golden Evenings Motel. She had come off the set half an hour before and was still tense and sweaty.

"So, let me see this notorious tool of yours," she said.

Without hesitation Ben unzipped his fly and pulled out his penis.

"*Oi!*" she cried. "The biggest one in California, right?"

Ben smiled. He let it hang out, making no move to put it back inside his pants. "Well, I haven't seen all the others in California, have you?"

"No. Only about half of them," she said.

"Have you ever seen another one that would rival it?"

"You're proud of it, aren't you?" Glenda asked.

He seized his penis and pulled it out even more. It was thick, as well as long, with prominent blue veins showing under the skin. He lifted it in the palm of his hand. "Girls ask me to show it to them, even if they don't want it."

"Do you show it to them?"

"Once in a while."

Glenda began to undress. "That's grotesque," she said.

He undressed with her. "The one thing it can't stand is unemployment."

"And your girlfriend's shut up in a psychiatric clinic."

"She asked for what you might call a conjugal visit. They said no, only if we were married. She's angry and frustrated, but she signed herself in and can't get out. Bat took care of Jo-Ann. He doesn't seem to be taking care of you."

"When he came out here to make the arrangements for her, he called me, but he couldn't spare an hour to see me."

She was naked now. So was he. He stood facing her. She reached up and touched his mammoth penis, then tipped her head to beckon him to sit down beside her. He sat down and began to fondle her breasts.

"We're gonna have a good time," Glenda said softly. "We don't need the Cords. We're gonna have a good time!"

"Damn right we are," he said. "A good time. Both of us have been screwed by the Cords—more ways than one."

"Anybody's been screwed by you's been *screwed*," she said, squeezing him gently to be sure he was rigid and ready. "So, c'mon. Make me the envy of every girl in California."

He kissed her on the neck and ran his hands over her body one more time. He nodded. "'Kay," he grunted.

Glenda scooted across the bed, lay down on her back, and spread her legs. He mounted her and slowly shoved his oversized organ into her until she groaned in protest. He pulled back a little but then began strokes, each one invading her a little more deeply. She moaned and whimpered—but only softly—and he continued until his belly touched hers and all of him was inside her. He was gentle. He had to be. And he didn't take long. By the time she decided he was hurting her too much, he was finished.

"My god, Ben!" She pressed both her hands to her crotch. She gleamed with sweat. "Like I said, a girl who's been screwed by you has been *screwed.*"

"You're bein' screwed more ways than one," said Ben. His thoughts had remained on what he had been saying before she called on him to perform. "You know somethin', kid. You *are* Cord Productions. You're the only successful show they've got. When the time comes for contract renewal, you ought to hold them up for a bundle."

"The thought has occurred to me," she said.

"The show was an experiment, a gamble," said Ben. "But you're a hot property right now. But showbiz is fickle, as I don't have to tell you, and you should make every dime you can *while* you can."

22

1

THE AIRPORT JUST ACROSS THE ARIZONA LINE SOUTH OF Las Vegas where Jonas had landed in 1951 when he was ducking subpoenas was still there and was still used the same way. A sleek, fast private plane landed about noon.

The first man off the plane was Carlo Vulcano, capo of the Vulcano Family that controlled Cleveland's East Side. Wizened and white-haired, he was of medium height, but he looked short because he walked with his shoulders hunched and his head thrust forward. His suspenders held his trousers up almost to his armpits, and he carried a white handkerchief in his left hand, which he pressed to his mouth from time to time because he drooled.

Next was John Stefano, underboss of Detroit's Cosenza Family. He was a swarthy, dark-haired man with shifting brown eyes, about fifty years old. He paused just outside the airplane to light a big cigar.

Morris Chandler was waiting on the tarmac. He strode forward to greet Vulcano and Stefano. Jimmy Hoffa, cocky, happy, and wearing a big grin, passed him and reached Vulcano first.

The four men walked to the private club in the house at the end of the ramp. They sat down in solid maple chairs at one of the tables covered with a red-

and-white-checkered tablecloth. Stefano reinforced
the fire in his cigar by holding it in the flame of the
candle stuck in a Chianti bottle.

"Not a bad place," said Vulcano, glancing around
the dining room. "Are those girls hookers?"

"For sure," said Chandler.

"Ah, good."

"A private place," Stefano remarked half sarcastically. "You're hopin' Cord won't find out you're
meeting with us, right?"

"Right," Chandler admitted.

"What's he do, hire private dicks?" Stefano asked.

"He doesn't have to," said Chandler. "He's got his
own guys. Nothing much happens that he doesn't
know."

"Well . . . we are sorry about Dave Beck," said
Vulcano to Hoffa. "Unfortunately, he was not a man
to listen to advice."

"Nobody's advice," said Hoffa. "The lawyers have
no confidence the appeals are gonna work. He'll die in
the slammer, I imagine." He shook his head.
"Nobody's advice."

"So. You will assume the presidency of the Teamsters Union now," said Vulcano. "Is there any
problem?"

Hoffa shrugged. "What problem?"

"Do you need any help?"

"There was never a man who couldn't use and
appreciate a little help," said Hoffa. "But I've got it in
line pretty good."

"Okay," said Stefano. "We came out here to talk
about something else."

"The Cords," said Hoffa. "I'm gonna kill that son
of a bitch, so help me!"

Carlo Vulcano, hunched over the table, leaned

toward Hoffa. *"Business,* my friend," he muttered, his lips fluttering so a trickle ran from the corner of his mouth. "Killing a man is very bad for business. If you want to work with us, you will have to subdue your temper and your resentments and put out of mind all thought of killing."

Hoffa smiled his toothy smile. "It was a figure of speech, Don Carlo."

Vulcano nodded, accepting the assurance. "We don't speak for everyone," he said to Chandler, "but there is agreement among many of the men of honor that further intrusion into Vegas by the Cords will be detrimental to our interests."

"To put the thing in the simplest words," said Stefano, "the revenues from the hotels are secondary to us. We need the casinos for money laundering and other purposes."

"You may not be able to count on Cuba much longer," said Chandler. "Meyer Lansky couldn't persuade the Cords to invest in the Riviera, and I'd have thought that was as sweet a deal as anybody could make, what with Lansky's connections and expertise. I can only figure the Cords know something even Lansky doesn't know."

"Which would be what?" asked Vulcano.

"Bat's mother is Batista's niece. Maybe they got inside information," said Chandler.

"Naah," said Stefano.

"It is essential," said Vulcano, "that we have a way and a way. I make it a point always to have a means to an end and a means in reserve." He was a man who was accustomed to pontificating and to being solemnly heard when he did. "These people the Cords threaten our interests. What is the best way to cope with them?"

"It's a shame we can't do it the old way," said Chandler.

"Put that from your mind," said Vulcano. "The question is How can we apply pressure to these people?"

"Jonas Cord has a daughter in a drying-out clinic in California," said Chandler. "She has given herself to a Hollywood hustler named Benjamin Parrish. The illegitimate son, Jonas Third, called Bat, sleeps with Glenda Grayson. Jonas Second himself keeps Angela Wyatt as a private and confidential secretary—and sleep-in lover. She has a federal criminal record." Chandler shrugged. "We may be able to find some advantage in one or more of those things."

"We can call down strikes on their heads," said Hoffa. "They can't build their InterContinental Vegas without—"

"Let's hold that idea in abeyance, Jimmy," said Vulcano. "The other ideas Brother Morris has just mentioned may prove the better solution. Crude tactics are not acceptable when foxy tactics will do as well."

"Let's have a means and a means, Don Carlo," said Hoffa, picking up the expression the don himself had used. "One of the things Maurie's thought up and my idea in reserve."

"Don't call me Maurie," said Chandler coldly.

Hoffa grinned. "Don't worry about it, buddy," said Hoffa. "You're the best-connected guy I ever heard of, whatever we call you."

"Gentlemen," said Vulcano. "We are in agreement. Before we go back aboard that uncomfortable little airplane, I want to enjoy a nice steak, a nice bottle of wine, and one of those nice girls who are eyeing us and looking for an invitation to join us at this table."

2

"Goddammit, I said *no*. I told you I didn't want Jo-Ann on our payroll—"

"Until she dried out," Bat interrupted. "Well, she dried out. I made her commit herself to a drying-out clinic, and she stayed there for a month."

"What makes you think she won't go right back to her old habits?" Jonas asked.

"She might very well do just that if nobody gives her a chance," said Bat.

"You should have checked with me first."

"What good is it to be number-two man in the company if I can't hire a public relations girl?"

"It's not a business matter," said Jonas. "It's a personal matter, a family matter."

"Are you telling me to butt out of family matters?"

"She's my *daughter!*"

"She's my sister."

"Half sister."

Bat nodded. "So. Not good enough?"

Jonas got up and walked to the window. He had learned Morris Chandler's little trick of staring through the telescope while he took a moment to control his emotions and put his thoughts in order.

Not good enough? What kind of question was that? Unhappily, he *knew* what kind of question it was. He knew what his son implied. What was he supposed to do? Apologize? He changed the subject.

"I have some information for you," he said, turning away from the telescope and returning to the couch where he had been sitting. "Your television star has been shacking up in your beach house."

"How do you know?"

"It's my *business* to know. It's *your* business to

352

know. She works for us. I've had men watching her. And you haven't? You don't *know* she shacks up in *your* house?"

"Well . . . That's *her* business."

"No. It's not her business. It's your business. It's our business. She works for us. She's a property. Besides, I thought you had some kind of personal commitment from her."

Bat shook his head.

"Okay. I don't care who she lets hump her. Except— Guess who the guy is?"

"Who?"

"Jo-Ann's friend Ben Parrish."

"Parrish! For God's sake! That son of a bitch!"

"Right. The guy who's screwin' Glenda Grayson is also screwin' Jo-Ann and also screwin' you."

"That son of a bitch," Bat muttered.

"I wouldn't be surprised if there's not more to it," said Jonas. "Parrish has a reputation for hustling. What you want to bet he's trying to get her agency contract or something like that?"

"What can we do about it?" asked Bat.

"I've already done something about it," said Jonas.

3

The offices for Cord Productions were on the grounds of the Cord soundstages in West Hollywood. Jo-Ann had a small office with a window overlooking the parking lot. Arthur Mawson, producer for the *Glenda Grayson Show,* was accustomed to handling his own public relations, but he had his orders from the younger Mr. Cord and gave Jo-Ann as much responsibility as he could. What she did mostly was take telephone calls from reporters and answer fan letters.

Glenda Grayson's interviews and mail were handled by her agent Sam Stein and his PR staff. Guest stars also had their own staffs. Jo-Ann's responsibilities involved only inquiries and mail directed to the production company. It was not a demanding job, and she looked for ways to give it more stature, to give herself a more active role in the business.

Whether she improved the job or not, Jo-Ann felt good about herself. For the first time since she was in school, she had a reason for getting up every morning, a reason for bathing and doing her makeup and dressing. She had lost weight during her stay in the clinic. They had insisted she play tennis and swim, and they served planned meals with calories counted.

She was still fond of Scotch, but for the time being she was able to recognize her limit and stop. "If you can stop when you should stop, you're not an alcoholic," she said. She'd be damned if she'd call for orange juice when everyone else was having a drink. That would be too humiliating. She wouldn't go to AA either, though the doctors at the clinic had urged her to. She'd gone to one meeting and decided AA was a cult.

Her father hadn't seen her, but at twenty-three she'd made a new image for herself. She had bought new clothes, and they fit her sleekly. She'd had her hair redone, too: cut shorter and curling under her ears. This morning she was wearing a cream-white flared linen skirt and a tight baby-blue cashmere sweater. Her bra lifted her breasts and thrust them out. Ben liked this outfit, so she wore it often, particularly when she expected to see him during the day.

Her telephone rang. The receptionist told her a young woman who had no appointment was asking to see her: a Cynthia Rawls, who said she was a reporter for the Hollywood *Sketch*. Jo-Ann was glad enough to have a call from a reporter and told the receptionist to send her in.

Cynthia Rawls was a gum-chewing bespectacled girl who seemed to think she played reporter by wearing a pencil in her hair above her right ear and carrying a steno pad in her left hand.

She handed Jo-Ann a card. "You know our paper?" she asked.

Jo-Ann nodded. The *Sketch* was a supermarket tabloid. "I've seen it," she said. "I'm not a regular reader."

Cynthia Rawls nodded. If she read derision in Jo-Ann's comment, she showed no reaction. "We like to check our facts," she said earnestly. "Believe it or not, we check our facts closer than most any other paper. In our line, you can't afford to publish if you don't check your facts."

"I can understand," said Jo-Ann.

"So . . . I tried to check with Mr. Stein, but he just won't talk. This has to do with Glenda Grayson, you understand. Your star?"

"What makes you think I can—or will—tell you anything Sam Stein won't tell you?"

"Maybe you can't—or won't," said Cynthia Rawls. "But I figure I have an obligation to run the story by you." She handed Jo-Ann a couple of typewritten pages. "If you want to deny any of that, we'll check the facts further."

Jo-Ann scanned the sheets.

Cozy, cozy, cozzy! Things have gotten really cozy between TV superstar /// Glemnda Grayson and Hollywood hiustler Benjamimn Parrish, otherwizse known as agent, sometime smalltime producer, and all-around man-about-town.

No more "quickies" in hot-sheet motels for the one-time stripper and her new man. She madkes Benny-boy welcome these days in the beachfront house she used to sheare with money-boy Jonas "Bat" Cord.

So far as we know, Mr. Cord has raised no objection. Like his notorious father, Jeonas Cord II, "Bat" has many irons in the fire. Monogany is not a Cord family tradition.

Our sources for this story are beyond question. Our informer nails it cold.

"I'm sorry about the way I use your family name," said Cynthia Rawls. "I guess it can't be any surprise, though, can it?"

Jo-Ann stared at the young woman with cold eyes, for the better part of a minute, before she said, "I want to know the name of your informer."

"Oh, you have to understand I can't tell you that."

"Yes, you can. You face two alternatives, Miss Rawls. I think you know that playing games with the Cords is not wise. If my father can't defeat you in a libel suit, he might just *buy* your newspaper. He's done it before, you know. It's not a freedom of the press issue. My father might decide to convert the Hollywood *Sketch* into the weekly *Dairy Reporter*. What do you know about cows, Miss Rawls?"

Cynthia Rawls tried at first to play the bold reporter. She shrugged and smirked. Then she licked her lips, deflated, and asked, "What is the second alternative?"

"Give me the name of your source," said Jo-Ann, "and I might be able to cooperate with you. You've got a little story. I might be able to make it a big one."

As the reporter pondered, Jo-Ann congratulated herself. She was a by-God Cord! This was the way

Cords played it. And she'd destroy Ben Parrish—for she had no doubt that what this girl reporter had written was true.

"Miss . . . Miss Cord, I—"

"Who is your source?"

"Miss Cord . . . You've got me between a rock and a hard place."

Jo-Ann raised her chin. "When you get a few more years behind you, Miss Rawls, you will become accustomed to that. This is an easy one. You've got alternatives. Most people don't."

"It's more difficult than you realize. The source called my editor. He recorded the call, like he records all that kind of calls. He played the tape for me. You're not gonna believe who it was."

"Well, try me," said Jo-Ann icily.

"Miss Cord . . . It was your father!"

Jo-Ann could not dissemble. The reporter saw her flush and stiffen. "So," she muttered. "My father. You think it was my father on the phone."

"Do you deny it?"

Jo-Ann considered for a brief moment, then shook her head. Of course she wouldn't deny it. It made sense more than one way. "I don't deny it. More than that, I can tell you that everything he said is absolutely true. I can tell you something more. Ben Parrish has a certain, uh, *reputation*. I'm sure you know what that is."

"That he's hung like a horse?"

"He'd make a stallion jealous. Do you want to know how I can testify to that?"

"I'm afraid to ask," said Cynthia Rawls.

"You can guess. At the same time, I'm glad you came here today. I'd suspected somebody was leaking a story, but I didn't know for sure. Especially, I didn't know who."

357

"But your father knew. How could he know what you didn't know?"

"I told you it's always a mistake to mess around with Jonas Cord. He finds out what he's interested in finding out. He didn't tell me. He wanted me to read it in the newspaper."

"How's he gonna react when he reads this extra stuff I'll be putting in the story?"

"He won't buy out the paper over that."

"Well gee, thanks, Miss Cord. I'm glad we met."

4

"He told her he was in love with her. She believed him."

Jo-Ann would meet Ben only over lunch, only in a public place where there could not be a scene. There was a scene anyway, of sorts. People stared at them. Some laughed. They were surrounded in the restaurant by people who would have sworn they never looked at a supermarket tabloid, but they glanced at Ben Parrish and Jo-Ann Cord and recognized them as two of the people shown on the front page of this week's *Sketch*.

The story had made front page, complete with photographs, none flattering. The picture of Glenda Grayson was one that Gib Dugan had distributed of her fourteen years ago, wearing her signature black hat and nothing more but bra and panties. The picture of Jo-Ann was one taken the night she was led under arrest and handcuffed into a Los Angeles police station. The one of Ben showed him at a swimming pool, paunch spilling out over the top of his trunks, cigarette in one hand, martini glass in the other.

The reporter was more clever, more devious than

Jo-Ann had realized. If she had seemed deferential toward the end of the interview, nothing of the sort carried over into her story. She had treated none of them kindly. She called Glenda Grayson "a one-time stripper," Ben a "Hollywood hustler," and Jo-Ann a "swinging rich kid." She called the three of them "a libidinous trio"—libidinous being one of the *Sketch's* favorite words.

"I believed *you*," said Jo-Ann, carefully holding her voice down. She had drunk more Scotch than her limit allowed, but she was in control of herself. "I was stupid. I hate myself for that. Cords are supposed to be a lot of things, but stupid isn't one of them."

"Bat told Glenda he loved her and wanted to marry her," said Ben, equally quietly. "Then he went off to New York and began to find excuses not to come back out here to spend weekends with her. She found out he was seeing Toni again, in fact that Toni was living part of the time in the Waldorf Towers apartment. Glenda was upset. *I* was upset. And *you* were in jail!"

"Yeah. I recommend that for a short, restful vacation sometime. It beats the drying-out clinic. A cellmate is not holier than thou. Mine was in for the same thing I was and could hardly look down her nose at me."

"We're the same kind of people, you and I," said Ben.

"Is that a suggestion that I forgive and forget?"

"We *are* the same kind. We enjoy the same things. We—"

"What are you saying to Glenda?" Jo-Ann asked.

"Nothing. She won't take my phone calls. She's moved out of the beach house, you know. Sam Stein is furious. I suppose your father is even more furious."

Jo-Ann smiled and shook her head. "Not at all."

She had decided not to tell him who had initiated the *Sketch* story. "I can think of a way to make him furious."

"Hey! He's not a guy to be played around with."

"What's he gonna do to *me?* Shut off my friggin' allowance? Make Bat fire me? What'd you say—that we're the same kind of guys?" She lifted her glass and gulped down Scotch. "Damn right we are. And I'm not going to let that son of a bitch dominate my whole life. I can handle you, *stud,* and I can handle him, too."

"The Consolidated deal went down the drain yesterday," said Ben.

"Sure. Of course. The fine hand of Jonas. We can screw *him.*"

"Honey, he's not a man to—"

"We fly over to Reno," she said. "Tonight. See how he likes *that.*"

5

Jonas paced the living-room-office in his suite in The Seven Voyages, his talk fast and angry. Bat, sitting on a couch with his legs stretched out before him, watched and listened. He had begun to worry about his father. Jonas, though as fully recovered from his heart attack as he would ever be, isolated himself more and more in the hotel and rarely ventured out. In the ten months since the attack he had not returned once to New York and had flown to Los Angeles only twice. He managed his businesses from the suite, using half a dozen telephone lines. In the suite across the hall, converted into offices for staff, a teletype chattered constantly, sending and receiving. The long coffee table that served as his desk was strewn with the yellow paper torn off the machine.

For a few weeks he had let his beard grow but had shaved it off when it came out grayer than his hair. He didn't wear business suits anymore, or even jackets and slacks. He wore wrinkled khakis with golf shirts and sometimes cardigan sweaters.

"How the hell can a man focus his attention on business when he has to contend with damned foolishness like this?" he barked.

The damned foolishness he referred to was the newspaper story reporting Jo-Ann's marriage to Ben Parrish. It was a short, factual story in the *Los Angeles Times*. Probably he had not seen the coverage in the *Sketch*, which featured a photo of the newlyweds strolling hand-in-hand on the beach, he in a pair of boxer trunks, she in a spectacularly brief bikini. The beach was the one below Bat's beach house. Since Glenda had moved out, he had turned the house over to Jo-Ann.

"What am I supposed to do now?" Jonas went on. "The next word I'll get, she'll be pregnant."

"It happens," said Bat. "People do live their lives. I don't like Ben Parrish. But we've got to face it; he's Jo-Ann's husband. And Jo-Ann is not to be taken for a dummy. I don't know what she thought she was doing, marrying that man. But there it is; she did it."

"She did it to defy me. And you."

"Well . . . maybe. Why not?"

"Whose side are you on?" asked Jonas sullenly.

"Are there sides? Do there have to be sides?"

"I am placed—*you* are placed—in a hell of a position," said Jonas.

"You didn't have to send the story to the *Sketch*."

"Who says I did?"

"Do you deny it?" Bat asked.

Jonas stiffened and flared with indignation. "I don't have to deny things," he said. "When did it get started that you hit me with challenges and I have to deny them?"

Bat shrugged. "Describe this hell of a position that we're in," he said.

"I didn't want her to have any part in the business," said Jonas. "Now she's married to that worthless son of a bitch, and anything she finds out he'll find out. Pillow talk. She's got to go."

"Why do you think she married him?"

"To shoot me a finger."

Bat grinned. "Why would she want to do that?"

"Why the hell do you think?" Jonas asked. "You know Parrish was trying to make a big deal with Consolidated. Well, I queered that for him. I let Goldish know I wouldn't take it kindly if Consolidated let Benjamin Parrish in on anything. So now where am I? The bastard is my son-in-law!"

"It'll have to be worked out," said Bat. "I've got a worse problem."

"Worse than that?"

"We've got one successful television production," said Bat. "The *Glenda Grayson Show*. It's showing a profit, and we're starting to get your investment back. But I've got one seriously unhappy star."

"You screwed the girl. It's a dumb dog that shits in his own bed."

"Forgive me," said Bat. "A chip off the old block."

"How much is it gonna take to make her happy?"

Bat nodded. "You have it figured."

"A word of advice," said Jonas. "Glenda Grayson is thirty-five years old and getting a little shopworn. Get your guys to write better stuff for Margit Little. Build her up. One of these days we can tell Glenda Grayson to go screw."

"Great minds run in one direction," said Bat. "If you'll forgive the cliché."

Jonas had stopped pacing and now he sat down. "Got something to show you," he said. He picked up a telephone and dialed a number. "Angie, have the guys wheel in that model." He spoke to Bat. "The new hotel."

Angie came in, and two young men wheeled in an architect's model of a new casino-hotel. "The Cord InterContinental Vegas," she said.

Bat stood and looked at the model. Since he had last involved himself personally with the new hotel, his father had authorized a substantial increase in its size. He had obviously acquired more land, since this hotel would not stand on the land they had originally bought.

"Okay?" asked Jonas.

"Beautiful," said Bat. It would have been pointless to say anything else. Except— "But it looks like a hell of a lot of money." His thought was that it was his father's plaything, but it would have been a major mistake to suggest it.

"Sixteen floors," said Jonas as if he didn't detect Bat's thought. "The executive offices of the company will occupy the top floor, the way they do here—only four times as big. A stage that can accommodate the most spectacular nightclub shows in the world. I've been in touch with the Folies-Bergère in Paris. It may be that we can stage an authentic Folies right here in Las Vegas."

"Problems?" Bat asked.

"Oh, yeah. The problems are beginning to show up. Coincidences that don't make sense. Oh, yeah. We're going to have problems."

23

1

JONAS ENJOYED ASSEMBLING PEOPLE HE CARED FOR AT THE ranch at Christmas. It wasn't always possible. The year Nevada died, and the next year, he didn't feel like it. He couldn't imagine the party without Nevada. He invited Jo-Ann the next year. And he brought Angie. Bat had felt obliged to go to Mexico for Christmas. Four sat down at the table: Jonas and Jo-Ann and Angie and Robair. It wasn't enough. He had actually considered inviting Monica, to fill the house. Then last year he was just out of the hospital for Christmas, so they spent the holiday in the apartment in the Waldorf Towers—the same four, plus Bat. This year there would be more people but no Robair, who had died in August.

This year Bat would bring Toni again. Jonas asked Jo-Ann to bring Ben Parrish. He had to face the man sometime. So did Monica, so he had invited her, too, and her cartoonist friend Bill Toller, if she wanted to bring him—or whoever was sleeping in her bed this year.

Since the heart attack Jonas had let his pilot's license lapse. He had not taken the biennial physical, because he doubted they would pass him. Bill Shaw was technically pilot in command of the Beechcraft Bonanza they flew from Las Vegas to the ranch, but

Jonas sat in the left seat and flew the airplane. He hadn't lost his touch and was exhilarated by having his hands on the controls of an airplane again.

He landed first at the Cord Explosives plant and went in to see once more the office where his father died. The plant manager didn't use it. It was kept as an office for the Cords, whenever one of them came to the plant. Jonas went out into the plant and shook hands with as many as he could of the workers, mostly Mexicans, who still operated this highly profitable seminal enterprise of the Cord empire. They hadn't seen him for a long time, and they didn't see Bat often either. His visit was good for their morale.

Bill Shaw carried Jonas's luggage into the ranch house and then took off in the Bonanza to be with his family in Los Angeles for Christmas. Angie was in the house, trying to do what Robair had always done: decorate for Christmas and organize the meals. She was a good girl and was doing her best, but Jonas realized she couldn't do what Robair had done, much less what Nevada had done; and he reached an abrupt conclusion that he would sell the ranch. This would be his last Christmas there.

2

Toni was dismayed by Jonas. She couldn't really like him, because she couldn't like his influence over Bat; but she was jolted by the change in the man. She remembered what Bat had told her when she came here for Christmas five years ago: that the household would live to Jonas's schedule, that probably consciously but even unconsciously *he* would dominate totally. He would be the center of everything. He still was, but not in the same way. Everyone gathered around him. Everyone deferred to him. But it was for a new reason—that they sensed he was a dying lion. What was worse he obviously sensed the same thing and had settled into the role. It was appalling. He was only fifty-three!

At Christmas in 1952 she had observed the immense energy of these people. Now she saw something else: that none of them loved Jonas, and he didn't love them. She was distressed by the thought that maybe they were incapable of love. They shared a sense of family, a stalwart loyalty toward each other; but it wasn't love; it was something else, a defensive family allegiance that inspired them to strike out at anyone who threatened the demesne. That was their only commitment to each other: to protect the turf. They would rush to each other's defense, not because they cared for each other, but to defend the empire.

Monica stood by the fireplace chatting with her friend Bill Toller, who had to have accommodated her to come here and be subjected to this evening. Monica patently didn't like any of the Cords, including her own daughter. She knew why Jonas had invited her here: to let her see what her daughter had married. Jonas was punishing her for something out of the past. He was succeeding. Monica was at no pains to conceal her antipathy for the Hollywood hustler her daughter had married, nor her indifference for the son Jonas had discovered.

Toni had done a little research into the life and character of Benjamin Parrish. She had a word for him. Slick. She had anticipated slick, and he *was* slick. He was a bulky man, ten years older than Jo-Ann, and he was all but absurdly protective of her. He was also playing a transparent game of deference toward Jonas and Bat. He smoked only when he stood by the fireplace, where the draft would carry his smoke up the flue.

Jo-Ann had matured since Toni last saw her at her graduation two years ago. Matured? No, she had deteriorated. At twenty-three, she was a damaged woman; heavy drinking and constant smoking had marked her. She had been an unhappy girl when Toni first saw her at the 1952 Christmas party . . . a bitter, cynical young woman at the graduation . . . a scarred woman now.

And, damn it, they were all responsible for it, except maybe Bat. Jonas had expectations of her, and he let her know she didn't meet them. Monica didn't want to acknowledge she had a daughter who looked nearly as old as the mother. The mother and father weren't proud of their daughter and had let her know it. What the hell did they expect of her?

Toni could see that Angie was devoted to Jonas, perhaps pitiably so. It looked as if Jonas accepted her devotion the same way he accepted the devotion of employees—he would reward it, but he thought it was no more than his due. Angie was realistic and probably comfortable.

Bat. He was of course the one most interesting to Toni. She had watched him change. He had always been a Cord, she understood. Some of the combined elements of his character and personality—the relentless drive, the focused and endless span of attention, the calm and unaffected egocentricity, all coupled with an unremitting erotic appetite—had been enigmatic until she met Jonas and saw the same combination of traits in him. In Bat, all but the last had been tempered by what he was of his mother, as Toni judged, but under the continuing influence of his father he was more and more a Cord, with the tempering influence diminishing. It was said of Jonas that he was not a man to be crossed, that he was remorseless when crossed. She wondered if Bat had not acquired that trait, too.

Bat had developed a slight farsightedness and carried in his breast pocket a pair of eyeglasses with dark horn rims, which he pulled out from time to time and settled on his nose, giving him an owlish aspect that was almost always submerged in his facile, active smile. He paid more attention to tailoring than his father did and wore clothes his New York tailors cut precisely to fit him. Time had not ravaged him the way it had Jo-Ann; to the contrary, it had caressed him; he was, if anything, more handsome than he had been before.

They were thirty-one years old. If they were going to marry and have a family, the time was now. But it was anything but certain it was going to happen. She was not certain, in fact, it was what she wanted. The demand he had made in Lexington, Massachusetts, nine years ago still stood. He wanted his wife to be a homemaker and mother. He wanted his wife to be an ornament to his life. He said he'd learned better, but she was not confident he had.

She had said she was willing to be wife and homemaker and ornament, in time. She had said she would in time give up her career and spend twenty years rearing children. And no man she had ever met matched Bat Cord. Still— He had too much Jonas in him. He seemed to be filling up with it.

3

Jo-Ann sat beside her father on a couch and drank Scotch. She was pleased with herself. Both her parents were pissed. She had married the man with the biggest cock in California and had made it plain to him that he had better, by God, cleave to her like the Bible said or she would, by Christ, cut it off. She was a Cord. He had better understand that. Jonas might not like it that she was a Cord, but she was, and she was just as much a bitch as he was a son of a bitch, and there was nothing he could do about it.

He was counting her drinks. So was Monica. So was Bat. To hell with all of them.

She *was* a Cord, but she didn't *need* the Cords. She had every quality they had, and she was married to a highly competent flimflam artist. Jonas wanted to destroy Ben but obviously was not so sure he wanted to destroy his daughter's husband. Anyway, the hand of Jonas did not reach everywhere.

4

His body rarely reminded Bat of the shattered rib and ripped flesh he had suffered on the Ludendorff Bridge. But occasionally it did: with sharp spasms, then throbbing in his right side. The pain came at odd times, usually not more than once every few weeks. He felt it tonight, and he related it to having lifted a heavy suitcase with his right arm as he left the plane that had delivered him and Toni to the ranch landing strip.

He moved to the fireplace and exchanged idle words with Bill Toller and Ben Parrish, studying the others in the room with the same intensity with which they were observing him and each other. He wore a gray tweed cashmere jacket and charcoal-gray slacks, a white shirt, and a narrow regimental-stripe tie.

He saw his father often, not less frequently than

once every other week, and he had seen him at his worst, depressed and probably frightened. He had seen him snatch a nitroglycerine pill from a bottle and jam it into his mouth. Lately, though, he had observed distinct improvement. Jonas had lost one-third of his heart capacity, the doctors said. He should moderate his activity, they said. Bat had watched him closely and knew what he was doing. Jonas was testing himself. He knew what he cared about, what counted for him; and he knew how much he was willing to give up to survive. He was the kind of man who wouldn't value life without bourbon, rare steaks, a lot of vigorous sex, and, above all, the satisfaction of challenging, competing, and winning.

"You know what?" he had said to Bat one day in the suite atop The Seven Voyages. "I get it up just fine. I didn't lose a bit of that. In fact, I had her go down on me before I left the hospital. The doctors would have—"

"How would *she* have felt if—"

"I know, I know," Jonas had said impatiently. "We talked about that. I told her it was okay with me. What a way to go!"

Bat had grinned. "You are irrepressible," he had said.

Jonas had laughed. "Damn right."

His father had given him authority to make the changes he had recommended; but, as he had expected, the older man looked over his shoulder every minute and intervened regularly. He won his father's approval often, but it was never unqualified approval. There was always some little thing that could have been done better.

For example—

"You passed up an opportunity. Lucky I saw it."

"What are you talking about?" Bat asked.

"Cord Aircraft."

"What the hell? You agreed to phase it out. I got eight million five for the plant and machinery, most of it obsolete. Sold the whole works to Phoenix Aircraft. Everybody I know says I got a damned good deal. We're out of the airplane business, and we got eight and a half million cash."

Jonas shook his head. "Well, you don't know anything about airplanes. You know what I did with the eight and a half million?"

Bat shook his head. "I'm afraid to ask."

"I bought twenty-five percent of Phoenix."

"*Why?* We were getting out of the airplane business. You agreed—"

"I asked the guys from Phoenix to stop by and show me what they were planning. I discovered I was talking to some aviation geniuses. They're gonna build a sleek little low-wing two-seater configured with the seats fore and aft, to be flown with a stick instead of a yoke. That little airplane will *sell*. I offered them their eight and a half million back, for twenty-five percent and a seat on the board of directors. God, were they happy!"

"So, are *we* supposed to be happy? We're back in the airplane business, where we were losing money, and—"

"Bat!" Jonas interrupted. "Can't you see a no-lose proposition when it's staring you in the face? All we invested in their airplane is the money they paid us for the plant. If this great little plane they want to build is a success, we have a percentage. If it isn't, all we invested is the old building with a lot of obsolete old machine tools. You've gotta watch for deals like that. They come along once in a while."

Another plaything. Another enthusiasm that would cost money. Another time when it would have been a big mistake to say so.

When the *Wall Street Journal* and other newspapers reported that Cord television sets would no longer be made, the market for the sets vanished. Retailers unloaded the sets they had at sharply discounted prices and ordered no more. Jonas was extremely annoyed and suggested someone had intentionally leaked the news. The family took a loss on the deal, and Jonas blamed Bat. He hadn't done it right. He'd let it get away from him.

"Somebody fucked us, Bat. Somebody who works for us. You've gotta be always on the lookout for that. You're too goddamned trusting. Look around for the guy that *owes* us, that we've bailed out of trouble. You think that wins us his loyalty? No. The other way around. He hates us. I'd first trust the guy we screwed, then the guy we saved from a screwing."

5

Jonas sat at the head of the table, Bat at the other end. The cook, without the supervision of Robair, had carved a big turkey, and a temporary man serving in a white jacket as a waiter set it on the table on a silver tray. Platters and bowls were filled with dressing, potatoes, gravy, vegetables, cranberry sauce, celery, radishes, olives, and hot rolls. Red wine, white wine, and champagne were in cradles or in buckets of ice.

Jonas surveyed the spread with a critical eye for a long moment, then seemed to be satisfied. He tapped a glass with a spoon. "Let me say how pleased I am that we are all together this evening. I wish we could do it more often. Let's plan on it. Next year we will gather in New York."

He didn't offer to say grace, and no one suggested it. The family and their friends set about eating.

Toni had noticed before that Jonas, Monica, and Jo-Ann—and five years ago, Nevada—ate like ranch hands: diligently filling their plates and moving food to their mouths as if they had but limited time. They spoke little while they were eating, and when they did speak it was usually to express satisfaction with a dish. ("This is good, isn't it? Tell Martha she did a first-rate job.") They were not rude in their manners; they just ate purposefully. They were purposeful people.

In this, Bat was not like them. He savored his food and wine and took his time. Toni was pleased that she and Bat and Bill Toller were still very much in the middle of their meal when Jonas, Jo-Ann, and Monica were finished and were allowing the man to take their plates.

"Well," said Jonas, glancing around the table. "Maybe this is as good a time as any, while we're all together, to announce a change or two I've decided to make in the organization of the businesses."

There could have been no more inappropriate time to announce a reorganization, and surely Jonas knew it. Bat went on eating, as if he knew what his father was about to announce—which he did not know.

"I've been reviewing this year's performance and this year's changes," Jonas went on. "On the whole, I'm satisfied. We stubbed our toes on a few things, but on the whole we've had a good year. Bat recommended reorganization, I accepted his recommendation, and I'm glad I did. Studying what we've done over the past five years, it has become apparent to me that Bat and I have complementary talents. Bat does some things better than I do. I do some things better than Bat does. For that reason, I want to change the structure a bit to take advantage of those disparate and complementary skills."

Bat glanced up at his father at intervals, but his attention seemed to remain focused on his dinner.

Jonas continued. "For myself, I'm very happy I got us into the hotel business. We're going to own two of the finest casino-hotels in Las Vegas, and they're going to make money like nothing else does! I will continue personal control over Cord Hotels. Bat recommended that we go into television production, and we've done reasonably well at that. I am oriented to show business more than he is. I made movies, after all, and we own Cord Studios because I established them. I am going to assume full executive authority over Cord Productions and relieve Bat of any responsibility in that area of the business."

It was obvious now that Bat's concentration on the remainder of his dinner was a facade against what his father was saying.

"I'm gonna run the casino-hotel business and the entertainment element of the business myself, hands-on," said Jonas. "Now, as to Bat, he has proved himself a shrewd businessman, an organizer, a man who understands how to finance things. As of the first of January he will be president and chief executive officer of Cord Enterprises. He will be president and chief executive officer of Cord Explosives, which incorporates Cord Plastics, and of Inter-Continental Airlines." Jonas paused and grinned. "With those offices he won't have enough work to do, so I'm handing him a new assignment. I'm creating a committee of the board of directors of Cord Enterprises— a committee on new ventures and acquisitions. Bat will be chairman. I'll serve on the committee, as will Professor Moynihan; and since the board is not really large enough to have committees, I am enlarging the board from five members to seven. Our general counsel, David Amory, will be a director and a member of Bat's committee. In addition I have asked my dear friend Angela Wyatt to serve as a director."

6

Two of the bedrooms in the ranch house had small fireplaces. Jonas had taken one for himself and assigned the other to Bat. Snow had fallen all during their dinner and was still falling. The sight of snow, the deep silence of a snowy night, made them feel cold even when the temperature in a room was the same as it had been a few hours ago. Jonas had asked Angie to build up the fire, and she squatted in front of the fireplace, already naked, and pushed splinters of kindling against the few hot coals that remained from an earlier fire.

"Congratulations, Madame Corporate Director," said Jonas.

She turned and smiled at him. "Thank you, Jonas. That was a wonderful thing for you to do for me."

"You deserve it," he said. "You've earned it. Anyway, you know all about what the board does, since you've been at every meeting, taking the minutes. Now you'll have a vote."

"I'll always vote the way you do," she said ingenuously.

Jonas grinned. "Well, I hope so." He was sitting on a tweedy couch in a long blue terry-cloth robe. He picked up a bottle and poured a splash of bourbon. "Nightcap," he said. "One last sip." She'd had the temerity to count his drinks and remind him of his promise to his doctors to cut down on the booze. He didn't sip. He tossed the bourbon down with a satisfied grunt.

With the fire beginning to catch, Angie came to the couch, sat down beside Jonas, and reached inside his robe to massage his penis.

"I wish I had the place wired," said Jonas. "I'd like to hear what they're saying out there." They had come to their bedroom as soon as they left the dinner table. "Actually, they won't say anything. None of them trust each other enough to say what they think in each other's presence."

"Bat—"

"I wouldn't want him to know how much he means to me," said Jonas. "What I really wish I had wired is that bedroom at the other end of the hall. I'd like to hear what he and Toni say when they're alone."

7

As Toni undressed, Bat stirred coals, added wood, and knelt and blew on the coals, coaxing up a lively blaze in the little fireplace.

"What was all that about?" she asked when he stood and began to take off his clothes.

"I *could* say much ado about nothing. Actually, it's about something. He gives me a more impressive title, but he isn't giving up an iota of control."

"Was it a sort of Christmas present?" she asked. "The title?"

"You could think of it that way," said Bat. "He wants my allegiance. He could have assured it better another way."

"What way?"

"He could have arranged a transfer to me of a block of the CE stock. I hold just ten shares. So does each of the directors, except Judge Gitlin who owns two hundred. All the rest of it, my father owns himself. That's how he keeps absolute control. Absolute control."

"He won't give up control while he lives. You know that. You couldn't expect him to."

"No, of course not. But if I held ten percent of the stock, I'd feel more secure."

Bat hung his clothes over a chair and sat down on the bed beside Toni. She beckoned him to lie back, to cuddle with her.

"If you held forty percent, he could still fire you any time he felt like it," she said.

"Right."

"But why did he shut you out of television production?" she asked. "The *Glenda Grayson Show* was your idea. You've done as much with Cord Productions as anybody could."

"I can think of two reasons," Bat said. "In the first place, he likes the glamour aspect of it. He was always bored with businesses like explosives and plastic, though for a long time they were his basic moneymakers. He liked the airline. He liked building airplanes and flying them himself as the test pilot. And he liked making pictures."

"That's one reason. What's the other?"

"As head of Cord Productions, I hired Jo-Ann. He's going to dump her. He doesn't want her anywhere near the business, any aspect of it."

"Does he hate her?"

"No, but he doesn't trust her. You can understand why."

"What kind of a job was she doing?" Toni asked.

"Good enough. Competent. But he won't let her

work for him, and I don't think Monica will give her a job, either."

"She has a good education," said Toni. "Nothing prevents her from getting a job not working for her parents."

"She doesn't have to work. She can live very comfortably on what our father gives her. Of course, I understand how frustrated she has been, living on an allowance."

"Bat . . ."

"Hmm?"

"You're not very happy, are you?"

"Well. I'm not accustomed to observing Christmas Eve by hearing a talk on the reorganization of the business."

"Yes, and you're full of tension. I've got a present for you. Just lie back and loosen up."

She put a pillow on his legs and laid her head on it, pressing her face against his belly. "I want to be comfy," she said in a low voice. "I figure on this taking a long time."

She opened her mouth and took his penis in. He saw what she meant by taking a long time. She licked very gently for a minute or so, then stopped licking and lazily nibbled his foreskin with her lips. She turned her big brown liquid eyes upward and watched his reaction. She smiled. Bat relaxed. She bent his penis to one side so she could lick along its length without having to lift her head from the pillow.

Bat moaned. He wouldn't think about his father anymore tonight.

24

1

JONAS ASSUMED PERSONAL CONTROL OF TELEVISION PRO-
duction. He began to fly regularly to Los Angeles,
where he stayed in the Cord hotel suite and spent days
at the studio. He did not fire Jo-Ann as Bat had
thought he would. He ordered Arthur Mawson, now
executive producer of the *Glenda Grayson Show,* to
give him frequent and detailed reports on what she
did, but he kept her in her job. He did not stop by her
office to see her every time he came to Los Angeles—
only occasionally.

Sometimes Angela came to Los Angeles with him.
Usually she did not.

St. Patrick's Day fell on a Monday. Jonas did not
celebrate it as a holiday, but he was conscious of it
and regretted being alone in the suite on an evening
when most people were drinking Irish whiskey, eating
corned beef and cabbage, and pretending to be Irish.
He had arranged not to be alone. Margit Little was
with him.

They sat on a couch, where he had invited her to sit,
with a bottle of Old Bushmill's, two glasses, and some
crackers and cheese. Margit was wearing what was
characteristic of her: black dance leotards with a

maroon skirt. Her light-brown hair was tied back in a ponytail. She frowned over the whiskey in her glass.

He had been working on this for some time—that is, on getting her to come alone to his suite. She had been just eighteen when Bat signed her up for the *Glenda Grayson Show,* and she was not yet twenty-two now. She looked sixteen, which was the age she was represented to be on the show. She had the lithe body of a dancer and a pretty, open, innocent face. It was hard to believe Bat had not had this girl, but he swore he hadn't.

"It's traditional," he said of the Irish whiskey.

She pinched her lips and wrinkled her nose. "It's strong," she said.

"Well . . . just a toast and then you can have something more to your liking. A toast— To you, Margit. To your career."

"Thank you," she said softly after she took a small and cautious sip.

"Can we talk in confidence?" he asked. "I mean in complete confidence. Neither of us will ever tell anybody anything we may say in the next few minutes."

"Yes . . ." she said hesitantly.

"Fine," he said, nodding. "In confidence. I took over Cord Productions because I decided my son had run out of ideas. The *Glenda Grayson Show* is a success, and it makes some money, but it's getting a little stale. Glenda is getting a little stale. And her money demands are becoming unreasonable."

"Mr. Cord—"

"Jonas," he interrupted.

"Oh, sir, I couldn't!"

"Please. Hearing you call me Mr. Cord or, worse yet, sir makes me feel a hundred years old." He put a hand on hers. "Please, Margit."

She nodded. "Jonas."

"Okay," he said with a reassuring smile. "Now. In any case, Cord Productions can't go on forever with all its eggs in one basket. Whatever we do about the *Glenda Grayson Show*, we've got to start producing new shows. Can you guess what I've got in mind?"

She shook her head, but her widened eyes suggested she had guessed what he was about to say.

"The *Margit Little Show*," said Jonas. "Maybe a half hour weekly. Say you did a comedy skit every week, with a guest star. Not a continuing family situation like on the old show but a different idea with you as a different character each week. With dancing, of course. I'm thinking of you as a solo, in a simple classic dance number to open the show, then something of a production number with your guest to close the show—with the sketch in between. I bet you can sing, too, huh?"

"Well . . . I have taken voice lessons."

"Okay. The *Margit Little Show*. You know, when I say I'm going to produce something, I'm going to produce it. I don't just play around."

Margit sampled the Old Bushmill's again, a little more boldly.

Jonas poured himself a second drink. "We will have to address a little problem," he said.

She nodded solemnly and fixed her eyes on him, waiting to hear what the problem was.

"What kind of a contract do you have with Sam Stein?"

She frowned. "None. He took me on as a kid and promoted a career for me, and we've never had a written agreement. I mean, he's been something like a father to me."

Jonas grinned. "He didn't want you to come up here alone, did he?"

"No, he didn't."

"And I bet you're supposed to call him when you get home."

She smiled and nodded.

"All right. I like Sam, but I don't know how he'll react to your leaving the Grayson show. There could be a conflict of interests there, if you see what I mean. He might think it will damage the Grayson show when I take you out of it, and after all Glenda's his chief client."

"I see what you mean. But I don't think Sam would stand in the way of my—"

"No, but he might lose Glenda. I'll talk to him. We'll talk to him together. If the whole thing is okay with him, then it's okay with us. If he has a problem, I think you should get another agent."

"Do you have somebody in mind?" she asked, and he could hear in her muted voice that she guessed he did. Margit was small, and she was quiet and modest, but she was shrewd. Far from being overwhelmed by the proposal he was putting before her, she was even thinking ahead of him.

"Yes, I do. My daughter is married to Ben Parrish. I don't like the guy, and I don't trust him. And you shouldn't either. But we can stick him out front as your ostensible agent. You and I will write the contract ourselves, whether he likes it or not. You can ask Sam to review it in confidence, if you want to. Or get a Hollywood lawyer to look it over. I'm thinking of a two-year contract. If the show flops, we'll put you back on the *Glenda Grayson Show,* with bigger billing, and I'll see to it that they write better stuff for you."

"Mr.— Jonas. I'm grateful to you."

He put his hand on hers again. This time he closed his fingers around her hand. "Will you do something for me? If you say no, it's okay. A no won't kill the deal we've been talking about. But ever since I first saw you on television I've thought about what a vision it would be if you danced nude. Would you do that for me, Margit?"

Her face flushed, and she nodded.

"I have all kinds of records," he said, pointing to a stereo system. "Pick out something for your music."

She undressed first, pulling the skirt over her head, then pulling off the leotards. She had no pubic hair. She saw his surprised stare at her naked pudenda, and she self-consciously covered herself with her hand. "I can't risk wisps of hair showing around the edges of leotards," she said. "So I shave it."

He nodded. "You're a vision," he said.

She went to the stereo cabinet and looked through his collection of records.

She chose the song "I'm in Love with a Wonderful Guy" from *South Pacific*. It was lively music, and she performed a lively dance. The next band on the record was "Younger Than Springtime," and to that she danced sinuously. Jonas was enthralled.

She came to the couch, sat down, and took another swallow of Irish whiskey. Her skin gleamed with a trace of perspiration. She made no move toward putting her clothes back on.

"Margit, you are the most beautiful girl I've ever seen," Jonas said in complete sincerity.

"I guess it's gonna be just like Sam told me," she said softly.

2

"Okay, fill me in, Eddie."

Angie sat at a table in the coffee shop of the Flamingo facing a man who had once been her brother-in-law. Eddie Latham. Jerry's brother. Seven years younger than Jerry, he was just thirty-one, and he looked like Jerry, though Jerry had been only twenty-five when he was killed in the Normandy Invasion. Eddie had been only fourteen when she saw him last, not long before she was arrested.

"Ma died a couple years ago," said Eddie. "She always thought you ought to've kept in touch."

"Maybe I should have," said Angie. "But she didn't keep in touch either. I was in jail three months in Manhattan. She came to see me once. I was in the reformatory thirty-nine months, and I got two letters from her. Anyway, I'm sorry you lost her, Eddie. How old was she?"

"She was sixty-four. Had a bad heart the last few years."

"So why have you come to see me?" Angie asked.

"I'd have looked you up a long, long time ago if I could've found you," he said. "I always thought Jerry married the prettiest girl in town. After Jerry was killed, I got the crazy idea I'd go to West Virginia and meet you when you came out of the slammer. But guess where I was: at Fort Dix, drafted, taking basic training. I was sent to the Pacific, but the war ended before I ever fired a shot or anybody fired one at me. I came home. I tried to find you. You won't believe this, but I hired a private eye. The last address the Federal Bureau of Prisons had for you was White Plains. You'd been given final release, and they didn't know where you'd gone. I gave up. Then a couple months ago I saw your picture in the paper: director of a big corporation. I said, Hey, that's Angie! So, first chance I got, I came to Vegas."

Angie smiled and shook her head.

"Simple story," said Eddie. He glanced around and frowned as if the bright bustle of the coffee shop offended him—not the right setting for what he apparently meant to be a solemn and significant conversation. "So where *did* you go in 1945, if you don't mind my asking?"

"I married again," she said. "Wyatt. We went to California, then came here. I've been here ever since."

"You and Jonas Cord must have a very friendly relationship," said Eddie.

Angie smiled and nodded. "Very friendly," she agreed.

Eddie took a package of Camels and a lighter from his jacket pocket. He offered her a cigarette, and she shook her head. Jonas had smoked little for years and had stopped smoking entirely after the heart attack. She didn't smoke in his presence, which meant in effect that she had stopped, too. Eddie lit the unfiltered Camel, drew the smoke down deep, and blew it out through his nose.

"I figured that," he said. He grinned. "I came along too early and then too late."

"You must be married."

"I was for six years. Two kids. She has them."

"I can't believe you came to Vegas to see me just for old times' sake, just because you're a romantic," said Angie. "What business are you in, Eddie?"

He stared into his coffee cup and took another deep drag on his cigarette. "That's the point, Angie," he said. "Somebody asked me to talk to you."

3

Captain Frank's was a fish restaurant on Cleveland's Ninth Avenue Pier. On a day on the cusp of spring, the view from the broad windows was of an angry green Lake Erie, its waves whipped up, spray flying and visible like snowflakes against the gray sky. The place was very well known in Cleveland, and well thought of.

A round table for six was saved every day for Carlo Vulcano, and rare was the day when he was not at his table. On days when he was not there, no one sat at his table, even his friends, for fear he would come in and find someone he did not want to talk to that day sitting at his table. People sat at his table only at his specific and personal invitation—usually four or five men, today only one.

That one was Eddie Latham.

"So. You are not able to report success."

Eddie shook his head. "I am sorry, Don Carlo. I did all I could."

"Did you offer to marry her?"

"I promised her what you promised: a villa on a Brazilian beach. I told her it was not too late to have children. But— She is loyal to the man. She thinks of him as her great benefactor. I think she is in love with him, Don Carlo."

"You invoked the memory of your brother?"

"She said we had to face a fact. Jerry was a grifter. That's what she called him, a grifter. She said that's what he was, at best."

"She told you nothing, then?"

"Don Carlo . . ." Eddie turned up the palms of his hands. "I did everything I could."

"Did you speak of exposing her criminal record?"

"She says Cord knows about it."

Carlo Vulcano turned his face away from Eddie and for a long moment stared at the pitching gray-green water of the lake. "The newspapers who were so intrigued with her appointment to the CE board of directors did not take the trouble to discover it. I wonder—"

"She is still a beautiful woman," said Eddie quietly.

"You were taken with her, Eddie. If you had succeeded, you could have had her."

"Don Carlo, I am afraid she is not the kind of woman who—"

"Who what? That was your problem, Eddie. You do not understand women. Businessmen trade in women like they trade in commodities, like oil or wheat or pork bellies. You say she is beautiful. So is every one of them, to somebody. You were *afraid* of her, Eddie!"

"I did the best I could for you, Don Carlo. I would never think of doing anything less—for you."

"Uhmm . . . Well, I'm told you're a good boy. We thought that being related to her you might be able to do more than the usual thing. But— Go now, Eddie. Go back to New York. I will not speak ill of you."

Eddie Latham wondered if he should not kiss the hand of the Don, but it wasn't offered to him, and already Don Carlo Vulcano was summoning others to his table. Eddie hurried out of the restaurant.

4

The *Glenda Grayson Show* was broadcast live, and when the star came off the set after her final number she was drenched with sweat. She was also high with exhilaration. She needed a shower, and she needed a drink.

Danny Kaye had come off the set just ahead of her and waited for her. He threw his arms around her. "We work good together, huh?" He laughed. "Hey!" He, too, was sweating and high. He seemed about to break into another song and dance.

"C'm in and have a drink, ol' buddy," she said, leading him toward her dressing room.

"What? Two more shows this season?" he asked as he walked beside her, holding her arm.

"Two more. Then, by God, contract," she said.

"Your producer was in the booth," said Kaye. "I thought he looked kinda grim. Does anything ever satisfy the man?"

"Nothing in this world ever entirely satisfies Jonas Cord," she said. "Bat you could satisfy. Not Jonas. Tomorrow I'll get a memo telling me it was a great performance but also telling me how it could have been better."

"Like a sponsor," said Kaye.

She threw open the dressing room door. "Scotch!" she cried. "Something for Danny!"

Sam Stein was sitting on the small couch in her dressing room, waiting for her to come off the set. Sitting beside him was a handsome, swarthy man she did not recognize. He was smoking a cigar and lounged comfortably on the couch, with his legs crossed. Glenda had no idea who he was, but if Sam had brought him he was okay with her.

Amelia had served as Glenda's dresser for the past two years. She was a handsome, formidable, slender black woman, maybe forty years old, so far as Glenda could estimate, and Glenda had learned to place confidence in her. She had a light Scotch with plenty of ice and soda waiting, and she handed it to the star and stepped behind her to begin unfastening her finale gown.

"It came down very well, Glenda," said Sam Stein. "The ratings will be—"

"Danny brings the good ratings," said Glenda. "Pour him a drink, for Christ's sake, and hand him a wet towel."

Glenda let Amelia take off her dress, leaving her standing in the middle of the dressing room in white nylon panties and bra. She took a gulp from her drink and stepped inside the shower. Her underclothes were wet with sweat, and usually she soaped herself and them together, then took them off, rinsed them, and hung them over the top of the glass door. The shower water steamed the glass, and a blurred image of her showed through the door.

"Didn't give you a chance to introduce your friend, Sam," she said.

"He's John Stefano," said Sam. "Got some ideas for us."

"Joke writer?" she asked.

"Not exactly."

"Well, nice to meet ya, John Stefano. Congratulate Danny on a great performance. When he comes on, we do the best show of the year."

Stefano nodded and smiled at Danny Kaye. "I've admired your work for many years," he said.

"Thank you," said Kaye. "Well . . . Sam says you're not a joke writer—which I didn't think you were. What is your business, Mr. Stefano, if I may ask?"

"Investments," said Stefano.

"The very best line of business," said Danny Kaye. He took the answer as ominously uncommunicative and retreated from the subject. "Anyway, I hope you enjoyed the show."

"Oh, yes," said Stefano.

Kaye took a sip from the Scotch Sam handed him. "I have to get on to my dressing room," he said.

"Don't you dare leave before I get outa here and give you a big kiss," said Glenda. "Time for a towel, Amelia."

Amelia handed her one towel and held up another while Glenda dried herself and pulled on a flowered silk dressing gown. She picked up the bottle and strengthened her drink.

"Well, you say Mr. Stefano has some ideas for us," she said to Sam.

"Some business ideas," said Sam.

"I'll be going," said Danny Kaye. "You'll want to talk in private."

Glenda threw her arms around him and kissed him on the mouth. "Thank you, lover," she said. "Give my best to Sylvia."

Glenda turned to Amelia. "Thanks," she said. "You can go get yourself some dinner now."

Glenda sat down at her dressing table and went to work on her hair and makeup. Her back was to Sam Stein and John Stefano, but she could see them in the mirror. "What ya got in mind, guys?"

"Some different things," said Sam. "To start with, I've got some news for you. Margit notified me this morning that she doesn't want me for her agent anymore."

"What the hell?"

"And guess who her new agent is gonna be," Sam continued. "Ben Parrish. How does that grab ya?"

"It grabs me that Jonas Cord is getting ready to give Glenda's show to Margit Little," she said angrily.

"No. He won't do that. You're still the only money-maker Cord Productions has got. I figure he'll spin her off, set up a *Margit Little Show*."

"Well, I guess you can't blame the girl if she takes *that* deal," said Glenda. "She'll get another deal with it, though—that she may not find irresistible. Jonas Cord will want in her pants."

"He's already in her pants," said Sam.

"And Ben'll be in 'em next," said Glenda.

"I doubt it. I think the Cords have chewed up Ben Parrish and spit him out. They queered some of his deals. For a guy like him, money dries up when the Cords put the word around that anybody who backs his deals will offend them. He can't do anything they don't want him to do. They've made him dependent on them."

Glenda turned and smiled over her shoulder. "Except in one important respect, Ben's a *little* guy. When he messed around with Jo-Ann, he brought down the wrath of a family that can buy and sell him out of pocket change."

"Which brings us to another point," said Sam. "John Stefano is here to offer us a deal."

"Let's say I'm here to do some preliminary talking about a *possible* deal," said Stefano. Now that he was going to talk, he put his cigar aside in a heavy glass ashtray. "When you came in from the set, you said you had to do just two more shows under your present contract with Cord Productions. When you go to negotiation with the Cords, it could be very helpful to you if you had an alternative."

"What might the alternative be?"

"Just thinking out loud," said Stefano. "I can book you into the best clubs in the United States, not to mention a run in one of the big rooms in Havana. You can make more money than you're making in television, and you won't have to work so hard, because you can use the same show for a whole year."

"The way I used to do," she said.

Sam interjected an idea. "Suppose you were off television for a year. There would probably be a big demand for you to return."

"Or maybe not," she said. "The public's got a short memory."

"You're a star," said Sam. "The public won't forget you."

"We can keep you in the public eye," said Stefano.

"Get you covered in the tabloids. Then maybe we form a production company—GG Productions, let's say—and package a return show. We go to one of the networks with a pilot tape. We can orchestrate everything."

"Where's the money for all this coming from?" Glenda asked.

"We can get it," said Stefano simply.

"I suppose I shouldn't ask where the money will come from?"

"Does it make a difference?" Stefano asked.

"Does it, Sam?" she asked.

Sam Stein shook his head. "Not to me it doesn't. This deal can be a great career boost for you, Glenda. And it gets the Cord family off our backs forever."

"Deal, then," said Glenda.

5

"Tittle Tattle" was a syndicated column, originating in Hollywood and written when she was sober enough to do it by a onetime bit player named Lorena Pastor. The column was syndicated in sixty-eight newspapers, thanks partly to heavy promotion by the syndicate, thanks also to Lorena's formidable reputation that persuaded people to confide in her. Gossip was her stock in trade, but it was also understood in the movie community that mention in "Tittle Tattle" often goosed new life into fading careers or into lusterless pictures.

—("Don't be surprised if you hear about a bust-up between La Crawford and her current. Her latest ex, save one, has been seen leaving in the golden light of dawn, and we hear that an old fire is hot again. After all, old flames often burn hottest.")

—("The town is ga-ga about Dan Armstrong's stellar acting in *The Condemned*. This little-heralded flick is a sure-fire winner. And don't forget—nobody else has been telling you.")

Lorena had the facial complexion of an Indian elephant: a tangle of wrinkles that lotions would not soften, sanding could not remove. She could only try to distract attention from it by wearing exaggerated lipstick and mascara, all obscured by veils that hung from her hats. She affected also an air of giddy ebullience: grinning widely, fluttering her hands, dancing about on her feet as if she were a girl of twenty, not a woman of seventy. Privately, people in the movie industry called her a viper, a harridan, and a lush.

Her usual turf was a table at the Brown Derby or another restaurant or watering hole, but this noon she ate a box lunch in the office of her publisher, Walter Richard Hamilton, Junior. He had accommodated her known penchant by providing her a pint of Beefeater gin, a bucket of ice cubes, and half a lime.

"I've got a story for you, Lorena," he said.

"Let's hope it's *true,* Walt," she said. "You know my policy—only to publish what can be—"

"Right, Lorena. Dad respected you for that. So do I. I can assure you this story is true."

"Well, *tell* me then!"

"Okay. You know the cute little dancer—ballerina-type dancer—who plays the teenage daughter on the *Glenda Grayson Show?* Margit Little? Okay. She sleeps with Jonas Cord."

"Oh, my dear! So did *I* once—when I was twenty-five years younger. How many women in America haven't—"

"Lorena. I want you to run the story. Not only that, I want you to give it big play."

She lifted the glass into which she had poured gin over ice and squeezed lime juice. "Of course, dear Walt! Don't forget, though, the man is a *menace!* You aren't ordering me to buy us a libel suit?"

"Let me worry about that," said Hamilton.

"You're the boss," she said simply.

"Here's the story. Her agent Sam Stein warned the girl not to go to Cord's hotel suite alone. She did anyway. She was supposed to call him when she got home. She called the next day. Sam's had her watched. When Cord is in town, she is not home nights."

"Sam's pissed," said Lorena Pastor. "You know he lost Margit Little as a client. To Ben Parrish. He might be—"

"Don't worry about it," said Hamilton. "I want you to play it. I'll run pictures with the column—sick old man and fresh young girl. That's the theme: old lecher taking the bloom of youth off pretty little dancer."

"Jonas Cord an old letch?" She shook her head. "I was in my forties. He was in his late twenties. Not a letch, Walt—a *stud!"*

"Write the story my way, Lorena," said Hamilton firmly. "Either that, or I'll write it and insert it in your column."

"Understood," she said sadly.

"Okay. Drink up. You see, your onetime friend Mr. Cord has run his ass up against some people who aren't afraid of him."

6

An hour later Hamilton was on the telephone to Detroit. "Done, my friend," he said. "No, I didn't have to; she'll write it herself, in her own inimitable style. Sixty-eight papers, Jimmy! Plus others that'll pick up the story as news. Sunday in thirty-five papers, Monday in the rest. This time next week every other American will know that Jonas Cord is screwing Margit Little. So— We got a deal, right? Your local will sign the contract. Right. Right. Sure, I know it's peanuts to what your pension fund is putting into the new Glenda Grayson. But you can understand a man's interest in— Right. Your word's good. I know that. So's mine. Look for the story on Sunday."

25

1

JONAS HAD RECONSIDERED HIS DECISION ABOUT A BEARD. It was gray, no question about that, but he had retained not just a barber but a hair stylist to trim it, and the man came to the suite twice a week to clip both beard and hair. With a straight razor he cut the hair low on Jonas's cheeks, to give him a beard and chin whiskers reminiscent of Abraham Lincoln's in the final Brady photograph—which indeed he acknowledged was his model. Unlike Lincoln, though, Jonas wore a mustache, which was the most difficult part of the trimming job.

Lest the beard seem to have turned him into some sort of bohemian character, Jonas returned to wearing jackets, white shirts, and neckties. A tailor came to the suite and measured him for half a dozen conservative single-breasted business suits. He abandoned the rumpled khaki slacks and golf shirts.

In April he flew to New York. In the Waldorf Towers apartment he did not reclaim his office but left it to Bat. Father and son met for lunch at The Four Seasons.

"I can break the bitch," Jonas said.

"No, you can't," said Bat. "She doesn't need us. Besides, she's got money behind her. She can walk away from us—"

"And shoot us a finger," Jonas interrupted. "How'd you think you were going to prevent her from doing that? By humpin' her? Well, it didn't work, did it?"

"That doesn't work very often, does it?" Bat challenged. "You haven't made it work any better than I have. You think you've sewed up Margit Little's loyalty by—to use your term—humping *her?*"

"Margit—"

"The *Margit Little Show* will not replace the *Glenda Grayson Show,*" Bat interrupted. "Not in ratings, not in revenue. Hell, she's got talent, she's appealing, and in time she'll be a winner. But next season we don't have a major show."

"Are you telling me I fucked it up?" Jonas asked irritably.

"I'm not saying it. *You* say it, if you think it's possible."

"You humped our star, then dropped her," said Jonas.

"You're humping Margit," said Bat grimly. "That's the problem. You started humping Margit, then you announced you were going to build a new show around her, and when Glenda asked for more money, you said no. What'd you think she'd do?"

"Son," Jonas murmured with mock patience, "Glenda didn't go off the reservation because I'm humping Margit and am going to make a new star of her. She'd have gone off, no matter what. *Two days,* just two goddamned days, after we broke off negotiations, she announced her nightclub schedule. She and Sam Stein didn't arrange that in two days. That took time to set up. When they came in to negotiate, they already knew she was going to do nightclubs all next season. Face it, Bat. The bitch sold out."

Bat drew a deep breath. "Margit is damaged goods," he said. "When the word got out that you were sleeping with her, the whole goddamned world took that as an explanation as to why you wanted to build a show for her."

"I told you last year to build her up, in anticipation that Glenda would jump. And you didn't do it."

"I had a few other things to do, if you recall. Anyway, we didn't announce a plan to build her up until the word was out that you and Margit—"

He paused for a moment. Senator Jacob Javits had come in, spotted Bat, and was coming toward their table. Bat introduced him to Jonas, and the three men chatted for a moment. When the senator moved on, Jonas and Bat picked up their conversation.

"There's more to this than just a performer with a wounded ego," said Jonas. "Sam Stein has been talking to Lennie Hirschberg about a new *Glenda Grayson Show,* for the '59 season. That's going to take a lot of money, and guess who's coming up with it."

"Who?"

"The Teamsters Union. Central States Pension Fund. Jimmy Hoffa."

"Yeah, and they're funding a Vegas hotel," said Bat.

"You have any idea how much money is in that fund?" Jonas asked. "Billions."

"But that's a trust fund," said Bat. "How can they invest it in a television show?"

"They play fast and loose with their fiduciary obligations," said Jonas. "Dave Beck did, and now Hoffa does. They don't invest just to make the fund grow; they invest to wield power. And they've formed an alliance with some damned unsavory guys."

"You think they approached Glenda Grayson, rather than the other way around?"

Jonas nodded. "And I hardly need tell you why.

Problems are beginning to show up at the construction site. They don't want the InterContinental built."

"Strikes?"

"No. That would tip their hand too much. Delays in delivery. After three days preparation for pouring a concrete floor, we couldn't pour because one of the five mixer trucks failed to show up. You can't pour four and add one later; that would make layers and seriously weaken the structure. The driver said the truck broke down on the road. I suspect he *made* it break down."

"Well . . . maybe," said Bat skeptically.

"If that was the only thing that's happened, I wouldn't be suspicious. Last week a load of steel fasteners disappeared from a warehouse in San Francisco, and our men had to stop work until we could get a load from another source. The warehouse said they'd accidentally delivered our fasteners to the wrong job. And so on and so on and so on. Too many coincidences. We're falling more and more behind. I don't need to tell you how much it's costing."

Jonas stood up to greet an auburn-haired woman who had literally trotted across the room to his table.

"Jonas, *dah*-ling!" she boomed in her all-but-patented smoky voice. "Back in town! And this is that mysterious son of yours who doesn't *go* where people *go*—which has deprived me of the pleasure of meeting him."

Jonas kissed her hand, then introduced her to Bat. "This is Tallulah Bankhead, in case you hadn't already figured that out."

"In the gossip columns again, naughty boy," she said, shaking her head. "Thank *Gawd* that wretched woman Lorena Pastor never found out about you and *me!*"

"Found out what, Tallulah?" Jonas asked, smiling and frowning at the same time.

"That we never *did it!*" She laughed. "That would have been a much more *scandalous* story than if we had." She turned to Bat. "Give me a ring, dah-ling. Come up to my place and play bridge sometime. Well . . . ta-ta."

As she hurried back to her own table and Bat and Jonas sat down again, nearly every eye in the room was on them.

"Whatever you do, don't go to her apartment and play bridge with her," said Jonas.

"Any particular reason?"

"She takes off her clothes and plays bridge nude. Not always, just when the spirit moves her. She's casual about it, makes no big drama. She goes on playing bridge as if nothing were different. Sometimes it's embarrassing as hell—depending who's at the table with you. She did it in front of David Sarnoff one night. He's a man not easily embarrassed, but she took him completely unawares, and he began to cough and turned red, and I thought maybe he was having a heart attack."

"She mentioned the Lorena Pastor column," said Bat. "How did Angie react to that?"

"Angie's realistic," said Jonas. "And if your personal life is none of my business, mine's none of yours."

2

Angie loved the black Porsche that Jonas had given her for Christmas in 1952. The hotel garage kept it washed and waxed, and she liked to go for drives in the desert. She'd had it up to 125 miles per hour and had sensed it had more in it when she eased off on the accelerator. Once she'd been chased by a Nevada highway patrolman, and he had simply given up after a few miles. He was getting all he could out of his special police Ford, and she was opening more distance between them. He knew who she was and meant only to give her a warning anyway, so he pulled off the road, and when she passed him on her way back to town, he just blinked his lights, and she blinked hers playfully.

Usually she drove alone, though sometimes Jonas rode with her. Today Morris Chandler sat in the right seat.

"Haven't you got it figured out?" he asked her. "You can't trust him. Nobody can trust him."

"He can sleep with another woman if he wants to," said Angie, staring at the road, not glancing at Chandler. "He never said he wouldn't. He made no commitment of that kind."

"He's not a nice man," said Chandler. "Nevada Smith was a good man, a true friend. He asked me to take Jonas in to help him duck a subpoena, and the next thing I know he owns the hotel and I'm his employee. And so are you. And you're sleeping with him."

"He's been good to me," she said firmly.

"Yeah, but Jonas giveth and Jonas taketh away. Whatever you've got from him, he can take away any time he feels like it. You've got no *security,* honey. What are you, forty years old? His new girlfriend is barely twenty."

"Twenty-two," said Angie dryly.

"Where you gonna be ten years from now?"

"What are you trying to say, Morris? Spit it out."

"I have friends who could do some very good things for you, Angie," said Chandler.

"Who are they? And why would they want to do anything for me?"

"Never mind who they are. They're the kind of people that, if you do something good for them, they'll take care of you for the rest of your life. Hell, that's what they've done for me. I'm gonna be seventy-six years old this year. If Jonas fired me, they'd take care of me. It's what you call loyalty."

"If I do 'something good for them,' huh? Just what do they have in mind?"

"They want information, that's all. Maybe copies of some papers."

"In other words, they want me to betray Jonas," she said coldly.

"The bastard has betrayed *you!*"

She shook her head. "No. He hasn't."

"Be realistic, Angie."

"The answer is no, Morris."

"Better think about somethin'. These guys I'm talking about are loyal and all that, but they're also the kind of guys you don't say no to. They have ways of getting what they want."

"That's a threat, I suppose."

"Angie, let's don't use bad words! You're being offered a good deal."

"The answer is no, Morris."

He sighed. "Jesus . . . I suppose you'll tell Jonas about this conversation."

Angie shrugged.

3

Dr. Maxim was at the wheel of *Maxim's III,* taking the boat home at the end of a half day's fishing, during which nobody had caught anything but a bonito.

Nobody was unhappy about that. They had come out to fish, but their real purpose, of getting to know each other better, had been accomplished.

Morgana Maxim had arranged the afternoon. As a prominent Democrat, she wanted to know all other prominent Democrats so far as possible and be influenced by personal judgment, not by what she read in the newspapers. Tanned and sun-bleached as always, she sat in the rear of the boat, relaxed and sipping from a gin and tonic.

Toni sat beside her stepmother, dressed almost identically in a red polo shirt and brief white shorts.

Sitting in one of the two fishing chairs, wearing tennis whites—shorts and shirt—with a Red Sox baseball cap and aviator sunglasses, smoking a small cigar, his face deeply wrinkled from squinting into the sun, was the man Morgana had wanted to meet: Senator Jack Kennedy of Massachusetts.

Senator Kennedy had barely failed to take the 1956 vice-presidential nomination away from the farcical Estes Kefauver, and it was widely supposed he would claim a spot on the 1960 Democratic ticket. He had only one hurdle to leap: reelection in Massachusetts in the fall.

Morgana had been impressed, as Toni had told her she would be. Toni had known Jack Kennedy from the time of his arrival in the Senate in 1953, when she was still an aide to Senator Holland. More recently she met with him from time to time as a political reporter for *The Washington Post*. She had learned to mimic his Boston-Harvard accent, and one time he had overheard her doing it. From that time, they counted each other as friends.

"You should hear Toni do *me*," he had said to Dr. and Morgana Maxim just after they came aboard the boat. "If I wanted to do a radio speech, I could let her do it, and I could take a day off."

Toni had laughed. "Let him explain to you that there's no such thing as a Harvard campus, just the 'Haa-v'd yaad,'" she had said. "Sometimes he takes his daag for a ride in the caa."

Kennedy had laughed heartily. "See? A little change in voice, and she could take my place at any microphone."

He had caught the bonito. They had tossed it back.

"Plans?" Morgana asked Kennedy.

He shrugged. "Life is short," he said. "Art is long. Who knows?"

4

Jack Kennedy remained astride Toni, though he had withdrawn from her and his drooping penis gleamed with their fluids.

"Would Dr. Maxim and Morgana be angry if they knew about this?" he asked.

"Morgana'd be disappointed if we didn't," said Toni. "She'll be a delegate for you, and she'll lead other delegates."

"What about, uh, Jonas Cord the Third?"

"Ask me no questions, I'll tell you no lies. I don't ask you—"

"No, you don't, and I appreciate that, Toni."

This was the third time they had been together this way, and each time it had been a completely satisfying experience, made more satisfying by their mutual understanding that they did it honestly: for the pleasure of the moment, with no thought of any kind of commitment. He was a handsome, personable, virile man, and her pleasure in him was enhanced by her hunch that one day she would look back on these hours and be glad she had fucked with one of the century's preeminent leaders, maybe even a President.

Another reason for their satisfaction was the certainty that they could trust each other.

"What can I do for you, Toni?" he asked.

"Uhhmm . . ." She chuckled. "You've done quite enough, thank you."

He grinned broadly, showing his teeth. "I had something, uh, different in mind. A different kind of thing. I mean—"

"Jack . . . I'm not from Massachusetts. You don't have to do me favors."

"You've done some very nice favors for me," he said.

"Meaning I did something I didn't enjoy so you could enjoy it?" she asked. "C'mon, Jack. Women like to play the old game: pretending they can hardly bear to do it and are making a big sacrifice for you, making themselves martyrs. But don't kid yourself. Women like it just as much as men do. Anyway, this woman does."

"I'm glad to hear it."

She nudged him playfully.

"Are you going to marry Jonas Cord the Third?" he asked.

"I haven't decided," she said.

"His father is like my father," said Jack Kennedy. "Life in that family would be exciting . . . but tough and demanding. Challenging, Toni. Challenging."

"Speaking of challenges. The Cords are being challenged to get out of Las Vegas."

"Mafia turf," said Kennedy.

"Hoffa," said Toni. "The Teamsters are making it difficult for Cord Hotels to build the InterContinental. No strikes. Just . . . coincidences."

"My brother Bobby would be interested. So would Senator McClellan. I'll talk to Bobby about it."

"Do that, will you, Jack? I'd appreciate it. And have Bobby keep me informed, okay?"

5

Ben Parrish enjoyed driving Jo-Ann's Porsche 356. He appreciated fine cars. It was the only car he'd ever driven in which you might actually turn off music on the radio and just listen to the engine. It handled beautifully, too. You didn't have to steer it around a turn; you just pointed it where you wanted it to go, and the little coupe would obediently slip through the curve—provided you didn't ask too much of it and make the rear end come around.

Because he was driving the Porsche, Ben had decided to return to Santa Monica by way of Mulholland Highway and Topanga Canyon Road. He was doing just fine, too, pushing seventy most of the time, up to eighty occasionally, and conceding sixty or below only when he had to.

His mind was on his wife. She was waiting for him, ready with an ice-cold vodka martini, for sure, and something more besides that would melt the ice in that martini.

He'd fallen into shit and come out smelling like roses. He could stand the old man: Jonas. He had to grit his teeth to be polite and deferential, but he could do it. He could function as a Cord errand boy. There was money in it. And status. And there'd be an inheritance. The girl—Jo-Ann—was a handful in more ways than one; but she was the most eager to satisfy of any piece of tail he'd ever had; and whether she'd married him for his long schlong or to shoot a finger at her father, she was a good wife in most senses of the term.

She was—

What the hell was this? A car had come up behind him and was blinking its lights. The guy wanted to pass. Yeah? Well, he'd play hell, too. Whatever that was back there, it was what men who knew cars called Detroit Iron, and no Plymouth or Dodge was gonna pass this Porsche, no matter how much somebody had souped it up.

On the other hand— He was in no condition to race, really, Porsche or no Porsche. He was in firm control of it, for sure, but he'd had too much vodka to stretch the car or himself. What the hell? Let the guy pass. If he had any brains, he'd know he'd been *let* past.

Ben slowed a little and edged to the right. The car came up on his left. It was a Plymouth—what a car to be passing a Porsche!—but obviously modified, its unmuffled engine roaring. He glanced, trying to get a look at the driver. What? Some crazy kid?

Crazy! Running alongside of him, the Plymouth suddenly lurched right and slammed the Porsche. Ben fought for control and kept away from the guardrail. He floored the accelerator, knowing he could, if he had to, outrun any goddamned Plymouth ever modified; but as the Porsche gained speed the Plymouth veered right again and slammed hard. Ben couldn't control it. The Porsche rammed the guardrail. Metal flew. Glass flew. He hurtled forward and felt his arm break against the steering wheel.

6

Jonas sat across the desk from a thirty-two-year-old assistant district attorney named Carter. The bespectacled young black man was sufficiently awed to have crushed his cigarette when he noticed that Mr. Cord did not smoke.

"Have you heard my name, maybe?" Jonas asked.

"Yes, sir, Mr. Cord. Absolutely."

"Well, don't think of me as a guy who's come in your office to throw his weight around. That's not why I'm here. You're going to do what you have to do, your duty, and I didn't come to suggest you do anything else. I'm hoping, though, that my name suggests to you that I'm not the kind of man who'd come to your office and make wild, stupid statements he couldn't back up."

"Your name suggests anything but that, Mr. Cord."

"So, what was his blood-alcohol percent?"

"Point-one-seven."

"Drunk," said Jonas.

"Yes. The statute says you shouldn't drive if you've got point-one-five."

"Marginal?"

"I took part in a test, drinking and blowing in the meter, so I could relate to those numbers when I have to present a case to a court," said Carter. "Frankly, Mr. Cord, if I had point-one-seven in me, I couldn't *find* my car, much less get the key in the ignition and start it."

Jonas nodded. "Okay, schnocked."

"Yes, sir. I'm afraid that's what Mr. Parrish was."

"Kinda depends on the man, doesn't it?" Jonas suggested. "I'd be willing to bet I could drink enough to make the meter show one-point-seven, and I could take a cop out in the car with me and pass a driver's license test."

The young district attorney smiled. "I'm skeptical about that, Mr. Cord," he said. "But what's the point?"

"When a man knocks back as much vodka every day as Ben Parrish has been doing for years, he develops a certain tolerance for it. I don't like the son of a bitch much, but I'd be willing to ride in a car with him after he'd had six drinks. My point is, I don't think what he had to drink is what caused the accident."

"I'm listening, Mr. Cord."

"I don't mean to put down your investigators. I know they're honest and did what they believed was right. But I have investigators, too, and I think yours missed some facts. They missed some because they'd made up their minds what had happened and only looked for the facts that sustained their theory. They missed others because they couldn't have known them and couldn't have found them—unless they know what I know."

The young lawyer reached for his cigarettes, then quickly put them back in his pocket.

"Go ahead and smoke," said Jonas. "I quit for good reasons, but you don't need to be uncomfortable."

"Thank you." Carter lit a cigarette. "So, what facts have we overlooked, Mr. Cord?"

"Ben Parrish's car was smashed in thoroughly on the right side, where it hit the guardrail, which your investigators' report emphasizes. But why was the driver's-side door smashed in, too? Doesn't that suggest something?"

"I suppose it does," said Carter. "What did you have in mind?"

409

"Simple enough. Somebody rammed Ben Parrish and forced him into the guardrail. The big dent in the left door is at the height of an automobile bumper. Right above that is a smaller dent, with traces of green paint in it. Somebody rammed him."

"Why would somebody do that?"

"To kill him," said Jonas. "If that guardrail hadn't held—held really beyond what they're expected to do—Ben Parrish would have gone into the ravine."

"And what are the facts we couldn't have known?"

"This is where I ask you to believe I'm not the man to come to you with wild and stupid accusations. Ben Parrish is my son-in-law, as I suppose you know. Off the record, I'm not very happy about that, but that's the way it is. I think somebody may have tried to kill him to get at me. I've made some tough people very angry."

"Can you be more specific?" Carter asked.

"Well . . . How much specificity goes with the smashed-in door on the left side of the car? If he'd gone through the guardrail and rolled down into the ravine, no one would have noticed that left door. Even my guys wouldn't have. It would have been *so* simple. Drunk driver hits guardrail, rolls down rocky bank. The guardrail fouled somebody up."

Carter used his cigarette to give him a moment to think. He inhaled deeply and let the white smoke trickle out of his mouth. "What do you want me to do, Mr. Cord?"

"Whatever is right," said Jonas. "Have your investigators look at the car again. If they and you conclude the accident wasn't an accident, then the drinking wasn't so significant. Was it?"

"He broke the law, Mr. Cord. Drinking and driving is dangerous."

"But if he was a victim of attempted murder, that

puts a little different complexion on the case, doesn't it?"

"You're suggesting I drop the drunk-driving case?"

Jonas shook his head. "I don't want to say anything that so much as *suggests* I'm trying to exert improper influence. I brought an additional fact to your attention: the left door. I brought you an idea as to why someone might have tried to force Ben Parrish off the road and kill him. I hope you'll agree the case may not be a simple matter of drunk driving. It may be more."

"All right. I'll look into it."

7

Dave Amory sat with Bat in the Chrysler Building office. Most of Bat's endemic clutter was hidden under the covers of the rolltop desks. He faced Bat across the big table that served as desk for the chief executive officer of Cord Enterprises.

"It's war now, Bat," said Dave. "Teamsters drivers in four cities—Detroit, Chicago, Cleveland, and Newark—have refused to make deliveries to Inter-Continental loading docks, claiming they are non-standard and unsafe."

"Let independents haul our air freight," said Bat.

Dave shook his head. "We tried it in Chicago, figuring that would be the safest. They hit the trucks. Somebody dropped concrete blocks on them as they went under overpasses. Non-union companies are afraid to touch our air freight."

"Well, Hoffa is not the only guy who can play that game," said Bat grimly.

"Be goddamned careful, Bat," said Dave Amory. "Be goddamned careful."

8

Detroit *Free Press:*

Jay Fulton, vice president of the International Union of Teamsters and Warehousemen, was seriously injured last night when a concrete block, dropped from an overpass on the Jeffries Freeway, shattered the windshield of his limousine and disabled his driver, causing the car to veer across the center divider and into the path of an oncoming sixteen-wheeler.

Fulton, 46, is also a trustee of the Central States Pension Fund. Hospital officials removed him from the critical list early this morning, but he remains in guarded condition with fractured ribs, a punctured lung, a concussion, and a broken arm.

Teamsters President James Hoffa described the attack as "A cowardly attempt on the part of certain bosses to prevent this union from protecting its members. Such outrages will never succeed."

9

Detroit *News:*

Early arrivers at the executive offices of the International Union of Teamsters and Warehousemen knew something was wrong as soon as they entered the building this morning.

That smell—

It was the stench from a gooey mixture of tar

and kerosene and maybe some other things, that had been poured into all the drawers in some sixty file cabinets.

Left atop one of the cabinets was a box of wooden kitchen matches, suggesting that the files could have been burned if the intruders had so intended. One secretary, who asked not to be quoted by name, said the files would not have been any more completely destroyed if they had been burned. "Who can separate one paper from another?" she asked. "Who can read anything?"

The Teamsters Union takes some pride in its security. An official who similarly asked to be unnamed said it was apparent to him that someone had been paid more to let the files be destroyed than that someone was being paid to protect them.

"If the bosses can do this to us," he asked plaintively, "what can't they do?"

10

"Bat . . . Did you do it?"

Bat drew a deep breath and blew it out noisily. They were in bed. In the past she had not wanted to bring up things like this when they were in bed. Priorities. Why now?

"Bat . . . ?"

"What do you want me to say?"

"I just want to know if— Off the record. I'm not asking as a newspaper reporter. I'm asking as the woman who loves you."

He sighed again. "Look. Jimmy Hoffa is a *thug*. Am I supposed to let thugs destroy my business?"

"Would you kill him?" she asked.

He shook his head. "I won't have to."

"That's not the answer. *Would* you? *Could* you?"

"No."

Toni lay silent for a moment, not sure if she believed what he had just said. "What does your father think?"

He turned his head on the pillow and looked at her. She was lying on her back, staring at the ceiling. "I had a Catholic friend once who used rubbers so his girlfriend wouldn't get pregnant. I asked him if that wasn't against the rules, and he said, 'The pope doesn't know everything.'"

"So . . . You out-Jonas Jonas."

Bat reached for the glass that sat on the nightstand and took a sip of Scotch. "Toni," he said. "Don't try to make judgments about what I do in business. Sure I mean to out-Jonas Jonas. I'm gonna out-Jonas him. I'm going to take it away from him. When he dies. Or sooner."

"Which would you rather?" she asked.

"Sooner," he said.

26

1

JONAS SAT ON THE COUCH IN HIS SEVEN VOYAGES SUITE facing a stack of files and two telephones on the coffee table that by now had become his favorite of all the desks he'd ever had. It was ten at night, and the suite was closed now to everyone but him and Angie. He still wore the blue blazer and crisply creased slacks he had worn during the business day. Angie was naked. That was what he wanted. He still had Bat on the telephone from New York, where it was 1 A.M., but his eyes were on her.

"He's gone," he said to Bat. "Gone like the legendary Arab who folds his tent and disappears in the night. It's good riddance, of course, but I imagine it has some meaning."

He was talking about Morris Chandler. During the day, Chandler had simply disappeared. His clothes were gone from his suite. He had taken little from his office, but Jonas surmised he had copied any papers he wanted. He had left no word. His departure had been abrupt and unexpected.

"What? Well, let me ask Angie." Jonas turned from the telephone and asked her, "Bat wants to know if we can supply anything that would have a clear set of Chandler's fingerprints on it. In his office, you think?"

"We don't have to look in his office," she said. "He left a bottle of absinthe under our bar. His private stock. He had the damned stuff smuggled in from Hong Kong, you know. Nobody else ever touched those bottles, except maybe me when I poured him a drink."

"Angie says we can send you a bottle that will have his fingerprints on it. I'll have her wrap it so the New York courier can deliver it to you in the morning. So . . . You can go to bed now. I'll talk to you in the morning."

Angie had already gone to the bar and was looking underneath for the bottle of the illegal liquor. She slipped a paper napkin under it and lifted it by the cork.

"Absinthe," Jonas muttered. "The stuff is supposed to fry your brains. I always wondered why he liked it."

"Why do you suppose Bat wants Chandler's fingerprints?" Angie asked.

She had picked up another bottle and was pouring them two bourbons. Jonas was aware of her little trick. She knew he would want a drink about now, and if she poured it, it would be smaller than if he poured it himself.

"He didn't say, and I didn't ask," said Jonas. "But if I were Morris Chandler I'd watch my ass. Bat's got a mean streak in him."

"Like you never did." Angie laughed.

2

Glenda opened her new club show in the Nacional Hotel in Havana. Sam Stein had tried to book her into the Riviera, but Meyer Lansky vetoed the idea. "The long arm of the Cords," Sam complained.

Glenda told Sam she was tired of television and wanted to do a bold act, in the kind of costume she used to wear, doing a monologue with words and subjects that were taboo on the little tube. Sam was dubious, but she swept aside his cautions, wrote her own lines, and designed her whole production.

"I'm gonna be a *sensation,*" she told Sam.

For the first half of the show, she returned to a costume that had always worked very well for her and was something of a Glenda Grayson signature: a simple black dance leotard, this one cut very high on her hips, dark sheer stockings, blood-red garters, and black hat. Her hips and upper legs were bare, emphasizing as always the theatrical contrast between white skin and black costume.

After she had danced and sung, she climbed on a stool, took off her hat and shook her blond hair, then put the hat on again, now on the back of her head.

"God, I feel like I've come home!" she cried. "Do any of you have any idea how goddamn *boring* making a television show is? The first guy who yells 'About as boring as watching it' is gonna get a kick in the nuts. Anyway, I feel like I'm back where I belong, entertaining a live audience. And, hey, you *are* alive! And I thank you."

Her audience applauded.

"Television is supposed to be *family* entertainment. But if you make any reference as to how families come to be, they cut that from the script. Right? The TV father nearly faints with surprise when the wife tells him she's preggers. 'Really? Really, honey? Gee, that's great! I can't believe it!' What the hell did he think was gonna result from what he's been doin' three times a night for the past six months?"

The audience laughed, then applauded again.

"Margaret Mead, I think it was—you know, the

anthropologist—writes that some primitive people just don't make any connection between doin' it and getting pregnant. But . . . *Americans,* in the twentieth century yet? Television. Jesus!"

She took a break, while an act featuring trained chimpanzees amused her audience.

When she appeared on the stage for the second half of her show, she walked out into the beam of a spotlight wearing fifty strings of tiny glittering black beads that cascaded from her neck to her ankles. Under the thousands of beads she wore a diaphanous straight black gown. When she moved, the strings of beads shifted, and her audience could see she was wearing nothing under the gown. The sheer fabric blurred what they saw of her, but no one doubted they were seeing everything. The applause rolled up as a roaring wave before she sang a note.

She did not dance in the second half of the show. Or do a monologue. She walked around the stage singing, while four handsome, muscular young men in skin-tight flesh-colored panty hose danced a balletlike routine behind her.

The audience called her out for two encores and four extra bows.

"I'm better than ever!" she exulted in her dressing room afterward. "Thirty-six friggin' years old, and I'm better than ever!"

"You're dead for television," said Sam grimly. "That deal that was made for you is dead. No network will touch you. You're too hot."

"I'm too *good!*"

"That, too. But television won't dare. This is the time of Billy Graham and Norman Vincent Peale, and of President Eisenhower, who thinks this country is a 'God-fearing one.' Presley appears on the Sullivan Show, and they don't let the cameras show him below the waist. You just went out there *naked*, sis. You're using bad words on stage. You think a network is going to let you in front of its cameras?"

"The great unwashed won't even know about it," said Glenda. "Only the people who can afford to come to clubs like this will know—and they will appreciate it."

"Let us hope you're right. And this act has got to be toned down before you take it back to the States."

3

"Never mind, never mind, never mind," said Jonas to Ben Parrish. "And I didn't put a fix in. Get that idea out of your mind. You see to it that Jo-Ann cooperates one hundred percent with those guys I've assigned to her. Until this mess is straightened out."

Ben nodded solemnly. His broken left arm was in a sling. He couldn't drive. Jo-Ann had delivered him to the airport in Los Angeles, and Angie had driven him from the Las Vegas airport to The Seven Voyages. He wore a lightweight blue-and-white checked jacket, a white polo shirt, and gray slacks. He was subdued.

Angie handed Ben a vodka martini.

"What?" Jonas asked. "You a public-relations guy? You got connections? You can plant stories?"

"Yes, sir."

Jonas flared. "Don't call me sir. Or Mr. Cord. Or, God forbid, Dad. My daughter calls me by my first name, and so do you. Now— I've got some pictures. And I've got a piece of tape. You don't have to be a genius to figure out what I want done with them. Here. Look at these."

Infrared flash had penetrated Glenda Grayson's bold sheer costume even more than bright stage lights did. In the six 8 x 10 prints Jonas handed Ben, she appeared to have gone on stage stark naked, with nothing covering her but the strings of beads.

"Jesus Christ," Ben murmured.

"It's her, okay?" Jonas asked. "I mean, you oughta know."

"It's her, all right. What did she have in mind?"

"Ask Angie."

Angie shrugged. "What do you suppose she has in mind? She thinks she's been had. I guess I don't need to say how and by whom."

"Listen to this tape," said Jonas.

Angie pressed the button and started a tape rolling between reels. The voice of Glenda came out clear. "So, the guy says, 'I got one like a baseball bat.' And his wife says, 'Naahh. More like a *soft*ball bat.' The old guy asks the cute young chick for a date. She says, 'I don't think so. You're too bald.' He says, 'No. What I'm gonna show you is, I'm two-balled.'" The tape rolled on silent. Then a little laughter broke out, then more, and then more and more. "Took you a while to catch it, huh?" asked the voice of Glenda Grayson.

Angie switched it off.

"Old burlesque routines," said Jonas. "They say she was once a stripper. I guess she was."

Ben nodded. "You want this stuff placed."

"You got it."

"Okay, Jonas. I can do it."

"Keep your ass outa trouble, Ben. When you signed on with this family, you signed on for a war."

4

"Goddammit! *Goddammit!*"

Jimmy Hoffa slammed his fist down on the table in

the dining room of the house on the private airport. There were only three men in the room—Hoffa, John Stefano, and Morris Chandler—and Hoffa's outburst drew the attention of no one but the single hooker sitting at the bar, forlornly hoping for business.

"You knew the Cords are bastards," said Chandler.

"Well, so am I! Aren't I? Aren't *I* a bastard?"

"It's been suggested," Stefano replied dryly.

"Am I supposed to be afraid of those bastards? By God, I came up from the *streets!* I *worked* to get someplace. My daddy didn't leave me *nothin'*. He couldn't. I wasn't handed *my* living on a silver platter. Were you?"

Chandler shook his head. "I never ate a mouthful of bread I hadn't earned."

Hoffa's mood made another abrupt swing, and he grinned. "That somebody else hadn't earned," he said. "I've heard stories about you."

"All right, guys," said Stefano. "A plane just landed. It's maybe the guy we're waiting for. Time for you to blow, Maurie. I mean, go. You can't have a look at this guy."

Chandler shrugged. He took a final slug from his drink and stood. "I'm gone," he said. "Have a good meeting."

Five minutes later a sad-faced man entered the room.

"Here's Malditesta," said Stefano nodding toward the door. "Be careful how you talk to him."

No one—with maybe an exception or two among the dons—knew the real name of the man called Malditesta. In street talk, to shoot a man in the head was called giving him a major headache. The Italian words for headache were *mal di testa*. Combined they made the pseudonym given this man after he had shot three or four people in the head. At fifty or so,

Malditesta was aging but still handsome, taller and broader in the shoulders than the average man, with gray at his temples but sleek black hair not in the least thinned. His face was long, his nose and chin sharp, his eyes heavy-lidded, and he wore a lugubrious expression. His long raincoat was rumpled, as if he had worn it on the plane. He wore a brown hat.

Before he came to their table to join Stefano and Hoffa he stopped to listen to a proposition from the hooker, and from her smile it looked as if he had agreed to visit her a little later.

Stefano and Hoffa stood and shook hands with the hit man.

"Well . . . Glad you're here," said Hoffa. "You talk with Don Carlo?"

"Don't ask who I talked to," said Malditesta. "I won't tell anybody I talked to you, either."

Hoffa fixed a hard glance on Malditesta, but he might as well have fixed a hard glance on a tree for all the reaction he got.

Malditesta was a pro. In the past twenty years he had killed eighteen men and three women. It was said of him that he had never failed to hit his target. What was more important, he had never so much as been suspected. He had never been arrested, never questioned. Stefano had heard of him but had never met him. Jimmy Hoffa had never heard of him, until now.

"This has gotta be done fast and clean," said Hoffa.

Malditesta summoned a waitress. "A Beefeater martini on the rocks with a twist," he said. "Medium dry. Tell the bartender I do like about a quarter of a teaspoon of vermouth in my martini—assuming he's using a good vermouth." He spoke to Stefano. "What do you eat here?"

"Steak."

Malditesta nodded. "Rare. And a good red wine? Whatever's the best you've got. Dry. I'd rather have a Bordeaux than a Burgundy."

"It may have to be a California, sir," said the waitress.

Malditesta wrinkled his nose. "If there's a problem, tell the bartender to come out and show me what he's got."

When the waitress had left, Hoffa spoke impatiently. "You wanta talk business or not?"

"There is nothing to talk about, Mr. Hoffa. I work one way and one way only. You name a person and set a date. You hand me money, the down payment. What happens after that is none of your business."

Hoffa grinned scornfully. "What if the guy dies of typhoid?"

"If by the date you set the man is shot by a jealous wife, you still owe me the balance of the fee," said Malditesta coldly.

"You mean even if you didn't do it?"

"How would you know I didn't do it? Things can be arranged in a variety of ways."

"How do I contact you?" Hoffa asked.

"You don't. You can't. When you hear word that the job has been done, you hand over the balance of my money to Don Carlo Vulcano."

"How do I know you won't take the money I hand you today and scram?" Hoffa asked.

Malditesta turned his heavy-lidded eyes on John Stefano.

"Jimmy," said Stefano solemnly, in a voice so low Hoffa had to frown and strain to hear it. "Don't even talk like that to this man."

Hoffa pondered for a long moment, then shrugged.

"No offense," he said. "But if Don Carlo is handling the payout, why am I sitting here with a briefcase full of cash I'm delivering personally?"

"I always meet personally with the people I do business with," said Malditesta. "I want to know what they look like, in case I have to hunt for them later."

5

Angie reached over from the driver's seat and put a hand on the hand of the weeping and trembling blond girl. "Look. We'll take care of you," she said. "It's over. We'll take care of you and protect you."

A little later she led the girl from the black Porsche to the private elevator that carried them from the garage under The Seven Voyages to the suite where Jonas waited.

"The bastard beat her," said Angie to Jonas as she brought the sobbing girl into the room where Jonas sat at his coffee table desk.

"What? 'Cause he found out?"

Angie shook her head. "No. Because it's the kind of guy he is."

Jonas stood and walked toward the trembling girl. "She need a doctor?" he asked.

"Nuhh," said the girl. Her lips were swollen and bleeding, her right eye was turning black, and she had a growing swelling on her right cheek. "Nuh doctor. Gimme a *drink!* Gin!"

He took her hand and helped her to sit down on the couch. Angie went to the bar.

"Did you get pictures?" Jonas asked.

The girl nodded. "I think so."

"The guys are souping the film," said Angie. "We should know before long."

"We had no idea he'd beat you," said Jonas. "I figured it was just a regular deal. This— What's your name?"

"Vicky," the girl mumbled.

"This multiplies our obligation to you, Vicky," said Jonas.

"The money will be better, and we'll get you out of Vegas, set you up someplace else. Maybe we can get you out of the business, if you want out."

Vicky nodded. "Want out. Second time I've been busted up."

"Are you really sure you don't want to see a doctor?"

The girl shook her head firmly. "Teeth okay," she said. "Just fat lip, cuts— Like new in a couple weeks." She seized the glass Angie handed her and drank three big swallows of gin. "'Gain," she mumbled, handing the glass back.

"Can you tell me what you saw and heard?" Jonas asked.

"Heard nothing," said Vicky. "Saw . . . Three guys came first. One of them was Chandler. Another one was Jimmy Hoffa, I think. I'd seen the third guy before, remembered him for his big cigars. Chandler left before the fourth guy—*the one*—came in."

"Set up a photo array," said Jonas to Angie.

Angie laid out half a dozen pictures. She identified the photo of John Stefano as the man she remembered for his cigars. None of the pictures was of the man who had beaten her.

Jonas's security men had located Chandler the day after he abandoned his office in The Seven Voyages. Thereafter they tailed him. He made no great effort to hide himself, and it was easy enough to keep track of him. They heard a rumor that Chandler was to be the manager of a big, new, as-yet-unnamed casino-hotel that was to go up next year. When he went to the airport, it was certain he was meeting somebody important.

Having used the private airport himself, Jonas knew the private club in the old house off the ramp was a meeting place for a variety of men coming into Las Vegas for a variety of reasons. Some months ago he had managed to place one of his men in the club as bartender. That man had recruited Vicky as a spy, at five hundred dollars a month whether she did anything or not. Jonas's men had installed a hidden tape recorder and camera that could be activated by a button in the girl's bed. Until now Vicky's tapes and film had produced what Jonas had described as "high entertainment" but nothing significant.

The bartender had given Vicky instructions to work especially hard to sell her services to anyone who came to the club with Morris Chandler. This was the first time she had earned the bonus Jonas had authorized if she got pictures and tapes of a Chandler associate.

"Did he say anything worth hearing?" Jonas asked.

Vicky shook her head. "You can listen, but—"

"You can sleep in Mrs. Wyatt's suite tonight," said Jonas. "Have a bath and some soup or something. Like I said before, we'll work something out for you. You don't need to go back to the airport, ever. Do you know who I am?"

"I know . . . Mr. Cord."

"Then you know that when I say I'll take care of you, I'll take care of you."

6

Half an hour after Vicky, now a little wobbly from gin, went to Angie's suite, the lab men brought the photographs she had taken.

The equipment was good, and Vicky had known when to press the button to take a picture and advance the film. From 35-mm negatives the darkroom technicians had produced 8 x 10 prints of a middle-aged, muscular, well-hung naked man.

"I want to know who he is," Jonas said grimly. "Send a set of these to Bat. Somebody take a set to Lieutenant Dragon at LAPD, and somebody show them to Detective Baker, Manhattan North. Show a set to Ben Parrish. That hustling idiot knows everybody. Any other ideas?"

"Send Bat two sets," Angie suggested. "He can send a set to Toni. Maybe somebody at *The Washington Post* will recognize the man. She might—"

"Good thinking," said Jonas. "Put two sets in the New York courier bag."

They listened to the tape. They heard the sounds of the punches Vicky took, of her screams and grunts and coughing and begging; but from the time he entered her room until he left the man had said nothing that suggested who he was—except that he was a vicious bastard.

7

Lorena Pastor lifted her veil and peered intently at the bland face of Ben Parrish. He smiled faintly at her and took a sip from his vodka martini. His left arm hung in a sling, and she had driven the car to bring them to this restaurant in Malibu.

"I really can't believe you, Benjamin," she said. "I really cannot believe that you threw in the towel and went to work for Jonas Cord."

"I don't work for him, Lorena. But I think you know that Jonas has a way of getting people to do what he wants them to do. Anyway, I'm married to his daughter."

"You two are naughty," said Lorena. "She married you to spite her father. I can't imagine what *your* reason was."

"If she married me to spite her father, it didn't work," said Ben. "He was furious at first, but he seems to have accepted it."

Lorena had ordered a vodka martini, too, to see if she would like them, she said. She lifted her glass and drained the last of her drink, and by a nod to the waiter she ordered a second round. "You say you have something for me," she said. "I can't imagine your motive. Why would you want to feed me a story? I have to know the truth, Ben. Is it really from Jonas?"

Ben nodded.

She smiled and for a moment closed her eyes. "I have a fond memory of that man. I was just making the transition from would-be actress to columnist, and he pumped me full of energy. He's ten years younger than I am, you know. I was all but forty, and to have a handsome rich young stud after me was a marvelous boost to my sagging self-confidence. He took me flying and nearly scared me to death."

"He's a scary man in some ways."

"Nevada Smith introduced me to Jonas," she went on. "Talk about studs, there was another one!"

"You didn't miss many, did you, Lorena?"

"In my day," she said. "If I wasn't so damn old and

hadn't got so damn ugly, I'd want a go with you. You could at least let me have a look at what you're reputed to have."

"In the car on the way back," he said.

"Promise? Look and touch?"

"Promise. Look and touch." He laughed.

Their second round was delivered. She took a sip, then asked, "Well, what've you got for me?"

"A piece of tape. And some pictures. Of the new Glenda Grayson nightclub act that opened in Havana. She's been going out on the stage all but naked. And wait till you hear some of her monologue. She's kissed television good-bye."

"Okay. I get it now," said Lorena. "What she kissed good-bye to was Cord Productions. So Jonas wants her ass."

"She's doing the show," said Ben. "The pictures and tape are real."

Lorena sighed. "I don't think I can do anything with it, Ben."

"Why not, for Christ's sake?"

"I don't think Walt will publish it. He's got something against Jonas. He wanted the Margit Little story. Off the record, he *ordered* me to use it. I don't think he'll want this one. I don't think he'll help Jonas hurt Glenda Grayson."

"I think I know why," said Ben.

"Then you know more than I do," she said. She sighed again. "Take the story to Edna. She won't have my problem."

"She doesn't have sixty-eight newspapers either," said Ben.

"She's got forty-six. That's enough to break a story. After she breaks it, Walt may have to let me do something with it. Let me see the pictures, anyway."

Lorena Pastor opened the big brown envelope that Ben handed her and glanced through the photographs of Glenda's nightclub costumes. "This is the end of her in television," she said. "The papers that won't publish pictures like this will publish descriptions. And if her monologue is raunchy the way you say, the guardians of our public morality will go into a frenzy."

8

Bat brought the FBI fingerprint report to Las Vegas. He checked the distant rooftop through the telescope while Jonas read the document Toni had obtained.

FEDERAL BUREAU OF INVESTIGATION
WASHINGTON, D.C.
J. EDGAR HOOVER, DIRECTOR

The fingerprint laboratory of the Federal Bureau of Investigation has examined the unlabeled wine bottle submitted this date and reports its findings as follows:

Four sets of fingerprints exist on the bottle, two indistinct and two distinct. The conditions of the indistinct prints make it impossible to state with certainty that they are not the fingerprints of a known person whose fingerprints are on file with this Bureau. The two distinct sets of fingerprints are those of the following persons:

(1) One set are the fingerprints of one Angela Burns Damone Latham. Angela Burns Damone Latham was born in Yonkers, N.Y., on May 21, 1918. She was arrested by Postal Inspectors on

March 11, 1941, in White Plains, N.Y., on a charge of stealing from United States postal facilities, i.e., mail boxes. Counterfeit money was also found in her possession. She pleaded guilty to mail theft and was sentenced to five years imprisonment. She entered the Federal Reformatory for Women on June 20, 1941—

Jonas flipped the sheet. He didn't want to read any more about Angie.

(2) The second set of fingerprints are those of Maurice Cohen. Maurice Cohen was born in New York, N.Y., on April 26, 1882. This Bureau possesses fingerprint records of Maurice Cohen as follows:

a. Subject was arrested on May 3, 1900, in New Orleans, La., on a charge of larceny by fraud. This charge was subsequently dropped.

b. Subject was arrested on August 8, 1900, in New Orleans, La., on a charge of larceny by fraud. Subject was convicted on this charge and sentenced to one year of imprisonment. Subject entered a Louisiana state prison farm on September 21, 1900, and was released on September 21, 1901.

c. Subject was arrested in Houston, Texas, on March 17, 1903, on a charge of public vagrancy. He was sentenced to thirty days on a road gang and was released on March 18, 1903.

d. Subject was arrested in Detroit, Mich., on June 4, 1927, on a charge of being accessory to murder. The charges were dropped for lack of evidence, and he was released from the Wayne County jail on August 19, 1927.

e. Subject was arrested on January 23, 1932, in Lucas County, Ohio, on a charge of violating the National Prohibition Act and the Ohio state laws prohibiting the sale of alcoholic beverages. Subject was convicted on this charge and sentenced to three years imprisonment. He was received at the Ohio Penitentiary on February 27, 1932, and was released on parole on May 2, 1934.

The subject Cohen is reputed to have been a member of the "Purple Gang."

This Bureau has no further record of the subject Cohen.

Jonas grinned at Bat. "So that's who Morris Chandler is," he said.

"It makes me wonder what we'd find out if we ran a check on Nevada Smith," said Bat.

Jonas's face darkened. *"No!"* he yelled. "Don't even think of it. Don't even— Son of a *bitch!"* He grabbed a vial, popped off the lid, and shook a tiny pill into his hand. He shoved the pill into his mouth and sat silently for a quarter of a minute, eyes closed.

"Can I do anything for you?"

Jonas shook his head. "The pills take care of it," he said.

Bat stood staring at Jonas, his mind filled with things he might say, with thoughts to which he would not give voice. God, it had to be hard on a man to—

"Listen to me," Jonas grunted. "Don't you ever think of running any kind of check on Nevada. He was a better man than you'll ever be."

"Better than you, too?" Bat asked. It was what popped out; he had not meant to challenge Jonas at this moment. "I mean—"

"Yeah," Jonas interrupted. "Better than me. Better than the old man. I mean my father. Some ways. Nevada knew some special things about . . . life. I wish you'd known him better. I wish—" He paused, as if his breath came hard. "So . . . Chandler is Cohen. Felony record. By *God!*"

27

1

BAT SAT ACROSS THE TABLE FROM MARGIT LITTLE, IN A cozy candlelit Czech restaurant in Beverly Hills: the kind of place more likely to be found on the Upper East Side than in Los Angeles. They had finished their dinner and were sipping the last of their wine. Bat's hand was on hers.

"Margit," he said in a low voice. "What I'm going to ask probably won't come as any surprise to you. Will you come to the hotel with me?"

"I don't think that's a very good idea, Bat," she said solemnly.

"Sometimes the best things in the world are bad ideas."

She sighed softly. "I'm not surprised. I knew if I came out to dinner with you again, you'd ask. I guess if I didn't want to hear you ask, I shouldn't have accepted your invitation."

This was the fourth time he had taken her to dinner. From their conversation over those dinners, he had learned that Margit was no naïf. To the contrary, she was cunning and focused; she knew what she wanted, and she thought she knew how to get it. What was more, he could detect no sign that she carried any burdensome emotional baggage. She was pretty and talented, and she knew it. She was fresh and vivacious before the TV cameras. She was potentially a bigger star than Glenda Grayson ever dreamed of being, and she knew that, too.

"If you're not offended by my asking, I won't be offended if the answer's no," said Bat.

"I'm not offended. I expected you to ask, sooner or later. Everybody does. It's just that I don't think it's a good idea," she said.

"Why?"

"Your father. He'd be furious. Wouldn't he?"

"Well, in the first place, he doesn't have to know. In the second place, he doesn't own you. Has he told you he loves you? Has he asked you to marry him?"

She shook her head.

"So . . ." said Bat. He tossed back the last of his wine.

Margit turned her hand over, palm up, and closed her fingers around his hand. "All right, Bat," she said. A faint but playful smile came to her face. "I guess a girl can never have too many friends."

2

They coupled on the couch, and when that proved too constricting, they rolled off onto the thick carpet and finished there, too fervently involved to interrupt long enough to get up and walk to the bedroom. He was enervated when they were finished and was astonished at how exuberant it left her. She scrambled to her feet and pirouetted around the living room of his suite. Bat watched her, fascinated. He'd never before had sex with a girl who shaved her crotch. She shook her head, tossing her ponytail around, and then she sat down on the couch beside him.

"Do you have any Old Bushmill's?" she asked. She had acquired a taste for the Old Bushmill's Irish whiskey Jonas had introduced her to and always ordered it for her before-dinner drinks. "I feel like a drink."

"I'm a lecherous seducer," he said. "I ordered a bottle put on the bar, expecting to get you up here and break down your inhibitions with alcohol."

He poured two drinks, on the rocks.

"To next year," he said, lifting his glass.

"To next year," she agreed.

"It will be a great year," he said.

For a moment Margit stared thoughtfully at him, then nodded and lifted her glass again.

"The *Margit Show*," he mused. It had been his suggestion that the show they were putting together be called that instead of the *Margit Little Show*.

Bat sat down beside her on the couch and drew her into his arms. He put a hand on the soft bare flesh of her genital lips and gently fondled them. Margit sighed contentedly.

3

The dressing rooms backstage at the Ocean House in Miami Beach were not as posh as the ones at the Nacional or those at the Flamingo in Vegas. Glenda had a shower anyway, and she stood under a refreshing stream behind a canvas curtain in a rusting steel cubicle. Amelia hovered outside the curtain with a huge bath towel, knowing that her star would have to dry herself and begin to dress in the close presence of two men.

John Stefano sat on a wooden chair—there was no

couch—puffing on a big cigar. Sam Stein sat on another chair.

"Hand me in a drink, Amelia. Jeez Christ, hand me in a Scotch!"

Amelia put aside the towel and stepped to the makeup table, where a bottle of Black and White waited. They had no refrigerator in this dressing room and no ice, but she had learned that Glenda was more interested in the Scotch than in ice or soda, and she poured a shot of the liquor into a water glass. She shoved the glass past the curtain, and in a moment Glenda shoved it back out, empty.

"What brings you to Miami Beach, John?" Glenda asked.

"Nothin' special," said Stefano.

She turned off the water and flipped back the curtain. For an instant Stefano stared at her naked, until Amelia covered her with the towel. As she dried herself, Amelia tried to keep herself between her star and the eyes of the men. She handed her a pair of panties and a bra, both simple white underwear, and Glenda pulled those on and came out into the room.

"Thank you, Amelia," she said.

Amelia knew that was an invitation to leave the room.

"'Nothin' special,' huh?" said Glenda. She sat down at her makeup table and poured another drink. "Good."

"Let's don't kid around," said Sam. "John is upset about the Edna Trotter piece."

"Part of the game," said Glenda dismissively. "Nobody can control the gossip hens."

"Pictures," said Stefano. "Not only pictures but a tape. It wasn't supposed to happen. Hotel security was supposed to—"

"Well," she interrupted. "I didn't *let* it happen. It's not my fault that—"

"Makes no difference whose fault it is," said Stefano darkly. "What? Thirty, forty newspapers. Then picked up by fifty more, plus magazines. It damaged our investment in you."

"What do you mean by that?"

Sam explained. "It's like I warned you, Glenda," he said. "You've killed yourself for television."

"Fuck television," she snapped. "I was sick of that Pollyanna bullshit."

"There is more damage," said Stefano. "You were in demand for the best rooms in the best hotels in the hemisphere . . . *because you were a television star.* Now—" He turned down the corners of his mouth and turned up his palms. "Now you're just another broad that sings and dances and recites an off-color monologue."

"'Just another broad.' I'm just another broad? Glenda Grayson is just another broad?"

John Stefano stood. "We made a deal," he said. "We said there'd always be a booking for you, and there will be. We're not dumping you, understand. You'll be working. But the very big rooms aren't interested in you right now. Maybe sometime."

Stefano stood and put a hand on her bare shoulder. "How 'bout dinner after the second show?" he asked.

Glenda glanced at Sam, who nodded almost imperceptibly. "Okay," she said. "Why not?"

"See you later, then," said Stefano. He left the dressing room.

"*Sam!* Has it come to this?"

Sam Stein stood and put a hand on her shoulder. "My bet's still on you," he said softly. "We've got to work on the act."

She looked up into his eyes, tears in hers. "Don't

tell me to start playin' the little old lady in the modest cocktail dress, who tells jokes about her husband and kids and stuff that happens at the supermarket. Sam, for Christ's sake! We had a thing goin' before the Cords came along and before the goddamned Mafia came along—"

"Don't speak of Stefano as Mafia," Sam warned her. "Don't talk that way."

"Which one of the Cords shot me down?" she asked. "Which one planted the story with Edna Trotter?"

"I don't know."

"If I thought it was Bat, I'd kill him! I swear to God I would!"

4

Bat walked through the casino of the Havana Riviera, led by Meyer Lansky and towering over the little man. Both wore tuxedos. Lansky continued to insist he was only the food-service manager of the hotel, but the deference paid him by staff and gamblers alike belied his self-definition.

"You don't gamble, do you, Bat?"

"Not like this."

"Don't start," said Lansky somberly. "Look at these people. This is an honest casino, but some of them are going to drop fortunes in here tonight. And you know why? They're *addicted* to it."

"There are other ways to gamble," said Bat.

"Yeah. I'm a gambler myself. So are you. So's your father. The thrill of the risk. I mean, risking more than you can afford. Do you mind if I drop a personal note into this conversation?"

"Shoot," said Bat.

"What you're doing is dumb. You think your father is not going to find out you've brought Margit Little to Havana?"

"Who's going to tell him, Meyer?"

"Not me. You can be sure I'm not gonna talk. But the pilot, the—"

"I've got it covered," said Bat curtly.

"You *think* you have," said Lansky. "But confess something. The thrill of taking her to bed is nothing compared to the thrill of knowing you're bedding down your father's—"

"Margit is not his," Bat interrupted.

"Try telling *him* that. But don't tell him I helped you."

"If he finds out, I'll say we stayed at the Nacional."

Lansky led Bat to his private dining room, with a window overlooking the show room. In half an hour he would go up and bring Margit down on a private elevator. He wanted this half hour to talk with Lansky.

"I'll get right to the subject, Meyer," Bat said when they were seated at a small round table for four, covered with thick white linen and set with heavy silver and delicate china.

Meyer Lansky poured Chivas Regal for Bat. He lit a cigarette for himself and held it under the table, trying to keep the smoke from rising to Bat's nostrils.

"I'm going to do you a favor, and I'm going to ask you one," Bat went on.

"A good way of doing business," said Lansky.

"I think so. You are not going to like what I have to tell you, but please believe me that I know what I'm talking about. You're an American—"

"A Pole," said Lansky.

"An American," Bat repeated. "And so is my father. But my mother is Cuban. And I . . . Well, I am

American, now. But I know Latin America. I know something about Cuba."

"You are going to tell me," said Lansky, "that these . . . unwashed ones in the mountains are about to come to Havana and overthrow the government."

"Make yourself a fallback position, Meyer. That's what I'm telling you. You are going to need it."

"I know you believe this," said Lansky.

"You think his niece wouldn't know?" Bat asked.

Lansky shrugged. "Anyway, there is no fallback position for me. Everything I've got is invested in this place."

"There's a job for you with us, if you need it. Look. At least be sure you can get out. There will be shooting."

Lansky nodded. "I am grateful for the warning," he said. "Now what is it I can do for you?"

"I want to show you some photographs," said Bat. "I want to know who the man is." He reached into his jacket pocket and pulled out a small envelope of snapshot-size pictures. "Know him?"

Lansky frowned over the pictures. "How'd you get these?" he asked.

"My father arranged it. I'm not exactly sure how."

"A hooker," said Lansky. "The guy must have been with a hooker."

Bat nodded. "Do you know who he is?"

Lansky crushed his cigarette. He closed his eyes. "I know who he is. Is he involved in something?"

"He met with Jimmy Hoffa and Morris Chandler a couple of weeks ago. Chandler, incidentally, is really Maurice Cohen."

"Right. A small-timer. But—" Lansky stopped and jabbed at the photographs with a finger. "This guy is not a small-timer."

441

"You know him?"

"I've met him. I don't like what he does, and I wouldn't want you to think he's a friend of mine."

"What does he do, Meyer?"

"He's a killer, what they call a hit man. I don't know his name. They call him Malditesta. You understand the reference?"

Bat thought for a moment, then nodded. "Shooting a man in the head is called giving him a major headache."

"I will trust you with some information the FBI would very much like to have," said Lansky. "Please don't think I speak from firsthand knowledge. What I tell you is hearsay. It was Malditesta who killed Albert Anastasia. I tell you so you'll know what kind of man you're dealing with."

"It's been called the perfect hit," said Bat.

"Right. He walked into the barbershop, emptied his gun into Anastasia, dropped the gun on the floor, and walked out. These pictures you got of him are probably the only pictures ever taken of him, that he didn't want taken. I bet the cops showed the barbers a thousand mug shots. None of them was Malditesta. He's never been arrested."

"Who is he?" Bat asked. "I mean, what's his cover?"

"I don't know who he is. I doubt six men in the country know his real name or how to get in touch with him."

"Suppose *you* wanted to get in touch with him," said Bat. "Could you?"

"I don't want to get in touch with him."

"Suppose you did."

"I'd have to talk to somebody. Carlo Gambino maybe. Vulcano . . . The dons don't like killing anymore, and they try to avoid it. But when they decide they have to get rid of somebody, Malditesta is their man. He charges a heavy fee, but he never fails. Or so they say. I'd guess he's failed sometime."

"The secret of that might be that he only takes the jobs he knows he can do," Bat suggested.

"That's a thought."

"If he met Hoffa and Chandler, that means—"

"You or your father," said Meyer Lansky grimly.

5

Bat sat down in the living room of his father's suite atop The Seven Voyages. Having judged his father's mood, he poured himself a heavy drink of Scotch. Jonas was working on a fifth of bourbon.

"Exactly how many women do you think you have to fuck?" Jonas asked Bat. He was as furious as Margit had warned he would be. "I don't give a goddamn how many, but I'd think you could keep your fingers off *mine!*"

"Who's *yours?*" Bat asked coldly.

"You goddamned well know who's mine. I tell you this—you touch Angie, and you're out on your ass: fired, disinherited, and I won't ever want to see you again."

"Let's draw a line," said Bat, lifting his chin and half grinning. "Angie's yours, Toni's mine, and all the rest of them . . . may the best man win."

"You saying I have to *compete* with you?" Jonas asked indignantly. He shook his head. "No way, boy. No way. If I tell you to leave Margit alone, you'll leave her alone. *Because I say so!*"

"Don't . . . count . . . on it."

"Oh? Well, maybe we'd just better call it quits right

now and have done with it. I wish I understood just what the hell you think you are."

"I'm your *son,*" said Bat. "Did you give up on Rina just because your father said to? That's not the story I've heard. He had to marry her himself to—"

"Quit talking about my father! You don't know anything about my father!"

"I'm told I'm like both of you," said Bat quietly.

"My father died in 1925. Who could have told you anything about my father? Only Nevada, and Nevada never had a chance to talk to you much."

"He talked to Jo-Ann, and Jo-Ann has talked to me."

Jonas nodded and sneered. "So. The two of you. A fine pair. Okay. To hell with you."

Bat stood and walked to the bar. He poured his Scotch into the sink. "Okay. To hell with me. But one thing . . . I found out about the man who beat up the little hooker. He's a very bad fellow. Nobody knows his real name, but he's called Malditesta. The name means—"

"I know what it means. A hit man."

"Right. A hit man," said Bat. "The worst of them."

"For?"

"One of us. Or both."

Jonas stood up. He pointed at the place where Bat had been sitting. "Sit down, for Christ's sake." He went to the bar and refilled the glass Bat had poured into the sink. "Look," he said. "I don't like you. And you don't like me. And I don't know how the hell we could ever learn to stand each other. But this is a question of getting killed or not getting killed, and I think we'd better tolerate each other till we get past it."

"Assuming we're going to," said Bat.

6

Senator John McClellan presided over the Select Committee on Improper Activities in the Labor or Management Field—usually known as the McClellan Committee. He placed much confidence in his committee counsel, Robert Francis Kennedy, and allowed the young man a great deal of latitude in pursuing whatever lines of inquiry he thought proper. The senator knew that his young counsel had chosen the Teamsters Union as his *bête noire,* but he didn't care; the Teamsters was a Republican union. Anyway, Bobby Kennedy's dogged investigation of the Teamsters and now Jimmy Hoffa had won the committee a vast amount of admiring publicity.

Two men could hardly have been more unlike than John L. McClellan and Robert F. Kennedy. The senior senator from Arkansas was a courtly but competitive gentleman with a tall bald dome of a head and dark horn-rimmed glasses. The lawyer from Massachusetts was a sandy-haired Irishman with chipmunk teeth and a flat Boston accent. But they worked together to their mutual advantage.

In the cocky, sarcastic Jimmy Hoffa they had found themselves a whipping boy both of them could use. When he appeared before the committee, the news media covered every word.

"Mr. Hoffa, in previous testimony you have identified the Central States Pension Fund as a trust fund in which money collected from union members and employers is deposited in trust to provide members of the Teamsters Union their, uh, retirement benefits. Is that not correct?"

In order to sit with his legs crossed and yet be close

enough to the microphone on his table, Hoffa sat with his chair turned to the left and spoke into the microphone over his shoulder. He grinned and nodded. "That's right, Counsel. You did hear me testify to that before."

"Yay-uss. And you are a trustee of that fund, are you not, Mr. Hoffa?"

"As I testified before," said Hoffa.

"How do you invest the pension fund?" asked Kennedy.

"In a variety of things. I testified about that before, too."

"Specifically, Mr. Hoffa, has the fund invested in a project to build a hotel and gambling casino in Las Vegas, Nevada?"

"Absolutely. There's a lot of profit in those hotels."

Bobby Kennedy's eyes shifted from Hoffa to the second row of chairs in the hearing room, where Toni Maxim sat. His glance met hers.

"In order for that investment to make a profit, though, you will have to get a license from the Nevada Gaming Commission," said Kennedy. "Isn't that so?"

Hoffa nodded. "That is so. But it's no problem."

"Well, let's see if it's a problem, Mr. Hoffa. You have already filed an application for the license, and in your application you list the officers and directors of the company you have formed to operate the casino."

"The stock will be held by the fund," said Hoffa. "The profits will be paid as dividends. That will enrich the fund. My members will benefit."

"They may if you get the license."

"We'll get the license," said Hoffa with a twisted, toothy smile.

"Well, let's see," said Kennedy. "Are you familiar

with the terms of Nevada Statute Number 571 dash 1302?"

"I don't try to memorize all the laws, Counsel. Maybe you do. I guess that's your business: to know as many laws as you can. I have other problems."

"The Nevada statute I'm citing to you, Mr. Hoffa, is the one that says a gaming license cannot be issued to any individual with a felony record—nor to any organization which has such an individual among its officers or on its board of directors. You *are* familiar with that, are you not?"

"I've heard of it, Counsel."

"Yay-uss. Aren't you concerned about the felony record of one of your corporate officers?"

Hoffa swung around and leaned toward the microphone. "None of my officers has a felony record, Mr. Kennedy."

"Way-ull, let's see about that. What about Mr. Maurice Cohen?"

Hoffa grinned. "You blew that one, Counsel. There's no Cohen associated with our company."

Kennedy opened a file folder that had lain before him all during the questioning of Hoffa. He glanced again at Toni. "The man who calls himself Morris Chandler," he said, "is in fact one Maurice Cohen. Mr. Cohen has a criminal record, supplied to this committee by the FBI. He served a year in prison in Louisiana many years ago for larceny. He served more than two years in the Ohio Penitentiary for violation of the National Prohibition Act. In addition to that he served time for public vagrancy in Texas. His FBI sheet says also that he was a member of the Purple Gang. Were you unaware of this when you made him an officer of your hotel corporation, Mr. Hoffa?"

"I sure as hell was," said Hoffa. "If all that's true— which I doubt—it's news to me."

Kennedy closed the file. "I believe the Nevada Gaming Commission will say it was something you were supposed to find out before you employed Mr. Cohen."

"Okay," said Hoffa. "Let me tell *you* somethin'. Cord Hotels owns one Vegas casino-hotel and is buildin' another one. One of the directors of that company is a Mrs. Wyatt. Okay. Mrs. Wyatt didn't do time 'many years ago' like you say Mr. Chandler did. She did hers not so long ago. And it wasn't for sellin' liquor during Prohibition, either. Mrs. Wyatt went to the federal pokey for stealin' mail outa mailboxes! Check it, Counsel. Check somethin' more. When she was arrested, she had counterfeit money in her possession. Who's clean, Mr. Kennedy? Not your friends the Cords either!"

7

Toni opened her door and welcomed Bat into her Washington apartment. They had agreed it might not be wise for them to meet in his hotel or to go to dinner in a restaurant—not right now.

"I'm sorry, Bat," she said. "I really am. I didn't realize I was opening a can of worms."

He tossed his coat on a chair. "My father's answer to that is to hell with it; he's glad we did it. So Angie resigned from the board."

"Poor Angie."

"She's getting something better," said Bat. "He's marrying her. Christmas Eve. At the ranch."

Toni sat down on her couch. "Jesus . . . Last year I wasn't sure he'd make it through 1958."

"It's been a good year for him. Being active in the

business again, having a fight on his hands . . . He thrives on it. It's what he cares about."

"I'm surprised it's at the ranch again," she said.

"He did talk about selling it," said Bat. "He didn't think there could be another Christmas there. Now he's glad he didn't sell. And I suppose the ranch is the closest thing he's ever had to a home. There'll be the party. We're all invited. Even Monica."

"I'm not sure I can come this year, Bat," she said. "My father and mother—"

"Toni," he interrupted. "You *must* come. My mother will be there. And my stepfather, Virgilio Escalante. My mother hasn't seen you since we were at Cambridge. She wants to see you. Besides . . . it may be the last time *I'll* be there for Christmas. The old man and I are pretty close to an end."

"I can't believe that."

"Do believe it. There's only so much I can tolerate."

"He's invited *Monica?"* Toni asked. "He's going to marry Angie in the presence of—" Toni shook her head. "I guess that's his style. A Roman triumph."

"I'm not sure," said Bat. "He may have it in mind just to collect around him the people he cares most about."

"For his wedding."

"Right. And more news. Jo-Ann is pregnant."

"Lucky girl," said Toni, half sarcastically, half not.

8

As she always did, Toni pulled her panties back on after they had sex. That was an idiosyncrasy of hers that had always amused Bat. He had first undressed her twelve years ago, and in those twelve years she had not gained weight; nothing had loosened or slackened. She wore her hair shorter. She had developed a few very fine lines around her eyes, but instead of detracting from the beauty of her face they lent it character.

He picked up his shorts, then smiled and tossed them aside. Another of her idiosyncrasies was that she enjoyed seeing him naked. He had gained a few pounds. The fact was, he had been too thin when he came back to Harvard after the war. Over the years his scars had faded and lost most of their color. Toni seemed not even to notice them anymore. In the small, warm, cozy rooms of her Georgetown apartment, he enjoyed being naked. Besides, he could expect she would want his penis again before long, for something or other.

They returned to her living room, where she poked at the coals in her little marble-faced fireplace and set the fire blazing again. Bat poured Courvoisier into two snifters, and they sat together on the couch.

"Bobby Kennedy will hang on to Jimmy Hoffa like a bulldog," she said. "One thing, though. We've got to worry about one thing."

"What's that?"

"The 1960 election. Dick Nixon is hand in glove with Hoffa. He'll drop the prosecutions. He might even pardon him."

"So your friend Kennedy has to be elected President. You'll have a tough time selling that idea to Jonas Cord."

Toni lowered her face to Bat's stomach, took his penis in her hand, and began to lick gently, languidly, manifestly not anxious to bring him along quickly. He caressed the back of her neck.

"I'll come to the ranch with you for Christmas," she said. "But I've got to go to Florida before or after and spend some time there. Morgana insists I must come."

"Problem?" he asked.

"You know Morgana. She's always thought it was her business to arrange my life."

"So what's she arranging now?"

"She's been talking to some people at the Miami *Herald*. There's a possibility I'll be the Washington correspondent for the *Herald*. There's even a possibility I'll be political editor."

"Meaning live in Florida," he said.

She had slipped his penis inside her mouth, so she answered, "Mmm-hmm."

"Toni."

"Hmm?"

"Do I have to remind you I love you?"

She pulled her face back. "I love you, too," she said. "I always have. I actually tried to stop loving you. You're not the ideal man to be in love with, you know."

"I am capable of being more than one kind of idiot," he said.

She ran the tip of her tongue from his scrotum to his foreskin. "This conversation is getting very serious, Bat," she said softly.

"I want to marry you. I want us to have a home and children."

"It can be arranged," she said. "You could take the Florida bar exam. You could do worse than live in a home on a Fort Lauderdale canal. We can work together, work it out. You don't need Jonas."

"*He* needs *me*," said Bat.

"Right," Toni sighed. "A thought like that can ruin everything."

28

1

JONAS CORD AND ANGELA WYATT WERE MARRIED WITH simple formalities at the ranch house on Christmas eve. A justice of the peace arrived about seven o'clock and performed the short ceremony in the presence of Bat and Toni, Jo-Ann and Ben, Sonja and Virgilio, Monica and Bill. Angie cut a wedding cake and fed the first slice to Jonas as was traditional. Afterward, the company did not sit down to a dinner but nibbled from a buffet. They mixed and talked.

Toni was touched to see how proud Jonas was of Angie—and how protective of her. He had changed still more. He was the picture of a man who had recovered from a heart attack but was alert for the signs of another one. He was thin. He was more economical in his movements, even with his words. But nothing diminished his force. He was, as always, the focus of the assembled group—no longer as the lion in winter; no, as the lion scarred but recovered from his wounds, fit and ready to do battle.

This was Angie's and Jonas's happy occasion, and Toni and Bat had agreed not to distract any attention from it by announcing their own plans to marry. They would keep that word for later. Bat had told his mother, and Toni had told her parents, but no one else knew.

Jonas saw Toni standing alone by the Christmas tree studying the ornaments—probably comparing them to the strings of popcorn Robair and Nevada used to put on a tree. He walked over, took her hand, and squeezed it warmly. "You're more beautiful every time I see you," he said.

"Why, thank you, Mr. Cord. You are more distinctively handsome every time I see you," she said.

Jonas grinned. "One of the things I most like about you," he said, "is that you're a first-rate bullshit artist. I wish Bat would learn something of that art from you. But I'm serious. You are an extraordinarily beautiful woman. And, for God's sake, quit calling me Mr. Cord. To be called that by the most beautiful woman in a party—with the *possible* exception of my Angie—is a complete put-down."

"Jonas . . . Do you really think so? Most beautiful—"

"Absolutely. The dress is exquisite."

"Bat bought it for me, for tonight."

"The boy learns . . . gradually."

In their bedroom before they came out for the ceremony, Bat had unpacked a peach-colored cocktail dress embroidered with silver thread. She was not so obsessed with modesty as to deny it was beautiful and she was beautiful in it.

Bat was as protective of Toni tonight as his father was of Angie, and seeing her in earnest conversation with Jonas, he broke away from Jo-Ann, Monica, and her friend Bill Toller, picked up two fresh Scotches, and crossed the room toward his father.

"I know where Chandler is," he said to Jonas, adding to Toni, "Sorry. A word about business."

"What about Chandler?" Jonas asked, not disguising that he didn't want to know this evening but was compelled to now, since his son had so insensitively mentioned it.

"He's in Rhode Island," said Bat. "Since gambling is not legal in Rhode Island, there's no such thing as a gaming license, and his felony record is no impediment to his managing a joint some people have there. It's quite a place. People come from Boston, even from as far away as Hartford to gamble and consort with the hookers."

"He landed on his feet," said Jonas.

"If you want to call becoming a big duck in a very little pond landing on your feet, I suppose he did."

Monica joined them. Toni renewed her judgment that Monica was a brittle bitch. "I love your dress," she said to Toni with the same condescending edge in her voice she had used when she said the same thing to Angie. She herself wore a black dress of undistinguished style—unless showing extraordinary cleavage was style. "Where's your bride, Jonas?"

Angie was at the bar pouring a small new drink of bourbon for Jonas. She came to Jonas and handed him the glass. She wore pink brocade and was easily the most beautiful woman in the house, Jonas's compliment to Toni notwithstanding. "I appreciate your all being here this evening," she said, directing the comment particularly toward Monica.

"I wouldn't have missed it for the world," said Monica.

"I'm taking Angie to London and Paris for a wedding trip," said Jonas.

"I haven't been to Paris in *ages,*" said Monica.

Bat had noticed his mother standing near the buffet table, glancing around, apparently briefly at a loss to know who to talk to, though she had already clearly demonstrated she was not in the least discomfited by the company. He broke away from the group around his father and led Toni toward his mother. *"Madre,"* he said opening his arms. She smiled and entered between his outstretched arms for a warm embrace.

"Boston," Sonja said to Toni.

"Yes, it's been a long time since we've seen each other," said Toni. "Too long."

"I'm very happy about your news," she said quietly. "You haven't told Jonas, though, have you?"

Toni shook her head. "Not yet."

Toni had met Sonja when she came to the States to visit Bat when he was at Harvard. She'd been in her forties then and was in her fifties now: a woman of presence and poise and possessed of a rare, almost unique beauty. With her form-fitting silver lamé cocktail dress she wore a massive turquoise-and-silver squash-blossom necklace. Toni had watched her talking with Jonas earlier. She yielded nothing to him but treated him as an old friend.

Jonas walked away from Monica and brought Angie to the buffet table. "I'm about to be made a grandfather," he said to Sonja. He nodded toward Jo-Ann.

"Congratulations to both of you," said Sonja.

During the flight to Nevada, Bat had told Toni that Jo-Ann was a defeated woman. She had married as an act of defiance, only to see her husband captured by the gravity of Jonas and now dutifully circling him like a satellite. He had said he wasn't sure she wanted to be pregnant, either. "The name is cursed," Bat had said bitterly.

2

Monica said something similar to Jo-Ann a little later, when they stood apart by the window, looking out over a bleak landscape where no snow lay.

The next thing she said was "He dotes on his bastard."

Jo-Ann shrugged. "A blessing from heaven."

"Remember something," said Monica. "More bastards may show up, especially when he dies. But you're the only legitimate child he has. He can't shut you out of your inheritance."

"Yes, he can," said Jo-Ann. "I've talked with lawyers about it. By will. If it's drafted right, and executed right, he can leave everything he's got to Angie, or to Bat, or to whoever he wants."

"You mean he can leave you to the tender mercies of his bastard?"

"You're not very observant," said Jo-Ann.

"Meaning what?"

"He doesn't like Bat as well as you think he does. Can't you see the tension between them? If it weren't for this wedding, this joyous occasion, they'd be at each other's throats. They may be heading toward a complete breakup."

Monica laughed. "We can always hope so."

Jo-Ann shook her head. "I'm not sure *I* hope so."

3

"A few minutes," Jonas said to Bat. "I want to talk to you alone for a few minutes."

Jonas ushered Bat into the little office he kept in the ranch house. He closed and latched the door. "This ought to be a happy day for me," he said as he sat down in a chair covered with cracked black leather. "I don't want anybody out there to see it isn't."

"What's wrong with it?" Bat asked. "You've just

married an extravagantly beautiful, conspicuously devoted woman."

Jonas shrugged. "And the fourth-quarter figures are good, and we're going to sell a sponsor a TV production starring a cute little girl we've both screwed. So . . . ?" He blew a loud sigh. "Maybe I don't want to go to Europe for just two or three weeks. What if I kept Angie over there for six weeks instead of two? What if we stayed six *months?* What would happen?"

"You'd go nuts, is what would happen," said Bat. "You're playing games with me."

"The point is, do you think you could handle it?" Jonas asked. "You got it all in your head now? You wouldn't pass up any more Phoenix Aircraft deals? You wouldn't make any TV shows we have to sponsor ourselves? You wouldn't make dumb changes in the *Margit Show?*"

"In other words, I wouldn't make any decisions while you're gone."

"Put it in a confrontational way. You always do. All right. I won't kid you. I'm tired. And I've got a great new wife. And maybe I haven't got unlimited time ahead of me. But I've gotta hurry home in two weeks because I'm not sure if you can run the whole thing for any longer than that. So, tell me the truth. You think you *can* handle it?"

Bat's face was flushed. "My idea was that we'd run it *together* for a while."

"That's what we've *been* doing."

"No," said Bat firmly, shaking his head. "I'm an errand boy. I'm sick of it."

"You haven't ever been a fuckin' errand boy!" Jonas yelled. "I can hire errand boys for twenty percent of what I pay you. I let you restructure the whole

damned business. What the hell do you think you
are?"

"I'm what *you'd* have been if your father had
lived," said Bat. "A son who can make suggestions
but had better not make decisions."

"You never pass up a chance to unload my father on
me, do you? No— Let's get back to the question.
Suppose I decide to retire at the age of fifty-five. You
ready to run the whole goddamned works?"

"I—"

"I'm not saying without mistakes. I made mine. But
are you ready to tell me, honestly, that you're ready to
take over all the stuff we call CE and run it without
me? I'll take your word on it."

"What do *you* think?" Bat asked.

"What I think isn't the point. Whatta *you* think?"

"You put me in—"

"Right," Jonas interrupted. "That's the whole
point. I put you between a rock and a hard place.
Which is where you'll be put every goddamned day
when you run the business. And then you gotta be
smart. And then you gotta have guts."

"You're smart, and you've got guts," said Bat
tentatively.

Jonas shrugged. "I'm here. I haven't lost it."

Bat lifted his chin high. "I've got in me what you've
got in you. You put it in my mother, and it came out
in me."

"Okay. You think you're ready?"

Bat nodded. "Yeah. Right. I'm ready."

Jonas's faced hardened. "Well, I don't think you
are—and the fact you think you are is the best proof
you aren't. When my father died, I knew better than
to think I was ready. But I didn't have any choice; I
had to do it. Every day of my life, almost, I've wished

I had the old man's help and advice. But not you. You throw it away. You resent it. You're an egomaniac, Bat."

"Where could I have acquired that gene?" Bat sneered.

Jonas reached for a bottle of bourbon. His hand trembled as he poured a shot. "Go on," he said. "Go get your cock sucked. Before I leave for Europe with Angie, we're gonna settle this. Tomorrow. Christmas day or no Christmas day, we're going to settle it. We're going to have a modus operandi, you and me. We're gonna be father and son. Or you're through."

4

Not long after midnight, Jonas led Angie to their bedroom; then Bat led Toni to theirs.

The room was warm, and Toni was not reluctant to undress, except as always for her panties. They had a bottle of Courvoisier in the room, and Toni poured them tiny final drinks as Bat stirred the fire and put on more wood. They lay down side by side in bed. Only when a blanket was pulled up over them did Toni slip the panties down and lay them on the nightstand. Bat laid his thirty-eight snub-nose Smith & Wesson revolver on the nightstand on his side of the bed.

"Are things that bad?" she asked.

"No. Just insurance."

"I don't want to have to think about it now," she said.

For an hour they thought of nothing but each other, and then they went to sleep.

She went to sleep. Only rarely did Bat suffer any pain in his old wound scars, but occasionally he did.

It happened after he had lifted too much weight with his right arm. He had lain sleepless in this house once before after lifting luggage off an airplane out on the landing strip. He'd done it again today, and he felt sharp twinges in the permanently damaged musculature of his chest.

He slipped off the bed and took a heavy shot of brandy.

Sitting in a chair, he stared at the flickering darts of flame rising from the red-hot crumbling coals on the andirons. He had said nothing to Toni about the confrontation he'd had with his father. He wouldn't, not until they were away from here. Fort Lauderdale ... Maybe.

A twinge stabbed him. Dave Amory had them, too. He'd been hit in the leg. It was the price you paid for being an infantryman, Dave said. And he said, too—

Maybe for the price you bought something. Bat remembered nights in Belgium when they had sensed something was wrong, just sensed it, without any real evidence. One night he had rolled quietly out of his foxhole, two minutes before an infiltrating German had struck into it with a dagger. The German died because an infantryman developed a sense— Oh, yeah. The Kraut was not an infantryman.

Like that night ... Bat heard nothing. But he sensed something. Something was goddamned wrong, just like it had been the night the German struck into an empty foxhole with a rune-marked SS ceremonial dagger.

He didn't take time to pull on his pants. He didn't have a robe. He grabbed the thirty-eight and slipped quietly out of the bedroom, wearing only slingshot underpants.

The household was asleep. It was dark. A few smoldering coals glowed in the big fieldstone fireplace. No electric lights burned. The silence was complete. Even so, Bat needed only a minute outside his room to confirm his suspicion that something was horribly wrong—

The front door was open.

5

Jonas slipped a nitroglycerine tablet under his tongue. He clutched his chest.

The man in the brown overcoat, wearing a brown hat, holding a small-caliber silenced automatic pistol leveled on Jonas and Angie, shrugged and said, "Maybe God's gonna do it for me. Maybe I have to do nothing."

"I can make you a better deal," Jonas whispered hoarsely.

"You'd be surprised how many men offer me a better deal," said the man. He was Malditesta. "The first time I bought that, *I'd* be the dead man." He shook his head. "I already made the deal."

Angie was naked. She had thrown herself across Jonas, to block a shot. She was sobbing.

"What's your deal?" Jonas asked. "Just me? Not her?"

Malditesta shook his head. "Just you, Mr. Cord. Not even your son."

"You'll do it and leave?" Jonas asked. "Can I believe that?"

"I am paid for one," said the hit man. "If they want another one, they pay again. And—I'm a pro. It won't hurt. If the little lady will get out of the way, I can make it very easy—easier than that heart attack you seem to be havin'. Push the little lady off, Mr. Cord."

"Do what he says, Angie," Jonas pleaded.

"NO!" she shrieked.

"You're a businessman, Mr. Cord," said Malditesta. "You understand, it's nothing personal. This is my *business*. It's what I do. It's how I make my living. A man has to make his living doing what he can, what he knows how to do. This is strictly a business deal. You can understand that. Make her understand it."

"Angie," Jonas whispered. "Get away. Let him do it. What he says is true."

Angie shook her head and clung more tightly to Jonas.

"It can be both of you, if that's what it has to be," said Malditesta.

6

"Like shit!"

Malditesta stiffened, then glanced behind him. "Mr. Cord Junior," he grunted. "With a gun pointed at my back. Okay. I've still got one pointed at your father and his new wife. You think you can drop me before I drop one of them? Or both? Even with a slug coming through me I can pull this trigger once or twice. Standoff, huh?"

Angie rolled off Jonas and lurched to her feet. She stood halfway between Jonas and Malditesta. "No standoff," she said. "The only one you can kill now is *me.*"

Jonas scrambled off the bed.

"No!" Bat yelled. "Stay behind her. He won't shoot her."

"You think so?" Malditesta asked Bat. "And who's this? We're attractin' quite a crowd here. With another gun, yet."

Toni had come through the door and was edging her way around Bat, to confront Malditesta from the side. She did have a gun: her .30-30 Winchester.

"So," muttered Malditesta. "I guess the question is Just how important is the new Mrs. Cord? I guess you're Miss Maxim," he said to Toni. "You better point that rifle down. It might go off. And if anybody's gun goes off, the new Mrs. Cord is dead. Her at least. Like I asked, how important is she to you folks?"

Bat pressed the snub-nose thirty-eight against Malditesta's lower back. "How important is your spinal cord?" he asked. "You kill her, I'm not gonna kill you. I'm gonna put a thirty-eight slug right through your spine. You'll spend the rest of your life in the Nevada pen and you won't be able to walk or piss. I'm not going to kill you, Malditesta. I'm gonna *cripple* you. You ever figure on that?"

Malditesta moaned, as if he were already in agony. "I drop my gun, you let me go?" he asked. "It was a business deal, strictly."

"Sure," said Bat. "A business deal."

Malditesta hesitated for a full half minute, as if running past in his mind whatever alternatives he might have; and then he dropped his pistol to the floor.

Bat grabbed for a half-full, heavy champagne bottle that stood on a table behind him. He raised it and brought it down hard on Malditesta's head.

Malditesta dropped to his knees, then sprawled on the floor. "You . . . made a *deal*," he moaned.

"I lied," said Bat as he raised the bottle and struck again.

7

"And *he* lied," said Toni as she pulled a revolver from inside Malditesta's coat.

Jonas sat on the bed. He breathed heavily.

"We'll get a doctor," said Angie as she covered herself with a flowered silk wrapper.

"No. I don't need a doctor. I needed the pill. That's all I need. You've seen me take those before. The nitroglycerine stops the pain."

"Pain you shouldn't have," she said. "You don't need—"

"We don't need an investigation either," said Bat grimly. He nodded toward the lifeless body of Malditesta. "Uh— You realize that nobody knows but the three of us."

"Whoever sent him knows," said Angie.

"And will be the last to call the police to help find him," said Bat. "I'll drag him out in the desert and bury him," he said. "No one is going to be looking for him. No one else is awake. There are no witnesses but us."

"I'll help," said Angie.

"Then we'll have to get rid of his car," said Bat. "He must have had one. Drive it fifty miles or so and abandon it."

"You can do that in the morning," said Jonas.

8

Bat and Angie dragged the body of Malditesta by a rope looped under his arms. Toni carried their tools: a pickaxe and a spade. Against the cold wind, all three wore sheepskin jackets and blue jeans, boots and gloves and hats.

The moon was setting. In half an hour it would be dark. They walked as the moon dropped toward the distant mountains and covered most of a mile before Bat stopped and began to chop at the frozen earth with the pickaxe. Frost had penetrated only a few inches, and he did not take long to dig a shallow grave.

Toni knelt over the hit man and went through his pockets. He carried no identification.

When the grave was ready they rolled Malditesta into it. Bat filled the hole, and together they shuffled over it until it was all but indistinguishable from the level desert around it. As they walked away the wind had already begun to scatter sand and dust over the grave and over their footprints.

9

Back inside the house they found Jonas sitting in the living room. He had put wood on the embers, and a fire was blazing.

"I'm hungry," he muttered. "And don't stare at the bottle. I'm entitled to a nip. The doctors say so. Bourbon helps reduce tension—and tension was what caused the pain."

"I'll see what's available in the kitchen," said Angie. "Anybody else want a snack?"

Bat and Toni shook their heads. Bat poured two Scotches.

"Well," said Jonas. "What I said had to be settled . . . is settled."

Bat stood beside his father's chair and put his hand on his shoulder. "How do you want to settle it?" he asked.

"I'm afraid I've missed something," said Toni. "What are you settling?"

Jonas looked up at her. She stood by the fireplace in her jeans and wool shirt. "If I'm gonna talk business in front of you, I need to know how it stands between you and Bat."

"We're going to be married," said Bat. "We would have told you before we went back to New York."

Jonas smiled and nodded. "That's the best news I've had for a long time. So . . . Tonight Angie offered her life to save mine. The least I can do for her is try to keep myself alive as long as possible. What the doctors tell me is I have to avoid tension and too much exertion. Well, you can't ride herd on a business empire without tension and exertion."

Bat moved over to stand beside Toni. He took her hand.

"You said I made you an errand boy," said Jonas. "Well, I never made you an errand boy. But I admit I kept a thumb on you. So, as from tonight the thumb is off. I'm taking Angie to Europe. I don't know how long we'll stay or when we'll be back. We may be gone six months. I don't know. When we do come back, I'll keep my nib out." He stopped, and a wry smile came to his face. "Out of whatever's left."

Bat, too, smiled, and he shook his head. "You never give up, do you?"

Jonas shrugged. "You're gonna have your chance. It's what you wanted, isn't it? I don't think you're entirely ready for it, but . . . well, neither was I."

"Stick your nib in one more time, Jonas," said Toni. "Order him to take a vacation."

Jonas pointed a finger at Bat. "You do that, son," he said. "I'm still chairman of the board, and I'm telling you: You take a vacation."

"As soon as—"

"Not as soon as, goddammit! My old man wasn't indispensable. I'm not, either. And neither are you."

Bat sighed. "There are things that—"

"Bat," Jonas interrupted firmly. "Marry Toni. Take a nice honeymoon. I mean, really nice: out of touch with the phones." He paused. For a moment he seemed to have difficulty with his voice. "You're my *son.* You're more important to me than things that might go to hell while you're away. I'm sorry I didn't say it before now, but . . . you see . . ." His voice broke. "I love you, son." His eyes shifted to Toni. "I love you, too. And Angie. Bat— It's not a business order. It's a father-to-son order."

"All right," said Bat softly. "And— And, I hope you understand— No, why should you understand? I'll say it, flat out. I love you, too."

Jonas grinned. "We've just broken a Cord family tradition." He laughed through tears.

EPILOGUE

Jonas and Angie returned from Europe for the grand opening show in the Follies Cabaret of the Cord InterContinental Vegas Hotel.

The headliners opening night were Maurice Chevalier, Glenda Grayson, and Margit Little. The theme of the show was Folies-Bergère, and the revue had been designed under the personal supervision of Paul Derval, owner and manager of the Folies in Paris.

Never before had so many showgirls appeared on a nightclub stage. Never before in America had so many showgirls performed in such elaborate costumes and yet so nearly nude. In one scene the showgirls swam in an onstage pool. In another some of them ice skated on real ice.

Margit performed a ballet solo. Though her leotards were high cut, they were modest by comparison with anything else in the show. Her television show was opening in October, and Bat would take no chance of damaging her television career.

Chevalier was his usual charming self with cane and straw hat, dancing a little but mostly singing his signature songs, such as "Valentina," "C'est Magnifique," and his new hit "Thank Heaven for Little Girls."

Glenda Grayson did her monologue in the first half

of the show, coming on a bare stage in the tightly focused beam of a spotlight, wearing her black hat, a black corselette, showing the white skin of her upper thighs above dark stockings held up by red garters. She sang, but mostly she kept the audience roaring with laughter with a string of original one-liners. She returned to one of her favorite lines—"Y' wouldn't b'*lieve* it!" She finished with a line she had killed and now revived—"Golda, change your name. *Please!"* That line had always been poignant. The audience, who knew something of her history, was moved by it.

"It's been said of a great comic that he can make you laugh, then make you cry," said Jo-Ann, who sat at the table with Bat and Toni, Jonas and Angie. This was her first night out since the birth of her daughter.

For Glenda's second appearance, she was delivered on the stage in the middle of the finale, by a three-quarter-scale helicopter that descended over the audience at their tables and landed on the stage—on wires of course but realistic enough to draw loud applause just for the helicopter.

Four young male dancers lifted her from the helicopter and put her down on the stage. She was wearing the costume that had made her poison for television: the fifty strings of tiny, glittering black beads cascading from her shoulders over her body, down to her ankles. Only now, she wore nothing underneath; the thousands of beads fell over her body, not over a sheer black gown. Her modesty, if any, was protected by the tight control of the light that touched her. Her audience understood she was naked; but peer and squint though they might, they got no clear view of her. As she moved, the light dimmed, it changed color; lighting technicians had worked for two weeks to achieve the effect.

Chevalier came onstage in white tie and tails. They sang together, songs identified with both of them.

The dancers of the chorus worked around them, they upstage in bright light. They wore feathered headdresses and feather boas, but their breasts, bellies, and hips were bare. The muscular male dancers wore feathered and jeweled jockstraps.

The music of the pit orchestra rose and overwhelmed the singing. The revue was ending. The helicopter came down on its wires again and landed on the stage. Chevalier led Glenda to it. Her four dancers surrounded her and made ready to lift her into the helicopter. At the final moment, Glenda reached behind her neck and unfastened a clasp. The beads fell to the floor. The dancers lifted her. Her back was to the audience, but she was completely naked. They stood to applaud as the helicopter rose and swept out of the room.

Jonas grinned at Bat. "You've made her a big star again. And she'll schnook you again."

Bat shrugged. "Maybe."

"I'll promise you one thing," said Toni. "She won't screw him."

Jo-Ann laughed. "He's a Cord," she said.

"Dad, I want to thank you for renewing your contact with Paul Derval at the Folies."

"Interrupted my vacation," said Jonas.

"Speaking of which, when are *you* going to take a vacation?" asked Toni. "When are *we* going to take one?"

"That's hard to say."

"Have you become the indispensable man, son?" Jonas asked. "Haven't you learned better than that? I thought for Christ's sake that you'd—"

"Easy . . ." whispered Angie, taking Jonas's hand.

Jonas pointed at Toni. "Before she gets too heavy," he said. "I never did get to Acapulco. Now, that'd be a good place for you two to go swimming—"

"I don't want to go swimming," said Toni. "I want to see Paris in the fall. I want to be able to take long walks in the streets, before the baby gets so big I can't do it."

"You do it, Bat," Jonas barked. "By God!"

"I thought you didn't give me orders anymore," said Bat gently.

"I don't try to be your boss anymore, but I'm still your fuckin' *father!* You take this girl wherever she wants to go!"

"You want to stay in Vegas and run things while I'm gone?"

Jonas shook his head. "Angie and I are flying to Honolulu on Monday. Then on to Tahiti. Then Australia and New Zealand."

Bat frowned at Toni. "Paris . . . A week?"

"Two weeks," she said firmly.